I0746415

Stories of Crime & Detection

Volume Ten

Counsel for the Defence

James Ronald

Edited by Chris Verner

Moonstone Press

This edition published in 2024 by Moonstone Press
www.moonstonepress.co.uk

Introduction and About the Author © 2023 Chris Verner

Counsel for the Defence originally published in 1932 by Gramol.
The Awakening of Theodore Wrenn originally published in 1934 by *Arthur
Gray (Books) Ltd.*
The Baby and the Gorilla originally published in 1935 in the
Linlithgowshire Gazette.
Stories of Crime and Detection, Vol. X: Counsel for the Defence © 2024 the
Estate of James Ronald.
The right of James Ronald to be identified as author of this work has been
asserted in accordance with the Copyright, Designs and Patents Act 1988

ISBN 978-1-899000-92-0
eISBN 978-1-899000-93-7

A CIP catalogue record for this book is available from the British Library
Text designed and typeset by Moonstone Press
Cover illustration by Jason Anscomb

Some stories have been edited to remove objectionable content to better
reflect contemporary standards, including references to ethnicity that
could be interpreted as racially insensitive or xenophobic.

Royalties from the sale of this book will be donated to MND Scotland,
who fund ground-breaking MND (motor neurone disease) research and
world-class clinical trials to combat an uncommon condition that affects
the brain and nerves, and causes weakness that gets worse over time,
eventually resulting in death.

Contents

INTRODUCTION

This tenth volume of *James Ronald, Stories of Crime and Detection*, contains two novellas and a short story.

The two novellas feature a respectable solicitor, Theodore Wrenn—of Gentry, Green and Gentry an old-fashioned but influential firm of solicitors—first making his appearance in *Counsel for the Defence*, followed up by the title role in *The Awakening of Theodore Wrenn*:

"At 36 years of age Theodore Wrenn managing clerk to the old established firm of Gentry, Green and Gentry, solicitors, has one ambition—to succeed old Daniel Gentry when he dies as its head. It is the only thing in Theodore's life that matters, and to fulfil that ambition he lives frugally in the dingiest of boarding houses, scraping together capital in readiness for the time when the opportunity to purchase the business will occur. He is mild mannered, rather unworldly and self-effacing: and although he looks older than his cousin, Sir Anthony Ravenal, the dissolute head of the family, he is actually three years younger."

Counsel for the Defence was published by Gramol in 1932, an Adelphi Novel number 22, priced at 2d. It is hard to believe that out of choice James Ronald began as a pulp writer for a prolific publisher of cheap fiction between the wars, Gramol Publications, 3 Duke Street, Adelphi, London W.C.2. The name Gramol was extracted from Arthur Gray (1889-1960) and Frederick Matthew Mowl (1887-1949), who ran the outfit. They were regarded as the worst-paying publishers of the period. They had begun publishing in the 1920s, originally as the Federation Press, operating since about 1926, from Gramol House, Farringdon Avenue.

Apart from Theodore Wrenn, *Counsel for the Defence* also introduces the fictional police officer Detective Sergeant Evans (later promoted to become Detective Inspector Evans C.I.D in several other stories).

The story is concerned with the murder of Moses Silverstein, pawnbroker and moneylender, who had been something of an old rogue:

> A hard old man whose emaciated frame was bent like a question mark and who wore a long silver-streaked beard that quivered when a customer had the temerity to ask a larger loan than his clock or candlesticks warranted. Everyone in the neighbourhood had known old Silverstein. And now Silverstein was dead—murdered!

This is the same story as *Murder!* by Michael Crombie, published by Arthur Gray (Books) Ltd 1935 and or Gramol (according to The British Library).

Arthur Gray published a number of Ronald's books under his own banner including the second novella in this volume *The Awakening of Theodore Wrenn*, written by James Ronald but published under his non de plume Michael Crombie.

When the rakish and dissolute Lord Ravenal introduced his staid and respectable cousin Theodore Wrenn to his fiancée Anne Wilding, it was to have a profound influence on all their lives. For it awakened in Theodore feelings and ambitions he had never experienced before. Anne Wilding was the most beautiful woman he had ever seen, and he felt dazed in her presence. From the moment his eyes had met the clear, frank eyes of Anne Wilding, he was lost to everyone but her...and a chain of events was to be set in motion that would embrace both love and death!

The Awakening of Theodore Wrenn by Michael Crombie was originally published in 1934 by Arthur Gray (Books) Ltd, 3 Duke Street, Adelphi, London W.C.2. with a wonderful art deco dust wrapper by talented postwar pulp fiction artist H. W. Perl (1897-1952) a contraction and pseudonym of Hyman Woolf Perlzweig, who exhibited three pictures at the Royal Academy between 1938 and 1940.

The amusing short story, *The Baby and the Gorilla*, first appeared in the *Linlithgowshire Gazette*, West Lothian, Scotland, 08 February 1935 and again in the Saturday Evening Express Launceston, Tasmania, 15 July 1939 and no doubt other newspapers.

ABOUT THE AUTHOR

James Jack Ronald, to give his full name, was born 11 May 1905, in North Kelvinside, Glasgow, Scotland. He was the son of James Jack Ronald, a Chartered Public Accountant, and Katherine Hamilton Ronald. He was educated at Hillhead High School, Glasgow, established in 1885.

Until he was five, James Ronald says he was chubby, happy, and irresponsible; but in 1911, his sixth year, he was run over by an automobile causing a very real morbidity to creep in. For ten years following the accident he suffered recurrent dreams about a wheel that became larger and larger as it turned faster and faster. He was invalided over a long period during which, with his mother Catherine's encouragement, he enjoyed a prodigious amount of reading. He later claimed he owed his literary gift and resultant career to this near-fatal automobile accident, which caused him to change from a sunny little extrovert to a cloudy introvert.

When he was fourteen he wrote an account of the accident, setting down all the details in a somewhat light vein, not forgetting to note that the candy he had purchased with such delight on that foggy morning was found sticking to the wheels of the car as he was being carried off. The piece won him first prize for composition and congratulations from the masters at the school and even the headmaster wished him well, but that did not prevent corporal punishment for his appalling handwriting. He was called into the headmaster's office, but kept waiting so that everybody knew that he, James Ronald, was going to receive a beating from the headmaster. This injustice obviously affected him very deeply, because it remained with him all his life, and crops up in interview after interview:

> After all, I taught myself to read before going to school and could see no reason for accepting a beating because they failed to teach me how to write, so I bolted.

In a spirit of rebellion against repeated punishments for bad handwriting for compositions for which he invariably got an 'A', Ronald came home from school one day announcing he would never return. It was time to leave. His mother Catherine was understandably distressed, concerned her elder son leaving school at such a young age would diminish his career prospects. Aware of the scarcity of jobs just then in Glasgow, she told him he could only stay away from school if he remained active in some useful employment, making it clear she would not condone an idler in the family.

Within three days James Ronald was an errand boy for the *Glasgow Evening News*, a paper into which he had smuggled a poem some months earlier. But there was 'no writing, nothing editorial' in his set up and he thoroughly disliked it and lost the job. He found another post immediately with the *Glasgow Sunday Mail* and kept this one until he printed his own rival paper on the office mimeograph. He broke the machine and, failing to cover his tracks by leaving a sheet in the copier, he was fired. Then came a dozen jobs, including one with an art dealer for whom he gilded statues and washed windows. His mother told him, 'It is no disgrace to wash windows, James, but it is a disgrace to wash them like that.'

By the age of seventeen, James Ronald had run through all prospective employers in Glasgow, including every newspaper.

He felt the need of open space—'a lot of it'—and after various and sundry abortive departures, finally won grudging permission to seek his fortune in the New World.

For some reason, Chicago stuck in the mind of the young Ronald as a magic word. He became determined to travel to the United States of America. The main method of crossing the Atlantic Ocean in the 1920s was by steamship and ocean liner. The passengers aboard the *SS Saturnia* included seventeen-year-old James Ronald, who arrived at his destination on 6 December 1922, at the Port of Québec, an inland port located in Québec, Canada. From there he continued his journey across the Great Lakes to Chicago, Illinois, United States. He managed to survive in Chicago; the fastest-growing city in world history, with a flourishing economy approaching three million people, attracting huge numbers of new immigrants from Eastern and Central Europe. Ronald stayed in Chicago for five years, wanting to write, but unable to afford the time because he was forced to earn money to live. He was taken on and fired from a variety of jobs with monotonous regularity. Like his experiences in Glasgow, he exhausted all potential employers, dabbling in some forty jobs ranging from short-order cook and dishwasher to muslin salesman; from dance promoter and theatre manager to washing dishes again in a Greek restaurant. He edited ten trade journals at one time for a Chicago publisher; and gave new life to a women's religious magazine. A chain-smoker, he confessed slyly to have worked for the Anti-Cigarette League, his excuse being 'a man must eat don't you know'—at that time eating being the only philosophy he could afford to practise. It was in the Windy City that he learned about life.

Working in the U.S. as 'a visitor' to avoid immigration may have caught up with Ronald because, in 1927, he returned to Britain on a more permanent basis, and secured a well-paid job with an English newspaper chain, and a promise of future advancement. However, during his first holiday in the job, a car accident disrupted this promising career trajectory. Whilst driving a small open two-seater Rover 8, Ronald was struck by a two-ton truck and thrown out against the radiator of another vehicle. Left with a broken hip and temporarily crippled (and without the newly acquired job), he settled down to write.

Ronald's writing developed in three stages. First, he hammered out serializations and short stories which were syndicated in newspapers, both at home and abroad; and a number were also published in obscure pulp magazines. Some stories then became lost and forgotten and this has unfortunately contributed to a lack of recognition for an impressive body of work. These early narratives were very difficult to track down, but searching has provided me with an enjoyable and rewarding task—a treasure hunt for lost tales. This was not made any easier because many of these stories were published under pseudonyms; Peter Gale, Mark Ellison, Kenneth Streeter, Alan Napier, and even women; Cynthia Priestley and Norah Banning—in addition to known pseudonyms Michael Crombie and Kirk Wales. Those I have discovered have all been gathered together for republication in this series.

A second writing stage followed; the full-length mystery stories which have made him so popular with Golden Age of Detection aficionados. They are out-of-print, elusive to find, and first editions are very expensive.

Finally, late in life, James Ronald embarked on his Dickensian-style life drama novels. He received enthusiastic praise for his ingenuity, freshness, and sharp sense of humour by many critics and writers of the time, such as August Derleth. Orville Prescott, the main book reviewer for *The New York Times* for 24 years, called James Ronald 'a born novelist', and that he 'has in full measure the two basic drives which inspire a writer of fiction—the urge to create characters and to tell stories about them. Mr. Ronald does both naturally, directly and well.' His work received praise and has been compared to William de Morgan, H. G. Wells, Rudyard Kipling, J. M. Barrie, and Somerset Maugham.

James Ronald is a writer who has not gained the long-term recognition he deserves. His work has received high praise for his ingenuity, freshness, and sharp sense of humour by many critics and writers of the time and current enthusiasts, highlighting him as one of the leading storytellers of the day, yet barely anything has been republished since his death in 1972. I hope the reader will enjoy these imaginative and entertainingly written stories as much as I have collecting them.

Chris Verner
Berkhamsted, Buckinghamshire, UK
April 2023

COUNSEL FOR THE DEFENCE

At one o'clock in the morning, Sergeant Daniel Regan turned in at the doorway of the Battersea district police station, leafing over the page of his notebook as he went, to be ready to make his report. The sergeant in charge looked up as the Irish officer came in, and his usually calm, expressionless face gleamed with suppressed excitement.

"Hello, Danny," he called. "Have you heard the news? Old Moses Silverstein has been murdered!"

Regan was thunderstruck. His thick, moist thumb poised in mid-air on its way from his lips to the notebook. In his amazement, his brogue became unusually pronounced.

"What are ye telling me? Och, Mary, but I was talkin' to him not two hours ago! Are yiz sure?"

The station sergeant nodded. "There's nothing surer. The constable on the beat found him less than half an hour ago, lying on the floor behind the counter of his pawnshop, with his skull cracked like a nut."

"Save us!" gasped Regan, shaken to the core. "Ould scoundrel that he was, that's no death for any man. May the Lord rest his soul!"

"You'd better get back to Stark Street, Danny," said the other in a sympathetic tone. "Superintendent Westcott from the Yard is in charge of the case, and he'll want a word with you."

Regan nodded silently, turned, and made his way out of the police station. He walked briskly towards the scene of the crime, a gloomy, dismal thoroughfare, aptly named Stark Street, which ran only the length of a single block connecting two brighter and more important streets.

Stark Street was lined on either side with dilapidated

stucco-fronted houses each, even in the stain and decay of time and neglect, exactly alike, except that at one end of the street a house front had been altered to serve the purpose of a shop. Over its door, three brass balls and a sign with faded gilt lettering proclaimed that here was the place of business and dwelling of Moses Silverstein, pawnbroker and moneylender.

This Moses Silverstein had been something of a character. A hard old man whose emaciated frame was bent like a question mark and who wore a long silver-streaked beard that quivered when a customer had the temerity to ask a larger loan than his clock or candlesticks warranted.

Everyone in the neighbourhood had known old Silverstein. And now Silverstein was dead—murdered!

"Rest his soul," thought Danny Regan. "Sure, he never did any harm."

Sergeant Regan was a tall, red-faced man whose chief interest lay in his cheery little home in a happier thoroughfare in Battersea, with his wife and his three bonny children. In his heart, the good-natured Irishman despised Moses Silverstein, but he had known him intimately and resented the violent nature of his passing.

On more than one occasion, the pawnbroker had been able to provide the police sergeant with useful information. Many queer folk came to Moses Silverstein with articles which they dared not offer elsewhere and if the return was large enough, and the risk not too great, the pawnbroker had accepted them readily without enquiring into their antecedents.

Sergeant Regan had been certain for years the old man was a receiver of stolen property, but the pawnbroker was wily enough to cover up all actual evidence of his dealings on the wrong side of the law, and so the sergeant had been unable to do more than to keep him under surveillance. Occasionally the sergeant would drop into the pawn-office in the evening and have a casual chat over the fire in the parlour with the old man. These evenings had occasionally born fruit, for the pawnbroker knew perfectly well that he was suspected and when some petty thief brought him a valueless trinket of a set of worthless spoons, he had no compunction in betraying him to the Irish police officer with implied insinuation: "See how honest I am. Always on the side of the law!"

An unsavoury old man, Silverstein, but a fascinating study. Like a bird of prey, he had pounced on the needy of the neighbourhood and turned their ill-fortune to his own profit.

Regan had little doubt that one of his victims had turned on Silverstein, and squared accounts drastically.

The pawn-office was dimly lighted when Regan arrived in Stark Street. At the door stood a constable, who stepped aside promptly to admit the sergeant.

Inside, Regan found Superintendent Westcott, who was questioning the constable who had discovered the murder. On the floor knelt a short, slight man in a fawn coat and bowler hat, who was examining the still, limp body of the pawnbroker. Regan's eyes were drawn to the body against his will, for the cruelly battered head was sickening to look at.

The dead man was sprawled out, face downwards, in an ungainly attitude, with one leg doubled under him, and the other stretched out rigidly. A foot or so away lay a blood-stained skullcap. The body was clothed in a nightshirt, and ancient green dressing-gown, and a pair of shabby red felt slippers. On the floor near the body lay a small enamelled candlestick, in which was a stump of candle, broken in the middle.

Superintendent Westcott checked the constable's narration of his story for a moment, and nodded to Sergeant Regan.

"Glad you turned up," he said pleasantly. "Knew the old man pretty well, didn't you?"

With an effort, Regan withdrew his eyes from the frail, pathetic looking bundle on the floor, with its nauseating mashed head.

"Pretty well, sir," he replied with a gulp. "I must have been one of the last to see him alive. I was in here at the back at twelve o'clock."

The superintendent nodded thoughtfully. "Take a look round if you like," he said. "I'll have a word with you shortly."

He turned back to the constable, who was consulting his notebook. "At exactly what time did you find the body?" he asked.

"About twelve minutes to one it would be, sir," replied the constable. "I reached the other end of Stark Street at a quarter to one, and had come slowly down the street. I tried the handle of the pawnshop door lightly as I always do. To my surprise, the door was unlocked and slightly ajar, and I went in to investigate. When I passed behind the counter, the light of my torch fell upon the body of Moses Silverstein, which was lying on the floor in exactly the same position as it is now. I did not examine the body, as it was obvious that he was dead. I swept the room with my light, and assured myself that there was no one else in the room. "I felt a bit seedy with seeing the blood, and all, and I went outside and blew my whistle for my mate, who was with me in exactly three minutes. I took charge of the premises, while he went to telephone the police station."

"And nothing has been interfered with?" asked Superintendent Westcott.

The constable shook his head. "Nothing, sir."

"Very good."

Superintendent Westcott turned to the dapper little man in the fawn coat, who had risen from his position on the floor beside the body, and was dusting the knees of his striped trousers.

"Satisfied, doctor?" he enquired.

The man in the fawn coat nodded. "He's been dead about half an hour," he replied. "Possibly a little less than that; it isn't easy to say. There are at least a dozen injuries on the skull, most of them unnecessary; one such savage blow would have been sufficient to kill him. I expect the murderer was nervy, and wanted to make sure. The injuries were inflicted with a blunt instrument, wielded with terrific force, either by a very powerful man, or a very angry man, almost a lunatic."

"A blunt instrument," echoed the Scotland Yard man. "Can you give me an idea what kind of blunt instrument?"

"Afraid I can't. Possibly a poker, or one of those heavy candle-sticks over there. It isn't easy to say, for the skull's been mashed to a pulp. It's impossible to identify the individual blows. If the weapon was a poker, it was a heavy, rigid one."

"There's a heavy, steel poker in the parlour," said Regan.

"Get it, please," said Superintendent Westcott.

Sergeant Regan went into the little parlour behind the shop, and returned in a few moments with a puzzled expression on his face. "It isn't there."

"Look round the shop and see if you can find it," directed his superior officer. "You might examine the candlesticks on that shelf for bloodstains as well. Use your handkerchief in handling them. We don't want to obliterate possible fingerprints."

The doctor picked up his little black satchel. "I don't think you'll need me again tonight," he remarked. "I'll send you my report first thing in the morning. Fact is, I'm anxious to get home and mix myself a stiff brandy-and-soda. I don't know when I've seen an uglier sight."

"That's alright, doctor" said Westcott sympathetically. "Goodnight."

"Goodnight."

As the doctor left, Westcott turned to Regan. "Anyone else

sleep in the house?" he asked. "I sent Sergeant Evans upstairs to investigate ten minutes ago and he's not back yet."

"Only the housekeeper," replied Regan. "He may be having a little trouble with her. She's very deaf."

At that moment, they heard footsteps coming down the rickety, creaking staircase, then Sergeant Evans of the C.I.D. came into the shop guiding an elderly woman who wore a faded blue dressing-gown, which did not conceal a flannel nightgown beneath.

Her mouse-coloured hair hung in drab wisps about her head, and her face, seamed and wrinkled, was drained of all colour. Her eyes wore a dazed, terrified expression like those of a trapped animal.

When they lit on the huddled figure on the floor, they widened, and with a shriek the woman swayed and would have fallen had not Sergeant Evans caught and held her in his powerful arms.

"She's fainted," he remarked laconically. "Don't wonder. Nasty sight."

"Take her into the parlour," directed Westcott. "She'll be off again if she sees the body when she comes round. Here you" —this to the constable— "see if you can rustle up a cup of tea for her. We don't want a hysterical woman on our hands."

Evans carried the woman into the parlour, and laid her gently upon a sofa, while the constable investigated the contents of the larder in the musty kitchen at the rear of the house.

Westcott looked at Sergeant Regan. "What's your theory?" he demanded brusquely. "Do you think one of his customers did this? Pretty tough lot, aren't they?"

Danny Regan thought carefully before replying. "They are all pretty poor," he replied at last; "or they wouldn't be customers of Silverstein's. But I don't think any of his 'regulars,' you might call them, would do that." He jerked his thumb toward the battered head. "Mind you, he drove some of them to a pretty desperate pitch, and I won't say he wasn't threatened many a time, for he was, and little enough notice he took of it. But none of them were the killing sort. They might have beaten him up, but they wouldn't have murdered him."

His blue eyes assumed a thoughtful expression.

"I've an idea," he said. "I'm remembering a well-dressed young man who was here late tonight, when I was back there in the parlour. He was confabbing with Silverstein, and not in any friendly terms either, if I'm any judge of expression. And I'm remembering something the old man said when he came back into the parlour."

"Spit it out," said Westcott impatiently. What did he say?"

Sergeant Daniel Regan turned his blue eyes reproachfully upon the man from Scotland Yard.

"I'm trying to remember his exact words—if I'm not mistaken, Silverstein said that the solid earth had crumbled beneath the young man, and that he did not like the sensation of dancing on air."

"Dancing on air?" repeated Westcott slowly. "Dancing on air? A peculiar phrase sergeant. I can only think of only one meaning it could have—"

Sergeant Regan had worked under Superintendent Westcott before, and he knew that the Scotland Yard man was no stickler for etiquette.

He drew a blackened briar pipe from his pocket. "With your permission, sir," he said. "The air in here is none too sweet." Permission granted, he methodically filled and lighted the pipe.

Exhaling a cloud of pungent blue smoke, which steadied his nerves, and overcame the nausea which had threatened him since he came into that room of death, he said: "As you say, sir. A peculiar phrase. I wonder, now, if it could have been a prophecy?"

On the floor in front of the high sloping desk on which Silverstein had done his bookkeeping lay a strip of worn red carpet. Superintendent Westcott moved the high stool which stood upon it, carried the carpet across the room, and gently covered the huddled figure on the floor.

"And now," he said, tell me about your visit here tonight."

Sergeant Regan tilted his uniform cap forward, and scratched the back of his head. He was trying to remember every single detail of the incident. "It would be about the back of eleven o'clock—"

Moses Silverstein had been putting up his shutters when the sergeant came down the street with his heavy tread. The old man looked up at his approach, and a fleeting smile crossed his features. He propped a shutter against the glass of the window, and opened the door of his shop, rubbing his hands together.

"Come in, sergeant," he said ingratiatingly. "I will leave the remainder of the locking up for a quarter of an hour. With me you shall have a glass of wine. Today I have done a bit of good business."

After a moment's thought, the Irishman went into the dingy shop and passed through to the shabby parlour with Silverstein at his heels.

"And what was the business, may I ask?" he enquired, sitting down heavily.

Silverstein looked at him craftily from beneath shaggy eyebrows. "You remember the pair of miniatures I bought six months ago. They have been in the window beside the brass warming-pan ever since."

Regan remembered the miniatures.

"You gave poor old Miss Manders thirty shillings for them," he grunted. "They were her grandmother's. It nearly broke her heart to part with them."

Silverstein shrugged his shoulders. "She was glad enough to get the money. Today, my friend, an American saw them, and offered me ten pounds for the pair."

"A nice enough profit!" commented Regan, drily. "You know how to make money alright."

The pawnbroker smiled and poured out two glasses of wine, one which he handed to the sergeant.

"But that is not all," he replied. "I refused his offer. He offered more—I refused again. He said 'Fifty pounds, take it or leave it'. I rolled my eyes and cried: 'Oi! You want to rob me!' But I took it. Fifty pounds, my friend!" He laughed shrilly, his grey beard quivering.

"Fifty pounds!" exclaimed Regan. "Holy Mary! But, look now, Silverstein, you'll share a bit of your luck with the old spinster who sold them to you? She's having the very devil of a time making ends meet."

"Why should I?" parried Silverstein. "Business is business, my friend."

"But you will?" insisted Regan, glaring steadily into the pawnbroker's shifty eyes. "You'll spare her a fiver, now, won't you?"

Silverstein's expression hardened, but his eyes dropped, and he nodded reluctantly.

"Very well. You want to ruin me, but for you I'll do it. Five whole pounds she shall have."

"Give it to me now," said Regan. "I'll take it over to her on my way to the station."

After a moment's hesitation, Silverstein shuffled out of the room, and returned with the money. It was just as well, in his business, to keep on the right side of the police.

Regan pocketed the money, and sipped his glass of wine with added relish.

"Ye've got a queer place here Silverstein," he remarked, glancing around him. "For all that I know little about valuable things, I can tell you have some expensive ornaments in this poky old parlour of yours, cheek-by-jowl with some trash that you couldn't get a tanner apiece for. You must be worth a rare bit of money to have your treasures lying around loose like this!"

"Not so much, not so much," muttered the old man softly, his eyes glistening with cupidity, "and yet, as you say, some of these things are valuable. Someday I shall sell them—when the price is right."

The huge Irishman shifted comfortably in his chair. "And what will you do with your money? Will you buy a fine motor, and ride around like a lord?"

Silverstein smiled slowly. "To you," he said, softly, "money means a fine motor car, and luxury; in my neighbour, Silas Taplow, it means more horrors for his museum; to a young man of my acquaintance—a very foolish young man—it means more pretties for his empty-headed sweetheart; to me, money means—just money. Who is right? Yourself, Silas Taplow, the young man, or myself? Who can tell? When I die, I will leave my money to my heirs, and they will treat it as it should be treated—as money, to be valued for itself. Money, is a sacred trust, my friend. It must not be treated lightly. Be good to it, value it, keep it, and it will bring you more. Fling it to the winds, buy motorcars, or the ears of a murderer, or dainties for a lady, and it will soon desert you. Who shall know the value of money, if not a pawnbroker, who sees every day in the course of his business the result of its misuse?"

The old man's question remained unanswered, for at that moment a piano wire which was suspended above the outer door emitted a resonant twang, the signal that someone had entered the shop. Silverstein hurried away silently to attend to the newcomer, closing the door as he went. Curious as ever, the big police officer arose and reopened it slightly, so that he could see the customer, although he could not hear all that was said.

The newcomer was a tall, thin young man, with eyes set a little close together, which spoiled an otherwise pleasing face, and he was pleading urgently with the pawnbroker, who listened passively, with an occasional shrug of the shoulders. The only words that the police officer could catch were: 'I must have it,' which the young man uttered in a high, strained voice in which fear and anger mingled. To this the ancient pawnbroker only replied with an expressive shrug of his shoulders.

Silverstein was turning away to terminate the interview, but the young man grasped his arm while he fumbled beneath his jacket, and brought forth a wad of notes, which he offered to the old man. Silverstein looked at the money quizzically, then shook his head slowly, with a dry smile. The young man pleaded, threatened and cajoled, but the old man was firm. Regan could not hear their conversation, but the pantomime of the young man's changing expressions and Silverstein's calm passivity was unmistakeable. Then the young man said something which his expression told he thought a trump card to be kept until the last, but was answered only by a shrug of the shoulders and the outstretched palms of the old man, who seemed to be very little concerned.

There was no misreading the finality of Silverstein's gesture, and the young man turned and slowly left the shop. With a peculiar expression on his face, the old man moved silently back to his parlour, and Regan had barely time to close the door through which he had been a silent witness before the ancient pawnbroker was with him again.

"Sure an' it's late for a customer?" Regan queried.

"Customers at all times come," Silverstein replied. "An old man's bedtime to them is nothing. Sometimes they bring me good business, at other they merely waste my time and theirs. That was the young man I spoke of, a very foolish young man who sees in money mere dainties for his sweetheart. A pretty dance she has led him, and now the solid earth has crumbled beneath him, and he does not like the sensation of dancing on air. What did you think of him, this young man? His eyes are too close together, are they not?"

"Why—I—" stammered Regan. How the devil did the 'ould fule' know he had opened the door, he wondered.

"There are mirrors in my shop," explained Silverstein suavely, "and the business of other people is the chief business of the police, is it not?"

There was no possible reply, Regan felt, to the pawnbroker's question, and he drained the last drop in his glass, and rose to go. Moses Silverstein saw him to the door, then recommenced the task of locking up. As he strode down the street, Regan's thoughts were of the old man and his fortune, which must run into thousands, and of the customer, the young man whose sweetheart led a wanton dance.

It was a quarter past eleven when he arrived at the house where Miss Manders, an elderly spinster who had seen better days, rented a single room. The old lady had retired an hour before, but her landlord was still up. The sergeant borrowed an envelope and a sheet of paper, and wrote 'with the compliments of Moses Silverstein' on the paper, and enclosed it with a five-pound note in the envelope, to be given to Miss Manders first thing in the morning.

There the material part of his story ended.

"I was round and about the neighbourhood for the best part

of two hours after that," he concluded. "Then I dropped in at the police station, and was told about the murder."

Superintendent Westcott nodded reflectively. "You mentioned Silas Taplow; who is he?" he asked.

Regan stared. "You must have heard of Silas Taplow, sir!" he exclaimed. "Why, everybody knows of him. The Scavenger, they call him. He's a collector of horrors."

"I remember," Westcott agreed. "He runs a private museum of criminal relics, doesn't he? I read about him in the morning papers a few weeks ago."

"That's him. He lives a few doors away, on this side of the street."

"Must be a queer fish," Westcott commented. "I should think that your story is going to be of considerable value, sergeant."

Sergeant Evans appeared in the doorway of the parlour to report that the murdered man's housekeeper had recovered sufficiently to make a statement. A cup of tea, and Evans' friendly manner had restored her shattered nerves.

Westcott decided the woman in the parlour; even when covered with the strip of red carpet, the shape upon the floor of the shop had a sinister, nerve-shaking appearance. He requested Sergeant Regan to continue a search of the shop with a view to finding the weapon with which the crime had been committed.

Sophia Levine, the pawnbroker's middle-aged housekeeper, was able to tell little of importance. At twenty minutes past twelve she had been awakened by the sound made by her master closing his bedroom door and descending the creaking, groaning staircase to the shop. She concluded that he had heard the doorbell ringing downstairs and had gone to answer it. She herself had not heard the bell, but then, she was very deaf, and the shop was considerable removed from the sleeping quarters, and Silverstein had exceptionally keen hearing. It was by no means out of the ordinary for the pawnbroker to have callers at a late hour, and she thought nothing more of it, and dozed off again.

She had heard nothing more—simply the closing of the pawnbroker's bedroom door, and his noisy descent of the stairs.

"You say that was at twenty minutes past twelve?" Westcott regarded her closely.

She nodded vigorously. "Yes, sir. At twenty past, exactly."

"How can you be so sure of the time?"

She was startled at the abruptness of his tone, but answered simply and convincingly: "I have an alarm clock with a luminous dial on the table by my bed. When I awoke, it was the first thing I set eyes on."

Westcott rose from the chair facing the housekeeper in which he had been sitting.

"That's all for the present," he said. "If you think you can sleep you had better go back to bed."

Sophie Levine rose with a gasp to her feet.

"Thank you, sir. May I lock my door?"

The Superintendent smiled: "Certainly."

Like a pale ghost, the withered little woman slipped out of the room and up the stairs without a glance at the thing which lay in the shop.

Superintendent Westcott went back to the shop. He found Regan looking inside the large single compartment of the Silverstein's desk.

"Look here, sir," said the sergeant. "It looks as though someone has been rooting about in here. Everything's jumbled up all higgledy-piggledy."

Westcott looked over his subordinate's shoulder. The papers in the desk were scattered in wild profusion, and on one of them there was the impression of four fingers of a bloodstained hand!

Superintendent Westcott picked up the paper and examined the bloodstained impression closely. "Pity he wore gloves," he commented in a disappointed tone. "Still, we could hardly expect the murderer to leave his fingerprint like a visiting card. Criminals are too cute for that, nowadays."

His tone changed. "Look into that desk, sergeant, and tell me what you see," he demanded brusquely.

It was evident that he himself had noticed something which interested him exceedingly. Regan could see nothing but the mass of distorted paper, and said so.

"For heaven's sake use your eyes man!" retorted Westcott.

Regan's large, red face remained as imperturbable as ever. "All I can see is the old man's papers all mixed up higgledy-piggledy like a dog's breakfast, some of them with bloodstains on 'em."

"Now we're coming to the point!" exclaimed the C.I.D. man triumphantly. "Some of them stained with blood. Some of them. Why not all?"

Sergeant Regan thought hard. "Because some of them were examined before the murder?" he suggested at last.

"That's the idea! Fairly evident, isn't it? All of the papers are mixed up in exactly the same way, but only some are blood-stained. Therefore, it would seem that the pawnbroker appeared on the scene while the midnight intruder was actually in the act of rifling the desk, and that the murderer completed his examination of the papers after he had killed Silverstein. Probably it was the noise made by the intruder which brought Silverstein downstairs.

"I wonder—there's a safe on the premises, isn't there?"

Sergeant Danny Regan nodded. "Bound to be," he replied.

"I don't know just where, for Silverstein was a secretive old devil, but it won't be hard to find."

"Look around then," Westcott directed, "and see if you can find it."

The superintendent himself made a careful survey of the shop and its contents. As the C.I.D. man strode across the floor a board gave beneath his weight and he stumbled and almost fell. Righting himself, he looked down and saw that the board had shifted, revealing a hollow space between two of the floor supports. Inside was a metal cash box about two feet long and a foot wide.

Using his handkerchief to avoid smudging any fingerprints there might be, Westcott lifted the box out of its hiding place and carried it to the counter. Then, methodical as ever, he returned and inspected the loose board and the hiding place it covered before examining the box. It seemed improbable to him that the pawnbroker would have concealed anything of value beneath a loose floorboard without nailing the board down. This assumption he found to be correct. The board was studded with nails at each end, but had been replaced in its position so clumsily that the nails had not fitted into their holes. Obviously, it had been the murderer who had replaced the board, for the pawnbroker would not have been guilty of such carelessness.

An examination of the box confirmed this. The lid had been battered with some blunt instrument until the flimsy lock had given way. The box was empty. On the bottom of the box was a number of bloodstains which looked as though they had been made by the groping fingers of a gloved hand. The box, therefore had been rifled after the murder.

On the lid were several impressions of gloved fingers, and an almost perfect set of recently made fingerprints!

Whose fingerprints? Not the murderers, for he had worn gloves. Could he have had an accomplice?

As a thought occurred to him, Westcott went into the parlour and thrust a small shovel which lay in the fireplace up the chimney. A considerable amount of soot fell down. He gathered up some of the soot and returned to the shop. Gently he rubbed it on the murdered man's thumb and fingers. He found a piece of clean white paper and pressed the dead man's hand upon it. The result was a clear set of fingerprints. On comparison, they proved to be identical with the recently made impression on the lid of the box.

Sergeant Regan tramped heavily into the room. "I've found the safe, superintendent," he reported. "It's hidden in a little cubby-hole under the stairs. Someone's been trying to batter it open, by the look of things."

"Show me," was the C.I.D. man's laconic reply.

The sergeant led the way to his find, a squat, solid-looking safe, old-fashioned and massively built. Regarding it closely, Westcott saw that clumsy attempts had been made to open it, obviously by a beginner at the job. Here, too, he found the bloodstained impressions of a gloved hand.

On the floor beside the safe lay a bag of tools, and scattered about were chisels, hammers, files and drills of various sizes, all marked with a tell-tale red stain.

Sergeant Regan picked up the tool-bag and examined the initials 'T.F.' which were painted in white upon its side. "This is Tommy Finnigan's kit," he remarked.

"Tommy Finnigan?"

"Yes, Tommy's a joiner; he lives in the next street. But that doesn't mean that he did the job. He's been out of work for months, and I happen to know that he pawned his tools with old Silverstein well over a month ago."

"Then that doesn't help us much," remarked the superintendent losing interest in the tools. "The murderer must have been pretty keen on opening the safe, though. He must have known that the task was hopeless, without skill and the proper tools for the job, yet he worked at it like a madman. I wonder what he was so anxious to find?"

He stood up and walked slowly back to the shop, followed by Regan. For several moments there was silence while the two men looked at the drab, unsightly scene of the crime.

Then the superintendent crossed to the front door and examined the lock. It had been forced with a jemmy or some similar instrument.

Westcott looked at it thoughtfully and nodded his head. "What happened seemed fairly obvious," he remarked, turning to Sergeant Regan. "I believe I could reconstruct the crime from the evidence the murderer left behind him.

He went outside and closed the door behind him, waited a few moments, then pushed the door open again and stepped in.

"I am the murderer," he said, in a serious, thoughtful tone. I have just gained entrance by jimmying the door. I am looking for something, presumably money. That desk beneath the window catches my eye first, and I tiptoe across the shop, raise the lid, and peer in. Probably I have a flash lamp, and I examine the contents of the desk with its aid."

Suiting the action to the word, the superintendent tiptoed to the desk and went through the pantomime of examining the papers in it. Suddenly he stopped and stood in a listening attitude. "Suddenly I hear the creaking of the stairs," he said. He discarded his role for a moment and added: "I suppose the stairs would creak even under the weight of a light man like Silverstein, Regan?"

"The stairs would creak if a cat tiptoed down them," Regan replied.

Westcott nodded. "I realise that the pawnbroker has heard me. He is at the head of the stairs, descending slowly. In another moment I will be caught. There is barely time for me to hide. "I—" Coming out of character again, he said: "Where would I hide, would you say, sergeant?"

Sergeant Regan glanced round slowly with a serious expression upon his stolid face. "In the parlour?" he suggested.

"Precisely!" I tiptoe to the parlour door and slip inside."

Again, he went through the pantomime of crossing the room upon his toes. "I can hear the creaking coming nearer. I can almost hear the old pawnbroker breathing. He come into the shop holding a lighted candle above his head—" The superintendent broke off again: "But, not unarmed Regan. He wouldn't come downstairs to face a burglar unarmed. Hadn't he a revolver or something?"

"He had. I've seen it many a time. It lay on a shelf under the counter all day, and under his pillow at night."

Westcott nodded briefly, and resumed his grim game of make-believe. "The revolver is in his other hand. He peers about him but sees nothing. He advances a step or two, but I am hidden in the shadows of the parlour, and he does not notice me. He crosses to the front door, and confirms his suspicion that his premises have been entered. He becomes afraid, not for himself, but for his precious money. Has the intruder found that? He must know at once. He stoops and examines a certain floor board, beneath which something he values is hidden in a metal cashbox. I make up my mind quickly. In another minute he will come into the parlour and discover me. At all costs I must prevent that. I find a weapon—what weapon, Reagan?"

"The steel poker from the parlour fireplace?"

"Yes, the steel poker. I seize it and glide forward. When I am almost upon him, Silverstein wheels sharply, and sees me. Swiftly I raise the poker and bring it down with stunning force upon his head. He topples forward, to all appearances instantaneously dead. But I must make sure. He has seen me, and must not live to identify me. I hit and batter him long after the need for violence is over."

Regan's face whitened as he visualised the picture his superior officer had created. "My God!" he gasped. "What a fiend the man must have been."

"A fiend, or a man driven crazy by fear," replied Westcott. "The pawnbroker must have known him, Regan. No ordinary burglar would have used such needless violence."

"What about the revolver?" asked Regan. "It isn't lying about the shop, or we'd have found it."

Westcott shook his head. "The murderer probably pocketed it after he had killed the pawnbroker. The impulse to make his escape at once must have been terrible. But he fought it down and remained. He prized up the board over which the old man had stooped, discovered the cashbox, and battered it open. He found something inside, probably money, but not the thing he had come to seek. He continued his examination of the shop without result, and, searching further, found the safe, which he made a determined effort to open. But that was hopeless, and at last he gave up. After that—well, probably his fears got the upper hand of him and he bolted. But why did he take the gun with him, if the poker was his weapon? It would be so easily spotted as he made his getaway. He must have taken it, though, for it isn't here. I expect he took it absent-mindedly, and threw it away when he got outside."

"It's marvellous to hear you tell it," Regan exclaimed. "Why I might almost have been here, watching the whole thing!"

Superintendent Westcott smiled fleetingly.

"It's all simple enough, on the face of the impressions the murderer left," he demurred. "If I am right, and the murder took place as I have suggested, it will be simple enough to fix the exact time. My calculation is that Moses Silverstein was killed within a minute of coming downstairs—and the housekeeper heard him leaving his room at twenty past twelve. It would take the murderer twenty minutes to search the premises, and do the amount of damage that he did to the safe. He could not have left the shop much before a quarter to one, just a few minutes before the murder was discovered. If the constable had happened to be in this part of his beat a little earlier, he might have caught the murderer red-handed.

"But the weapon, Regan," he said suddenly. "Why should he take the weapon with him?"

Sergeant Regan shrugged his shoulders.

"There's no saying, sir," he replied. "Criminals do odd things on the spur of the moment. The steel poker's gone, sir, that's a fact. Why he hampered himself with it, God only knows."

At that moment they heard the policeman on duty outside challenging someone, then the door opened, and a little, thin man appeared in the aperture. So emaciated was he that the skin of his face was drawn tightly over his features; giving his head the disconcerting appearance of a skull. His almost complete baldness heightened the illusion. His hands were withered and bony like talons. He was clad in shabby grey trousers, an old velvet smoking-jacket, a grey flannel shirt, and carpet slippers.

He advanced slowly into the room, his sharp little black eyes darting about keenly. At the sight of the thing which lay on the floor, covered by a strip of carpet, his lips twisted a little.

"I knew it! I knew it!" he exclaimed in a shrill voice. So, the old man's been murdered, has he? I knew that would happen someday!"

Chuckling ghoulishly and rubbing his skinny hands together, the diminutive newcomer approached the covered body, and stood over it peering down intently, as though trying to imagine the full horror of the thing which lay beneath the carpet. He even stooped and raised the carpet a little, where it covered the battered head of the corpse.

With a sudden exclamation, Westcott seized the intruder by the neck and jerked him unceremoniously to his feet. "What are you up to, you little freak?" he demanded, menacingly. "And who are you, anyway?"

His captive giggled in a servile way. "That's rich!" he exclaimed hoarsely. "Oh, yes, that's rich. Asking who I am. Why, everyone knows me!"

The superintendent shook him savagely. "Who are you?" he repeated.

"Ask—ask him," gulped the captive, pointing at Sergeant Regan.

The sergeant took a step forward. "It's the chap I told you about, sir," he explained. "Silas Taplow."

The collector of grim curiosities chuckled. "Silas Taplow, that's me," he averred. "Everyone knows me. I'm famous."

"What do you want here at this time of the morning??" snapped Westcott.

His captive wriggled convulsively. "Let me go, you're strangling me," he gasped. "Let me go and I'll tell you."

Westcott relaxed his grip and Silas Taplow, suddenly released, sprawled awkwardly on the floor. When he picked himself up there was blood upon his hands from the spattered floorboards, but he did not attempt to wipe it off. Instead, he looked at it with evident pleasure.

"I knew I could smell blood," he shrilled. "I could smell it right down the street. What a nose I've got!"

Westcott grasped his arm fiercely. "We'll have no more nonsense," he rasped. "Come on, out with it. What are you up to at this time of the morning?"

"I can take the air when I like, can't I?" Taplow demanded. "There's nothing odd about a man stepping to his own front door for a breather when he pleases, is there? I'm often about at this time. The sergeant can tell you that."

"That's right, sir," agreed Regan. "The little mummy never seems to go to bed. Spends hours pottering about his house late at night. It's by no means unusual for him to be having a stroll about this time."

Taplow flashed a triumphant glance at the superintendent. "There you are!" he exclaimed.

"That doesn't explain what you're doing here," Westcott retorted. "Don't tell me again that you smelled blood, as you put it. I'm not swallowing that story. You knew something was up before you came through that door."

"Of course, I did. Didn't I see the lights on in the shop? Why, you could see them right down the street. Do you suppose I imagined old Silverstein had turned on every light in the place? Not he, the old skinflint! I knew something was up when I saw that! And when I came down the street, I saw a copper at the door. I didn't have to be Sherlock Holmes to smell trouble, did I?"

He leered up at the tall C.I.D. man. "Simple my dear Watson!" he exclaimed shrilly. "Quite simple."

Westcott grunted. "You didn't happen to be taking the air about twenty past twelve?"

Silas Taplow's brain was alert enough. "That was when the murder was committed was it? Yes, I see from your face that it was. I was in my museum at that time. What a pity! A murder in my own street, and I knew nothing about it. I'll never have a chance like that again. Why, if I'd been about I might even have seen the murder committed! The opportunity of a lifetime, and I missed it!"

Westcott turned away with an exclamation of disgust. "Ugh! You make me sick! Regan, tell the policeman at the door to escort this man to his own house."

Sergeant Regan went to the door to call the constable. When he turned, he noticed Silas Taplow bending again over the covered body. The constable took Taplow's arm none too gently, and marched him up the street to his house.

Regan returned to the shop, and looked at Westcott with a disgusted expression. "Doesn't it make you sick that a thing like that can call itself a man?" he said hoarsely. "I don't feel clean after layin' him!"

"An odd specimen, certainly, sergeant," Westcott agreed.

He lit a cigarette and puffed thoughtfully for a few minutes.

"It has just occurred to me that we may be missing something," he said at last. "Silverstein had a safe, but he hid something valuable in that cashbox under a floorboard. Doesn't it seem feasible that he may have had other similar hiding places?"

Regan nodded thoughtfully. "It does, indeed," he agreed. "If all the old man was suspected of was correct, he did more than a bit with stolen property. He wouldn't leave warm goods in the safe where a search-warrant could find them any time."

"Exactly what I thought," responded Westcott. "It may be worthwhile to look around a bit and see whether—" He broke off sharply, and stared at the floor where the body lay. "Sergeant, wasn't Silverstein's skullcap lying there just a moment ago?"

The sergeant's eyes followed the direction of Westcott's pointing finger. For a moment both men looked in silent stupefaction at the spot where the skullcap had been. Then—

"The clever scoundrel!" Regan bellowed. "He pinched it right under our very eyes!"

"Silas Taplow?"

"Who else? I saw him bending over the body, but I didn't realise what he was up to. I'll be a Dutchman's uncle if that doesn't beat all. Who'd have thought the devil would take the chance to do a bit of collecting for his museum right under the eyes of the police?"

"What's the number of his house?"

"Number eight. I'll go along now and drag him out."

Westcott shook his head. "No, I'll go. You remain here, and see if you can find any other hiding places. Have the constable and sergeant Evans help you. Rip up every floorboard in the place, if need be."

With determination expressed in every line of his face, Superintendent Westcott left the shop and strode down the street to number eight. He had read of this Silas Taplow, and of his strange hobby, and he began to remember some of the things he had read.

In his way, Silas Taplow was something of a celebrity. People pointed him out in the street as he passed; errand boys gazed in awe at his dingy house; on several occasions reporters from the big morning papers had interviewed him. He was famous—or notorious—for his collection of gruesome relics. He loved them as a miser loves gold, and spent the larger part of his small independent income upon them. Like a carrion bird, he was to be found where death was—violent death—and the place he loved above all others was the morgue, dark and evil-smelling.

Arriving at Silas Taplow's house, Westcott ran briskly up the steps and pounded again and again upon the door.

A window on the second storey was thrown up, and Taplow's skull-like head appeared. "What is it?" he cried shrilly.

"Come down at once and open this door."

With a muttered curse, the peculiar little man withdrew his head and slammed down the window. A few minutes later Westcott heard the sound of shambling footsteps approaching, and the door was curiously opened a little. Westcott put his shoulder to the door, thrust it back unceremoniously, and walked in.

The hall was in darkness but for the glimmer of light afforded by a gas jet turned down so far that the flame was barely the size of a pea. Westcott turned the gas up full. To his surprise, Silas Taplow was dressed in faded pink pyjamas and a fawn dressing gown.

"Quick work," commented the Scotland Yard man. "You were fully clothed a few minutes ago. Why were you in such a hurry to undress and get into bed? 'Fraid one of us might be along to ask you awkward questions, eh?"

Taplow spread his skinny hands and shrugged his shoulders. "A few minutes ago, you impressed the lateness of the hour upon me," he replied with a smirk. "Can you complain if I have taken your hint?"

"Well, you can slip upstairs and dress again," retorted Westcott. "You're going for a walk with me. You can fetch the skullcap at the same time."

"The skullcap?" Silas Taplow looked quite mystified.

"Yes, old Silverstein's skullcap. You stole it just before Sergeant Regan threw you out of the shop."

"My dear sir," responded Taplow, in a sneering tone, "you flatter me, you do really. I'm not nearly clever enough to commit a theft right under the eyes of a celebrated officer of Scotland Yard."

"You took the skullcap, and the sooner you hand it over the better it will be for you."

"What a nasty, suspicious nature you must have, my dear superintendent! I assure you that you are quite wrong!"

With an exclamation of annoyance, Westcott shot out his arm, grasped the collector of horrors by the shoulder and shook him until his eyes watered.

"Don't lie to me you little freak! Where have you hidden it?"

The sneering mask of civility behind which Taplow had hidden his real feelings fell away from him, and he literally snarled into Westcott's face. "Find it yourself, if you're so sure I took it. But lay another finger on me, and I'll—I'll—I'll—"

He shook and stuttered with rage. Westcott released him, and for a few moments the two stood eyeing each other, one curiously, the other malevolently. Then a change came over Taplow's features, and he smirked up at the detective in an oily, toadying manner.

"We mustn't lose out tempers, my dear superintendent! If you wish to search for the skullcap you persist in suspecting me of stealing, you are perfectly welcome to do so. I waive the formality of a search warrant willingly—for you, my dear sir."

The C.I.D. man clenched his fist and took a step forward, then, with a shrug of his shoulders, relaxed his attitude and nodded his head.

"Very well," he said slowly. "I'll look around the place, and if I find it, you sleep in the cells tonight, my man. Let's see this museum of yours first."

Silas Taplow gestured towards the stairs with a leering grin. "This way, my dear superintendent."

In the largest room of the house Silas Taplow kept his morbid treasures. Among them was a jemmy which had belonged to Charles Peace; a lock of hair from the head of Hannah Martin, who was slaughtered in a basement in Limehouse; the rope which had hanged a notorious murderer; an axe which had featured in the 'Bow Street Horror' and a scale model of a morgue in papier mâché, with horribly realistic corpses laid out upon slabs.

To Westcott, unemotional though he was, there was something very awesome about these grim curios, with their dark histories of human passion and bestiality. The air of the room seemed to team with unmentionable horror that its gruesome inanimate inhabitants exuded.

"No good will come to you from these things," he said in a voice that was little more than a whisper. "If there are ghosts, this house must be full of them. The air here is charged with a malignant force."

Taplow rubbed his bony fingers together. "So, you think I can boast of a ghost or two, in addition to my other treasures? Capital! What a show they would make, if we could only see them!"

Westcott did not reply, but went on with his close inspection of the exhibits. At last he turned away with a shrug of his shoulders.

"The skullcap's not here, then?" murmured Taplow, with his eyes on the others face. "How strange! You were so certain it would be! I admit I should like it. A prize, superintendent, a prize! Why, he was wearing it when the murderer crushed his bony old skull! I must make a bargain for the rope they string up the old man's murderer with. It is not every day one has a murder in one's own street!"

With a grunt of distaste, Westcott went out of the room. There were three or four other rooms on the landing, and he searched each of them without success. On the floor above he discovered two doors. Opening one he found himself in a tiny bedroom, in which a maid-servant was snoring loudly on a dishevelled bed. He flashed a light round the room and under the bed without revealing the thing he sought.

The other door gave entrance to a large room, the floor of which was piled high with rags of every description and colour, mixed up higgledy-piggledy as though someone had been making hay with them.

"There is money in rags," murmured Taplow, at the superintendent's elbow. "I do quite a little business in that sort of thing. You are at liberty to turn them over if you choose, but I warn you, you will find fleas in abundance, and nothing else."

To search that rag-pile without assistance for a skullcap which was little better than a rag itself would have taken hours. With a groan of exasperation, Westcott slammed the door and went downstairs. The ground-floor rooms were equally disappointing. When Westcott opened the cellar door he heard a scuffling, scampering noise.

"Rats," explained Taplow, with a smirk. "Go down if you like, but it seems hardly probably that I'd hide a prize like the skullcap down there, where it would be torn to shreds in five minutes, granted, of course, that I was clever enough to steal the thing."

"You stole it all right," snapped Westcott.

"Then your duty is plain! Why don't you arrest me?"

"Oh, got to hell," snarled Westcott in a disgruntled tone.

He went out the front door, and slammed it behind him. There was not the slightest doubt in his mind that Taplow had stolen the skullcap, and that it was hidden in his house, but without being able to find it, he could not take the risk of interfering further with the oily-mannered little sadist.

Returning to the pawnshop, he found Regan waiting for him with triumph written plainly on his large, red face.

"Your hunch was a winner, superintendent!" cried Regan. "Look what we found under a loose board in the kitchen cupboard!"

He held up a glittering diamond necklace.

At half-past nine on the morning after the murder of Moses Silverstein, Superintendent Westcott sat in his office at Scotland Yard examining a little bundle of papers. He had remained at the Stark Street pawnshop until almost four a.m., and his latter efforts had been hampered by streams of reporters who arrived and poked into everything, but he was feeling tolerably fit for the work ahead of him. A Turkish bath, a few hours' sleep, and a huge breakfast had worked wonders with his tired tissues.

A uniformed messenger came into the room, laid a sheet of paper which smelled of fresh printers' ink on the desk before Westcott, and stood waiting for the superintendent to read and check it.

Blue pencil in hand, Westcott picked up the proof, and scanned it closely. It was Sergeant Regan's description of the young man he had seen arguing with the murdered pawnbroker on the previous night. Detail by detail, every point of the young man's appearance had been carefully written by the observant officer. Colour of eyes, and hair, shape of nose and mouth, complexion, height and build, everything that one man could note about another man in a few minutes of inspection was there, down to a description of the wanted man's nervous habit of plucking at his ear with the forefinger and thumb of his right hand and a complete inventory of the clothes he had worn.

Superintendent Westcott nodded his head approvingly as he came to the end of the proof, and wrote a large blue pencilled 'OK' at the bottom of the sheet. Within an hour or two the circular would be distributed to police stations all over London, and several thousand policemen would be on the lookout for the young man it described.

The orderly left the room, and Westcott turned back to his work. He was not left undisturbed for long, however. In a few moments the telephone bell rang.

He lifted the receiver. "Well?"

"A Mr. Cadman to see you, sir. Shall I send him up?"

"Yes, do, please, at once."

He leaned back in his chair with his eyes upon the floor, and in a few moments rose briskly as a tall, distinguished-looking man of about forty, with large, regular features and iron-grey hair was ushered into the room by a uniformed orderly, who immediately withdrew.

Henry Alain Cadman was a jewel expert employed by a world-famous insurance company. He smiled genially, and accepted the superintendent's outstretched hand, giving it a cordial pressure.

"I received your message on arriving at the office, Sooper," he remarked, "and I decided to come straight over. What is it? Something in my line?"

Westcott nodded. "Very much in your line, I should say," he replied, taking the diamond necklace discovered on the murdered man's premises from a drawer and laying it on the desk.

"I'm heartily obliged to you for coming to see me so promptly," he continued. "Take a look at these, and tell me what you think of them?"

Cadman took the necklace and examined it carefully with the aid of a jeweller's glass.

"Fairly valuable," he commented, "although by no means perfectly matched, and there are flaws on several of the diamonds. Worth about nine hundred pounds, I should say."

Westcott was frankly disappointed. "Is that all?"

The jewel expert laughed. "My dear Westcott what did you expect? Necklaces worth fabulous sums are few and far between, you know." He replaced the diamonds on the desk. "Stolen property, I presume?"

The detective offered his friend a cigar and a light, chose a cigar for himself, and in a few moments the two men were comfortably wreathed in fragrant blue smoke.

"There's something peculiar about this necklace," remarked Westcott, when his cigar was drawing to his satisfaction. "It must have been stolen, for one of my men found it under a loose board in the pawnshop of Moses Silverstein last night, and Silverstein had the reputation of being a fence."

"You mean the old pawnbroker who was murdered last night? I read something about in the papers at breakfast."

"That's the man. Now, you can bet your boots that he didn't come by that necklace honestly. It must have been stolen, yet we've ransacked the files this morning without finding it listed anywhere."

"Which means that the owner may not be aware of the theft?" suggested Cadman.

"Exactly. Although how anyone can be robbed of a diamond necklace worth nine hundred pounds and not be aware of it beats me!"

"Odd, certainly," agreed Cadman, thoughtfully.

"It means that I've got to reverse the usual procedure, and look for the owner," Westcott continued. "I wonder if you can help me? Have you ever seen the necklace before?"

The jewel expert shook his head in a positive manner.

"Never," he replied. "I'm certain of that. Diamonds are almost as distinctive as human beings, when you get to know them. If this necklace had been through my hands at any time I'd be pretty sure to remember it. But it never has been."

"Then that's that," said Westcott, in a disappointed tone. "Your people do a large percentage of jewellery insurances, and

I had a fugitive hope that you'd recognise it. But it wouldn't be my lot to have a stroke of luck like that. I'll have to send some of my men on a round of the big jewellery establishments to see if they can find the firm that stole the necklace. I've had it photographed with that purpose in mind. There's one thing you can do for me, though."

"I'll be only too pleased. What is it?"

Westcott handed his friend a piece of paper and a pencil. "Write me a proper trade description of the necklace, to supplement the photograph, will you?"

"Certainly."

For some minutes Cadman scribbled busily then he rose and handed the result of his labours to Westcott. "There you are," he said. "I wish you luck. And now if there's nothing else, I'll go along. I've got a busy day ahead of me."

The C.I.D. man took the other's hand and shook it cordially, promising to let him know the result of his canvass of the jewellery firms. As Cadman took his departure, Westcott rang a bell which summoned a typist who came almost immediately.

"Type a dozen copies of that," he said, handing over the description which his friend had written out. "I'll send Sergeant Evans for them in a few minutes."

He telephoned through for Sergeant Evans as the door closed upon the typist. While waiting for Evans to come, he put through a message to the Yard's photographic expert.

Evans and the photographer came into the room simultaneously. Westcott waved the former to a chair while he examined the dozen photographs of the necklace which the latter had brought with him. They were fine, clear prints, strikingly like the original.

"Good work," said Westcott, approvingly. "Thanks very much. That's all for the present."

"Evans," he rapped out, wheeling round in his chair. "We've got a warm trail to work on, but we've got to work fast while it's still warm. I've got a hunch that this necklace was the thing which the murderer went to Silverstein's last night to find. If I'm right, the sooner we identify it the quicker we'll get on the trail of the murderer. Mark you, this is delicate work. The necklace hasn't been reported to us as stolen. The owner himself or herself may have pawned it—and done murder in a vain attempt to regain possession of it. We can't do much until we discover the owner, anyway. That's your job. Here are twelve photographs. Go along to room 44, and one of the typists will give you a dozen typed detailed descriptions to supplement them. You and detectives Drummond and Hay will make the flying round of the big jewellers this morning and see if any of them can identify the necklace. If any of them can, get me on the 'phone at once. I'll be waiting here for a call. Give instruction to that effect to Drummond and Hay as well. Is that clear?"

"You bet," he said, unemotionally. "Is that all?"

"That's all. Be on your way."

The telephone bell rang shrilly, and with a sigh the superintendent picked up the receiver. "Well?"

"Three reporters to see you, sir."

A quick twist of his lips rolled his cigar to the corner of his mouth. "Tell them to go to hell!" he rapped out. "No! Wait a moment."

He reviewed the position quickly. Reporters were anathema to him; they had a habit of nosing about on their own, getting in the way, writing more than he wanted published. He knew that his message would not send them about their business. They would simply hang about waiting for him, and follow him wherever he went. If he could only put them off the scent for a few minutes—

An idea occurred to him, and he went into the corridor and summoned one of his assistants who was awaiting instructions there.

"Dodson," he said swiftly, "there are some nosey devils downstairs, and I want you to lead them off on a false scent. I'm having them sent up, and when they come into the room, do your best to look as though you'd just been receiving important instructions. I'll slip you an address in a secretive sort of way, as though I didn't want them to hear, and you go straight to the address, and wait there for an hour or two. Question people in the neighbourhood, if you like. Ask what time it is, or something of the sort. But look important, whatever you do. Is that clear?"

"Quite clear, sir."

Followed by the smiling detective, Westcott re-entered his office and picked up the telephone receiver. "Send the gentlemen up," he said, in so sweet a tone that the constable at the other end could hardly believe his ears.

When the reporters were ushered into the room, the superintendent was handing Dodson a paper with a secretive air (it was a circular which had come in the post that morning).

"Come right in boys," he said. "I'll have a word with you in a minute."

He walked to the door with Dodson, well aware that three pairs of ears were strained to catch his parting remarks.

"If my information is correct," he said, in a low (but not too low) tone, "the man we want is at 175 Gerard Street. Make a mental note of the number—175 Gerard Street. Don't attempt to make an arrest, but nose around, and 'phone in if you spot him."

"Very well, sir," replied Dodson, with an air of importance.

He touched his hat and strode smartly off down the corridor.

Taking a batch of typewritten papers from his desk, Westcott handed one to each of the reporters.

"This is the official report of the crime last night," he remarked. "You are at liberty to print it, if you like."

One of the reporters glanced at his paper quickly. "But we already know all this!" he expostulated. "It's identical with the verbal report that was given out at Battersea Police Station early this morning!"

"Then you know as much as we do," replied Westcott, suavely (but not truthfully, for the report made no mention of the diamond necklace). "Sorry, that's all the help I can give you, boys. We haven't a thing to go on so far."

After an exchange of ironic courtesies, the reporters filed out of the room. Westcott tiptoed to the door and listened.

"Well, I don't know about you chaps," he heard a reporter remark, "but I'm going to beat it up to 175 Gerard Street as fast as a taxi will take me!"

The others murmured agreement. The superintendent permitted himself a gentle smile. 175 Gerrard Street was the address of a steam laundry!

Half an hour later the telephone bell range and he answered it, to hear the voice of Sergeant Evans at the other end of the wire. "I've struck oil, sir!" Evans exclaimed. "The firm of Snaith, in Bond Street, recognised that necklace as one they sold three years ago!"

"And the name of the purchaser?" demanded Westcott. "Quick, man, don't keep me waiting all day!"

"Lady Agatha Daventry. Her address is number sixteen A, Lowndes Square."

"Good man!" exclaimed Westcott, jotting down the name and address. "Where are you 'phoning from?"

"A shop in Bond Street. The number is Bond 89341."

"Wait there, then. I'll give you a ring in a few minutes."

Sergeant Evans hung up, and Westcott jiggled the hook

at his end impatiently. In a few moments, the Scotland Yard operator had found Lady Agatha Daventry's number, and was put through to the house in Lowndes Square without delay.

"This is Superintendent Westcott of Scotland Yard. May I speak to Lady Agatha?" he asked the butler, who answered the telephone.

"I'm sorry, sir, but Lady Agatha been ill, and is unable to come to the 'phone."

"Is there a secretary or companion I can speak to?"

The butler coughed deprecatingly. "Lady Agatha has a secretary, sir," he replied stiffly. "But he has not arrived this morning."

"Is that usual?" demanded Westcott, trying hard to keep his excitement out of his voice.

"Hardly, sir. I 'phoned the young gentleman this morning, but he was not at his flat and had left no message."

"Hold the wire for a moment," exclaimed Westcott, fumbling with the papers on his desk. He found the one he sought, and continued: "Is this description at all like Lady Agatha's secretary: height, about five feet eleven; build, slight; eyes, dark and set close together; nose, prominent and aquiline; mouth, small and thin-lipped; complexion sallow? And has he a nervous habit of pulling his ear with his thumb and forefinger when excited?"

"The description tallies exactly, sir," replied the butler, with a note of interest creeping into his tone. "And I have frequently noticed the habit to which you refer."

"Thanks," snapped Westcott, hanging up the receiver abruptly.

Less than a minute later he was 'phoning Sergeant Evans at Bond 89341. "The trail's becoming hotter, Evans," he exclaimed. "I'll meet you at 16a Lowndes Square within fifteen minutes."

Sir Joseph Parker, Lady Agatha's doctor, was a sound, if old-fashioned physician of the family doctor type, who made up for his lack of modern theory with his wealth of common-sense. He was paying a visit to his patient when Westcott and Evans arrived at her house in Lowndes Square, and decided to interview the Scotland Yard man before permitting them to see Lady Agatha.

He listened patiently to what Westcott had to say, nodding intelligently at intervals, his alert grey eyes occasionally travelling to the detective's face with an appraising look.

"If you are right, and the necklace belongs to Lady Agatha, it is just as well that you turned up now," he commented, when Westcott had concluded his remarks. "Lady Agatha has been very ill, and it is one of her peculiarities that she doesn't care twopence for jewels when she is ill. Now she is convalescent, and in convalescence she has a habit of trying them on and playing with them for hours, hardly letting them out of her sight, in fact. She is about due to send for her jewels and heaven knows what would have happened had the diamond necklace been missing. The shock would have been terrific. However, since you have recovered it before she knew it was stolen, she will hardly be very upset—except by the fact that she must have been harbouring a thief in the house. I'll go upstairs and prepare her; I've no doubt that she'll see you."

Only a few minutes elapsed before Superintendent Westcott was summoned to Lady Agatha's bedroom. He found the old lady (she was over seventy) sitting bolt upright in bed, cheeks flushed, nose quivering a little, and with a belligerent look in her eyes.

"Sir Joseph says that you are under the impression that my

diamond necklace is in your possession," she snapped. "That is absurd, of course. My necklace is in the library safe."

"I am afraid you are mistaken, Lady Agatha," replied Westcott soothingly. "I have reason to believe that it was stolen some time ago."

"Nonsense!" quivered the old lady. "Who could possibly have stolen it? All of my servants have been with me for over twenty years. They are all perfectly honest and reliable."

Beneath the mask of anger which cloaked her face, Westcott believed that he could read fear. Lady Agatha was terrified of the possibility that the necklace had been stolen (which was strange, considering that she had been told that it had already been recovered), and seemed to believe that if she said it loudly enough that it had not been stolen, it could not possibly have been.

"What about your secretary, Lady Agatha?" asked Westcott, gently. "He is only a young man, isn't he? He can't have been with you for very long."

Lady Agatha shook herself.

"Arnold Hemingway? The suggestion is absurd! He is my nephew. He could not possibly be capable of such an action. Oh, I know people have been horrid about Arnold. There have been all sorts of stories—but one need only know the boy to realise how untrue they are. After all, that's all he is, only a boy."

"There is the necklace, Lady Agatha," said Westcott, taking the glittering string of diamonds from his pocket and handing it to her. "Do you recognise it?"

Lady Agatha took it gingerly as though afraid that it might burn her fingers. She examined it closely for a moment, then dropped it with a cry. "It is my necklace!" she cried, pathetically. "Oh, Arnold! Arnold!"

Sir Joseph Parker moved toward his patient with a worried frown, but she waved him aside, and squared her frail shoulders.

"I am quite all right," she murmured. "A little hurt, that is all. Faith is a precious possession, and it pains one to have it trampled on." She turned to Westcott. "If Arnold took the necklace, superintendent," she said in a shaky tone, "I should prefer not to prosecute him. I never wish to see him again, but I cannot invoke the law against a blood relative."

"I'm afraid the case is out of your hands, Lady Agatha," replied Westcott, gravely. "The necklace is evidence of a more serious charge." He hesitated, then nodded: "I should like to ask you a question, but I am afraid that it may cause you further pain. I you prefer that I should leave you a moment—"

"Thank you, but I feel perfectly alright," said Lady Agatha, "please put your question to me and I will answer it to the best of my ability."

"Last night, a man answering to the description of your secretary, was in possession of a considerable amount of money," he stated. "Can you suggest any way in which Mr. Hemingway could have obtained that money?"

"I'm afraid I can't."

"He handled no money in the course of his duties?"

"Very little," replied Lady Agatha, with a shake of her head. "Only the household petty cash, which is never much."

"Did he ever cash cheques at the bank for you?"

"Yes, frequently, but he always gave me the money when he returned."

"He would be well-known at your bank?"

"Oh yes. He did business for me there once or twice every month."

"Did he have access to your cheque book?"

"Yes," said Lady Agatha, in a low voice. "He filled out the cheques to my instructions, and I signed them. During my illness, I have not seen my cheque book, only individual cheques.

The book itself is in my desk downstairs, to which Arnold has had a key for some months."

"Will you be good enough to send for the cheque book?"

When it was brought, Westcott examined it closely. He gave an exclamation of interest when he found that one of the cheques near the end of the back was missing. It had been torn out, counterfoil and all. He wrote down the number of the cheque, D4719375.

"When did you last sign a cheque?" he asked, "and for what amount?"

"About ten days ago," she replied. "The amount was fifty pounds."

He found the particulars of the cheque written on the counterfoil previous to the first blank cheque. Closing the book, he handed it to Lady Agatha.

"That is all for the present," he said. "I am sorry that has been necessary for me to upset you."

"One of the cheques is missing?" she asked, watching his face nervously.

"Yes. It may mean nothing. I hope so. I will let you know when I have definite information on the point. Good-day, Lady Agatha."

"Good-day, superintendent," she whispered, and slipped back upon the pillows with an ash-grey face.

Downstairs, Westcott found the telephone, and put a call through to Lady Agatha's bank. When connected to the manager, he gave his name and business.

"When did you last cash a cheque on Lady Agatha Daventry's account?" he asked.

There was a short pause while the books were consulted.

"Yesterday morning," came the reply at last.

"For what amount?"

"Two hundred and fifty pounds!"

"And the number of the cheque?" demanded Westcott, eagerly.

"D4719375," was the reply.

"Who cashed it?"

"Mr. Arnold Hemingway."

"Thank you, that's all I wanted to know," said Westcott, in a satisfied tone.

"Here, hold on a moment!" the bank manager protested. "Is there anything wrong with that cheque?"

"You should be able to answer that question better than I can," retorted Westcott. "Does the signature look genuine?"

"Our teller accepted it without hesitation," replied the manager in a doubtful tone. "But now that you mention it, it doesn't look quite right. The lines are a little heavy."

"I'd advise you to have it examined by an expert," said Westcott. "I've a hunch that you'll find that it's a forgery."

Hanging up the receiver, the C.I.D. man summoned the butler, and obtained Arnold Hemingway's address, and a good photograph of the secretary from him. Then he took his departure, followed by Sergeant Evans, who plodded along stoically, without betraying the slightest interest in his superior's discoveries.

Arnold Hemingway lived in one of a small block of service flats in Half Moon Street. The porter on duty in the hall told them that the man for whom they sought had left the building at nine o'clock that morning.

"I took 'im up his breakfuss, an' the mornin' paper at eight o'clock this mornin'," he explained. "Did it to oblige the missus, who 'ad an 'eadache. Abaht an hour arter, Mr. 'Emingway comes boltin' down the stairs wiv a suitcase in 'is 'and an' goes flyin' out the door wivout a word."

Westcott looked at his watch. It was now a little after one

o'clock. If Hemingway had bolted, he had just over four hours' start. The trail was still warm!

"Any idea when Mr. Hemingway came in last night?"

"Las' night!" scoffed the porter. "'Twasn't las' night, it was s'mornin'. 'Alf past one, 'e come in. I was still awake, for the missus 'ad given me a bad night wiv 'er bleedin' 'eadache."

The two detectives went upstairs, and entered the secretary's flat with a passkey which the porter had handed them. The place consisted simply of a sitting-room, bedroom, and bathroom, and all the rooms were in wild disorder.

The fireplace was heaped high with charred papers. Suit-cases and trunks had been pulled from underneath beds, and from cupboards, and half-filled with clothes and other personal belongings. Evidently, Hemingway had been in the middle of an extensive packing when he took fright and bolted with a single suitcase.

Sergeant Evans knelt by the fire, and started to sort out the half-burnt papers. In heaping them into the grate in wholesale fashion and putting a match to the pile, Hemingway had defeated his own purpose. The papers had been too closely packed to burn, and half of them had survived unscorched.

Westcott examined the living-room with interest. There were at least a dozen photographs of different girls arranged upon the mantelpiece, all of them autographed lovingly in the corner. It was plain that Hemingway had been a believer in love, not only at first sight, but at every encouraging glance!

As Westcott turned over clothes and opened drawers haphaz-ardly, Sergeant Evans rose to his feet with a bundle of slightly scorched papers in his hand. He handed them to Westcott without remark.

The superintendent examined the papers, and emitted an exclamation of triumph. Among them were a number of pawn tickets, some burnt until they were hardly recognisable, other almost intact. Some acknowledged small articles of jewellery, a watch, cigarette case, tie-pin, and so on, which had been pawned for a nominal figure; others were for clothing, and one was for 'a violin, in good condition.' And they each bore the printed heading: 'Moses Silverstein, pawnbroker, 1 Stark Street, Battersea'.

Sitting down on a trunk, with a sheet of paper and a pencil, Westcott wrote briskly for a few minutes. Then he went to the telephone, rang up Scotland Yard, and requested that a messenger be sent to the flat to collect copy and a photograph to supplement the description provided by Sergeant Regan, which had been circularised early that morning.

Within two hours, the circular which Westcott had drawn up would be broadcast through London, and on its way to the provinces—

'WANTED FOR MURDER'
'ARNOLD HEMINGWAY, AGED THIRTY-TWO
HEIGHT FIVE FEET ELEVEN...'

The telephone staff at Scotland Yard worked efficiently and methodically, but at top speed nevertheless. All afternoon the wires hummed with the description of Arnold Hemingway wanted for the murder of Moses Silverstein.

The wanted man had four hours' start, but the net was ready to close in on him, to wherever he might flee!

At each of the London stations the railway police were watching for him. One of them questioning a booking-clerk at St. Pancras, elicited the information that a tall young man who stood nervously pulling his ear with his thumb and forefinger while waiting for his change had taken a ticket for Glasgow at a quarter past nine. A porter was found who remember seeing a man who answered the description of Hemingway getting into the carriage of the Scottish train at twenty-five minutes past nine, with a small suitcase in his hand. The train had left at ten minutes to ten.

It was five minutes to four when Westcott received the information. Consulting a timetable, he found that the train was due at Carlisle at 4.15p.m. He telephoned at once to the Carlisle police, giving instructions to meet the train when it arrived, and to arrest Hemingway if he was a passenger.

At 4.30p.m., the Chief of Police at Carlisle telephoned that the wanted man was not to be found upon the train when it arrived at his town. He added the information that the guard had some recollection of a tall man, carrying a suitcase, leaving the train at Leicester.

A telephone call to the station at Leicester produced the information that a man corresponding to Hemingway's description had come through the barrier from the Scottish-bound train at ten minutes to twelve, and had paid his fare in cash. After putting through a message to the Leicester police headquarters, Superintendent Westcott left for Leicester in a flying squad car with three other detectives.

A little after half-past six he walked into the central police station of the Midland city, to find the chief of police awaiting him with some information.

"Just before one o'clock," said the chief, after cordial greetings had been exchanged, "a Morris-Oxford saloon car was reported missing from one of the main streets. Enquiries were made, and we discovered that a little after half-past twelve a tall thin man carrying a suitcase had walked up to the car, stepped into it with an air of proprietorship, and driven away. The constable directing traffic on the corner particularly noticed the incident, for he had his eye on the car, which had been parked longer than our bye-laws permit. When I got your message, I decided that the thief must be the man you are after. We could find no other trace of him after leaving the railway station. I got in touch with the police of some of the neighbouring towns, and ten minutes ago I received this wire."

He handed Westcott a buff slip on which a few words were typewritten.

"Blue Morris-Oxford saloon car registered J.U.69103 found abandoned in Orchard Street, wire instructions," ran the telegram, which had been sent by Inspector Harkness of the Birmingham police.

Westcott nodded his head knowingly. "He's a hop ahead of us still. We'll get him, though, there's nothing surer than that."

The Leicester chief of police nodded. "I'm sending a constable and the owner to Birmingham to identify the car and bring it back," he said. "But if you're after the man who took it on a murder charge, we won't bother our heads about him any longer."

"I'll be moving along then," said Westcott, rising to his feet. "Thanks for your help."

"Next stop Birmingham," he remarked to the driver as he stepped into the flying squad car, outside the police station.

The driver let in the clutch, and the car was off with a roar, doing thirty-five miles an hour through the town, and accelerating to close on sixty when the country was reached. As they hummed along, Westcott explained the next move in the game of hide-and-seek which they were playing to Sergeant Evans who shared the rear seat with him.

"The police station first," he said, "to see if Hemingway's repeated his Leicester trick and stolen another car. Then the railway stations, and the long-distance bus stations. I expect our man will have lost no time in getting out of Birmingham. He won't expect us to be on his tracks so soon, though."

At the Birmingham police-station they drew a blank; no cars had been reported missing that afternoon, and no trace of Hemingway had been found, neither did any booking clerk or porter at New Street Station remember seeing anyone who corresponded with the description of the wanted man. At the booking-office of a bus company, however, they picked up the trail again. A young man whose appearance tallied with that of their quarry had taken a ticket for the bus which had left for Liverpool at three o'clock in the afternoon.

It was now a quarter past seven. Westcott dispatched one of his men to send a wire addressed to the Liverpool police, and proceeded to question the employees at the bus station, and the loafers who congregated about it.

"I remember him," stated a stockily-built individual whose uniform cap had 'Inspector' written across it. "He hung about the bus station from half-past two until five to three, when the Liverpool bound bus come up. He went into it and took a rear seat."

A newsboy who had been hovering about eagerly drinking in the conversation, and staring at the detective and their real flying squad car pulled Westcott's sleeve urgently.

"I saw that bloke, guv'nor," he cried shrilly. "I noticed 'im particklery, for his fust of all ast me for a paper, then, as I was 'anding it to 'im, he pushed it away, gave me a tanner, an' said he didn't want no paper. 'E didn't travel with the bus, guv'nor. At the last moment he climbed out and 'ooked it in the direction of the lavatories over there. 'E never come back, either, leastways, I never saw 'im."

Followed by a little crowd of bus company officials, his own men, and the excited newsboy, Westcott strode in the direction the boy had indicated. They found one compartment in the lavatory premises which was locked; the indicator at the handle showed 'engaged.' There was no reply when Westcott pounded on the door. One of the bus company officials went into a neighbouring compartment and climbed over the partition.

"It's empty!" he cried.

The next minute he opened the door, and they saw that his statement was not altogether correct. Lying on the floor was the wanted man's hat, overcoat and suitcase.

Westcott dragged the suitcase into the light and rummaged in it. To his disappointment, it contained only shirts, and a change of underwear. The shirts were marked with initials 'A.H.' which showed they were on the right track.

At that point they lost the trail for several hours. It was probably that Hemingway had carried a cloth cap in his bag, or in one of the pockets, which he had slipped on in the lavatory, then waiting until the bus station was temporarily free of loungers, had walked off to mingle with the crowds in Birmingham's busy streets. The hiding-place he had found for his discarded belongings was a simple, yet cunning one. If the sharp little newsboy had not seen him leaving the bus at the last moment, the locked compartment in which he had left them might have remained undisturbed for days.

The Birmingham police co-operated with Superintendent Westcott in his search for the wanted man. The hotels were combed without avail. In the end it was Hemingway's own fatal weakness which led them to his hiding-place.

At half-past ten that night, Westcott and Evans and Inspector Harkness of the Birmingham force were in the latter's office at the Central police station, when the telephone bell shrilled its summons.

Inspector Harkness answered it with a hopeful glance at his guests, who sat up in their chairs.

"Hello? Yes, this is the Inspector. What's that? Oh, I see. Just hold the wire a moment, please."

He turned to Westcott:

"Sorry to dash your hopes, old man, but the fellow at the other end of the wire is only a conscientious chemist who's afraid he's broken one of the regulations. The desk sergeant couldn't give him any information, so he's put him through to me. Excuse me, please, while I see what's on his mind."

Turning back to the telephone, he said: "Just tell me all about it, will you?—You say he was a complete stranger to you eh?— With a prescription from a London doctor?—Well, I shouldn't worry any more tonight if I were you. I'll send a man out in the morning to check up on your customer. He left his address, didn't he? I expect it will be alright. Goodnight."

Hanging up the receiver, he wheeled round in his chair, reaching for his pipe and tobacco pouch.

"The poor devil was in a blue funk," he remarked, carelessly. "An hour ago, a stranger came into his shop with a prescription for morphine made out by a London doctor. He wouldn't fill the prescription at first, but the fellow was so persistent, and he looked up the doctor's name in a medical directory, and found it there right enough, so against his better judgement he parted with the drug. After he had done it he got the wind up badly, and felt that he simply had to ring us up to find out whether he had committed a crime or a misdemeanour."

Westcott looked thoughtful.

"A stranger with a London prescription, and for morphine," he muttered under his breath. "I wonder—"

"Look here," he exclaimed suddenly. "If you've no objection, I'll just get that chemist on the wire again and ask him a question or two."

"Go ahead," said Harkness, with a wave of his hand. "You'll find his number in that directory over there. Name's Bernard Altman."

In a few moments, Westcott was in conversation with the nervous chemist.

"Can you describe your customer to me," he asked.

"Oh, yes, yes! I noticed him particularly. He was a neatly-dressed, respectable-looking man. That's why I let him have the stuff. I'll never forgive myself if I've made a mistake."

"Never mind that," retorted Westcott, brusquely. "What colour of eyes had he? What shape was his nose? How tall would he be?"

"I didn't really notice his eyes. He had a rather large nose, if I remember correctly, and I think I do, though it isn't easy to be quite certain. I think he would be about my own height, or an inch or two taller."

"What height are you?" Westcott shouted irritably. "I can't see you through the telephone you know."

"I am so sorry. I—I—I'm afraid I didn't think of that. Stupid of me. My height is five feet ten inches and a quarter.

Or is it a half? No, that can't be it, for my son is taller than I am, and he—"

"Never mind that," snapped Westcott. "Had he any peculiarities?"

"Now that you mention it," stammered Mr. Altman, "he had. I distinctly remember being struck by the odd habit he had of pulling his ear with—"

"—with his thumb and forefinger!" Westcott supplied, triumphantly.

"That's it! How did you know?"

"What address did he leave?"

"94 Hanover Avenue," he replied, at last.

"Thanks!" Westcott slammed down the receiver and turned to Evans and Inspector Harkness. "It's our man," he declared, "but I'm afraid the address is phony."

"Hanover Avenue?" said Harkness, thoughtfully. "That's a short street out in the suburbs. Let's see. Yes, it runs between Elm Street and Orange Road numbered from one to fifty, there isn't any number ninety-four."

"I didn't think there would be," replied Westcott. "And if there was, he wouldn't be within a mile of it. But he may be in the neighbourhood just the same."

"Walsall!" said Harkness suddenly. He took Westcott by the arm and led him to a map which hung on one of the walls.

"But why Walsall?" queried Westcott. "Why not West Bromwich or Atherstone? Aren't they equally likely—or unlikely?"

"He probably needs to lie low by day, and take his exercise at night," replied Harkness. "Now it wouldn't be long before the average landlady would become suspicious of a lodger with these habits. But there is one type of landlady who'd think nothing of it. One who lets rooms to theatrical people. There are no theatrical lodging houses in the two towns you mention, but there are four or five at least in Walsall, and it wouldn't be difficult for him to find them; they usually have their cards displayed in the window of a stationer's shop near the theatre."

Superintendent Westcott rose to his feet and beckoned to Evans to rise as well. "I've been following hunches all day," he remarked, "and they haven't led me far wrong. I might as well check up on this hunch of yours. I'll run out to Walsall and take a look around, in any case."

"I'll come with you," said Harkness. "I'd rather like to see whether I'm right or not."

Near the Walsall variety theatre they found a stationer's shop, in the window of which were three cards with crudely lettered inscriptions proclaiming 'clean, comfortable rooms to let' at three adjacent addresses. On two of the cards, the words 'no objection to theatricals' were added and underlined.

When they called at the first address, they drew a blank. The house was full, but the landlady was able to vouch for all of her lodgers, who comprised an acrobatic team, a sister act, and a conjuror.

At the second house a slatternly-looking woman, who smelled strongly of drink, regarded them suspiciously.

"Well, what if I did take in a new lodger today?" she demanded, "what business is it of yours, nosey?"

Inspector Harkness thrust his warrant card under her nose. "Not so much of your lip, ma," he snapped, "or I'll run you in for obstructing the police. We want a look at this lodger of yours."

The untidy harridan's lips twisted in a servile leer. "Why didn't you say you was police? I don't want no bother with the cops. You'll find him in the back bedroom upstairs. Second door on the left as you go up."

Westcott, leading the two men, went upstairs on tiptoe, to prevent their quarry receiving warning of their approach. On the landing they found the door, threw it wide open, and walked in.

A shirt or two and some other articles of wearing apparel lay in a suitcase, obviously newly-bought, on a chair. On the dressing-table was a collar and tie, and a gleaming nickel hypodermic syringe.

On the bed lay the man they sought, clad only in undershirt, trousers and socks, and with a drowsy, contented look on his face, which quickly disappeared and was replaced by a look of mingled surprise and fear as they entered.

"Who—who the hell are you?" he demanded.

As he spoke, one hand dived under his pillow and came out holding a revolver, which he pointed at the newcomers.

"You are Arnold Hemingway?" said Westcott, making a statement rather than asking a question.

Westcott took a step forward, and the fugitive's finger tightened on the trigger. "Get—get back," he stammered. "Back or I'll shoot!"

The detective advanced again with his eyes on Hemingway's face.

The hammer fell but no report followed. The gun had misfired. With a curse, Hemingway threw the revolver full in the detective's face and sprang for the window.

As he went through in a shower of splintered glass, Inspector Harkness dived for his feet, caught his ankles, and held him. With the assistance of Westcott, the fugitive was pulled back into the room, badly cut about the face and hands, and trembling spasmodically.

He stood in a daze while handcuffs were fastened on his wrists.

"Arnold Hemingway," said Westcott, distinctly, "I arrest you for the murder of Moses Silverstein, and it is my duty to warn you—"

R obert Harvey, barrister-at-law of some eight years' standing, was breakfasting on kidneys and bacon in his chambers in Fountain Court on a morning some three weeks after the arrest of Arnold Hemingway, when his valet came to him with the information that Mr. Wrenn, of Gentry, Green and Gentry, an old-fashioned but influential firm of solicitors, wished to speak to him on the telephone.

The dry, precise voice of Mr. Theodore Wrenn came to him from the other end of the wire. "I sent you a brief the other day, Mr. Harvey. Have you had an opportunity of reading it?"

"I'm afraid not. I've been abroad for a month and only returned this morning. What is it?"

Mr. Wrenn coughed slightly in a deprecatory manner. "A murder trial, Mr. Harvey." Wrenn's tone was apologetic, for Gentry, Green and Gentry is not at all the type of firm whose clients do murder. "It is a brief to defend Arnold Hemingway."

"Oh, the Stark Street case," said Harvey, quickly. "I noticed something about in one of the Continental papers. Have you briefed a K.C. as senior counsel?"

"We—er—wish you to take the case on your own."

This was staggering news, for it is only very rarely that the defence in a murder trial is left to a junior.

"Can you come and see me this morning?" asked Wrenn.

"Certainly—if you don't mind my finishing my breakfast first. I arrived at Victoria about an hour ago."

"In that case," replied Wrenn, "I think I'll just come across to your chambers myself. I want to see you as soon as possible."

"Yes, do."

Harvey returned to his breakfast, but could not concentrate

upon the business of eating. The news which Wrenn had given him occupied his mind to the exclusion of all else. The Stark Street murder—even the Continental papers had been full of it—was very much in the public eye. A brutal murder, a sordid, almost melodramatic setting, a quick arrest, there were all the elements in the case to provide sensational reading for a thrill-loving public. And he was to defend Arnold Hemingway on his own!

Harvey was thirty-three years old, and a certain measure of success had already fallen to his lot. Called to the bar eight years before, he had risen rapidly owing to his ability and his willingness to accept any brief no matter how small and un-remunerative.

In the morning paper, he found fresh details of the Stark Street murder case, and a photograph of Hemingway, which looked distinctly unprepossessing. He was engrossed with the article when Mr. Wrenn was announced.

After greetings were exchanged, the two men sat facing each other, Harvey smoking his first pipe of the day, and Wrenn with a cigarette.

"I've marked the brief with a fee of three hundred guineas," remarked the solicitor, with a quizzical look at his friend.

"That doesn't interest me as much as the fact that you've offered it to me at all," replied Harvey. "Hasn't Hemingway any money?"

"None whatever."

"No friends, then?"

Wrenn smiled. "That's where I come into it," he responded. "He has a number of very distinguished relatives, among them one of our clients, Lady Agatha Daventry. They are paying for his defence."

Harvey drew sharply on his pipe. "Then why don't they do

the thing properly, and brief a K.C.?" he asked. "I'm asking you to be perfectly frank, Theodore."

"Very well, I'll be as frank as you can expect. They don't think that Hemingway has a chance in a million, and they're naturally not anxious to throw money away. They're defending him for the sake of the family, that's all."

"Prominent men have been known to accept briefs which offered little money," Harvey remarked drily.

"Yes," agreed Wrenn, "but only when there is a chance of adding to their own glory by doing so. This case offers no such opportunity. Frankly, I believe the man's guilty, and certainly the public has already condemned him. It was rather a beastly murder, and nothing but a miracle will save Hemingway's life. The inquest has been postponed until after the trial, so the police haven't had to produce all of their evidence yet, but there's no doubt that they've a cast-iron case. It may do you some good, perhaps, to conduct a case which will loom largely in every paper in the civilised world, but no K.C. would take it without any record fee."

"I see," said Harvey, reflectively. "Then the plea is—"

"Insanity," replied Wrenn quickly, "at least that's what the family wish."

"Have you seen Hemingway? What's his view in the matter?"

"I've seen him several times without any satisfactory result. He wishes to plead 'not guilty.' He protests that he didn't do it."

"Is there a chance that he's telling the truth?" Harvey asked.

"Not a chance," Wrenn replied emphatically. "If he pleads not guilty, he'll hang, there's nothing more certain than that."

"You've pointed that out to him, of course?"

"Half a dozen times. But it isn't the slightest good talking to the man. He keeps on saying 'I didn't do it' and 'for God's sake find Lucy Hemmerde.'"

"Who is Lucy Hemmerde"

"One of Hemingway's former mistresses. One of them, mark you. He had several—probably that's why he is where he is now. He claims to have been with her at the time of the murder." The solicitor made a hopeless gesture. "That's the strange part of it all," he added. "Lucy Hemmerde has disappeared, utterly and completely, as though the earth had opened and swallowed her up. I've advertised for her and had private detectives on her trail for two weeks, without finding the slightest trace of her. I'd begun to think that no such person exists, but we have positive proof that she did exist up to a day or two before the murder. After that, she seems to have vanished completely."

"And you don't think much of Hemingway's claim that this woman can establish his alibi?"

"I think that he'll hang unless he pleads insanity," replied Wrenn positively.

"Is there any ground for such a plea?"

Wrenn smiled. "If you had seen him a few days ago, you would have said that he was insane without the slightest hesitation," he replied. "Hemingway is a drug addict, and they've been trying to break him off it in prison. He hadn't had an injection of morphia for forty-eight hours and he was climbing walls and literally foaming at the mouth. Now he's in the prison hospital, and they're giving him injections twice a day." He looked quizzically at Harvey, and added: "Rather a piece of irony trying to break a man of a powerful habit, when he may be dead in a few weeks."

The two men smoked in silence for a while.

"You'll take the brief?" asked Wrenn at last.

Harvey nodded. "Yes. When can I see my client?"

"Today probably. If I may use your 'phone I'll find out the hour."

The barrister waved his hand in the direction of the telephone.

After a few moments Wrenn spoke over the wire to the Governor of Brixton prison, then he returned to his chair.

"We can go over to see him in an hour," he said. "And for heaven's sake persuade him to agree to a plea of insanity. If he pleads 'not guilty' he'll hang, without a doubt!"

Arnold Hemingway was an unpleasant sample of that unsavoury type of human being, a bully who is also a coward. Throughout his life he had never felt pity for any of the women whose lives he had wrecked and whom he had lightly discarded when their charms had ceased to attract him; their fates had not concerned him, but lying on a steel cot in the prison hospital, with the shadow of the gallows upon him he felt an overwhelming pity for himself. He spent little time in regretting the possibilities he had wasted, but much time in bewailing the fact that his neck was in danger.

Half an hour before Harvey and Wrenn called at the prison to see him he had been given an injection of morphia and in consequence he was in a bold and brazen mood.

"I don't care what evidence they've got against me," he said, "I didn't do it and they can't prove I did. What if I did steal the beastly necklace? That doesn't prove that I'm a murderer. The police have 'framed' me, but their case will collapse if it ever goes before a judge and jury."

With a hopeless gesture, Wrenn turned to Harvey, who had taken no part in the conversation, but contented himself by closely watching his client.

"This is our man immediately after an injection of dope," Wrenn whispered. "A few hours from now he'll be a grovelling wreck, and certain that nothing can save him." Aloud he said:

"Hemingway, you've got to realise your position. You are a betting man, and I'll put it to you in the language you understand. It's a hundred to one against any jury finding you 'not guilty'!"

The eyes of the man in the narrow cot assumed a more serious expression as they travelled from Wrenn to Harvey, noting the gravity which was written plainly on their faces.

"But I didn't do it," he whispered, hoarsely. "They can't hang an innocent man, can they?"

Looking straight into Hemingway's eyes Wrenn said: "They can hang a man if a jury is satisfied as to his guilt."

"Do you think I'm guilty," he whispered.

Theodore Wrenn hesitated for a moment. "What I think mean nothing," he said, slowly, at last. "I recognise the strength of the evidence against you."

"Then you do think I'm guilty!" He raised himself almost off the bed. "But there's no evidence!" he cried. "Nobody saw—"

"Nobody saw you commit the murder," Wrenn responded. "But circumstantial evidence has been too strong for a man before this. Hemingway, you stole that necklace, and sold it to Silverstein and would have gone to desperate lengths to get it back. At eleven o'clock on the night of the murder you threatened Silverstein when he wouldn't sell it back to you. Don't deny that, for you were seen. There are two hours of that night which you can't account for—"

"I was in Hyde Park with—" whispered Hemingway.

"Hyde Park!" snorted Wrenn. "Hyde Park! As if anyone will believe that story! If you told it in the witness-box it would be enough to condemn you. You've got to realise your position, man. Only a plea of insanity can possibly save you."

Hemingway shrank back, with his eyes wide and staring wildly. "I'm not insane I tell you, I'm not," he gasped. "I'm not, and I won't let you pretend that I am. I didn't do it, I tell you!"

Harvey seated himself on the bed and looked seriously at his client.

"You've got to be frank with me," he said. "I want you to tell me truthfully whether you murdered Silverstein or not; and bear this in mind, if I think you are lying, I will refuse to defend you. I must know the truth, whatever it is. Wait a minute, don't reply yet. I want to impress upon you that we three are alone, and that two of us are your legal representatives. Anything you say to us is sacredly confidential. Your secret is as safe with Mr. Wrenn and myself as it is with you. Now tell me truthfully—did you murder Moses Silverstein?"

The reply came with lightning rapidity: "I swear I didn't!"

"Did you break into his premises that night?"

"No."

"Supposing for a moment that you had broken into the pawnshop," he said, at last, "and had been trapped by Silverstein, as the police claim, would you have gone the length of killing him in order to escape?"

Hemingway's eyes searched the barrister's face, and what he saw there decided him that it was best to tell the truth. "I'm afraid I would," he muttered.

"I see. Were you drunk that night?"

"No. I only had a couple of large whiskies."

"So that you were perfectly aware of your movements?"

"Oh, yes."

"You went to see Silverstein about eleven o'clock with the money you had obtained by forging a cheque on Lady Agatha Daventry's account?"

"Yes." The reply was given in a low tone.

Wrenn was slightly bewildered. Previously Hemingway had strenuously denied this. "Did you visit the pawnshop again that night?"

Hemingway hesitated slightly before replying. "No."

"Are you quite sure?" asked Harvey, keenly.

"Yes." Without hesitation Hemingway plunged eagerly into his narrative, to which Harvey listened intently.

About half-past eleven, he said, he had met a girl named Lucy Hemmerde in Piccadilly Circus, a girl he had first met almost two and a half years before, who had lived with him for some months, and whom he had not seen for fully two years. She had insisted on a private conversation with him, and they had gone to Hyde Park together, remaining there for almost half an hour.

"Why didn't you take her to a more suitable place; a restaurant, for instance?" Harvey asked. "Why Hyde Park, of all places?"

"We would have attracted too much attention. She—she was very shabbily dressed."

"I see. Where does this woman live?"

"She said that she was homeless. That was what she wanted to speak to me about."

"And did you help her?"

"I gave her a pound."

"A pound?"

"I was in a terrible hole myself," said Hemingway, with a shrug of his shoulders.

"Is Lucy Hemmerde her real name?"

"Perhaps not. I've always suspected that it wasn't. Once I said as much to her, and she didn't deny it, but on the other hand she didn't admit it."

"Did she correspond with relatives or friends while she lived with you?"

"No."

"Where did you first meet her?"

"At Brighton."

"Was she using the name Lucy Hemmerde then?"

"I can't say. That was the name she gave me, but we were at different boarding-houses, so I didn't have a chance to check up on her. Girls often use fictitious names when they meet stray acquaintances at the seaside. It saves complications, I suppose."

"Did you leave Brighton together?"

"Yes, she came with me to London."

"Have you a photograph of her?"

"Unfortunately, I haven't. I destroyed her photograph two years ago."

"That's a pity."

Hemingway clutched his arm feverishly.

"You do believe me?" he demanded hoarsely. "You know I didn't do it, don't you? My God, you've got to believe me!"

Harvey looked at him with serious, troubled eyes.

"I do believe you," he said firmly.

"Thank God! And you'll find Lucy Hemmerde, won't you?"

"If it's humanly possible."

William Corkran, former Scotland Yard Inspector, and sole proprietor of the Corkran Private Intelligence Bureau, was broad and stout of build, stolid and unimaginative of mind, slow of thought and drawling of speech. He had a large red face, a heavy nicotine-stained moustache and a habit of speaking without removing his cigar from his mouth.

"Say you were broke and destitute, had maybe slept on park benches for a few nights, and someone gave you a quid just when you were feeling like making a hole in the river, what would you do with 'it'?" he asked, shifting his cigar to the corner of his mouth with a twist of his lips.

The question was directed at Robert Harvey and Theodore Wrenn, who were in consultation with the private detective in Wrenn's office in Chancery Lane. Neither of them could think of a suitable reply.

"I'll tell you," said Corkran, jabbing a stubby finger on the desk before him. "If you had a friend or a relative in the world, you'd spend that quid on railway fares to get to him or her. Of course, you would."

"But you've traced Lucy Hemmerde's life over a period of two and a half years, and found no trace of any relatives."

"That's true, and I'll explain it. She was a well-brought-up young lady, we have Hemingway's word for that, and when she'd disgraced her folks by living with Hemingway, as she did, she'd naturally steer clear of them. She'd be ashamed to face them. Rather than ask them to help her she'd work her fingers to the bone, starve herself even. But every human being has a breaking-point, and on the night of the murder, Lucy Hemmerde came to her breaking-point. She was down and out, and absolutely desperate. It's my guess that she either swallowed her pride and went home, or—

"—or drowned herself!" he said with awful emphasis.

"In the latter case," said Harvey, refilling his pipe, "in the latter case, our chance of establishing Hemingway's alibi will be nil."

"Exactly," agreed Corkran. "And in the former case, they're almost as slight. Gentlemen, my office staff has searched the directories of every city and town of over a thousand population in England, Scotland and Wales for people called Hemmerde. Every Hemmerde we could find has been written to regarding the woman we're looking for. We've sent out thousands of letters, and every one has been useless. None of these people called Hemmerde has a daughter or sister called Lucy."

"Which means," said Harvey, thoughtfully, "That Lucy Hemmerde has not gone to relatives, because she has none to go to."

He threw away his limp, chewed cigar-end, and selected a fresh cigar. "It bears out what I discovered in Brighton," he continued. "I went to a boarding-house where this woman stayed two and a half years ago when she met Hemingway. The proprietress had a vague recollection of her, but was almost certain that she had stayed there under another name. Unfortunately, they kept no record of their guests at this place, so she was unable to say what name, but it stands to reason that she'd have remembered a guest named Hemmerde—it isn't an everyday name by any means."

"What's to be done now?" inquired Wrenn.

Corkran shrugged his shoulders. "Nothing, so far as I can see," he replied. "If she's staying with relatives under a different name, there's no way we can trace her, and if she's made a hole in the river there's no point in tracing her."

Wrenn gathered up the private detective's report and put it in a wire basket on his desk marked 'For immediate attention.'

"I'll examine the facts, and let you know," he replied. "Good day, Corkran."

"Good day, gentlemen."

"That's that. You can't go into court with a plea of 'not guilty' without Lucy Hemmerde. It would be simply putting Hemingway's neck in the noose."

"May I see these papers?" asked Harvey.

"Certainly." Wrenn passed over the detective's report.

"I shan't find time for luncheon," he observed. "I've a pile of work to get through. Sandwiches and coffee must suffice for the present."

An office boy sent out to the nearest restaurant soon returned with a parcel of cut sandwiches and a large cup of coffee. Wrenn ate and worked his way through the pile of papers on his desk simultaneously.

Harvey sat in a corner, deep in his perusal of Corkran's report.

Wrenn's last sandwich was being demolished rapidly when there was a knock at the door and the office boy entered.

"Miss Priestley to see you, sir."

"Great Scott!" Wrenn put down the half-eaten sandwich with a ludicrous expression of consternation on his face. "Cynthia Priestley! I had forgotten all about her."

A tall, graceful woman appeared in the doorway. "How awful, Mr. Wrenn!" she exclaimed, in an amused tone. "I simply hate to be forgotten. That sort of thing makes me feel so terribly small."

The solicitor rose hurriedly to his feet. "I don't know what I can say," he remarked. "The truth is I've been terribly busy, and somehow—I can't understand how it happened exactly—but I—I forgot all about our luncheon engagement. However, I've just had a sandwich, and I'm still quite hungry, really."

"Just a sandwich! But such a large sandwich! And the extensive paper wrappings suggest several sandwiches. Three or four at least, all of impressive proportions. You can't possibly eat a bite more."

"I—I shan't be able to eat much," stammered Wrenn. "But you mustn't let my lack of appetite spoil your luncheon. If you don't mind waiting a moment, I'll just get my hat."

"You'll do nothing of the sort, Theodore Wrenn," Cynthia retorted. "I won't have any man, stuffed to the eyes with ham sandwiches, watching me at luncheon and marvelling at the amount I eat. I'm disappointed in you though. Now I must lunch alone, and I hate lunching alone. It will be a miserable meal. I can't go home, for my maid isn't expecting me, and there won't be a bite to eat in the house."

Harvey, who had risen to his feet, was staring at the newcomer in frank admiration. Cynthia Priestly was a woman of perhaps thirty, and she had the poise and charm of maturity. She had a long straight nose with a thin bridge and fine sensitive nostrils, a small delicately-formed mouth, and oval jaw. Her lips were carmine velvet, her dark eyes, like deep pools, had a questioning look which was intensified by the quaint angle of her arched eyebrows.

Wrenn suddenly realised the presence of his friend. "Cynthia, may I present Robert Harvey?"

Harvey took the slim white hand that was offered to him. "I'm delighted to meet you, Miss Priestly," he mumbled.

"And have you, too, been lunching on gargantuan sandwiches, Mr. Harvey?" she asked mischievously.

"I have allowed nothing to spoil the excellent repast I intend to indulge in shortly," he replied.

She raised her eyebrows whimsically. "How attractive that sounds."

Mustering his courage, he made a little bow. "Won't you make the meal perfect by joining me?"

"I'd love to, but"—with a glance at Wrenn—"there's some wretched business to discuss."

"It can wait, surely," said Wrenn. "Go my children, and leave me to my shame."

"To the last bite of the sandwich you mean," Cynthia retorted with a laugh. "You know you're simply dying for us to leave so that you can finish it."

"In that case," said Harvey, "we'd better go at once, hadn't we?"

Over luncheon at Henrico's, they chatted gaily and impersonally, but at times Harvey's attention wandered a little. In his favour it must be said that the strange disappearance of Lucy Hemmerde was very much on his mind. On one of those occasions, Cynthia recalled his wandering attention with a gay remark. "A penny for 'em?"

"I'm terribly sorry," he said, with a start. "I'm afraid my thoughts were wandering."

"They were. To a woman?"

"I'm afraid so."

"I knew it! A beautiful woman?"

"I don't know. I've never seen her."

Cynthia leaned forward, supporting her chin on her cupped hands, her elbows resting on the table. "How intriguing!" she exclaimed. "Do tell me about this woman whom you have never seen, but is so much in your thoughts."

After some slight hesitation, Harvey told her of the missing Lucy Hemmerde, and her connection with Stark Street murder case.

"I'm afraid," she commented, gravely, "that suicide is the more likely alternative. Tragic, unhappy girl! Having suffered so much, she would have killed herself rather than return in the end to the relatives she was ashamed to face in the beginning."

"In that case there isn't much hope for my client."

Cynthia's pale brow was furrowed by a frown. "That doesn't

worry me much," she replied. "A man like that doesn't deserve to live. But that poor girl! What was the last trace of her the detectives discovered?"

"She left her most recent lodgings three days before the murder."

"Three days—but she was in London on the night of the murder. It's reasonable to presume that she was in London for the three days before it. Where could she have spent these three nights?"

"There are places. Cheap lodging houses, even free shelters. Corkran visited all of them, but no one recognised her description."

"Her description!" Cynthia repeated, thoughtfully. "How did he describe her?"

He read Lucy Hemmerde's description from the report. "Height, five feet, three inches. Build, slight. Complexion and hair, blonde. Eyes, blue. Appearance prepossessing—"

"Appearance prepossessing!" Cynthia exclaimed. "How ridiculous! She had been through two years of misery and hard work. Her complexion would be dull and muddy. Her hands would be reddened and rough. Perhaps her hair would be more grey than golden. Certainly, it would be drab and lustreless. That isn't a description of Lucy Hemmerde today. It's a description of her as she was two and a half years ago!"

"You're right! Someone might have recognised your description of her, but not the one that Corkran had! I wonder if it would be worthwhile to go round these lodging-houses again! I've simply got to find her," added Harvey. "There's a man's life at stake."

"A man like that!" Cynthia made a grimace of disgust. "Will you let me help you?" she demanded.

"Of course, if you wish."

"I feel I must," she replied, simply.

They went that afternoon, the grave-faced barrister and his charming companion, to number twelve Redman's Row, the last known address of Lucy Hemmerde. They went in a taxi, which stopped at the end of the street, and one look at the grimy narrow thoroughfare was enough to make Harvey do his best to persuade Cynthia Priestley to remain in the taxi while he made enquiries, but she refused to do so. She descended from the sanctuary of the cab, and submitted herself to the staring eyes and whispering tongues of the slatternly women who clustered in groups upon the pavement and the ill-clad, undernourished children who played in the gutters.

"That human beings should live here!" Cynthia whispered, in a voice that trembled a little.

"Go back to the taxi," said Harvey. "This is too much for you."

"They bear it don't they?" was her murmured reply. "She lived here. I can stand it for a few minutes. It will be good for me. One is too complacent about this sort of thing when it isn't brought directly beneath one's nose."

As they reached number twelve, followed by an inquisitive crowd of children, the door was thrown open violently, and a young woman came out with a rush, speeded by a large, untidy harridan, who waved a broom menacingly.

"If you set foot over my door again, I'll brain you, you baggage," the woman in the doorway screamed. "I've had enough of keepin' you while my kids starve. Take yourself off elsewhere, and see if can find someone else as'll keep you for nothing, the way you expect me to do."

She turned and favoured Harvey with a look which embraced his appearance from head to foot, then her eyes travelled past him to Cynthia who was also submitted to a searching scrutiny.

"Mrs. Throop?" asked Harvey.

The woman scowled. "That's me," she snapped. "But I've got no time to be bothered. I've been bothered enough already. That hussy! French, if you please! With her airs and her parley vous."

"I wish to speak to you about Lucy Hemmerde—" Harvey began again.

"Don't ast me where she's gorn orf to," retorted Mrs. Throop. "I been bothered enough about that already. Gorn off she has, and owing me twelve shillins', too, an' I'm holdin' on to her luggage until she stumps up, but I don't know where she's gorn orf to, and that's flat!"

She turned away, and would have slammed the door, but Harvey produced a ten-shilling note, and held it suggestively between his fingers. "We'd like to come in and speak to you for a few moments," he said.

Holding the door open, she beckoned with a grimy hand. "Come in, then," she said, grudgingly, "but I ain't got all day to waste."

They followed her into a tiny kitchen, which evidently did duty as sitting room, dining room, bedroom and bathroom as well. A living room, in the most pathetic sense of the word, squalid, dirty, unaired, and with a foul odour of human breath, and cooking, and rank tobacco and perspiration. "Siddown, Miss," she said.

Cynthia ignored the ruin which the greasy surface of the chair would work with her dainty dress and sat down.

"Now, sir?" said Mrs. Throop, tucking the ten-shilling note away in a pocket in her voluminous petticoat.

"I wonder if you can suggest any reason why Lucy Hemmerde left you?" asked Harvey.

"She was broke, and couldn't pay me the few shillin's what she owed," replied Mrs. Throop. "There's some as waits until you throws them out, but 'Miss 'Emmerde wasn't that sort. She'd got pride, I'll say that for 'er. 'S'pose she jus' cleared out w'en she saw she couldn't square up for 'er room."

"Have you any idea where she might go?"

Mrs. Throop shrugged her shoulders. "That I can't say. I didn't know she 'ad left until I found 'er bed 'adn't been slep' in. 'Er things were still in 'er room, though. I'll say that for 'er, she didn't try to do me down."

"Do you suppose—might she have gone away with a man?"

"'Ere, what are you gettin' at?" she demanded. "Lucy 'Emmerde weren't that sort. She 'adn't no goings-on with men. As clean a girl as ever lived, that way, she was. Even when drunk, she never 'ad no truck with men."

"When drunk!" whispered Cynthia.

"Yes, drunk!" she exclaimed. "And wouldn't you get drunk, too, if you 'ad to wear yourself out washin' clothes for four shillin's a day, like she did? And even lorst that job, poor thing. She weren't no fancy piece," she added. "If she 'ad gone with men she wouldn't 'ave needed to work so 'ard, but she'd rather 'ave died than go with a man. Drink was 'er trouble."

"Poor girl!" Cynthia murmured. "Poor, poor girl."

"Would you let us see her belongings?" asked Harvey. "It is just possible that there may be some clue to her present whereabouts among them."

"I don't mind," said Mrs. Throop. "I'll fetch 'em. Upstairs they are."

She lumbered heavily out of the room. Harvey looked round with an expression of disgust on his face. "Awful!" he muttered.

"Life!" Cynthia whispered. "Tragic and sordid, but life."

Mrs. Throop returned with a large cardboard box. She opened it, and spread the contents on the kitchen table. A pair of stockings, darned until there was practically nothing of the original foot and heel left lay uppermost.

There was nothing likely to assist them in their search among Lucy Hemmerde's belongings. Just rage. Mended over and over again, but rage. A powerful story of a woman's misery they told.

"She 'ad better stuff when she came 'ere at fust," said Mrs. Throop. "But she pawned it—"

Cynthia picked up the few garments and made mental calculations of their sizes. "That poor girl has had her share of misery," she said, in answer to Harvey's enquiring look. "When we find her, I'm going to have a stock of new things, dainty, fresh things for her to wear."

"Can you give me a description of Lucy Hemmerde?" Harvey asked.

Mrs. Throop thought for a moment. "I don't know as I can," she replied. "She looked pretty much like everyone else." She glanced at her guests. "Around this way I mean."

"What colour was her hair, for instance?"

"I don't know that you'd call it any colour, exactly. She 'ad a good few grey 'airs, and the rest was, well, mousy, you might call it."

"Her complexion?"

Mrs. Throop laughed. "After you've working in a laundry, with all the chemicals they use, you ain't got no complexion!" she retorted.

"I see." Harvey was thoughtful. "Can you suggest anywhere a woman without money might go for the night?"

Mrs. Throop scratched her head. "Not offhand I can't. 'Ere, wait a bit, there's an old church on Bow Road, near 'Awkin's Rents, where they lets 'em doss for the night. You might try there."

"Thanks, I will."

They rose to go. Harvey pressed a piece of paper that crackled into Mrs. Throop's hand. She looked at it with startled eyes.

"Gor! It's a fiver. Sir—" They left her speechless with gratitude.

In the taxi, Harvey turned to Cynthia. "You should have remained in the cab," he said, reproachfully.

"No, I shouldn't," she replied. "That place was good for me. It made me realise all sorts of things. Heavens! What a selfish life one leads!"

The church on Bow Road was locked when they arrived. After much pounding on the heavy oak door, Harvey was rewarded when it opened, and a young man in a grey flannel shirt, open at the neck, shabby grey flannel trousers, and tennis shoes appeared. When they explained what they had come about, he opened the door and let them in.

The place was no longer used as a church, and the pews and other church furniture had been taken out. Along one wall was heaped straw, which still bore the impression of human bodies. In the centre of the room was a long unpainted trestle table which flanked an old-fashioned iron stove. In the farthest corner a camp-bed with a single blanket, a chair, and a small table. By the stove a zinc bath full of water, in which lay a number of enamelled mugs.

"Here they come, the down and out, the destitute, submerged humanity," said the young man. "If they are lucky, I have bread and margarine and tea to offer them. They eat it ravenously, for many of them have not eaten all day. They sleep in their clothes on that pile of straw, not even removing their overcoats, and huddle together for warmth all night. Some of them have not taken off their outer garments for months. In the morning, there is lukewarm water for those who care to wash, but it is rarely used. What is the good of washing your face when your belly is hollow with hunger? After they have gone I clean up their filth, and rake over their straw, and then I go begging among people who have money, for a few shillings to buy bread and margarine so that my guests shall not go supperless to bed. At eleven o'clock every night I open the doors again, and in they come. I have to close the in the faces of some, for there isn't room for all who are homeless and hungry."

He had sad eyes and a pale ascetic face; the face of a poet.

"Women come too?" asked Cynthia.

"Yes. Women and men, they sleep there together," he replied.

There were a dozen questions they would have liked to ask him. About himself, for he had a sensitive cultured voice, and clean, manicured hands. About the ambitions he had sacrificed to do this work, for he had the eyes of one who dreams and sees visions. But there are questions which may not be asked.

They asked about Lucy Hemmerde, and described her as well as they could.

"I am almost certain that she came here," the young man said. "About the time you mention, a women who spoke in a different voice from the rest, and ate her bread less savagely, and washed in the morning. She came here for three consecutive nights, and has not appeared since. I was interested in her, for there was something indefinable about her which suggested that she had once known comfort and happiness. But one does not speak of the past here. That is a subject which must never be mentioned. I don't know her name, for names are also taboo."

Cynthia opened her handbag and gave the young man a banknote.

"For bread and margarine?" he suggested gravely. "Or, for once, shall I buy a little jam?"

There was a lump in her throat and she could not reply.

Outside, Harvey turned to her. "We have traced Lucy Hemmerde until the night of the murder," he said. "I wonder what happened to her afterwards. If she went home, at last, —or—"

"To the river," said Cynthia, and added, with a trace of bitterness in her tone: "I almost hope she did. At least she would find rest and peace for her poor troubled soul in the river."

CHAPTER 12

The scuffling of feet, rustling of paper, murmuring of many tongues ceased in the body of the court as Mr. Justice Saintley entered, and the court rose in a silence which would have rendered audible the dropping of a pin.

When the judge was seated, there was a subdued rustling as the people in court settled themselves to await the opening of the trial. The Clerk of the Court rose and cleared his throat portentously.

"Arnold Hemingway," he intoned, in a high, clear voice, "you stand charged upon indictment for that you on the 14th day of February in the present year, at number one Stark Street, Battersea, murdered Moses Silverstein. How say you, are you guilty or not guilty?"

The man in the dock ran a finger round the inside of his collar, as if to relieve a pressure that was suffocating him.

"Not guilty," he whispered, in a breathless voice, through lips that twitched nervously.

While the jurors were sworn, Robert Harvey turned his eyes upon the judge. It was the first time that Harvey had appeared in a case before Mr. Justice Saintley.

He saw a face, immobile and waxen, with a large sharp nose, and sunken grey eyes, which was already familiar to him through photographs in the illustrated papers, and a masterly caricature which had appeared in the 'Law Journal.' The face of an old man, wise, stern, and austere; the face of one who ranked Justice above Mercy.

Turning his eyes from the face of the judge, he glanced keenly down the double line of jurors, and decided that nothing was to be gained by challenging any of them.

Sir Herbert Nash K.C., was conducting the prosecution. A deadly opponent, and an untiring fighter; perhaps a little too much of the actor, too inclined to stage elaborate effects designed to sway the emotions rather than the brains of the jury.

It was the first time Harvey had faced a barrister of Sir Herbert's standing on his own. He reflected ruefully that even had the case been less hopeless, he himself was scarcely the man to win it against so redoubtable an opponent. At the same time the jaw hardened and he determined to put up the strongest fight of which he was capable. It should not be said afterwards that he had been like a child in the hands of Sir Herbert Nash.

The Counsel for the Defence raised his eyes to the public gallery, and saw Cynthia Priestley there, her pale oval face framed by a smart, wide-brimmed hat. She caught his eye and smiled.

During the days before the trial, they had been constant companions. Theirs was a friendship which had developed rapidly. He found her irresistible, and she seemed to take great pleasure in his company.

Only one shadow lay between them, and that was the missing Lucy Hemmerde. They had come no nearer to finding her, and she was seldom out of their minds; on Harvey's part, because his case depended on her, on Cynthia's part, because the tragic story they had discovered had inspired her with sympathy for the missing woman.

After the initial formalities were concluded, Sir Herbert rose, rustling a sheaf of papers in his hands. A tall man, with a fine presence, and an air of complete self-possession, a shrewd clever face, and flashing magnetic eyes, he made an impression upon the court from the first.

He wasted no time in opening his case, speaking briskly yet distinctly and articulating every word so that it was heard in the farthest of the public benches as well as in the jury box. In less than an hour he had given a concise summary of the things he intended to prove. "Gentlemen of the jury," he finished, his voice rising slightly, "if at the end of this case you are satisfied that the facts I have enumerated are proved, it will be my duty to ask you for a verdict of murder against Arnold Hemingway."

He sat down and the first witness for the prosecution was called. The Crown Junior, Mr. Siegfried Higgins, a distinguished counsel of some twenty years' experience, conducted the examination.

"Your name is Aaron Silverstein?"

"Yeth."

"You are the nephew of Moses Silverstein, who was murdered on the 14th of February?"

"Yeth."

"Were you called upon by two policemen some hours after the murder and requested to accompany them to the Battersea morgue?"

"That's ri'."

"What transpired?"

"They showed me a body, and asked if I could identify it."

"And could you?"

"Yeth. It was the body of mein Uncle Moses."

"You had no doubt whatever of the identity of the corpse?"

"Not the slightest."

"Thank you."

Mr. Higgins sat down, the Counsel for the Defence intimated that he had no questions to ask, and the witness left the stand, and was replaced by a uniformed constable.

The prosecution's junior council rose again. "Your name and number?"

"Constable George Mackinlay, number G.G.436."

"Where does your beat lie?"

The policeman mentioned the boundaries of his beat, one of which was Stark Street.

"Where were you on the morning of the 14th of February at about a quarter to one?"

"I was at the far end of Stark Street farthest from and heading toward the pawnshop."

"Tell us what you found when you arrived at the premises of Moses Silverstein?"

Consulting his notebook, the policeman repeated word for word the statement he had made to Superintendent Westcott on the morning of the murder, including his discovery of the body, and the summoning of the constable from the next beat.

"I remained in charge of the premises until the arrival of Superintendent Westcott of Scotland Yard," he concluded.

"You interfered with nothing until the Superintendent arrived?"

"Nothing, sir."

Siegfried Higgins sat down, and the Counsel for the Defence rose to his feet. "Where did you stand while blowing your whistle to summon the other policeman?" he asked.

"On the doorstep, sir."

"You didn't move from the door of the shop for so much as a moment?"

"No, sir."

"There is only one door to the premises, I believe?"

"Yes, sir; the rear door was bricked up several years ago."

"I see. So that, had the murderer still been on the premises, he would have had to pass you in order to leave the shop?"

"Exactly, sir."

"Also, to enter the shop from the street, it would be necessary to pass you?"

"Yes, sir."

"But no one did pass?"

"No, sir."

"Thank you."

The next witness was a dapper little police surgeon who had been called to the scene of the murder shortly after the discovery of the body. He gave his name and occupation in a brisk, distinct tone.

Sir Herbert Nash conducted the questioning of this witness. "On the night of the murder you were called to Stark Street premises shortly before one o'clock?"

The doctor nodded. "At four minutes to one, to be precise."

"Were you in bed at the time?"

"No, I had been playing bridge at my club until half an hour or so before, and had just returned home."

"How long did it take you to cover the distance between your house and the scene of the murder?"

"About five minutes, I should judge. I arrived there a few minutes after one o'clock."

"Tell us what you found on your arrival."

"Superintendent Westcott was in charge of the premises. He indicated the body of an elderly man which was lying on the floor and asked me to examine it. I did so, and found that life had been extinct for about half an hour. Death had been practically instantaneous, and was caused by one of a series of severe blows inflicted by a blunt instrument. There were about a dozen injuries to the skull, any one of which would have been sufficient to cause death. The skull was badly smashed."

"You say that Moses Silverstein had been dead for 'about half an hour' when you arrived on the scene a few minutes after one o'clock?"

"Half an hour, more or less."

"What do you mean by that? For just how much more or less than half an hour might he have been dead?"

"Not more than five or ten minutes either way."

"I see. Did you form any conclusions about the weapon which might have caused the dead man's injuries?"

"A heavy poker, or similar instrument."

Sir Herbert Nash went to a table in the well of the court and returned with a heavy brass candlestick. "This was found upon an open shelf in the room in which Moses Silverstein was murdered," he remarked. "Please examine it and tell me whether it could have been used to inflict the injuries to the dead man's skull."

The doctor took it, examined it closely, and nodded his head. "It could," he said.

"Turn it round slowly. You see the dents upon it?"

"I do."

"In your opinion, are they consistent with the candlestick having been used for the purpose I suggested?"

"As to that I cannot say. It is not unlikely, but I cannot speak as an expert in the matter."

"We understand that."

Sir Herbert replaced the candlestick upon the table, lifted a .32 Colt revolver which lay among a number of other exhibits, and held it out to the doctor. "This is exhibit fifty-four which was found in the possession of the prisoner when he was arrested. Please take it for a moment and hold it firmly by the barrel. Now, in your opinion, could the injuries to Moses Silverstein have been caused by the butt of that revolver, if the weapon was held in that manner?"

The doctor looked at the revolver doubtfully.

"It is possible, I should say," he replied, slowly at last. "Although considering the shortness of the striking surface I do not consider it likely, unless it was wielded by someone of considerable strength."

"A normal man under the influence of an unnatural stimulus—cocaine, for instance—might have the strength to do it?"

"Perhaps," agreed the doctor in a doubtful tone.

"This ruler, which was found on Moses Silverstein's desk, would have been a sufficient weapon to cause the murdered man's injuries?" he suggested.

"Quite," replied the doctor, in a decided tone.

"Thank you."

Sir Herbert resumed his seat, with a satisfied expression upon his keen face. Harvey rose with a determined air.

"You said that a heavy poker, or similar instrument occurred to you when you viewed the body as having been the weapon with which the murder had been committed?"

"I did."

"The nature of the injuries suggested a poker to you immediately?"

"A poker, or some similar weapon."

"Did you mention your opinion to the police?"

"I did."

"And did they find such an instrument?"

"As to that I cannot say. I believe one of them did remark that there was a heavy steel poker in the parlour fireplace."

"A heavy steel poker would be quite the most likely weapon, in your opinion?"

"Yes."

"Thank you, that is all."

Sophie Levine, Silverstein's aged housekeeper, was called to the witness box, but could give no evidence of any importance, except that at twenty minutes past twelve on the night of the murder she had been awakened by the closing of her master's bedroom door. It had not seemed unusual to her at the time; she had simply concluded that he had heard the bell ring in the shop and had gone to answer it. She had not herself heard it, but then she was almost deaf, and the shop was considerably removed from the sleeping quarters, and her master had exceptionally keen hearing. It was by no means out of the ordinary for the pawnbroker to have callers at a late hour, and she had thought nothing more of it, but had gone back to sleep. She had heard nothing more—simply the closing of her master's door.

At the moment of waking her eyes had fallen on the luminous dial of the clock which stood on a table beside her bed, and the hands had stood at exactly twenty past twelve. The clock was right by Big Ben.

The Counsel for the Defence cross-examined the witness. "Was there a poker in the fender of the parlour fire?" he asked.

"Yes, sir."

"Describe it, please."

"Vell, it was shiny, like silver, except for the end, which was in the fire too much. Over two feet long, I tink. It was pretty heavy, too, I tell you. I dropped it on my toe once, and it wasn't no joke."

"I see. A pretty hefty poker, evidently. When did you last see it?"

"I can't say for sure. Las' time I clean out the parlour. Maybe two, three days before the murder."

"Then you can't tell me if it was in its place on the night of the murder?"

"Of course, it was. Where else would it be?"

Harvey walked to the table, picked up the brass candlestick, and handed it to the woman. "You've seen this before?"

"Too many times; I used to clean it."

"Examine the dents on it and you will see that they are partly covered by a green chemical. Can you tell me what that is?"

"Sure, I can. That's metal polish. It ain't easy gettin' it all out of the dents, after you've cleaned the candlestick."

"We can understand that, I'm sure. Examine every dent upon the candlestick, please. Can you find a single one that is not partially coated with the old metal polish?"

"Of course not!" snapped Sophia Levine, turning the candlestick round in her hands.

"Then all the dents are old ones, at least they date back to your last cleaning of the candlestick?"

"Yes, and before that, too. I'm a careful worker, I am, and I don't make no dents on ornaments I handle."

"And when did you last clean the candlestick?"

"Two weeks before the murder."

"I thank you. That is all."

Harvey sat down, feeling quite pleased with himself. He had established the fact that the dents on the candlestick were not made on the night of the murder. It was going to be part of his defence to urge that the crime was committed with the steel poker, which was missing, and which it would have been suicide for his client to carry away, had his client committed the crime. Disposing of the candlestick as a possible weapon was one step in the right direction.

"Sergeant Daniel Regan," called the Clerk of the Court, and the Irish police officer appeared through a side door into the court, and made his way to the witness box.

After Regan was sworn, Sir Herbert rose to his feet. "You are Sergeant Daniel Regan?"

"Yes, sir."

"Attached to the Battersea division of the Metropolitan police force?"

"Yes, sir."

"You were visiting the late Moses Silverstein in his parlour behind the shop shortly after eleven o'clock at night, on the

13th February, and hour and a half or so before Silverstein was murdered?"

"I was."

"Tell us of your visit."

In simple, straightforward language, Regan recounted the story of his visit to the old man, and of the caller who had disturbed their chat. He admitted frankly that he had spied upon the pawnbroker and his caller, and had observed the newcomer's first pleading, then threatening manner towards Silverstein.

"Describe the caller," said Sir Herbert Nash.

"He was about five feet eleven inches tall, slightly built, with dark eyes set fairly close together, dark hair, and wore a grey felt hat and blue overcoat. I noticed that once or twice he pulled nervously at his ear with his thumb and forefinger."

The eyes of most of the people in the court were turned upon Arnold Hemingway, whose hand dropped instantly to his side, from the ear at which he had been tugging.

"Look about you," said Sir Herbert Nash. "See whether you can identify the young man you saw among the people in court."

Without hesitation, Regan pointed to the man in the dock.

"There he is, sir," he replied.

With a dramatic gesture toward the dock, Sir Herbert Nash K.C., spoke in a clear high voice which rang resonantly through the courtroom:

"You saw the prisoner threatening Moses Silverstein less than two hours before the murder took place?"

Almost before the words were uttered the Counsel for the Defence was on his feet. "I object," your lordship," he cried. "The witness has stated that he watched the scene through the slight aperture of a door which was all but shut. He was able to distinguish only a few words out of a conversation lasting several minutes. I submit that he cannot truthfully say that my client uttered a threat against Silverstein."

The judge leaned forward slightly. "Objection sustained," he said in a dry voice. "You must question your witness on what he knows, Sir Herbert, not upon what he may have fancied."

As the Counsel for the Defence sat down, Sir Herbert smiled his apologies in his usual bland manner. He was quite satisfied that his question should be stricken from the record, for it had certainly impressed itself on a more indelible record—the minds of the jurymen.

"Did the pawnbroker make any comment on returning to the parlour after taking leave of his visitor?" he asked calmly.

Sergeant Regan flushed; he was remembering the old man's dry remark which showed that he knew he had been spying on him.

"He said the caller was a very foolish young man who squandered his money on dainties for his sweetheart, that the solid earth had crumbled beneath him, and that he did not like the sensation of dancing on air."

A hush had fallen over the body of the court. The spectators were silent and immobile, many of them watching the strained white face of the prisoner. There was little pity for the trembling fellow-human in the dock in these hundreds of pairs of eyes; the man was guilty, they were telling themselves, and what mercy had he shown to old Moses Silverstein?

"Dancing on air!" Sir Herbert's eloquent voice repeated the words, and breathed life in them. He went no further, after repeating the words, and impressing them upon the jury; further stress might have spoiled the effect he had created.

He sat down and Harvey rose to cross-examine.

"Were Silverstein's premises lit by electricity or gas?" he asked.

"Gas, sir."

"Would you say that they were well illuminated?"

"No, sir. Silverstein was very economical in that respect; he only used one jet in the shop."

"So that from where you stood you could not have seen the man at the counter very distinctly?"

"Distinctly enough to give a description afterwards that enabled Mr. Hemingway to be readily identified," retorted Regan, in a stubborn tone.

"But you were not near enough to accurately observe shades in expression? At a distance from the two men, and with a flickering gas jet throwing shadows on their faces, you could not have distinguished between the emotions of fear and anger, or instance?"

"Perhaps not, sir."

"Certainly not, I should say." Harvey leaned forward dramatically, and raised his right hand. "You cannot swear before God, with a man's life resting on your words, that the prisoner actually uttered a threat against Moses Silverstein?" he demanded, in a clear, compelling tone.

"No, sir, but I thought—"

"What you thought is not evidence. Now, on returning to the parlour from his talk with my client, did Silverstein appear to be worried?"

"No, sir, he did not."

"He dismissed his caller lightly as being a very foolish young man?"

"Yes, sir."

"So that, granting for the moment that a threat had been uttered, it could not have been a very terrible one?"

The witness did not answer.

"Come, surely you can answer that!" Harvey exclaimed. "A threat to kill him, for instance, would surely not have left an old, weak man unmoved?"

"He may not have taken it seriously," said Regan. "Whatever he was, he was no coward."

Harvey took up a new line. "You were intimate with Silverstein; the visit you have described was not your first visit to the parlour?"

"No, sir."

"You must have often seen the bright steel poker on his fender?"

"I did."

"When did it occur to you to look for it?"

Regan scratched the back of his head. "The doctor had said that the weapon had been a blunt instrument, a poker, or the like."

"And, of course, Silverstein's own poker suggested itself immediately?"

"Yes, sir."

"But you couldn't find it anywhere, although you searched the premises from top to bottom."

"No, sir."

"Thank you, that is all."

Superintendent Westcott next entered the witness box and gave evidence in a clear, concise manner, describing the trail which had led him to the prisoner, from Regan's description of Silverstein's late caller, to the necklace found under the loose floorboard.

One of his points was that there was a wired connection between the pawnshop door and a bell by Silverstein's bed, so that the door could not be opened at night without waking the pawnbroker.

"What did you infer from your discovery of that fact?" asked Sir Herbert Nash.

"I decided that Silverstein had heard the intruder the moment he broke in, had slipped on his dressing-gown, armed himself with his revolver, and went downstairs to investigate. This theory seemed to be borne out by the fact that there were bloodstains on everything that the murderer had examined, except some of the papers on the desk, which were in great disorder, but not bloodstained. I decided that the intruder had started on the desk first; been disturbed almost immediately, and returned to his examination of the desk after the murder."

Sir Herbert took a little bundle of pink papers from the table on which his exhibits were grouped and held them up. "What are these?" he asked.

"Pawn tickets."

"You have seen them before?"

"Yes, sir. One of my subordinates found them among some partially destroyed papers in the fireplace at Hemingway's flat."

Sir Herbert replaced them on the table. "When you arrested Hemingway, did you examine his effects?"

"I did."

"What did you find?"

"Certain papers, a hypodermic syringe, a quantity of morphia, and a little over two hundred pounds in cash."

Sir Herbert took an envelope from his table of exhibits, produced a wad of notes from it, and handed them to Westcott. "Are those the notes?"

"They are."

"Did you take steps to trace them?"

"I did."

"What did you find?"

"They were issued to Hemingway at the Kensington branch of the Midwestern Bank, in payment of a cheque purporting to be signed by Lady Agatha Daventry."

"Thank you." Before sitting down, Sir Herbert addressed a few words to Mr. Justice Saintley: "I shall refer to both notes and cheque, and bring evidence regarding them, at a later period."

Robert Harvey rose to his feet. "You have had charge of this case from the beginning," he asked.

"From the time it was reported to Scotland Yard, yes."

"When did you arrive on the scene of the crime?"

"A minute or two before one o'clock."

"How much later would it be when Sergeant Regan described to you the caller he had seen earlier in the evening?"

"Perhaps half an hour later."

"Did he suggest to you that the caller had threatened Silverstein?"

"He did."

"So that you were prejudiced against the caller within about half an hour of your arrival on the scene?"

"No, sir," replied Westcott firmly. "It is my invariable rule to keep an open mind until the case is closed."

"Do you mean that you keep an open mind until after

the trial, or until you have turned over your discoveries to the Director of Public Prosecutions?"

"Until I have finished working on the case."

"So that you have tried and convicted the prisoner yourself before he appears before a jury?"

"If I have enough evidence for a trial there isn't much doubt of his guilt."

"In your mind, perhaps. You have heard of more than one man who was tried for murder and not convicted, haven't you?"

"Oh, yes."

"Have you conducted an investigation of such a case?"

"I have."

"And had no doubt that the man you arrested was guilty?"

"None whatever."

"But the judge and jury disagreed with you?"

"Yes."

"So, your judgement of guilt is not infallible?"

"Perhaps not."

Harvey produced a paper on which was printed the photograph and description of Arnold Hemingway, and the ominous words: 'Wanted for Murder.' "Did you order this circular to be printed?"

"I did."

"At what time?"

"About one o'clock on the afternoon of the murder."

"You would not issue a circular of that nature without being pretty sure in your own mind that the man it described was guilty?"

"It isn't likely that I would."

There was a dramatic pause, then raising his voice, Robert Harvey thundered: "So that barely twelve hours from the time you first appeared on the scene of the murder you had tried and convicted Arnold Hemingway in your own mind?"

"Hardly. The case had developed rapidly, and I thought—"

"You thought you had your man in the record time of twelve hours, but you have agreed with me that you are not by any means infallible, haven't you?"

"I have."

Mr. Justice Saintly leaned forward. "Is this an attack on the methods of the police, Mr. Harvey?" he asked.

"Yes, my lord, it is," replied Harvey steadily. "In this case, at least. I intend to show that the police were prejudiced against my client from the first, and that they shut their eyes to every factor of the case that did not fit in with their theory."

"You may proceed, Mr. Harvey," said the judge, after a slight pause. "But unless you can substantiate your claim, I shall not allow you to continue on that line."

"Very good, my lord." Harvey turned again to the witness. "The police surgeon who examined the corpse suggest that a poker might have inflicted the injuries to its skull, did he not?"

"A poker, or a similar blunt instrument."

"Did you search for the poker?"

"I detailed Sergeant Regan to do so."

"Without result?"

"That is correct."

"Granting for the moment that the poker had been used, what interpretation would you put on the fact that it was missing?"

"I should conclude that the murderer had carried it away."

"That would be foolish would it not? Wouldn't he be more likely to be seen, carry a heavy instrument of the sort?"

"Not if he disposed of it before encountering anyone."

"In the immediate neighbourhood of the scene, you mean?"

"Yes."

"Have you searched for the poker outside the premises where the murder took place?"

"I detailed a constable to do so at dawn that morning."

"How long did he search?"

"About two hours, I should think."

"Where?"

"In the surrounding streets, the areas of houses, dustbins, and the like."

"In the drains?"

"Yes, later that day."

"But he did not find it?"

"No."

"And the search was dropped?"

"Yes."

"Although you regarded the poker as the weapon used in the murder?"

"I thought it a likely weapon, yes," replied the Superintendent, grudgingly.

"Did that not suggest the possibility of the murder having been committed by someone who lived near enough to the scene of the crime to reach his house with the poker unobserved?"

"No, sir. I was by no means convinced that the poker had been used. A heavy candlestick, or the butt of a revolver would have been just as effective."

"But if the poker had been used, the theory that someone who lived near enough to have taken it home without attracting attention would be feasible?"

"It might."

"But you did not investigate the theory?"

"It did not seem necessary."

"Quite—for you had already decided on your man, and to investigate other possibilities would not have helped your case against him!"

"I object, your lordship!" exclaimed Sir Herbert Nash,

springing to his feet. The judge ordered Harvey's remark to be stricken from the record.

"Your theory is that Silverstein heard his alarm bell ringing, and went downstairs, revolver in hand, to investigate?" continued Harvey, quite unperturbed.

"It is."

"Did you find the revolver?"

"No."

"What did you make of its absence?"

"I decided that the murderer had carried it away."

"He seems to have a passion for carrying things away," commented the Counsel for the Defence, drily. "Does it not strike you that he must have looked pretty bulky as he made his escape, with a fairly large revolver and a heavy poker 'concealed' upon him?"

"I do not agree that the poker was the weapon of the murderer. It may have been missing before the murder."

"It may, of course, but since it was definitely seen a day or two before, your theory is not likely."

Going to the table of exhibits, Harvey picked up the candlestick in one hand, and the revolver in the other.

"You decided that one of these was the weapon used in the murder?"

"I considered it probable."

"Did you have them expertly examined for traces of blood?"

"I did."

"What was the verdict?"

"No blood was found upon them."

"So, neither could have been used after all?"

"It is possible they were wiped after the crime."

"But not so thoroughly as to have deceived an expert, with his microscopes and other testing instruments. Believe me, had the murder been committed with either of these weapons, definite traces of blood must have been found upon them."

Replacing the exhibits on the table, Harvey continued: "What clue first pointed definitely to my client in this open mind of yours?"

Westcott smiled grimly. "I discovered the necklace he had stolen from his employer on the scene of the crime."

"That proved my client was a thief."

"Yes."

"But a thief is not necessarily a murderer? Is it not correct that very few thieves commit murder?"

"It is, but I decided that the murder had been committed through the thief being trapped by Silverstein while searching the pawnshop for the necklace."

"So that if your theory is tenable, the murder was unpremeditated?"

"Yes."

"Thank you."

Counsel for the Defence took his seat, and Sir Herbert Nash rose. "You searched the scene of the crime very carefully?" he asked.

"I did."

"But found nothing to suggest any other train of investigation than the one you took?"

"Nothing whatever."

"If you had, you would have investigated it a thoroughly as you did the clues leading to the prisoner."

"Certainly."

The Counsel for the Prosecution resumed his seat, and Superintendent Westcott left the witness box.

So ended the first day of the trial for murder of Arnold Hemingway.

The public benches in the court were rapidly filling up. Almost a score of people had waited outside the Old Bailey since the night before, squatting on stools like a first night queue. Among those in court was a white-haired old man with a benign cast of feature who sniffed the air appreciatively as he came in, as though with keen enjoyment of the odour of the law; a middle-aged spinster who had attended every trial of any magnitude within fifty miles of London in the last twenty years, and who brought her lunch done up in tissue-paper and blue ribbon so that she might not miss a moment's atmosphere; two stout women in fur coats who compared the present trial with the last one they had attended, in the manner of moving-picture patrons; a neat little man with a tiny moustache and horn-rimmed spectacles who had written down every word of every murder trial that had taken place at the Old Bailey since 1919; and a 'flapper' whose frivolous clothes were given the lie by her wrinkled face and withered hands, who 'followed' the trials in which handsome Sir Robert Nash as flappers of more suitable years followed Tallulah Bankhead. These were the 'regulars' and knew the procedure inside out. They scuffled not, neither did they rustle papers, but sat still with avid eyes focussed on the dock—waiting for the prisoner to appear.

Others there were, mere novices at court-going, who made noises with their feet, with their parcels, their tongues, and with the wrappings of the chocolates which they had brought to relieve the tedium of the waiting period.

Chocolates at a murder trial! Like a jazz band at a funeral… At the height of a brilliant piece of cross-questioning or at an emotional moment in speech of the Counsel for the Defence, a speech on which rested a man's life, crackle! would sound a crinkled paper wrapping, and, pop! A large chocolate cream would be sucked into a red mouth and gobbled greedily by some fat woman whose heart and imagination were in her stomach.

The hum of conversation grew louder when the wigged-and-gowned Counsel entered, accelerated again when the prisoner appeared, then died away to a murmur when silence was demanded for the entry of Mr. Justice Saintley. Scraping of feet as several hundred spectators rose, more scraping and shuffling as they reseated themselves, then a subdued murmur as the trial commenced…

The Counsel for the Defence looked anxiously at his client. Hemingway looked white and strained, but he stood erect, looking steadily in front of him, without flinching or fidgeting.

He would be like that for an hour or two, perhaps more, while the effect of the injection of morphia he had been given lasted, then his hands and lips would begin to twitch, and by noon he would be a physical and mental wreck. During the luncheon recess, he would be given another injection, which would help him to weather the afternoon. It did not help Harvey to respect his client, this drugging and doping the man, so that he should not be a screaming lunatic in the dock…

Harvey's clerk put a slim white envelope into the barrister's hand. Tearing it open, Harvey found a single sheet of notepaper in which a few lines were written in Cynthia Priestley's well-formed handwriting.

"You are dining with me at my house," it ran. "You needn't change, and I won't bother you to talk or be bright. A quiet little dinner and a restful evening. I'll send you home to be back about ten."

He looked up at the public gallery, saw Cynthia's beautiful face, and nodded gratefully.

William Pryde, porter and man of all work at number eight 'a'

Half Moon Street, was the first witness of the day. Siegfried Higgins, Crown Junior Counsel, conducted the examination. "Do you remember the night and early morning of February 13th and 14th?"

"Yessir!" This emphatically.

"Why do you remember the date particularly?"

"Becorse the p'lice called nex' day an' axed me an 'umber of questings!"

"Where were you on the night in question?"

"In me quarters in the basement of the buildin' where I work."

"Asleep or awake?"

"Awike."

"Until what hour?"

"Abaht 'arf pars three."

"Indeed. Why?"

"Becorse the missis wos seedy-like, an' kep' me runnin' abaht arter 'er most of the night."

"Mr. Hemingway had a flat in the building?"

"Yes. 'E still 'as far 'as I know."

"Did you see him return on the night in question?"

"No sir. 'Twas nix mornin' before 'e came 'ome."

"About what time?"

"'Arf pars one, it would be."

"You are certain of that?"

"Yes."

The Counsel for the Defence rose as the Crown Junior Counsel resumed his seat. "You say that you sat up until half-past three in the morning because your wife was out of sorts?"

"Yessir."

"What is your usual bedtime?"

"Abaht 'arf pars ten."

"You must have been tired between half-past ten and half-past three?"

"I was, sir, an' no mistake."

"Are you usually so considerate a husband that you will sacrifice five hours of sleep because your wife has a headache?"

Bill Pryde grinned broadly. "You don't know my missus, sir," he retorted cheerfully. "W'en she carn't sleep, she tikes jolly good care that I don't!"

"When did the prisoner usually return to his flat?" asked Harvey, after a pause.

"Abaht one o'clock in the mornin', more or less."

"So, there was nothing unusual in his return at half-past one on this particular morning?"

"No sir, 'cept that he wasn't drunk."

"You say that he was usually drunk?"

"Yessir."

"At about one o'clock in the morning?"

"Yessir."

"But you have stated on oath that you usually go to bed at half-past ten; how can you tell us in what condition one of the tenants of the building usually arrived home two and a half hours later?"

Bill Pryde grinned again. "W'en a man wakens the 'ole 'ouse by fallin' over the mat, an' tumblin' over the stairs an' singin' songs at the top of 'is voice, I don't 'ave to see 'im to know that 'e's bl—drunk!" he retorted.

"Thank you."

The last witness for the Crown was an extravagantly over-dressed woman of about twenty-five, who entered the witness box with a defiant air.

Her name, she said, was Sonia Dering, her address, number twelve Paradise Row (a grimy canon of tenements adjacent to Stark Street) and her occupation 'actress'.

Sir Herbert Nash led the witness through her evidence,

handling her with gloves, for she was not at all the type with which juries are usually in sympathy.

"You remember the night of September 13th?" he asked.

"I do."

"Where were you on that night?"

"Out with some friends."

"At what time did you leave your friends to return home?"

"About half-past twelve, I should think."

"Does Stark Street lie on your way home?"

"Well, I pass a corner of the street."

"The corner where the pawnshop is situated?"

"No, at the other end of the street."

"At what time did you pass Stark Street on the night in question?"

"About twenty to one I should think."

"Did you see anyone in Stark Street as you passed?"

"Yes, a man I knew by sight."

"Do you see him in court?"

"Yes."

"Please point to him."

"That's him in the dock!"

"Tell us about your encounter with the prisoner."

"He came round the corner very fast—"

"Walking or running?"

"Well, half-walking, half-running. Sort of striding along quick. He had his hat drawn over his eyes, and his hands in his pockets."

"Did he recognise you?"

"Maybe he did and maybe he didn't. If he did, he didn't show it."

Robert Harvey's mind was in a chaotic, bewildered state. Hemingway had sworn that his visit to Stark Street at eleven o'clock on the night of the murder was the last visit to it which he had paid. Under the circumstances the Counsel for the Defence was entirely unprepared for this witness. As he met the eyes of the prisoner, Harvey frowned. Quickly, Hemingway took pencil and paper in hand and wrote a few lines, which were handed down to his advocate.

"This girl is lying," the hurried scrawl ran. "She saw me in Stark Street, but not at the time she says. I was there at twenty past one. I didn't think she recognised me, although I had seen her frequently before. She frequents a pub called the 'Eagle' in Shaftesbury Avenue."

Harvey rose to cross-examine Sonia Dering without the slightest idea how he could break down her evidence.

"Your name is Sonia Dering," he asked.

"I said so already," she replied in a cheeky manner.

"Is that your right name?"

"It's my stage name," she retorted defiantly.

"What is your right name?"

"Mary Fynn."

"You are an actress?"

"Yes."

"When was your last appearance on the stage?"

She hesitated. "I was in the cast of 'Gilded Wings'."

"The run of that play ended over four years ago, didn't it?"

"Perhaps it did, I don't remember exactly."

"What other stage work have you done since then?"

"Times are hard in the profession just now—"

"To tell the truth, you haven't been on the stage for over four years, have you?"

"No."

"I see. So 'actress' is really a polite euphemism for some other profession? You wear good clothes?" he asked.

"Well, I gotta right to, ain't I?" She became a typical street gamin in accent and manner. "I bought them, didn't I?"

"You live in a poor neighbourhood?"

"I gotta live somewhere, ain't I?"

"What do you work at?"

"I ain't workin' just now."

"I suggest that you haven't worked for four years."

"Well, and what if I haven't?"

"You haven't starved exactly and you are able to wear expensive clothes."

"What's that got to do with you?"

"I suggest, my poor child, that living has cost you more in these four years than if you had worked hard with your hands every day. I suggest your profession is a tragic one."

Her lips twisted. "I'm not askin' your sympathy," she snarled.

"You do not need to ask. You have it already." There was short pause. "You were at the 'Eagle' public house a part of the night in question?"

She stared. "How did you know?"

He ignored the question. "You left it with a man?"

"What if I did? I left him outside the 'Eagle' see?"

"Did you go home then?"

She hesitated. "Well, I did. I'd a ladder in my stocking, and I wanted to fix it."

"That would be shortly after eleven o'clock?"

"Perhaps it would."

"I put it to you that you saw the prisoner then—at eleven o'clock and not at twenty to one, as you say."

"I saw him at twenty to one," she replied, doggedly.

"I will remind you again that you are on your oath, and I put it to you that you were out that night as late as half-past one."

"What if I was? My affairs don't concern you!"

"So that you passed the end of Stark Street three times that night at least."

"Well, what of it?"

"Was there a fourth time?"

"How should I know? I can't remember exactly."

"You remember just as much and as little as you please. Remember a man's life hangs on your words. Do you swear that you saw the prisoner at twenty-past one on the 14th February?"

"Of course, I do!" Then, the force of his words coming home to her. "No! It was—"

"My mistake. You meant eleven o'clock, of course. That was the time you saw him, wasn't it?"

"Yes! Damn it, no. You are trying to—I saw him at—"

"That is all," said Harvey. "The jury will have no difficulty in interpreting your evidence."

Sir Herbert Nash rose.

"Is there any doubt in your mind as to the exact time when you saw the prisoner?" he asked.

"No, there ain't."

"At what time did you see the prisoner?"

"At twenty minutes to one," she snapped.

"Thank you."

So ended the second day of the trial for murder of Arnold Hemingway.

After a restless night, Robert Harvey rose at eight o'clock on the third morning of his client's trial for murder. Sleep had come to him only in snatches, and even these brief periods had been troubled by vivid nightmares.

Hemingway's was a hopeless case, and the next day or two would see the end of the trial, but Robert Harvey had not yet lost hope that something might happen which would enable him to save his client's life.

Something did happen—and the thing that happened turned Robert Harvey sick with horror.

Lying by his place on the breakfast table were perhaps a dozen letters, and the barrister glanced through the pile in a desultory fashion while he buttered a piece of toast. There was one among them in a familiar handwriting which made him forget his breakfast.

It was from a women he had not seen or heard of for years. At their last meeting she had still been in her 'teens, a merry slip of a girl with saucy eyes and dancing feet, whose kittenish ways had captured the heart of the staid young man he had been at that time.

Robert Harvey had been her devoted slave for ten years.

Her mother had brought her to live in a tiny house in the village of Maronlea, in Hampshire where the Harvey's had lived for generations, when Sheila was nine and Robert a manly fifteen. The dancing sprite of a girl had made him forget the dignity with the inferior sex which three years at Eton had taught him. She had made him play games with her, climb trees with her, listen attentively to the romantic narratives she was for ever making up. In a half-hearted, wholly ashamed fashion he had looked forward during school terms to the holidays when he would see her.

Then came the period when he was very much a man at twenty and she a jolly kid of fourteen, to be romped with occasionally, and frequently put in her place. Even then, her candid appraising eyes had kept him from having too great an opinion of himself. It was disconcerting when one was grown-up, and having tea in a grown-up fashion with one's equally grown-up guests (smooth-cheeked undergraduates like himself), to have a tousled mop of hair pop in through the open window, and a painfully clear voice cry:

"Come on Bobby, you old frowst, let's go birds'-nesting."

His long-legged little pal had vanished two years later, and a young lady took her place who sometimes forgot her dignity, it is true, but who made up for it by being very dignified indeed at the most unexpected moments. With this new version of Sheila Lavery, he had fallen wholeheartedly in love, and he had remained in love with her for three glorious years. Then Sheila and her mother had moved away from Maronlea, and after a bit, the lovers had lost sight of each other.

For nine years he had carried a picture of her in his heart, like a ray of sunshine dancing in a staidly-furnished room.

The envelope which had started his train of thought gave him a feeling of vague anxiety. It was made of cheap white paper, quite unlike the dainty scented envelopes which once carried Sheila's brief, frivolous letters to him. It made him wonder what the years had done to her.

It was postmarked 'Danbury', which was a small town five miles from Maronlea. His heart stood still when he turned the envelope over and read on the back the words 'Danbury General Infirmary.'

"Dear Robert," the letter began (it was the first time she had ever called him 'Robert'; she had insisted on 'Bobby,' because she knew men considered it childish). "When we were children and I hurt myself, you were always there to help, to pick me up, and put me on my feet again. You never failed me, though I was responsible for most of the scraps you got into.

"I've got myself into a terrible mess now, and I've been trying to steel myself to ask you to help me. You are the only person I can turn to, for I couldn't face anyone else. I should face it out alone, my dear, but I'm a coward, and I want you to lean on. If only I'd take my trouble to you years ago, everything would be different, but I always did go my own way until I fell with crash—and here I am.

"At the very bottom of the ladder, sick, hopeless and I think a little mad. I've been here for weeks, fighting death and worse, delirious for most of the time and scarcely conscious that I was alive until yesterday. The person who should be standing by me called me all manner of names when I asked for his help. I went mad that night, and with God knows what crazy notion I set out for home. Maronlea where I haven't been for nine long years. Something was calling to me; the child I once was, I suppose, and the green, shady lawns where we played together, you and I.

"I never got there, but somehow, I landed here. Thank God I never told" —the name was scored out— "my real name. When we first met, at Brighton, I gave him a false name for a joke. I took the name of that dear old lady who used to live in the grey house at the end of the village, 'The Elms' she called it, I think. After I had gone away with him, I continued to keep my secret. He fascinated me but I never trusted him.

"This pitiful scrawl is all incoherence and loose ends, I know, but it means simply—I need you.

"Your old friend,

"SHEILA LAVERY"

Robert Harvey's breath was coming in short, jerky sobs as he finished the letter, and his face was grey, for he remembered the name of the old lady who lived in 'The Elms', and he knew that he had found Lucy Hemmerde. It seemed impossible but it was true; Sheila Lavery, dainty and gay, fragile as a flower, and as beautiful, had become the drunken charwoman who was Lucy Hemmerde.

With knowledge, peculiarly enough, the first thought that came to him was that Arnold Hemingway's innocence of murder was proved. That thought was succeeded by a surge of bitter rage against Hemingway. In his fruitless search for Lucy Hemmerde, Harvey had seen to what red hell she had been brought by the man who betrayed her.

If the man had been in the room with him Harvey would have killed him with his bare hands. Death and worse than death he deserved, and walls of stone and bars of iron saved him from his just merits. The law had Hemingway in its grasp, and the law would punish him only for his transgression of it.

Then began a battle for possession of Robert Harvey's soul, and the warring elements were the memory of the girl he had loved and his horror of the wrong that had been done her against the ethics which had governed his life since he had entered the legal profession.

The truth stood revealed in its stark nakedness. If he suppressed his knowledge of Lucy Hemmerde's existence, Arnold Hemingway would hang. He would be innocent of the crime for which he was put to death, but guilty of a crime which morally was greater.

Robert Harvey K.C., had taken an oath to uphold the laws of his country, and to fulfil his duty. His duty was to save the life of his client, if it was humanly possible. On him a great trust was imposed: the cause of justice.

He put his hands to his face, as though to shut out the vision his imagination had conjured up.

"Let him hang!" he cried in a tortured voice. "He deserves nothing better. Let him hang!"

*

With unsteady footsteps, Robert Harvey entered the court on the third morning of the trial and, like a lifeless thing, he dropped into his seat. The boundless vitality which had been his greatest asset throughout his career at the Bar had left him and he was as limp as a wet rag.

When the formalities were concluded, there was a pause while the court waited for Harvey to open his case for the defence. For some moments there was silence, then whispering and shuffling of feet sounded.

The Counsel for the Defence did not move.

A hand tugged at his arm and a slip of paper was placed before him. He looked at in a dull, uncomprehending manner. It was in Hemingway's handwriting and said briefly, 'I wish to give evidence.'

The day before, Harvey had warned his client of the danger of his going into the witness box, and had said that he would not summon him unless expressly instructed. The slip of paper brought his mind to the present from its morbid contemplation of the past. He rose unsteadily to his feet with the paper in his hand. His lips moved but no sound came forth.

Mr. Justice Saintley leaned forward and looked at the barrister with compassion in his eyes.

"Are you ill, Mr. Harvey?" he asked.

Harvey shook his head listlessly.

"No, my lord, not ill," he replied.

With an effort he pulled himself together. "Call Arnold Hemingway," he said.

While the prisoner was being transferred to the witness box, Harvey turned his eyes to the gallery. He saw Cynthia Priestley there, and she returned his gaze anxiously. He did not realise that she was worried for his sake, because of the oddness of his manner.

There was a question he must ask, the question which he had decided to put to the prisoner at the beginning of his examination.

"Arnold Hemingway, before God, are you guilty of the murder of Moses Silverstein?"

"I am not."

The answer did not penetrate to Harvey's brain. He started to ask the question again, then checked himself as he remembered that it had been answered.

He wavered uncertainly on his feet, then sat down abruptly.

"I cannot defend this man," he said, and buried his face in his hands.

For a moment the world seemed to stand still. The Judge, startled out of his customary serenity, stared at Harvey with an odd expression. The prisoner trembled and his eyes were wildly anxious. There was a hum of eager whispering all over the court.

Harvey's clerk leaned forward and whispered hurriedly into the ear of Sir Herbert Nash. The Crown Counsel nodded and rose to his feet.

"Your Lordship," he said. "I have just been informed that my learned friend is most unwell. If I may suggest—"

The Judge adjusted his pince-nez.

"I shall adjourn the court for an hour," he replied, "in order that Mr. Harvey's condition may be ascertained. I suggest that a doctor be called."

Guided on one side by his clerk and on the other side by Sir Herbert Nash, Harvey stumbled out of the court.

Harvey's clerk helped his employer out of his wig and gown and into his outdoor clothes. Like an anxious mother Cynthia shepherded the barrister out of the building and into a taxi. When they arrived at Harvey's chambers in Fountain Court, she urged him to go straight to bed, but that he refused to do.

"But you're ill," she remonstrated. "You need rest."

"Ill!" he said, in a queer tone. "Ill! I'm not ill. There's nothing wrong with me."

"Then what on earth—"

Harvey went to the door of his study and summoned his man.

"I'm not at home to anyone," he said. "I can't speak on the telephone, and I can't see anyone."

"Very good, sir."

The barrister re-entered the study and closed the door. For a few moments he stood looking at Cynthia with an anxious, puzzled expression.

"I think I can trust you," he said at last. "I shouldn't dream of trusting anyone else."

"Thank you," said Cynthia, simply.

He went to his desk and found some snapshots. One of them, a photograph of a dainty girl of about sixteen playing with a Sealyham Terrier, he put into Cynthia's hand.

"That is a photograph of Lucy Hemmerde," he said, "taken about eleven years ago."

Cynthia looked at it closely, taking in the lithe, beautiful figure of the girl, her delicate features, the graceful animation of her pose.

"How charming!" she exclaimed.

Then a vision of the hovel in Redman's Row where Lucy Hemmerde had lived for months, and Lucy Hemmerde herself, worn out with work, and drunk every other night, came before her eyes, and she added:

"Oh, the poor, poor girl! To go from this to that horrible slum!"

Without a word Harvey handed her a photograph of the same girl taken about three years later, with a young man by her side. After a brief glance at the girl, Cynthia looked closely at the young man. She started suddenly and looked up.

"You!" she gasped.

The barrister nodded dumbly.

"But what does it mean?" she asked.

"It means that I have found Lucy Hemmerde," he replied. "Her real name is Sheila Lavery. I have known her since she was a child of nine. At one time we were sweethearts."

Cynthia rose and put her hands on his shoulders.

"My dear," she said, looking into his eyes, and seeing the misery that looked out of them. "You must have been through hell since you discovered this."

"I have," he groaned. "Now do you understand why I cannot defend Hemingway? Why, I'd like to kill him myself."

Cynthia moved away a little. "Where is this girl?"

"In a hospital at Danbury. She's been ill. She wrote to me—I got her letter this morning. She doesn't know anything about the trial, and if I can help it, she won't know."

"Her evidence might save Hemingway's life."

"It probably would," said Harvey, fiercely. "But would you ask her to condemn herself to further shame and misery to save a man who ruined her?"

She shook her head.

"I don't know," she replied. "I don't know."

"That's what I've been trying to decide since I read her letter," said Harvey. "I'm nearly out of my mind with worry."

"I can understand that. What are you going to do?"

"There's a train to Danbury at three o'clock. I'm going to catch it."

"May I come? You know I want to help."

He looked at her fondly. "I knew you'd say that," he observed, "and I'm more than grateful than I can express. I think Sheila would like you to come."

There was a discreet knock at the door, and Harvey's clerk entered. "Mr. Wrenn is on the 'phone, sir," he said.

Cynthia picked up the telephone.

Wrenn's voice came to her from the other end of the wire. "Is that you, Cynthia?" he said, in a surprised tone. "Is Harvey there?"

She put down the telephone and, turning, grasped the barrister's arm. "I want you to tell him that you'll be ready to appear in court in four days' time," she said.

"I can't defend Hemingway," he replied.

"Robert," she insisted, "you must. We'll do our best to restore Sheila to health and happiness, you and I, but you can't right one wrong with another. I'm not telling you to put that poor girl in the witness box, but you must defend Hemingway by every other means in your power. You've got to fight for him, tooth and nail. You'll never be able to respect yourself again if you don't!"

He moved to the telephone and picked it up.

"Alright, Wrenn," he said, in a colourless voice, "I'll be there."

They found her lying in a white enamelled ward filled with similar beds. The snowy linen which draped her meagre body seemed to enhance the pallor of her face, which was bloodless and waxen. Her hair was well brushed, but lustreless, and literally besprinkled with silver. There were lines of suffering one her face. At twenty-seven she looked fully ten years older.

"Sheila!" said Harvey, in a hoarse, strained voice.

"Bob!" she whispered.

Kneeling by her bedside, it was all he could do to keep back his tears. The sick woman's face was curiously passive, almost indifferent.

"I knew you'd come," she murmured, stroking his head gently with a coarse, calloused hand.

"If only you'd sent for me sooner!" he cried.

She shook her head. "No. I made my bed and I lay on it. But I should have had the courage to hold out till the end alone."

Her eyes wandered to Cynthia's face and stayed there, with a curious expression in them.

"Sheila," said Harvey. "This is Cynthia Priestley, a very dear friend of mine."

"I want to be your friend too, my dear," said Cynthia softly, coming forward.

Sheila's expression remained passive. "You're very good," was all that she said.

Sheila was as lifeless as a person may be who is not actually dead. Without enthusiasm she listened to their plans for her, allowed herself to be dressed and half-carried to the long limousine which waited outside for them, and sat silently throughout the journey to London, neither looking to right or left of her.

At Cynthia's little house in Cheyne Walk, she submitted with the same indifference to being put to bed, drank a glass of champagne and a cup of warm soup, and went to sleep without asking a single question, or making a remark.

During the next few days, there was no change in Sheila's condition. She was taken for a drive every morning and after-noon, ate nourishing food, and slept a great deal, but nothing seemed to restore her spirit. One thing Harvey stipulated: she was not to hear of the trial of Arnold Hemingway; she had enough to bear without that.

One evening Cynthia and the barrister went in to see their patient. For the first time Sheila took the initiative in the con-versation. "I've been thinking a good deal," she said. "I seem to have done nothing else for weeks. You're being very good to me, both of you, but you're wasting your kindness. Don't think I'm ungrateful. I'm just tired, that's all. Sick and tired of living. I've gone through too much in the last two years to have any illusions left about life. It's a weary sort of game that you are condemned to play any longer. They told me at the hospital that without the will to live I'd die. Well, that suits me. I don't want to live. I've nothing to live for, and just living isn't enough. Besides, there's the past, and I can't get it out of my mind. I made a mess of things. I made a low thing of myself. Look at me. I'm twenty-seven years old and I look forty at least. I've nothing left but a craving for drink, and a lot of rotten memo-ries. That's a poor foundation for a new life. I know what you're going to say, both of you; that I can always depend on you. In simple language that means that I'm to be a drag on you both as long as I live. You don't look on it that way now, but in time you'd begin to see things as they are. I'm sorry I wrote to you from the hospital, Bob, but it took more courage than I've got to pass out there—alone.

"I've been remembering our childhood together, and wondering if there was anything essentially bad in me at the start. I don't think there was. I was wilful and reckless but not bad. After mother died, I led a butterfly sort of life. I had some money—mother left me a little—which I spent in as idiotic a manner as any frivolous girl could spend money. Then at Brighton I met Hemingway. I didn't trust him, but I thought it was fine to flirt with him. I thought I could look after myself, but I couldn't. The inevitable happened, and when he left Brighton, I went with him. I couldn't face anyone else. We ran through my money in a few months living fast and furiously while it lasted and, in the end, he threw me over. I wouldn't ask anyone for help—I was too ashamed—so I did the best I could on my own, and a damned poor best it was. It landed me in the gutter. They say we all find our own level in this world, and I found mine. The gutter. But I'm not going on. If it's possible to die by just wanting to die, I'm going to apply my mind to it. The Coué method backwards. Every day I get worse and worse. If that doesn't work, I'll find something that will. I'm sorry to hurt you, but there it is. I'm tired, tired, oh, so terribly tired!" She finished the sentence in a flood of tears.

There was nothing to be said. With tears in his eyes, Harvey left the room.

Half an hour later, Cynthia came to him downstairs.

"My God!" he cried. "Isn't there anything we can do?"

"Don't lose hope," Cynthia replied. "She's worn out and nervous, but we'll pull her round somehow. She's crying now and when a woman cries, there's still life left in her."

She put two hands on his shoulders. "You've got a fight ahead you, my friend," she said. "Tomorrow the trial continues, and you've got to do your best to save that man. Your best, do you understand? You've got to fight for him, as you've never fought in your life."

On the second morning of the resumed trial, Robert Harvey rose limply to his feet and said, "Call Sheila Lavery."

For a moment there was complete silence in court, then the whispering of many voices, as a white-faced woman whose age was not easy to estimate, came through a side-door into the court, and made her way to the witness box. At sight of her the man in the dock swayed forward, a little cry of relief rose in his throat. The woman looked at him steadily for a moment, then turned away, her eyes smarting with tears.

The Counsel for the Defence stood with bowed head and with a hand over his eyes while the new witness was sworn, and there was quite a pause while she waited for him to question her.

Pulling himself together at last he looked at her with sorrowful eyes.

"You are Sheila Lavery?"

"I am." The answer came in a low, yet composed tone.

"Known for two and a half years as Lucy Hemmerde?"

"Yes."

The dropping of a pin could have been heard in court, so enthralled by this revelation were the spectators. Sir Herbert Nash leaned forward in his seat with his eyes fixed on the woman's strained white face. Mr. Justice Saintly adjusted his pince-nez to enable him to view the witness more accurately.

"You are acquainted with the prisoner?" asked the Counsel for the Defence more steadily than he had previously spoken.

"I am."

"When did you last see him?"

"On the thirteenth of February."

"At what hour?"

"I met him at half-past eleven, and we parted a little after one o'clock in the morning."

"The morning of February 14th?"

"Yes."

"Where did you meet him? Tell us how you occupied the time between half-past eleven and one."

"I met him in Piccadilly Circus, outside the pavilion. I noticed him first when he came out of a public-house opposite and came across the street. I went up to him and said that I wanted to speak to him. At first, he refused, but I threatened to make a scene, and to avoid that he gave in. We went on a 'bus to Hyde Park where we could talk without creating attention. My—my clothes were shabby. I—I provided a decided contrast to him." She faltered, and then continued. "We talked for quite a long time in Hyde Park. When we came out of the park I heard one o'clock striking."

"Mr. Hemingway was with you every minute of the time between half-past eleven and one?"

"Yes," she said, definitely and firmly. "Every single minute."

"You have not seen him since?"

"No."

"Thank you."

A prey to conflicting emotions, Robert Harvey sat down. He had just done the thing he had imagined so often with horror and loathing; examined the girl he had once loved, in defence of the man who had ruined her life. Now he was to sit calmly and watch her evidence being torn to pieces by the Crown Counsel, watch mud being thrown at her, with the certainty that much of it would stick.

In silence, Sir Herbert Nash rose slowly to his feet. So slowly did he rise that he seemed to be preposterously tall, and coming up out of a trapdoor in the floor of the court.

"Why did you not come forward with your evidence at the beginning of this case?" he asked in a smooth purring tone.

"I was ill in hospital."

Robert Harvey stood up again. "If my learned friend allows, your lordship," he said, "I have here documentary evidence in the shape of a signed statement from the resident physician of the Danbury General Infirmary to the effect that the witness has been in the infirmary in a serious condition since the afternoon following the murder, that she was admitted in a delirious condition, and that she was discharged only four days ago."

He held out a paper which Sir Herbert Nash waved away.

"I am perfectly satisfied," said Sir Herbert.

The Counsel for the Defence resumed his seat.

"Where have you been for the last four days?" asked Sir Herbert.

"At the house of a very dear friend," Sheila replied in a grateful tone.

"Why did you not come forward at the time of your discharge?"

"Because I knew nothing about this trial or about the murder until last night."

"Who told you last night?"

"I read about the trial in an evening paper."

"Last night's evening paper?"

"Yes."

Sir Herbert turned to his junior and whispered a few words. Mr. Higgins rose, and made his way to the door of the court, where he gave certain instructions to a messenger, then returned and resumed his seat.

"You were friendly with the prisoner at one time?" continued Sir Herbert gently.

"I was." Her lip quivered but her voice did not falter.

"Very friendly?"

"Yes."

"In fact," said Sir Herbert, with awful distinctness, "you were his mistress for a period of six months?"

Sheila trembled, and her eyes were like the hurt eyes of a stricken animal. "Yes," she whispered.

"You were then in love with the prisoner?"

"I was."

"Was your affair with him your first of that nature?"

"My first and only affair of that nature," whispered Sheila, in a pitiful tone.

"You must have been very much in love with him indeed?"

"I was."

"I suggest that you still love him."

"No."

"Oh, come, love of that sort does not change easily. You trusted him with your honour, did you not?"

"I did."

"You loved him enough to live with him, although you were not married, and he had no intention of marrying you?"

Her assent was almost inaudible.

"You did a great deal for him because you loved him, did you not?"

"I did."

"Because you loved him, you would have done a great deal more for him had he asked it?"

"Yes."

"You would have scrubbed floors for him, slaved for him, as women do for the men they love?"

She nodded, her face ashen and strained.

"You would even have lied for him?"

Sheila gave a little moan, but did not answer.

"You would have lied for him?" Sir Herbert persisted.

This time the answer was wrung from her in a tortured, terrible, way: "My God, I would!"

Sir Herbert turned towards the jury, as much as to say, "You see!"

"After you left him, how did you live?" he continued after a brief pause.

"I had some money."

"How long did it last?"

"About three months, or so, I think."

"And after that?"

"I worked."

She put the whole history of her months of poverty and misery into those two words.

"I was a mannequin at one time."

"And after that?"

"I made shirts in a Whitechapel factory."

"And then?"

"I washed clothes in a steam laundry."

Sir Herbert Nash was puzzled. He had hoped to prove that, after her parting with Hemingway, she had earned her living in another way. This record of menial toil was not at all what he wanted. It reflected upon the prisoner, but did not help him to discredit the witness.

"You say that you met the prisoner at Piccadilly Circus, on the night of the murder? Had you an appointment with him?"

"No."

"You just happened to run into him?"

"Yes."

"Was that not odd? That of all places in London, you two should meet there on the night of the murder?"

"I have told the truth," she said in a low voice.

"A great many women frequent Piccadilly Circus unescorted at a late hour."

"I suppose so."

"You wouldn't call them respectable women."

Sheila's eyes blazed suddenly. "Whatever they are men made them!" she cried passionately.

Just then a messenger came through the court to the seat where the junior counsel for the Crown was sitting and handed him a folded newspaper. The junior read a report on the front page eagerly, underlining certain passages in blue pencil, then handed it to Sir Herbert, who glanced at it, the held it up with a dramatic gesture.

"This," he cried in a clear, penetrating voice, "is a copy of last night's paper. On the front page is a report of the prisoner's evidence which was given yesterday. Are you aware, Miss Lavery, that this statement of his movements on the night of the murder, which is given here, is almost word for word identical with your evidence today?"

He shook the paper in front of her eyes. "This is the issue of the newspaper in which you first saw an account of this trial?"

"It is," she said in a low voice.

"You saw it last night?"

"Yes."

"And this morning you come here and tell a story which is identical with the report in the newspaper you read?"

"I have told the truth."

"That is for the jury to decide," he said with careful emphasis. "It is for them to say whether you have told the truth, or whether your love for the prisoner, the love you admitted might prompt you to lie for him, brought you here today in an attempt to save his life by a story without foundation, copied from the only report of the trial which has come into your hands."

"I do not love him now!" she cried. "It was my duty to come forward and tell the truth when I read that he was on trial."

With a dramatic gesture Sir Herbert pointed to the man in the dock.

"Look at that man!" he almost shouted. "The man responsible for all your misery. There he stands, in the shadow of the gallows. What are your emotions when you see him there, fighting desperately for his life?"

For a moment the woman did not answer, then she drew in her breath with a sob.

"I pity him!" she whispered.

"You pity him! And you once loved him! And pity is akin to love!"

He leaned forward. And took her hand gently. "You love him, don't you?"

She swayed, her lips twisting, and in her eyes was a haunted look.

"God help me, I do!" she moaned, then collapsed with a moan in a dead faint.

*

A folded slip of paper was handed down from the dock to the Counsel for the Defence.

On it, Arnold Hemingway had written: 'I would rather have been hung than see that poor girl tortured like that.'

Robert Harvey wrote a line or two on the bottom of the page in pencil, then passed it back to the prisoner, who read it, crumpled it up, and covered his face with his hands.

For the Counsel for the Defence had written: 'I would rather have seen you hanged than put her in the witness box.'

The sensation in court produced by Shelia Lavery's testimony had died away; the witness had been led in tears from the witness box.

Robert Harvey rose to make his speech for the defence.

Finishing his speech, which ended on a dramatic note, he was followed by the Counsel for the Prosecution.

Then calmly and coldly the judge summed up.

Too much stress had been laid, he felt, on the steel poker. Though it had been in constant use by the pawnbroker, even his housekeeper had not been able to say for certain that it was in its place on the night of the murder. The sergeant, who had visited the dead man on the very night of the murder, was uncertain on that point. It was possible, therefore, that the poker had not been in its place. The jury must not feel that the steel poker must necessarily have been the murderer's weapon because the steel poker was missing. Had there been positive evidence that the steel poker was in its place at the time of the murder and was missing directly afterwards, their conclusions might be different. There was no such evidence, and the possibility of the poker being the weapon had been magnified out of all proportion.

The police had not been prepared to say what actually was the weapon used. The premise had been advanced that the murder might have been committed with the butt of the prisoner's revolver, which he might afterwards have cleaned. That was possible. Any one of the possible weapons that were present in the shop in profusion might have been used and hurriedly cleaned. After such cleaning they might show traces of blood, or they might not.

It was true that the evidence in the case was circumstantial, but the evidence in murder trials was almost invariably circumstantial. Murders were not committed before witnesses. If murderers were not to be hanged upon circumstantial evidence, no murderer would ever hang.

If the jury believed the witness, Sheila Lavery, they must find the prisoner not guilty. If, however, they believed that she had concocted her evidence, had deliberately lied to save the man she loved, they must not take that to mean that the prisoner was necessarily guilty. They must examine the other evidence and bring in a verdict on such testimony as they were prepared to accept.

On and on the judge droned, blowing it seemed now hot, now cold.

"It must be borne in mind that—"

"On the other hand—"

"—the jury must not be misled by—"

"—benefit of reasonable doubt."

As the judge summed up, the Counsel for the Defence was watching his client's face. Hemingway had the strained, appalled expression of one who feels the solid earth crumbling beneath him. With a start, Harvey remembered Silverstein's words: 'He does not like the sensation of dancing on air.'

'Dancing on air!' The phrase had an ominous sound.

*

There was silence in court while the jury resumed their places, then a little murmur of conversation when the grim, determined faces of most of them were noticed.

The Clerk of the Court rose.

"Gentlemen of the Jury, are you agreed upon your verdict?"

"We are," said the foreman of the jury in a strained voice.

"Do you find the prisoner at the bar, Arnold Hemingway, guilty or not of the wilful murder of Moses Silverstein?"

With a tremor in his voice, the foreman said: "Guilty!"

The world seemed to stand still while the judge adjusted a little square of black silk upon his head, and pronounced the sentence, culminating in the soul-shaking words:

"To be hanged by the neck until you are dead, and that your body be afterwards buried within the precincts of the prison wherein you shall have been last confined before your execution, and may the Lord have mercy upon your soul."

Harvey went straight from the Old Bailey to Cynthia's house in Cheyne Walk. He found Cynthia alone in the drawing room and told her the news of Hemingway's conviction.

"So, her ordeal was in vain," said Cynthia.

Harvey nodded his head wearily. "The jury didn't believe her," he replied.

"Oh, the fools! Couldn't they see that she was telling the truth?"

The barrister made a hopeless gesture. "Why blame them? Sir Herbert persuaded them that she was lying to save her lover's life," he said. "What a grim joke! The idea that she'd lie to save the man who ruined her whole life." His fingers twined nervously. "What I can't understand is why she admitted in the witness box that she still loves him. It's incredible. She can't possibly have meant it. She was worn out and hysterical, that's all. But the jury believed that part of her evidence, or course, and decided that she was lying for love."

"It's quite true," said Cynthia quietly.

"What? But we know—"

"I don't mean that she lied. I mean that she told the truth when she said that she still loves him."

"But she couldn't!"

"She does. Oh, I know it's unreasonable and impossible, but there's no reason in love. She still loves him, why, God only knows."

"And he hangs in three weeks!"

Cynthia took Harvey's arm. "You've got to save him," she said earnestly. "If he hangs, Sheila will die."

"We've done everything we can," he replied, tonelessly.

"An appeal to the Home Secretary—"

He shrugged his shoulders. "Oh, we'll appeal all right, but it won't be much use without further evidence. Where is Sheila now?"

"In bed, asleep. I made her go to bed, and nurse has given her strong injection of morphia. I was afraid that the verdict would be unfavourable, and I didn't want her to know of it until I had a chance to prepare her."

He ruffled his hair uneasily. "This is hell," he said.

They were silent for a few moments. Then—

"We know he's innocent," she said slowly. "Isn't there any way of proving it?"

"If we could find the person who really did it," he replied. "But that isn't likely."

"Won't you try?"

"Of course, I'll try." This with a nervous shrug of his shoulders. "But I don't know where to start."

Without much hope, but with the feeling that anything was better than inaction, he went down next morning to Star Street to have a look at the scene of the crime. The pawnshop was already under new management. 'Aaron Silverstein' was the name above the door. Apart from the change of proprietors nothing had been changed, from the exterior view at least.

Harvey saw a familiar figure coming down the street with slow, ponderous strides. A figure in a heavy greatcoat and a bowler hat, with the firm solid tread of a policeman. Sergeant Regan. The Sergeant smiled when he recognised Harvey.

"Having a last look round, sir?" he said.

"Something of the sort; doing a little detective work," replied the barrister, genially.

The Irish police officer gave Harvey a shrewd glance. "Then you don't believe your man's guilty?"

"No, I don't," replied Harvey positively. "In fact, I know he's innocent. But he'll certainly hang unless I can discover the real culprit, and there's not much chance of that."

"It would be a terrible thing for an innocent man to hang," said Regan, thoughtfully. "Not that I'm your way of thinking, but even the law makes mistakes at times. I was in court the day you made your speech for the defence, and it set me thinking. I've been trying to think of anyone in the neighbourhood who had a strong enough motive for murdering the old man." He shrugged his shoulders. "But, sure, I can't think of anyone."

"I've thought of something," said Harvey, suddenly. "It is almost certain that the empty cashbox Westcott found contained money, but you failed to trace it to Hemingway. Now, supposing that someone who was deeply in debt to Silverstein had committed the murder and stolen the money, but failed to find the papers he was after, what would you expect him to do?"

Regan scratched his head. "By the Lord Harry," he exclaimed, as the idea penetrated his thick skull, "I believe I gather your meaning, sir. You mean he's wait until the coast was clear, then redeem the papers with the stolen money?"

"Exactly."

The sergeant took the barrister by the arm. "We'll soon test your theory, sir," he said. "Step inside with me, and we'll have a word with the young man that's the new proprietor."

Aaron Silverstein was a younger edition of his uncle, long-nosed, bearded and shabby, but his beard was black instead of grey, and he had still to acquire the wrinkles with which time had furrowed the face of the old pawnbroker.

"It's a nice day, sergeant," he said, ingratiatingly. "What can I do for you?"

"This is Mr. Harvey," said Regan, with a jerk of his thumb in the direction of the barrister. "We want to know if any large repayments have been made since you took over the business."

The younger Silverstein's eyes were shrewd. "For why should you want to know?" he asked, blankly.

"Never mind that," said Regan, impatiently. "All you've got to do is to tell me what I want to know."

The pawnbroker shrugged his shoulders. "It depends on what you mean by big repayments," he said. "Tommy Callahon was in a week ago, and paid a debt of thirty pounds—"

"Callahon's alright," said Regan. "I know where he got the money. Anyone else?"

"Mrs. Milligan came in with eighteen pounds the other day—"

"Her son's just back from two years at sea," interrupted Regan. "Get on with the list."

"Mr. Taplow—"

"Taplow!" exclaimed Regan. "Now you're talking! How much did he pay?"

The pawnbroker's brow darkened. "There ain't nothing phoney about the money, is there?" he demanded. "It ain't snide, is it?"

"No, the money's alright," snapped Regan. "It isn't counterfeit. How much did he pay?"

"Eighty quid," said the younger Silverstein.

Regan turned to Harvey with a curious expression on his large red face.

"If there's anything in your theory, sir," he said. "Taplow's your man."

"How can we find out?" asked Harvey, trying to keep his excitement from becoming evident in his tone.

"We'll go along and see him. I was on my way there in any case. I've a summons for him for letting his chimney catch fire."

They went along the street and pounded on the blistered, shabby door of Taplow's dingy house. They hammered loud and long enough to waken the dead before the door opened and Taplow's cadaverous head appeared in the aperture. When he recognised Sergeant Regan, he opened the door wider.

"Come in," he said. Then noticing the barrister, added: "This is an unexpected pleasure, Mr. Harvey."

"Then you know me?" said Harvey.

"Of course, I know you. I was in court every day of the trial, and very interesting it was, too. Very interesting."

"Mr. Harvey would like a look at your chamber of horrors," said Regan.

"Well, please come in, both of you."

They went up the narrow stairs in single file. The stair rail was thick with dust, and the dingy carpet had evidently not been swept for weeks."

"What's your servant girl up to?" asked Regan. "Neglecting her work a bit, ain't she?"

"She's gone," replied Taplow. "My little treasures were getting on her nerves, so she left and went home to her family at the end of February."

"I thought I hadn't seen her about," commented Regan.

They went into the room where Taplow's criminal relics were displayed. The air in the room was rank and foul.

"There is one relic which I hope to acquire which would interest you, Mr. Harvey," said Silas Taplow, rubbing his hands together. "I'm going to try to make a bargain with the hangman for the rope he strings up your client with."

Harvey shivered, and Taplow glanced at his pale face with eyes that glistened with malignant joy.

"This murder has a special interest for me," Taplow said, huskily. "The first that has been committed in my own street. What a collection I'll have soon! With every murder it grows bigger and better!"

Sergeant Regan crossed himself superstitiously.

"Mark my words," he said, in an awed voice. "No good will come to you from these fearful things. Who knows what wraiths ye have around ye, with horrors like these in the house?"

Taplow rubbed his hands together. "So, you think I can boast a ghost or two, in addition to my concrete treasures?" he asked jestingly. "Capital! What a show they would be, if we could only see them!"

"God forbid!" said Regan, hastily. He drew an official paper from his pocket. "While it's in my mind," he said. "Here's a summons for you, for lettin' your chimney catch fire on two occasions, the fourteenth of February and the first of March."

Taplow took the paper with a wry expression on his face. "Ten shillings fine!" he exclaimed. "Besides the expense of having the chimney swept!"

"That needn't worry you," retorted Regan, drily. "Come in for some money lately, haven't you?"

Silas Taplow started and wheeled sharply. "What do you mean?" he demanded.

"Just that I was chatting with young Silverstein, and he told me that you had paid him eighty pounds the other day. That's a large sum."

"Young Silverstein should learn to keep his mouth shut," said Taplow, vindictively. "It doesn't pay to chatter about other people's business. Not that it matters in this case. That money was a dividend payment."

"Well, if you get dividend payments like that," said Regan, cheerfully, "don't grouse about a ten bob fine."

A little later, Regan and Harvey took their departure. Out in the street the police sergeant turned to the barrister with a wry smile.

"A dividend payment!" he commented. "And there's no reason

to suppose that he's lying. He looked a bit queer when I touched on the matter, but few people relish having their private affairs bandied about. Probably his story is straight enough. I know he's got some sort of a private income."

Harvey grasped Regan's arm tightly.

"On February 14th and March 1st his chimney went on fire," he said, in an excited tone. February 14th was the day after the murder of Moses Silverstein—and his servant girl 'went home to her family' at the end of February. On the day after the murder, and on the day after the girl 'went home' he burned so much his chimney caught on fire."

"What do you mean?" asked Regan, hoarsely.

"What do you think I mean?"

"You mean—you mean—" Regan stammered.

"I'd like to know what he was burning on those two days," Harvey replied.

Robert Harvey and Sergeant Regan called at Scotland Yard and were closeted with Superintendent Westcott for the better part of an hour. He listened attentively to what they had to say. After a while he took a box of cigars from a drawer in his desk and passed it round.

"A present from my wife," he said, and added, drily, "but I stipulated the brand."

For a few moments he devoted his attention to the delicate task of piercing and lighting his cigar.

"You gave me it hot and strong at the trial, Mr. Harvey," he remarked, with a twinkle in his eyes. "But I don't have any malice. If there's the slightest possibility that your man is innocent, I'm willing to do all I can to help. What you've just told me about Taplow is interesting, I'll admit, but I don't see just what I can do. Your facts are too slight a basis for a search-warrant, I suppose that's what you want."

"It is," said Harvey. "If our suspicions are correct, a search-warrant might enable us to find more formidable evidence."

Sergeant Regan leaned forward with an apologetic laugh.

"Well?" demanded Westcott.

"You'll remember Silverstein's skullcap, sir?" said Regan, awkwardly.

"The one that was missing just after Taplow left the pawnshop on the night of the murder?"

"The very one, sir," said Regan, earnestly. "He pinched it all right. I'd bet real money on that. But you couldn't get anything out of him when you went to see him."

"Well?"

"Well, I thought—sure, now, couldn't you get a search-warrant on the pretext of looking for the skullcap?"

Superintendent Westcott was very thoughtful for a moment. "By George, I believe you've hit it!" he exclaimed, suddenly.

Within an hour the three left the Yard in a flying squad car with two plainclothes men and a search-warrant.

Just before they left, Harvey put through a telephone call to Cynthia. "I don't want to raise false hopes, my dear," he said, "but I couldn't refrain from letting you know that there's a chance—just a chance—mark you—that we're on track of the real murderer."

"That's splendid news," gasped Cynthia.

"Don't build on it," he warned. "I'll let you know definitely as soon as I can."

There are few streets in London, or anywhere else for that matter where the presence of the police in more than everyday numbers will not cause a crowd to collect, but Stark Street is one of them. It is inhabited by people who believe that minding their own business (especially where the police are involved) is a profitable policy. So, the flying squad car drawn up outside the house of Silas Taplow attracted little attention. An errand boy and a stray cat were the sole audience when Superintendent Westcott pounded on Taplow's door with a search-warrant in his hand.

The door was opened cautiously at first, then wider when Taplow recognised his visitors. "So!" he said, with the ghost of a sneer in his voice. "A visit in force, superintendent?"

"I'm going to make a search of the premises," said Westcott, stepping inside the house. "Here's my search-warrant."

Taplow did not even glance at the official paper. "A search, eh?" His tone was mildly speculative. "A search for what?"

"For a certain skullcap, which I suspect you of stealing from No.1 Stark Street on the morning of February 14th."

The collector of gruesome relics smiled. "Dear, dear! So, you're still barking up that tree, superintendent!"

Without replying, Westcott beckoned the others in and closed the door.

"Harker, you are detailed to the basement," he said crisply. "Evans, you will search the ground floor. Regan, you and I will investigate the upstairs rooms."

"Thorough!" commented Taplow, ironically. "Very thorough indeed. And all this trouble for a ragged-old skullcap."

His eye fell on Harvey. "Back again, Mr. Harvey! Perhaps you have not seen all you would wish of my treasures. My museum is still at your disposal."

With admirable thoroughness they searched the house from top to bottom. Not a nook or corner was left un-investigated. The room on the second floor which Westcott had found full of rags on previous visit still held its filthy store. They turned the rags over and separated them, but found nothing, except some slight traces of blood, which might mean that a bloodstained article had at one time been hidden under them, or might mean nothing but a long-healed cut finger.

"It's no good," said Westcott, at last. "If the devil's hidden anything, he's concealed it too well."

"Wait a minute," said Harvey. "What feature of this house strikes you most?"

"Why, filth," said Westcott, disgustedly. "Age-old dirt and filth. The place is lousy."

"Then go into that little room," replied the barrister, "and tell me what you see."

With a wondering expression on his keen face, Westcott went into the room which Harvey indicated. He returned in a minute.

"Do you mean that the wallpaper is practically new?"

"Exactly. All over the house the paper is dilapidated, torn and dirty, but in that room it's fresh and unstained."

They went into the room again. Regan remained on the

landing to divert Taplow, who was in his precious museum below, should the collector chance to come upstairs.

Westcott slid the blade of his knife into the wallpaper and ripped a section away. It revealed merely a layer of stained wallpaper beneath. He ripped again and again, then stopped and peered closely. "For the love of—" he exclaimed.

Harvey looked over the detective's shoulder, and saw a rust-like stain which he had uncovered.

"Blood, by all that's holy!" said Westcott.

The two men ripped and tore at the paper, and soon uncovered a large, bloodstained patch. Then Westcott investigated one of the other walls. He tapped it sharply with his knuckle.

"By George, that's not the sound of laths and plaster!" he exclaimed. "There's brick behind here!"

He tore away a strip of the wallpaper, and revealed, directly beneath, an expanse of brick. Without waiting to investigate further, he ran out on the landing and seized Regan's arm.

"Go downstairs and keep your eye on Taplow," he said. "Don't let him out of your sight for a moment. And tell Harker to find an axe, if he can, and bring it up here."

A few minutes later, Detective Harker came upstairs with an axe which was ominously coated at the blade with a dark brow substance.

"This is the only axe I could find," he said cheerfully. "The old blighter raised a holler when I grabbed it out of his precious museum. Seems it's one of his choicest exhibits."

Without comment, Westcott took the axe and commenced to batter at the bricked wall. Suddenly a brick fell in, and a rush of foul air came out which sickened the three men in the room. The stench was appalling. Only by opening the windows wide were they able to continue the work of demolishing the wall. When that was completed, they discovered that the bricks had closed up a large wall-cupboard. In it lay a heavy steel poker, a revolver, the murdered man's skullcap, and the decomposing body of a young woman.

The sight was nauseating. Harvey began to feel sick.

Westcott went out to the landing. "Regan," he called. "Bring Taplow upstairs."

The next moment the heavy tread of the Irish police officer and the catlike step of his captive were heard, and they came into view round a bend in the stairs.

Taplow's eyes darted to the half-shut door of the little room where the gruesome discovery had been made, like the eyes of a cornered rat.

"That was your servant's bedroom," demanded Westcott.

"Yes."

"Where is she now?"

The collector of grim relics moistened his lips nervously. "She went home to her people," he stammered.

"In Folkestone?"

"Yes, that's right."

The superintendent produced a buff envelope from his pocket, and drew a telegram form from it.

"This is a wire from Folkestone police in answer to an inquiry I wired to them before leaving Scotland Yard," he said. "It runs, 'Girls parents report that she has not been home, and has not answered letters since end of February.'"

"That's queer," said Taplow, in a strained voice. "She certainly said she was going home."

"I think I should tell you," said Westcott, slowly and deliberately, "we have found the bricked-up cupboard in that room, and broken down the wall you erected."

Taplow licked his lips again. "In that case," he said hoarsely, "the game's up."

"Yes," said Westcott. "The game's up. It is my duty to arrest you for the murder of Moses Silverstein, and the murder of—"

Quick as a flash, Taplow threw himself backwards, and went head over heels over the bannisters, landing in a huddled heap at the bottom of the stairs on the floor below. Westcott was after him immediately, but as the Scotland Yard man pounded down the stairs, the little collector picked himself up and limped into his museum room, shutting and locking the door.

"Bring the axe!" Westcott shouted at the top of his voice.

The others came running down the stairs, Regan carrying the axe. At the first blow he struck the door, however, there was a sharp report, and a bullet narrowly shaved his head and thudded into the wall behind him.

"Back from that door!" cried Taplow, shrilly. "Back, or I'll shoot again!"

"You can't escape," Westcott called. "We'll get you sooner or later."

"You'll never take me," shrilled Taplow. "Never. The old man deserved what he got. He nearly drove me mad with his threats to sell up my museum, the swine! I'm glad I killed him. I enjoyed doing it. But you'll never hang me for it, never."

They could hear him dragging something heavy across the floor.

"The girl knew," he continued. "She saw me burning my clothes after—they were covered with blood—and I was afraid she'd squeal. I had to kill her. It was her life or mine."

A thin wisp of smoke curled from beneath the door. Was caught by a draught and whirled upwards.

"What's that noise?" said Westcott, sharply.

They listened and heard a crackling sound.

"Stay!" cried Taplow, shrilly. "Stay, and die with me, like the rats you are!"

"He's set fire to the place!" shouted Regan. "Saints alive, the whole street will burn to the ground in no time! There's dry rot in all of these houses. They'll burn like matchwood!"

"Outside and raise the alarm!" said Westcott sharply.

In an incredibly short space of time the whole house was a blazing inferno. While the officers ran about warning people in the neighbouring houses, and sending in an alarm to the nearest fire station, Harvey stood in the road looking up at the window of Silas Taplow's museum. He saw a cadaverous face, like the face of a mummy, at the window for a brief moment, and it was contorted by a look of indescribably torture. Then it disappeared, the glass shattered and fell outwards, and a burst of smoke and flame belched from the window.

Soon the fire brigade was on the spot, and hoses were playing on the house and its neighbours, but the fire seemed to defy water. It roared as though Hell itself was in the dingy old house.

Harvey felt a hand on his arm and turned to find Westcott standing by his side.

"You win, Mr. Harvey," said the superintendent. "Your man was innocent after all."

H is Majesty was graciously pleased to confer a free pardon on Arnold Hemingway.

Hemingway came out of prison, grey-faced and grey-haired, with a dozen lines on his face that had not been there before, cured of his addiction to drugs, but silent and morose. He spent much time thinking about the past, brooding over it. A potential suicide if ever there was one.

His relatives took counsel of one another. He must go abroad and start afresh under a new name, they decided. Somewhere really far off, where he could drink himself to death if he wished, or murder half a village or live on opium sandwiches without disgracing the family. It was going to take the family ten years at least to survive the pitiless publicity of the Stark Street murder, and certainly longer if Arnold Hemingway remained in London.

Harvey was rather disgusted by their lack of consideration for the man himself; they wouldn't even leave him alone to make what he could of his ruined life. Nothing suited them but that he should go away, preferably to an unexplored part of the world, where an undiscovered wild animal might speedily and fortuitously make a meal of him. For the family's sake, the family was gratified that Arnold had not brought shame upon them by being hanged, but if he could have been destroyed quietly, without publicity, they would have been even more pleased.

One afternoon, Harvey met his former client in a little Fleet Street restaurant.

"I won't offer to shake hands," said Hemingway, gloomily. "I know what you think of me, and you're right. I'm an unmitigated cad."

Harvey put out his hand. "You may have played Hell with

your own life, and the lives of other people," he replied, surprising himself as much as his former client, "but you've been through Hell since. I think we can shake hands."

They shook hands gravely.

That evening, Harvey spoke of the meeting to Cynthia.

"It's a shame," he said. "The man's been a rotter, certainly, but he's suffered for it. He only wants to be left alone now, but the family won't have it. They want to hound him out of the country as fast as they can—all but Lady Agatha, who hasn't put her oar in so far."

"All but Lady Agatha," murmured Cynthia. "I believe that gives me an idea."

They had their own problem to face, the problem of re-awakening Sheila's interest in life. Now that her former lover was a free man, Sheila had relapsed into a state of listless disinterest in everything. She was quite well, but gloomy and silent.

A few days later, Cynthia telephoned to the barrister at his chambers in Fountain Court. "I want you to find Hemingway," she said, "and bring him to Lady Agatha Daventry's house at three o'clock this afternoon. Lady Agatha wants to see him."

"I'll bring him if I can find him, and if he'll come," replied Harvey.

"Bring him if you have to carry him," retorted Cynthia.

He found Hemingway in dairy lunch room, of all places, after having looked in a dozen public-houses without success. The man who had escaped the gallows was staring moodily at a glass of milk and a bun.

"I do this as a sort of penance," he explained. "I've always loathed milk, but I think it's about time I forced myself to try the things which are distasteful to me. By holding my nose, I manage to drink four glasses a day. Laugh if you like, but I haven't touched anything stronger since I came out of gaol."

"I'm not laughing," said Harvey. "But if you can tear yourself away from your morbid self-hypnotism, with that glass of milk, I'd like you to come with me. Your aunt wants to see you."

Hemingway stared at him. "Aunt Agatha?" he whispered.

"Yes."

"I can't face her," he said. "She's such an old dear, and I've been such a rotter. I couldn't hold my head up in her presence."

"It took the barrister almost an hour to persuade Hemingway to come with him.

They arrived at Lady Agatha's house in Lowndes Square a little after three. The old lady received them in her old-fashioned, cosy drawing room. Cynthia was in the room, and she beckoned Harvey to her while aunt and nephew had their talk.

"You're not looking well, Arnold," said Lady Agatha, gently.

Hemingway kept his eyes averted. "Oh, I'm alright," he muttered huskily.

"You're looking run down and London can't be good for you. Fog and smoke aren't good for anyone. You need sun, and plenty of fresh air. I've always found Torquay wonderfully bracing. Perhaps a spell there would do you good."

Hemingway was silent.

"If money will help," said Lady Agatha, softly, "I have plenty."

"I couldn't touch a penny of your money," said Hemingway, in a choking voice. "I'm a rotter, but not quite such a swine as that."

"But just look at it from a sensible point of view, Arnold," the old lady protested. "In a way, I believe we are responsible for the—er—unfortunate shape your affairs are in."

"You! Responsible!"

"The family, I mean. You were left an orphan at an early age without a penny of your own. The family was not content with bringing you up and giving you a sound education. No, you had to be educated in keeping with your position in life, or rather, the family's position. Your position was simply the position of a young man who must earn his own living in a hard world. Instead of educating you for it, we educated you to be an idler, to spend money, to have extravagant tastes. Then we expected you to settle down to a steady, hard-working life. We were quite wrong, of course. But in a long lifetime I fear I have very seldom found the family to be right in its judgements."

Hemingway looked up.

"Thank you for finding excuses for me," he mumbled. "But I'm afraid I'm just a rotter."

"You were a very dear child," said Lady Agatha. "A very dear child."

She fumbled in the pocket of her dress and produced a letter.

"This is from Harold Digby," she remarked. "If you remember, he was at school with you. A year or two older, I think. He is working very hard trying to make a success of a fruit and poultry farm in South Africa, and he seems to think that there's a very good future in it. My lawyers have examined the financial report he sent me and pronounce the proposition to be a sound one. Harold requires a partner with a little capital who is willing to work hard. I think it would be ideal for you."

"I—I can't—"

She held up a thin white hand arrestingly. "Don't make up your mind too quickly, Arnold," she said. "Here's a cheque for five hundred pounds. I'll really feel much happier if you'll take it. And here is Harold's letter. Go into that other room and think it over."

She put the cheque and the letter into his hands and pushed him towards a door leading from the drawing-room to an anti-room.

"Oh, by the way," she said, as Hemingway opened the door, "Harold wants his partner to be a married man. He says that married men are steadier than bachelors."

Hemingway emitted a gasp as he stepped into the ante room. Lady Agatha tiptoed across the drawing room and closed the door behind him.

"I'm an interfering old woman," she said to Cynthia and Harvey. "But I do hope my interference has been for the best."

"You're wonderful!" said Cynthia enthusiastically.

"Thank you, my dear," said Lady Agatha, kissing the other woman tenderly on the cheek. "And now I'm going to lie down for half-an-hour. Tea is at four."

As she went out of the room she paused for a moment and said sternly: "Tea is at four, young man. You have just half-an-hour."

The door closed behind her.

"Now, I wonder what she meant by that?" said Harvey in a puzzled tone.

Cynthia moved over to the fireplace. "I don't know," she said, in a slightly unsteady voice, "unless she's interfering in your affairs, too."

"Unless—" Harvey thought for a moment. Then—"Cynthia!" he exclaimed, striding across the room.

She warded him off and tiptoed across to the door through which Hemingway had gone, and opened it gently. Harvey looked over her shoulder.

Sheila Lavery was sitting in a chair by the fire, and on the floor in front of her Hemingway was kneeling with his head on her lap. They were both crying a little.

"Dear, interfering old thing!" she murmured. "What a wise old lady she is!"

"But remember," said Harvey, solemnly, "that we have only half-an-hour."

The half hour was not wasted.

THE END

THE AWAKENING OF
THEODORE WRENN

John Dodson, valet to Sir Anthony Ravenal, regarded his master's recumbent figure with disfavour. The hour was half-past ten in the morning, and Sir Anthony was still sleeping soundly. More, he was snoring.

His features in sleep looked heavy and bloated, and his complexion was a repulsive, unhealthy red. The loose mouth; the thick, sensual lips and the weak chin, were at their worst. The collar of his pyjamas was open, and displayed his fat, lobster-red neck. The morning sun shining on his head provoked no responsible glint from his canary-coloured hair, which was lustreless, seemingly lifeless.

There was a little sneer upon the valet's lips as he bent over to shake his master's shoulder. There were few things about Sir Anthony Ravenal's life and deeds which John Dodson did not know—and he knew little to his master's credit. He had a wealth of contempt for the man he served.

He shook his master roughly. There was little danger that Ravenal would waken up quickly and resent this treatment; for he was a sound sleeper, and his valet had put him to bed at three o'clock this morning, with more strong drink within him than any man should have been foolish enough to attempt to carry.

Dodson shook Ravenal's shoulder again and again, with increasing violence.

Ravenal grunted, and turned over. As he did so, a spasm of pain twitched his forehead. He opened his bloodshot, blue eyes, closing them again immediately, as the morning sun seared them like a red-hot poker. He passed a shaking hand over his forehead, with a groan of pain.

"Go away," he growled, and buried his face in the pillows.

"Miss Dean is telephoning," said the valet respectfully.

Ravenal sat up shakily, shielding his eyes from the sun with one hand, and rubbing his forehead with the other.

"Tell her I'm out." He groaned, as a spasm of pain like a thousand red hot needles pierced his brain.

"I informed Miss Dean that you were out," replied the valet suavely, "but she refused to believe me."

"Tell her I'm ill, then. Confound it, I am ill!"

Dodson left the room noiselessly.

Still shielding his eyes with one hand, Sir Anthony scrambled out of bed and pulled the blinds down as far as they would go. As he walked shakily back to bed, he cursed the valet who had called in the sun to help in weakening his master.

After a short absence, the valet came into the bedroom again. He carried a glass in which was a concoction consisting of the two raw eggs, a tablespoonful of Worcestershire sauce, and a liberal sprinkling of red pepper. He handed the glass to his master.

"Ugh!" Sir Anthony Ravenal tilted his head and swallowed the mess. His eyes watered, and he coughed several times. Dodson was just in time to catch the glass as it dropped from his master's fingers.

"Miss Dean wishes you to call on her this afternoon at four o'clock," he remarked, when Sir Anthony had concluded a series of horrible grimaces.

Sir Anthony glared. "You should have told her that it was impossible."

Dodson's face was expressionless. "I did, but she replied that in that case she would come here immediately."

His master made no reply. He climbed wearily out of bed, and put on the dressing-gown which the valet held for him, then wobbled to the mirror to look at his reflection, which judging from his disgusted expression completely failed to please him.

"Bring me a brandy-and-soda!"

In an incredibly short space of time the drink was presented on a tray at his elbow. He gulped it down, and began to feel better.

Breakfast he could not face, but when Dodson brought a slice of dry toast and a cup of coffee, he consumed them grumblingly. He began to feel well enough to face the rigours of bathing, being shaved, and dressing.

He lay for a long time soaking in his bath, which was warmer than usual, and scented agreeably with fragrant bath salts. Then Dodson shaved him smoothly and expertly. Sir Anthony scarcely felt the action of the razor, but, as his nature dictated, he grumbled that it had an edge like a saw. Above the level of his master's eyes, Dodson permitted himself a slow cynical smile.

Dressed in a grey lounge suit, with a regimental tie, and shoes polished to mirror-like brightness, Sir Anthony Ravenal was revealed as a fine figure of a man. Six foot tall he had massive shoulders, and a straight, broad back. He owed his handsome carriage to his eight years in the army.

The lines and the sagging of his facial muscles which had betrayed him in sleep were now eradicated, and his complexion has assumed a healthier colour. Only the slackness of his mouth, partially concealed by a crisp, military moustache, and his bloodshot eyes, hinted at the life which he had led for about fifteen years.

He was thirty-nine years old, and if he looked no younger than his age, at least he looked no older; his physical resources were remarkable. He was almost unrecognisable now as the man who had lain bloated and flabby on the bed, while his valet looked down at him with scorn and contempt.

His waistline, which had melted years ago into a frank 'corporation' was corseted, and laced so tightly that it was almost painful for him to breathe.

There was a neat pile of letters, perhaps a dozen in all, awaiting him in his comfortable sitting-room. Seven were bills, and he put them aside unopened for future attention. Five were in an interesting variety of feminine handwritings. After a casual glance at the envelopes, he threw four of them in the fire with a bored air, and opened the fifth which he read with eager attention.

This letter was written in a frank flowing hand-writing, in green ink on a snowy and expensive paper. From the handwriting, one might have judged the writer to be candid and straight forward, and one would not have been wrong. The letter was from Miss Anne Wilding, a lady of quality.

Sir Anthony read it through twice, then laid it aside with a sigh of contentment.

Dodson came in and handed his master a copy of a morning paper. Sir Anthony took it turning first to the announcement that a marriage had been arranged between Miss Anne Wilding, of Cheyne Walk, Chelsea, and Sir Anthony Ravenal, Bt., of Gay Ladies, Dorcombe, Hampshire. This paragraph he read not once but several times.

It would create a considerable amount of talk, he reflected. Mayfair knew little about Miss Anne Wilding, but much about Sir Anthony Ravenal. Season after season with unfailing regularity, Sir Anthony had provided society with scandalous tit bits to gossip about and dissect. His reputation would have been sufficient to bar him from the homes of Mayfair, but for the fact that he was the head of one of the oldest families in England, and so had a standing that even the worst scandal connected with his name had failed to shake.

Society would talk about this wedding of his, he knew. It would become a nine days' wonder. The fact of his fiancée's spotless reputation would add fuel to the flames of gossip. The worst of men, the gossips would say, invariably contrive to marry the best of women.

"The best of women"; the phrase admirably described Anne Wilding. She was fine in mind and body. Since meeting her, no other woman had any attraction for him.

There would be many who would wonder why Anne was marrying him. Let them wonder. Probably they would think that she was marrying him to reform him.

He laughed dryly. No one knew better than he the impossibility of changing his nature. He could never be divorced from the delights of the flesh to which he had been wedded so long. Until after the wedding however he intended to make an appearance of having changed. Afterwards—well, let afterwards take care of itself.

He stood up and rang the bell for Dodson.

"My hat and stick," he said when the valet appeared.

Dodson was at his elbow with hat, stick, and gloves, in a few moments. Sir Anthony took them slowly.

"While I am out," he said, "I want you to pack my things."

He was silent for so long, that Dodson ventured to prompt him. "For a few days, sir, or longer?"

"Pack everything."

"Everything, sir?"

Sir Anthony nodded. "Yes, all of my personal effects, clothes and photographs, and so on." he replied. 'I'll attend to my desk when I return tonight. Tell Brown's to send up some men to put dust covers on the furniture. I'm going down to Gay Ladies tomorrow and I shan't use this flat again for a year at least."

The valet's expression was inscrutable. "Shall I prepare to accompany you, sir?" he asked.

Sir Anthony shook his head. "No," he said. "I shall have to dispense with your services Dodson."

"I see," said Dodson quietly.

His master looked intently into middle distance.

"I think you do," he remarked. "You are an excellent valet, Dodson; quite the best I have ever employed, but I have permitted you to know a great deal too much about my personal affairs. This is not good. My next valet's knowledge will be confined to his own province, I hope." He glanced at Dodson. "It is not that I have doubts of your loyalty—"

He waited for the valet to say something, but Dodson was silent.

"—but it is not well to rely too implicitly upon the discretion of others."

There was a little silence.

"Perhaps not," said Dodson quietly.

Sir Anthony looked at his servant, and the man returned the look squarely.

"In a moment of confidence," said Sir Anthony, "you once told me that it was your ambition to own a small hotel. You were saving a considerable part of your salary to that end, I understand."

The valet nodded.

"It is kind of you to remember my poor ambition," he replied.

Sir Anthony looked into middle distance again.

"You must have saved quite a sum by now."

"Quite a sum," agreed Dodson.

"I wonder whether two hundred pounds would help you to realise your ambition?"

Dodson bowed slightly. "Thank you, sir. You are very good."

He held the door for his master to pass through.

CHAPTER 2

Sir Anthony dismissed his taxi at the Fleet Street end of Chancery Lane, and walked up that narrow thoroughfare swinging his walking stick vigorously.

Outside a dingy, two-storey building which was sandwiched between two taller and more imposing edifices, he halted and surveyed a worn brass plate with mingled pity and amusement. The brass, from constant polishing, was worn very thin, and the lettering was almost indecipherable. He knew the inscription by heart, however: 'Messrs. Gentry, Green and Gentry. Solicitors-at-law and Commissioners for Oaths.' He turned in at the narrow doorway, and made his way up a flight of creaking wooden stairs, which were uncarpeted, but scrubbed clean enough to eat a meal on, and worn by the passage of many feet.

At the head of the stairs was a stone landing covered with a threadbare red carpet, from which led three doors labelled 'Private' and one labelled 'Enquiries.'

He knocked on one of the doors which bore the legend 'Private,' turned the handle, and walked in. A thin, pale-faced man, who appeared to be about 40, was seated at a desk littered with papers in the centre of the room. He looked up at Sir Anthony's entrance, removed a pair of tortoise-shell rimmed spectacles, rose to his feet with a slow, shy smile, and said: "Hello!"

Sir Anthony laid hat, stick and gloves upon a chair, and advanced with his hand outstretched. They shook hands cordially, at the same time submitting each other to a searching scrutiny.

"You're looking well, Theodore," said Sir Anthony jovially. "It must be quite three years since we last met. Lord, how time flies!"

Mr. Theodore Wrenn nodded quietly. His eyes were frankly

upon Sir Anthony, noting every detail in his appearance, every slight change since their last meeting. There were new lines under Sir Anthony's eyes, his lips were looser than before, and his chin inclining to flabbiness. Mr. Wrenn drew a chair forward for his visitor, who sat down and produced a fat cigar case.

"No, thanks," said Mr. Wrenn, "I never smoke between meals."

Sir Anthony laughed as he selected a cigar and carefully lit it.

"Still the same creature of habit, Theodore!" he exclaimed. "Wrapped up in rules and regulations. Do you ever do anything simply because you want to do it?"

Theodore Wrenn smiled whimsically. "I've grown out of the habit of wanting to do things," he replied. "It makes life less adventurous to be contented to remain in one's rut, but it is much more peaceful."

Although they were entirely dissimilar in appearance and taste these two were first cousins. Theodore's mother and Sir Anthony's father were brother and sister. In appearance, Theodore took after his father, a mild scholarly man whose wealth of learning was coupled with financial poverty. Sir Anthony's appearance was typical of the Ravenal strain.

Theodore had a high forehead, thoughtful brown eyes, a straight, undistinguished nose, and a firm mouth and chin. His hair, which had been mouse-coloured in youth, was now sprinkled with grey, and one lock of pure white was brushed straight back above his left temple. He was three years younger than his cousin, but the repressed, quiet life which he led made him look at least three years older. Few casual observers would have estimated his age at under 42 or 43. He was five feet ten inches in height, but looked less; he was slightly and not muscularly built.

During his father's lifetime, the Wrenn household had been a happy but never extravagant one, and after his death Theodore and his mother had had to struggle to pay their bills and live decently. Somehow, they had managed it, and Theodore had studied law at London University.

On his twenty-first birthday he was taken in as a clerk to the firm of Gentry, Green, and Gentry, which was at that time thriving and prosperous. His mother had died nine years later, a martyr to the necessity for keeping up appearances without having realised her ambition to see her son a partner in the firm which employed him. Theodore had since applied himself to hard work and modest living, and had become indispensable to the firm, which could not have continued without him, but which had been slow to recognise the fact.

"Still the same dusty mausoleum," commented Sir Anthony dryly. "Have they made you a partner yet?"

Theodore shook his head. "Not yet; I'm beginning to think they never will. Still, I ought to be content. I've a comfortable berth, and that's a lot. I'm managing clerk."

"All responsibility, and little return." said Sir Anthony quizzically. "What do they pay you?"

"Four hundred-and fifty-pounds a year."

Sir Anthony whistled. "Good Lord! My yearly wine bill comes to more than that."

Theodore smiled. "Must be bad for your liver," he responded. "Don't waste your pity on me. I haven't had your training in expensiveness, you know. I live on about half my salary, and save the rest. I shouldn't know what to do with more money."

"Spend it, damn it!" exploded Sir Anthony. "Spend it, and live while your arteries will let you. Good lord, man, you're not living—you're only existing. What on earth are you saving for?"

Theodore shrugged his shoulders. "The present firm," he replied serenely, "consists solely of Daniel Gentry, who must be 85, if he's a day. The other partners have gone the way of all flesh. Daniel Gentry can't live forever, although I admit that it sometimes seems improbable that he will ever die. When he dies it may be useful for me to have a little capital."

"To buy a share in this musty old law firm?"

"This musty old law firm, as you regard it, is my life," said Theodore quietly. "I've given my youth to it, and some day it's going to be mine."

Sir Anthony rose, grunting with exasperation. "Come out to lunch; I can't bear this atmosphere any longer."

Theodore found his hat and umbrella, informed the office staff that he would be absent for an hour or two, and joined his cousin on the landing. They proceeded down the echoing wooden stairs in silence, and passed along Chancery Lane to the roaring chasm of Fleet Street.

As they walked along together, they presented a strange contrast. Theodore, who wore a black jacket and waistcoat, striped trousers, a black bowler hat, and carried a rolled umbrella, walked briskly but mechanically, the picture of sober respectability. His cousin, attired in a suit made by the prince of Saville Row tailors, and carrying himself with an arrogant air, strode with militant aggressiveness like a man who knows his world and is master of it.

In the Strand, Sir Anthony hailed a taxi, and they drove to his club in the Haymarket.

Among the luxurious appointments of the club, Theodore looked peculiarly incongruous. He was a gentleman, but there are varieties of gentlemen, and he presented a strong contrast to the sleek, overfed members, who emanated an air of expensive opulence. The club was by no means exclusive. Its criterion of membership was wealth. Sir Anthony, who belonged to half-a-dozen superior clubs, preferred the cuisine at this one, which catered for those who made gods of their stomachs.

During an epicurean meal, the cousins spoke very little to each other. They had few interests in common, and such remarks as they made concerned the most commonplace of topics. Over coffee, liqueurs, and cigars, however, Sir Anthony explained the mission which had taken him to Chancery Lane that morning.

He leant back in his chair with the contented sigh of a man who has lunched to repletion.

"I'm going to be married, Theodore," he said, watching his cousin's face.

Theodore was faintly surprised. Somehow, he had never pictured his cousin marrying. "Congratulations. Who is she? Do I know her?"

Sir Anthony shook his head. "I fancy not. Name's Wilding— Anne Wilding. Lives very quietly. Paints miniatures."

Theodore who knew very few people outside of his own sphere, had never even heard of Miss Wilding, whose miniatures of children had attained a certain mild celebrity.

"Allow me to congratulate you again," he said. "This is good news. You ought to marry, Tony. Marriage is a duty you owe to your position."

His cousin laughed heartily. "An heir to carry on the family?" he suggested jovially. "I suppose something of the sort is expected of me, but frankly, I never thought I'd marry. I had anticipated leaving the provision of an heir to you. Marriage has always frightened me. It is so very definite. But that's life, Theodore. Six months ago, I would have offered a woman anything but marriage; a month or two from now, and I'll be roped, tied and branded. A man can't escape his fate.

"Someday a pair of bright eyes will lure you from your deed boxes."

Theodore smiled. "I think not," he replied. "I have so little to offer a woman."

"How typical that remark is of you," said Anthony. "A woman who loves you will find in you the qualities she wants. I have been loved by many women, and I know."

A frown furrowed his brow as he spoke. "That reminds me." he continued irritably. "I'm in a devil of a mess, Theodore, and it's all on account of the women who've loved me, and whom I've loved. I want you to help me out, if you will."

"If I can, I will," responded Theodore readily.

"Good man!" Sir Anthony cleared his throat and commenced to explain the difficulty. As Theodore had guessed, a woman was at the root of the matter—or rather, three women, and the thing which Ravenal wanted his cousin to do was to see these three women—Esther White, Diana Marquis and Naomi Dean—and persuade them to give back or sell, certain compromising letters he had written to them. Also, they must be given to understand that they must leave Sir Anthony Ravenal severely alone in future.

"It won't be easy," said Ravenal, thoughtfully. "They'll have seen the announcement of my engagement in the morning paper, and they'll probably try to force up the price. Blackmail, you know. But I've got to have the letters, all of them, and I'll have to pay whatever's necessary. Confoundedly expensive business, getting married."

Theodore's expression was grim and thoughtful. "It's work that I don't particularly care for," he said slowly.

Sir Anthony looked rather awkwardly at the ceiling, and from his expression Theodore realised that more was yet to come.

"There's one thing I haven't mentioned." said Sir Anthony slowly, "one of the women—Diana Marquis, to be exact—has the Ravenal pearls."

Theodore sat up very straight with an expression of incredulous amazement in his eyes.

"You gave her the Ravenal pearls?" He enunciated the words slowly and distinctly. Sir Anthony threw his half-smoked cigar in the fireplace.

"Not exactly. I lent them to her, and she refused to return them."

"But the Ravenal pearls are an heirloom!"

Sir Anthony nodded his head wearily. "I know. It's all a confounded mess. I've got to get them back. Get them for me, old man!"

Theodore stood up. "I'll see what I can do," he said brusquely. "In law, of course, if you can prove that you only lent them to her—"

"We daren't call in the law!" his cousin protested. "You know the sort of unsavoury scandal it would create. They've got to be recovered some other way."

Theodore sighed. This sort of thing was quite out of his line.

"Very well," he said with an air of finality "I'll do my best."

Sir Anthony wrung his hand warmly. "I knew I could rely on you, old chap." he exclaimed. "You've got carte blanche. Recover the pearls and the letters, and I'll foot the bill, whatever it is."

He jotted down on paper the names and addresses of the three women, with a few other particulars, and handed it to Theodore.

"Call on me for whatever money is required." he said.

The lawyer looked at his cousin oddly. His manner was peculiarly strained.

"Money!" he said in a particularly distasteful tone. "You think that all the problems of this world can be settled with money. If I were you, I should be careful; you may get into a scrape someday that money won't get you out of."

He marched away in search of his hat and umbrella. Sir Anthony looked after him with a peculiar expression in his eyes.

"What in thunder was he driving at?" he wondered, then added, half aloud: "Queer, dry stick. He might just as well be dead for all he gets out of life."

A passing waiter engaged his attention. He snapped his fingers, and the man stood respectfully to attention.

"A large brandy-and-soda," said Sir Anthony Ravenal.

At 3 o'clock that afternoon, Daniel Gentry, sole surviving member of the firm of Gentry, Green, and Gentry, came into Theodore Wrenn's dusty little sanctuary. He was a fussy little man, and he came fussily and jerkily, as though a calamity had just befallen him. It was his nature to make mountains out of molehills. Nothing was unimportant to Daniel Gentry.

He was an old man; how old Theodore had never been able to decide. At times he seemed startlingly youthful; at others the picture of failing old age. The worn brass plate which was screwed to the office door affirmed that Messrs. Gentry, Green, and Gentry were 'established 1875.' And Daniel Gentry had been the founder of the firm.

Theodore had never known his employer's habiliments to vary. He wore sponge-cloth trousers, a Prince Albert coat, a formidable, starched, high collar like a wall round his shrunken throat, a black silk cravat, which passed through a gold ring, and patent leather boots with dove-coloured cloth uppers.

The old lawyer usually had a remarkable control of his faculties; this afternoon, however, his memory had played a trick on him and had carried him back almost thirty years.

"You must go to Richmond tomorrow afternoon, Norman," he said querulously (Theodore was occupying the room in which Norman Gentry sat thirty years ago). "Miss Gambit wants to make a new will. The woman's mad—always making new wills, but it can't be helped. You'll have to go. She's a good client."

Theodore disguised his astonishment and concern. Miss Gambit was a former client who had died ten years before leaving her heirs to fight their way through Chancery into bankruptcy.

He had a strong affection for Daniel Gentry, and he did his best to prevent the old man from receiving an unpleasant shock.

"Very well," he said quietly. "I'll write and arrange an appointment."

Perhaps it was something in his tone which brought the old lawyer back to the present. He looked at Theodore intensely.

"Young Wrenn," he said tonelessly. He looked around the room, as though in search of something, or someone.

"Where's Norman, Young Wrenn?"

Before Theodore could answer, the old man trembled.

"I'm not feeling very well," he said wearily, "It's a hot day, Young Wrenn. Norman and Miss Gambit, they're both dead. I thought…"

He turned, and went shakily from the room. Theodore followed the old lawyer into his own sanctuary.

"It is a warm afternoon, Mr. Gentry," he said soothingly. "Don't you think you ought to go home? There's very little to do today."

The old man turned on him fiercely. "Don't be a fool, Young Wrenn," he snapped, "you can't build up a business by going home in the afternoon. I know what it is. You think I'm losing my grip. You think I'm too old."

He went over to his desk and rung furiously for the typist. When she came, he began to dictate letters at lightning speed, completely baffling Miss Maudsley whose shorthand notebook was soon filled with meaningless scrawls.

Theodore returned to his own room, and telephoned to Daniel Gentry's daughter, who promised to come for her father at once.

Shortly, Miss Maudsley came into his room. She was 61 years old, and had a personality like a mouse, shy and timid and retiring. She had been in Daniel Gentry's employ for almost forty years, and was devoted to the old man.

"What shall I do, Mr. Wrenn?" she cried. "I haven't been able to take down half of what he said, and he wants all these letters typed at once. Most of them are to clients who are" —she lowered her voice—"who are dead, Mr. Wrenn!"

Theodore patted her arm. "Type them as well as you can from memory," he suggested gently, "and lay them on his desk."

A tear fell upon his hand. "He's so queer," she cried piteously. "Oh, if anything should happen to him, Mr. Wrenn! It would be the end of the firm, and of all of us."

She went out of the room, walking a little unsteadily. A few minutes later, Gifford, the clerk, came in. His pale face and watery eyes testified to ill health and overwork in unhygienic surroundings. He was a year or two short of 70, and had started work with Daniel Gantry as an office-boy at the age of 14. As usual, he had ink upon his fingers, and a wet pen behind his ear.

"What's the matter with the guvnor, Mr. Wrenn?" he asked his voice trembling a little. "Is he ill?"

"I think he's feeling the heat," said Theodore soothingly. "It's a hot day, you know."

Gifford wiped his forehead with an inky handkerchief held in a shaky hand.

"Oh, dear, it's hot, all right. I'm feeling it myself."

Theodore looked at the clerk. He was a pathetic little figure, frail and old, and tired.

"I should take it easy this afternoon if I were you," he suggested, in a kindly tone.

Gifford shook his head. "Oh, dear, Mr. Wrenn, that would never do. There's so much to do. I must put up with the heat, that's all. I can't expect to feel right at my age. In the winter it's rheumatism and lumbago, and chilblains, and in the summer, I feel sick and dizzy. But I'm not past my work yet, Mr. Wrenn. Only my head aches now and then."

As he went out of the room, he looked back with a shy little smile.

"I hope it's autumn when I die," he said in a low one. "I like autumn, Mr. Wrenn. It's kind to old folks."

Theodore sat at his desk for a long time, thinking. He was 36 years old, and these three, Daniel Gentry, Miss Maudsley, and Gifford had been working here in these offices before he was born. They had given life and youth to Gentry, Green, and Gentry, and now, when they had little left to give, they were still giving, and would continue so until the end. Carrying on. Doing their job with such puny strength as was left them, without complaining.

What would he be like in 30 years? he wondered. Like Gifford, or Miss Maudsley, or the old lawyer? Or a pale ghost of all three?

He admired the way they carried on. Their spirit was courageous and indomitable. Once the old lawyer, realising how age had crept upon them, had offered Gifford and Miss Maudsley pensions on which to spend their last years in comfort and leisure, but they had both refused tremulously, preferring to remain in harness.

Theodore felt that there was not a great deal of difference between these three and himself. Life had made him older than his years. He was part of Gentry, Green and Gentry, 'established 1875,' and worn with age.

With a sigh, he addressed himself to the papers on his desk. Work must go on!

At half-past five he tidied his desk, put on his hat, and, umbrella in hand, went into the office labelled 'enquiries' to say "good night" to the staff. Miss Gentry had called over an hour before and taken her father away.

Theodore lived in West Kensington, and had resigned himself

long ago to the impossibility of finding a seat in his train at the rush hour. Not that he resented the crowded condition of the compartment. The nightly jostle with packed humanity from Temple to West Kensington was one of his few personal contacts with his fellow men, and he looked forward to it. It was a pleasant in a way to mingle with the crowd and feel that he was part of it. At heart Theodore, was a lonely soul.

It eased his loneliness to feel at one with humanity for 20 minutes every evening. It did not occur to him to resent the fact that one of his fellow humans was breathing a strong smell of stout into his nostrils, that another was blowing rank tobacco smoke in his face, or that a third, in opening an evening paper, was digging bony elbows into his ribs. He accepted these petty annoyances as the price he paid for the precious companionship of his kind. Man is a gregarious animal, and Theodore was still a man, not yet a machine.

He occupied two cheerless rooms in a dingy house in an unprepossessing street. As he opened the front door, the smell of boiled cabbage and stale cheese was thick in the air, but he was accustomed to it and his nostrils conveniently ignored the familiar odour. He went upstairs to his rooms on the second floor.

His sitting room was filled with smoke, and his landlady was on her knees before the fireplace, trying with the aid of a sheet of newspaper to coax a blaze out of damp paper, a few thin pieces of wood, and a large lump of coal. It was her custom to leave the lighting of this fire to the last minute, and grumble when her lodger came in that she was "fair wore out wrestling with it."

Theodore put his hat and umbrella in their accustomed place, removed his shoes, and put on his slippers. His landlady left the room to fetch his tea, expressing as she went, the hope that the fire would "do nicely now."

It did as it usually did; went out dismally, and he patiently broke the lump of coal into small pieces, found fresh paper and re-laid it. By the time his landlady returned, the fire was beginning to show encouraging tongues of flame.

"Didn't I say it wouldn't take no time to burn up," she triumphed.

She laid his table with a great deal of fuss and clatter, then left him to the contemplation of three scorched sausages, a discouraged-looking fried egg, a pot of weak tea, some slices of thinly buttered bread, and a stale seed-cake.

Theodore regarded his meal sadly.

"Here I am," it seemed to say. "I'll give you dyspepsia and heart burn and biliousness, and probably insomnia, but you might, as well eat me. It's too late in the day for you to become fastidious."

CHAPTER 4

Miss Diana Marquis lived in a flat in Mayfair which was sufficiently luxurious for a star of much greater magnitude. Among those who were in a position to know the extent of Miss Marquis's modest earnings on the stage, there was considerable speculation on the question of how she managed the flat, a limousine, and a maid of French origin.

Although she had been apprised of his coming (or perhaps because of it) the actress received him in a crepe de Chine negligee, which displayed her slender form to the best advantage. This faintly disturbed Theodore. The deliberate appeal to his senses was less an allurement to him than a warning.

"I am here on behalf of Sir Anthony Ravenal," he began.

A frown disturbed the serenity of Miss Marquis's pale face.

"That man—!" she said. "Am I never to have any peace from him? Must he annoy me always?"

"It is not his intention to annoy you further," replied Theodore quietly. "But there is a certain matter to be adjusted—"

Miss Marquis offered him a cigarette, and, on his refusal, lit one herself, and blew out a cloud of fragrant blue smoke.

"I see that he is to be married. I should never have considered him a marrying man. It interests me very much."

"There are some letters—" said Theodore.

Miss Marquis pressed her tiny palms together ecstatically. "Ah, yes, those letters," she exclaimed. "They are the most delightful I have ever received. So intimate! So ardent! I read them often. They are a great consolation to me when I feel depressed."

"—and a certain pearl necklace," continued Theodore doggedly.

The actress shot him a quick, appraising look. "I value it very highly," she murmured. "It is the nicest thing he ever gave me."

"Lent you," suggested Theodore swiftly.

She shook her head. "No, gave me," she reproved him. "I am quite clear on that point He most certainly gave it to me."

Theodore coughed. "Sir Anthony assured me that the pearls were a loan," he said.

Her green eyes challenged him. "You will have difficulty in proving that."

"I trust that proof will not be necessary," he parried. "Surely we can come to an understanding?"

She shrugged her slim shoulders. "Any understanding which will enable me to keep the pearls will be entirely satisfactory to me."

At that moment, there was a discreet tap on the door, and the maid entered, holding a slim envelope in her hand.

"A young man from Snaith's, mam'selle," she murmured. "He wishes to see you."

The actress shot a swift glance at Theodore, then looked angrily at her maid. "Tell him that I am engaged," she snapped.

The girl made a little move. "He is very insistent, mam'selle."

Snaith's: Theodore was racking his brain to recover where he had heard the name before. Of course! —Snaith was the name of a famous Bond Street jeweller.

The actress tapped her foot impatiently. "Tell him I will write to his firm this afternoon."

The maid withdrew, and Miss Marquis turned to Theodore with a little smile. "Maids are such stupid creatures!" she exclaimed. "Please continue, Mr. Mr.—" she looked at his card—"Wrenn. You were speaking of my pearl necklace."

"We were speaking of the necklace which Sir Anthony lent you," retorted Theodore firmly.

The actress laughed. "Oh, dear, what a provoking man you are! I've told you several times that Sir Anthony gave me the necklace."

Theodore looked straight at those green eyes of hers. "The necklace is not Sir Anthony's to give. It is an heirloom."

"How awkward!" she exclaimed. "For Sir Anthony, I mean."

"You realise, of course," said Theodore, "that the law could force you to return the pearls?'

Her eyes assumed a guileless, naïve expression. "Oh! Would you really drag me into a horrid, musty court?"

"If necessary."

She laughed again. "How perfectly charming of you, Mr. Wrenn! Nothing would please me more. The case would be the sensation of the year. The Papers would be full of it. An actress lives on publicity, you know. I should be offered simply stupendous contracts. And these passionate letters Sir Anthony wrote me! I had considered using them eventually in my auto-biography, but, of course, it would be much more effective to have my lawyer read them out in court."

Theodore began to realise that it would be necessary to lay his cards upon the table. "How much?" he said brusquely."

She stared at him. "Oh, Mr. Wrenn, how blunt you are?" she protested. "I thought that lawyers used finesse in these matters."

"I am prepared to offer you five hundred pounds for the immediate return of the pearls and Sir Anthony's letters."

"Five hundred pounds!" She laughed. "My dear Mr. Wrenn. I value the pearls and the letters at five thousand pounds."

He rose to his feet.

"Then there is no more to be said," he replied. "My client is not prepared to pay that sum. It will be necessary for him to sue for the return of the pearls. You will get your publicity, Miss Marquis, but you will forfeit the sum my client would have paid to keep the matter out of court. Good morning."

He turned to the door, but her voice, clear and cold, arrested him. "Please don't go so soon. Won't you sit down again, and tell me just what your client is prepared to pay? Please don't mention five hundred pounds again. The sum is too ridiculous."

Theodore faced her again, but remained standing. "The sum you suggested is quite as ridiculous." he replied. "Suppose we say a thousand pounds?"

"Two thousand," she retorted.

He reflected a moment. "Shall we compromise on fifteen hundred?"

The actress shrugged her shoulders. "I hate quibbling. Very well, fifteen hundred let it be. But I shall want the money today."

Theodore thought for a moment. His bank balance was slightly over five hundred pounds (it would have been less, only he had recently sold certain shares) and his cousin had gone down to Somerset early that morning. It would probably take a day at least to raise the other thousand.

"I am afraid I cannot pay you the entire sum today," he replied. "If you will let me have the pearls and letters, I am prepared to give you a cheque tor five hundred pounds at once, and a written promise to pay the balance within forty-eight hours."

She shook her head. "Oh no, my friend. You will receive the pearls and the letters when you pay in full; not before."

"Very well, we can do nothing until tomorrow, in that case."

"But I need money today!" she protested.

"I cannot pay you a penny." he replied, "without the security of both pearls and letters. After all, Miss Marquis, I have no wish to offend you, but if you were so inclined you might quite easily cash my cheque for five hundred pounds, and refuse afterwards to part with the pearls. On the other hand, my written promise to pay the balance, which is backed both by my firm and Sir Anthony Ravenal, is as good as money in the bank."

Her expression, grew thoughtful. "Very well," she said. "Write out your cheque, and the agreement."

He sat down at a writing desk in a corner of the room and wrote busily for a few minutes. Then he rose, waving the two pieces of paper, to dry the ink upon them.

The actress took them, glanced at what he had written, and nodded her head in a satisfied manner. She opened a drawer in the desk, and produced a jewel case, which she opened to show him that the necklace was inside, and a bundle of letters.

Theodore was familiar with the appearance of the Ravenal pearls, and a quick scrutiny convinced him that this was the heirloom. He counted the letters, and found that their number was complete.

It was a shock to one of his meticulous carefulness that the actress had kept so valuable an heirloom as the Ravenal pearls in an unlocked drawer. A pretty mess would have resulted had it been stolen while in her possession!

Diana Marquis rang for her maid to show him out, and they parted amiably.

On the way out, Theodore turned to the maid. "Your mistress is very careless," he remarked.

The girl stared at him. "M'sieu?"

"I mean, that she is careless with valuable things."

The girl rolled her eyes. "Non, non, M'sieu, she is not careless with so much as a farthing! She is more careful than anyone I have ever known! Every time she takes off as much as a leetle ring, she puts it away in a secret place which even I do not know. She is not careless! Mon Dieu, non."

Here was food for sober reflection! Theodore was buried in thought on the journey by taxi from Mayfair to Chancery Lane. Why had the actress, so careful with even a "leetle" ring, been so careless with a necklace worth ten or twelve thousand pounds? She must have known of its value, of course.

Then he remembered the "young man from Snaith's" who had called on the actress that morning, and had been, according to the maid, so very insistent. What could the young man have been so insistent about, if not an unpaid account? That would be the thin envelope which the maid had held in her hand when she announced the caller.

Still, he could see no connection between an unpaid jeweller's account, and the actress's strange carelessness with a valuable necklace.

Suddenly, he put on his hat and went out. His uneasiness demanded action. He took a taxi to Snaith's in Bond Street.

At the jeweller's, he presented his professional card, and asked to see the manager. The name Gentry, Green and Gentry was still a respected one, and gained him immediate entry to the manager's office, where a grave faced elderly man received him.

Theodore placed the necklace on the desk. "I want you to examine these pearls and give me your opinion of them."

The manager put a jeweller's glass in his eye, and inspected the necklace closely. When he looked up, his face wore a curious expression.

"In the first place," he replied slowly. "these are not pearls, but excellent imitations."

Theodore felt dizzy. "Are you quite certain?" he demanded.

"Quite certain." responded the other dryly. "We made this necklace ourselves, copying it from a string of very perfect genuine pearls. The imitation is excellent. It would take an expert to tell that this string is not genuine."

"Do you mind telling me," said Theodore, "whether you have been paid for making this—this imitation?"

The manager coughed dryly.

"We were beginning to be alarmed about our account," he replied. "But the lady sent her maid with a cheque half an hour ago."

It was in a state of considerable perturbation that Theodore Wrenn sat in his office that afternoon. His luncheon hour had passed by unnoticed. On his desk lay the string of imitation pearls, and in a secret hiding place in Diana Marquis's flat reposed the genuine Ravenal pearls, worth probably twelve thousand pounds. It was evident that she had no intention of giving them up, otherwise she would not have gone to the expense of having imitations made. But for her careless handling of what was supposed to be a valuable heirloom, Theodore would certainly have handed the fakes in good faith to his cousin who, equally unsuspecting, would have placed them in the vault of his bank among others, for years, possibly not until the death of Sir Anthony. The imitations were good enough to deceive any but expert eyes. With Theodore's promise to pay one thousand pounds 'for value received' in her hands, the actress would certainly insist on her pound of flesh (she had already cashed his cheque for five hundred pounds). And, just as certainly, she would not part with the pearls, which was her part of the bargain.

It was natural that Theodore should first consider the recovery of the pearls by legal means, but that solution he set aside, as a last resort. A court of law would certainly order the actress to return the necklace, but a tremendous amount of publicity would ensue, which was the last thing Sir Anthony wanted. Diana Marquis knew this, of course, which gave her a considerable advantage.

With the suddenness of a flash of lightning, inspiration came to him.

The plan which he conceived almost took his breath away by its daring simplicity. He turned it over and over in his mind, and at last decided to adopt it. Perhaps it would not work, but in that case, the position would be little the worse, and there still remained recourse to the law.

It was past the closing hours of banks, but Theodore's greatest, almost only, friend was Samuel Marbury, manager of the branch bank with which he transacted all his financial business. Theodore had two minutes conversation over the telephone with his friend, ten minutes more in Marbury's private office, and was shortly in possession of a thousand pounds in five-pound notes, in exchange for which he had given a batch of war bonds as security.

He deposited the money for safety in the ancient iron safe at his office, and the following morning called at the Mayfair flat of the Diana Marquis at the unheard-of, hour—for the actress—of half-past nine. The French maid received him with wide, surprised eyes, and said in tragic tones that "Mam'selle" never rose before eleven at the earliest.

Theodore explained that his business was urgent. 'By the way,' he added, with feigned anxiety, 'I wanted to bring Miss Marquis some flowers.'

"Mam"selle loves flowers," she whispered, "all her friends breeng flowers." Theodore nodded comprehendingly.

"But I didn't know what kind to get."

"Oh, carnations, m'sieur!" the girl confided. "Mam'selle loves carnations. They are her favourite flowers, always."

Theodore nodded abstractly, as though deep in thought. "I wonder," he began hesitatingly, after you have announced me to Miss Marquis, would you mind slipping out and getting some carnations?"

The girl shook her head. "Mam'selle would not like me to," she whispered. "She would be veree angry."

Theodore produced two crisp five pound notes. "Miss Marquis will never know that you have left the flat. You will be back before she wants you for anything. This" —presenting one of the crisp notes— "is for the carnations. "And this" presenting the other— "is for your trouble."

The maid's eyes lit up with cupidity, and she took the notes and tucked them away among the mysteries of her underwear. She showed Theodore into a tiny sitting room, and went into the bedroom to waken her mistress. There was a short, low-voiced colloquy and 10 minutes later the girl passed through the sitting room again.

"Mam'selle weel see you in a few minutes," she said to Theodore, and added in a whisper: "I go now to get the carnations."

Theodore had little longer to wait before the actress appeared. She was in a negligee even more revealing than the one in which she had received him the previous morning.

"You're an early bird, Mr. Wrenn," she said, masking her peevishness with a dazzling smile. "If you earned your living between the hours of 8 p.m. and midnight, you wouldn't pay calls in the early morning."

Theodore's expression was dutifully contrite. "I am sorry, but I have a great deal to do this morning, and I wished to conclude my business with you as soon as possible. I have brought you the money—in cash."

She smiled again. "That was very thoughtful of you, Mr. Wrenn. If you wait a minute, I'll get your promissory note."

She left the room, and Theodore experienced a moment of anxiety, fearing that she would discover the absence of her maid. The actress returned directly, however, with the paper Theodore had signed on the previous day.

He gave her the money and received the document in return. His satisfied expression was a masterly piece of acting of which Theodore had not realised he was capable. It deceived the actress into believing that her plan had succeeded and that he had accepted the false pearls as genuine.

She stifled a yawn. "I am glad I do not do much business with lawyers," she said. "I am afraid I could not stand such impossible hours."

They laughed together.

"I mustn't detain you any longer," said Theodore apologetically. "You probably wish to return to bed."

"I do," she replied frankly. She rang a bell to summon her maid.

Hoping that this step in his plan would not fail him, Theodore shook hands with Diana Marquis and left the room, closing the door behind him. In the hall he spoke a few words in a fairly loud tone, to deceive the actress, if she were listening, into thinking that he was speaking to the maid. Then he opened and closed the door of the flat a little noisily. He remained, however, on the inside.

He waited for a few moments, then, noiselessly tiptoed across the hall, and gently opened the door of the little sitting room. It was empty, but the door of the actress's bedroom which led off it was open. Crossing the room silently, he looked in cautiously, and was rewarded by seeing Diana Marquis, with her back toward him, putting the bundles of five-pound notes into a small wall safe. One of the wall panels stood back on hinges, indicating the method by which the safe was normally concealed from curious eyes.

About to close the safe, Diana Marquis heard a step behind her, and wheeled round abruptly. Theodore Wrenn stood behind her with an apologetic expression on his face. He was regretting exceedingly the necessity for intruding himself in a lady's bedroom, but the rudeness was unavoidable.

As quick as a flash, she turned to shut the safe, but Theodore had anticipated the move, and thrust her aside gently, interposing himself between her and the hiding place.

"What do you mean by this intrusion?" she demanded in a voice that quivered with rage.

"I want the Ravenal pearls," he replied quietly.

"I gave them to you yesterday!"

He shook his head politely. "You gave me imitations. I want the real necklace."

Suddenly she flung herself upon him in a furious onslaught, biting and scratching like a wild cat. It took all of his strength to resist her without fighting back. Blind fury had lent her physical strength which was almost overwhelming.

When at last her frenzy had worn off, and she lay sobbing and panting on the bed, Theodore felt sick and faint.

He staggered rather than walked to the wall safe and found the necklace after a few moments search. Slipping it into his pocket, he left the room.

On the way downstairs, he met the actress's maid, who was carrying a large bunch of flowers.

"See, m'sieur, the carnations!" she said, holding them up. "Mam'selle will love them."

"Give them to her," said Theodore calmly, "with my respectful regards."

He proceeded down the stairs. Below, an awkward situation awaited him. The burly commissionaire, whose massive presence lent impressiveness to the hall of the building barred Theodore's way with a belligerent expression upon his face.

"Excuse me, sir," he growled. "But a lady on the second floor 'as 'phoned down to say that you 'ave abstracted a pearl necklace from her flat. I shall 'ave to hask you to accompany me hupstairs for a few minutes."

"I refuse to do anything of the sort," replied Theodore.

He produced his professional card, and handed it to the commissionaire, who inspected it critically.

"In that case," said the man uneasily, "I shall 'ave to call a cop. In the meantime, I can't allow you to leave the building, sir."

Theodore had an unpleasant vision of the results which might ensue if the majesty of the law were invited into the affair. Unpleasant publicity would result and his professional reputation would certainly suffer. The situation was decidedly awkward.

It was further complicated by the appearance on the scene of the furious Diana Marquis, in her skimpy negligee. She pointed a shaky accusing finger at Theodore.

"That's the man!" she cried in a voice which trembled with rage. "He stole my necklace. Search him at once. He put it in his side pocket."

The commissionaire eyed Theodore uncompromisingly. "What is it to be?" he demanded. "Shall I call a cop, or will you return the lady's property?"

Accepting the inevitable, Theodore put his hand in one of his pockets and drew out a gleaming necklace, which the actress triumphantly snatched from him.

"Well, Miss Marquis, it's up to you," said the commissionaire, favouring Theodore with an ugly look. "Shall I call a cop, or are you going to let 'im go?"

The actress laughed shrilly. "Let him go," she said bitterly, and added: "Better luck next time you go in for burglary, Mr. Wrenn!"

Theodore left the building quietly, and took a taxi to Chancery Lane. In his dusty little office, he sat down at his desk, and put a hand in one of his pockets.

With a suppressed chuckle, he drew out the Ravenal pearls and laid them on the smooth surface of the desk.

"I wonder how long it will be before Miss Marquis discovers that the pearls I returned to her were her own excellent imitations?" he pondered aloud.

The following day, Theodore lunched with his cousin, gave him the Ravenal pearls, and received in return a cheque for the money he had paid to the actress.

"That's a load off my mind," said Sir Anthony, when they had concluded the business.

"You know, I was half afraid that she wouldn't give them up."

"So was I—at one stage of the proceedings," said Theodore dryly.

Sir Anthony directed a shrewd glance at him. "You had some trouble with her?"

"A little."

"I expected as much. But I knew you'd be able to deal with her. You'll see Naomi Dean as soon as possible!"

Theodore nodded: "At once."

"Good. The woman's a nuisance. She's just the wild, impulsive type that would make trouble. And nothing must interfere with my marriage of Anne. Nothing."

Theodore rose. "I'll do my best," he said. "Good day." With that he left.

Miss Naomi Dean lived at No. 9 Potiphar"s Mews, which was a converted stable in an alley near King's Road, Chelsea. She wrote poetry for highbrow magazines, and little stories which were very praised—by her friends.

At 11 o'clock sharp on the morning after his meeting with Sir Anthony, having previously apprised Miss Dean by letter of his intended visit, Theodore rapped on the emerald green door with a brass knocker provided for the purpose. He heard a snatch of a song in a language foreign to him, sung in a rich but untrained contralto, which broke off at the sound of the knocker, and in a moment or two, the door was opened by a tall, dark girl in an orange-coloured smock.

She held the door slightly ajar and looked through the aperture at Theodore, eyeing him from head to foot. Her glance eventually came to rest upon his black bowler hat, which she regarded with marked distaste. Theodore raised the offending headgear.

"If you are Miss Naomi Dean, I wrote you yesterday."

She nodded slightly and opened the door a little further.

"I'm Naomi Dean," she admitted, and added suspiciously: "You're not a bill collector?"

"Oh dear, no."

"Then why," she demanded, "do you wear a hat like a bill collector?"

Theodore could think of no adequate reply, so he remained silent.

Naomi opened the door wide. "Come in; but please leave that hat outside. It is ridiculous, absurd, and sordid. If I were forced to look at it for five minutes it would spoil my work for weeks. And the umbrella too, please. I can't bear umbrellas. You may leave them upon the door step."

Completely at a loss, Theodore laid his hat and umbrella on the doorstep, and followed her into a large room, the walls of which were white washed and decorated with a frieze of dancing nymphs silhouetted in black.

The only comfortable seat in the room was a divan piled with cushions, which stood in the centre of the floor.

Naomi Dean gestured to Theodore to sit upon it. She herself squatted, cross-legged upon the floor on a square of thick Oriental carpet which was littered with sheets of manuscript, and looked to Theodore to commence the conversation.

"I wrote to you," repeated Theodore, "stating that I wished

to call, and asking you to 'phone me if my visit was not entirely convenient."

Naomi's pale, oval face assumed a thoughtful expression.

"Was your letter in a squarish, white envelope with a name embossed upon the flap?"

Theodore nodded: "It was."

Her face cleared: "Oh, that! I tore it up unopened. It was typewritten, and I loathe typewritten letters. So often they are bills. My work suffers for days if I open a bill."

"I see."

"You don't see at all," she said. "But it's polite of you to pretend you do." She looked at him frankly. "What is your name?" she asked.

Theodore produced his card-case, but she waved it aside.

"Don't give me your card; tell me yourself."

"My name is Wrenn—Theodore Wrenn."

Naomi clapped her bands gaily. "A delightful name!" she cried, "Theodore Wrenn! It's delicious, and it suits you perfectly. You have an intelligent, bird-like look, Mr. Wrenn."

Theodore coughed. "I called on behalf of Sir Anthony Ravenal," he murmured tentatively.

Her hand travelled swiftly to her heart, and her eyes assumed a tragic, stricken look. "He is ill? You are a doctor?"

He shook his head. "As far as my knowledge goes, Sir Anthony is in the best of health."

"Then what do you mean? You look like a doctor. If you are not a doctor, what are you?"

"A lawyer," said Theodore simply.

Naomi's high, pale forehead was furrowed.

"A lawyer," she repeated. "I don't understand. Why should he send a lawyer to see me? He hasn't been near me for a whole week. I 'phoned him a few days ago, and he promised to call that afternoon. He didn't come and now his flat is shut up and he's gone away without a word. Why does he send you to see me? Why doesn't he come himself?"

Before Theodore could frame a reply, she stood up and paced up and down the floor.

"We've meant so much to each other. Why, we're as good as engaged. How can he treat me like this?"

Her oval face seemed even paler than before, and her eyes seemed darker.

She halted in front of Theodore, and stared at him blankly. "We're as good as engaged," she repeated.

Theodore was at a loss what reply to make. He decided that the blunt truth was best in this case. "I am afraid you are mistaken," he said gently. "The announcement of Sir Anthony's forthcoming marriage appeared in the Press a few days ago."

She stared at him uncomprehendingly. "His forthcoming marriage?" she repeated dully. "It can't be true!"

He felt truly sorry for her. "I am afraid it is."

"Who is he marrying?" Her voice sounded unreal and remote.

He hesitated, but did not see how the question could be evaded.

"A Miss Anne Wilding."

Naomi's expression became suddenly fierce. "That insipid little fool! He can't possibly prefer her to me! She paints beastly pictures of horrid fat children."

She walked up and down restlessly, her fingers twitching. Suddenly she turned on Theodore. "She shan't take him from me!" she cried. "She shan't, I tell you, she shan't! I'll kill her! I swear I will! I'll kill her!"

Theodore was shocked at the quivering intensity of her passion. "Miss Dean, please—" he murmured distraughtly.

"We've been so much to each other!" she wailed.

With a little cry, she threw herself upon the floor, sobbing as though her heart would break. Her shoulders heaved convulsively and she struck fruitless little blows on the floor with the palms of her hands. The situation was more delicate than any in Theodore's previous experience. He felt distinctly uncomfortable, but his sympathy for the girl outweighed his personal uneasiness. Her long, slender body looked so pitiful as it lay upon the rug, writhing in a paroxysm of sorrow.

He bent over Naomi, murmuring words of comfort which he knew as he uttered them, were futile and useless. Words were powerless to console such grief as this.

Suddenly, the girl sat up, and brushed away her tears with a grimy hand. "I'm a little fool. I'm sorry, Mr. Wrenn."

There was a pause, then she added: "Tell me, why did he send you?"

Theodore felt like an unmitigated cad. He blushed to the roots of his hair.

"There are some letters—" he stammered.

Naomi's eyes flashed.

"Letters! Letters!" she laughed hysterically. "That's good! He's broken my heart, and all he can think of is the few letters he wrote me! And he meant so much to me! I loved him."

Her sobbing was renewed. Now it was a dry, voiceless, sobbing, tearless and terrible, which shook her slight frame. She rose to her feet, swaying and trembling.

"I loved him; do you hear?" she gasped. "I loved him."

There was a piteous expression in her dark eyes. "I'll kill myself!"

Theodore held out his hand mutely. He felt powerless, helpless; completely useless.

"I'll kill myself!" she cried again. "He shan't have the chance to laugh at me!"

She turned and ran into another room. The door slammed, and the key turned in the lock.

Theodore followed and rattled on the door handle.

"Miss Dean—" he shouted. "Miss Dean!"

There was an ominous silence, and he pounded on the door and shouted again.

"Miss Dean! Miss Dean!"

Still there was silence. He pressed his ear close to the door, and was relieved to hear her moving about inside. She was sobbing still, breathlessly and incoherently.

"Please open the door!" he cried.

There was no answer.

He was faced with a terrible problem. If the girl really contemplated suicide, it was up to him to stop her.

The door was too massive for him to smash down, even if there had been anything solid enough in the room to use for the purpose. And he dare not summon help, or the police, because of the consequences which might result to the poor girl.

For five terrible, seemingly interminable minutes he waited anxiously at that door. He could hear his heart beating, like the pounding of a hammer. He had one frail hope; he could still hear the girl moving about inside. Thus far, at least, she was alive.

When the door opened, he was almost overwhelmed with relief. His relief was succeeded by equal amazement.

Naomi came into the room dressed in a canary-coloured frock, with a bright red little hat upon her head. She had repaired the damage her tears had done to her looks, and presented a cool, attractive appearance.

"Take me to lunch," she said calmly.

With lightning rapidity, Naomi Dean transferred her affections from the man who had deserted her to his quiet, dependable cousin. To one of her frothy, fantastic nature, Theodore Wrenn's serene disposition was irresistibly attractive. She liked him for his reticence, his sincerity, his singleness of purpose, for all of the qualities in him. In fact, which were lacking in her own composition. Mercurial of temperament, after the wild hysteria to which she had abandoned herself on learning of the faithlessness of Sir Anthony Ravenal, she wasted no time regretting her former lover, but devoted herself to the wholehearted pursuit of Theodore.

Of this, Theodore was not fully aware for some time.

Naomi wrote letters to him, and telephoned, and called at his office, insisted on being taken to lunch, to the theatre, to supper in Soho, stormed at him when he would not see her during business hours, and sulked all evening when he insisted on taking her to a restaurant to dine instead of going to her maisonette in Potiphar"s Mews.

On one occasion, much against his will, she made him take her to a night club.

"But I don't know how!" he protested, when she insisted on dancing with him.

"You can learn; I'll show you." she retorted.

Once on the floor, and after his initial embarrassment was over, he found that it was not unpleasant to walk slowly, with her soft yielding body in his arms, to the intoxicating rhythm of the Black jazz band. Naomi was delighted with his docility as a pupil, and complimented him upon the ease with which he picked up the steps. A few minutes later, when they returned to their table, she ranted at him for preferring cider to champagne.

She had not yet given him the letters. Once he mentioned them tactfully, doing his utmost to spare her feelings, and she looked at him frankly.

"I expect Sir Anthony told you to offer me money for them," was her scornful conjecture. "I'm right, aren't I?"

"I'm afraid so."

"I thought so. Well, he can keep his money; I don't want it. And I never wish to see him again."

"Then why don't you give back the letters, and be done with him?" Theodore was emboldened to ask. A little smile flickered across her lips.

"If I gave you the letters, Theodore," she said candidly, "you would never come near me again."

For two days, she left him severely alone. He decided that she no longer needed him, and he was loath to trouble her again for the letters. He was about to turn to the third and last name on the list which his cousin had given him, when he received a letter from her, written in violet ink on mauve stationery, and scented faintly with heliotrope. Her handwriting was characteristic of her, sprawling, and erratic.

Marley-on-Thames, Thursday.
Dear Theodore,

I fled from Chelsea two days ago and came to rest here in a quiet little houseboat. It belongs to a friend, who has lent it to me for as long as I like. Moored on a backwater, three miles from the village, and far from the favourite haunts of trippers. The water is calm and still and serene, and some of its serenity has found its way to my troubled soul. I am at peace with myself at last. Do come and spend the afternoon with me on Saturday! You will love the solitude and quiet.

Come in flannels; I'm sure they will suit you: and a soft shirt. Do you realise that I have never seen you in anything but that horrible black jacket and striped trousers, with that beastly high collar, and your dinner clothes, which smell disagreeably of camphor?

Don't disappoint me, I really want you.

—Affectionately,

Naomi

There was a postscript, hurriedly scrawled across the back of the sheet:

"Oh, and I'll give you those wretched letters."

When he had finished reading the letter, he laid it upon his desk, and sat still for a long time thinking.

Naomi Dean meant nothing to him, and he could never be anything to her. Friendship was the most he could offer her, and she was not the sort of woman who is content with friendship. On the other hand, her letter contained a definite appeal to him to see her, probably for the last time, and he could not conscientiously fail her. Surely, in an afternoon upon the river he would be able to show her painlessly that their acquaintance was fruitless thing. In addition, he had promised his cousin to secure the letters. If it were humanly possible, and her postscript definitely promised them.

He looked up a diary for trains on Saturday to Marley-on-Thames, and having found what he sought, wired Naomi that he would be with her at three o'clock in the afternoon. Having made his decision, he went out and bought a ready-made flannel suit, a grey silk shirt, a brown felt hat, and dark tan shoes. He did not dare contemplate appearing at the office on Saturday morning in these garments. So, he left them at the shop, deciding to call for them half an hour or so before the time of his train, and change into them at a Turkish baths.

At a quarter to three on Saturday afternoon, he arrived at the sleepy riverside village of Marley-on-Thames, and was accosted at the entrance to the station by an elderly Individual in blue trousers and jersey, who had "Waterman" written all over him.

"If you're Mister Wrenn, the young lady engaged me, sir, to take you up the river to 'er 'ouseboat," this worthy explained.

Theodore admitted his identity, and meekly followed the man to a rowing boat which lay at a small wooden jetty by the river's edge. He took his place in the stern, and the waterman unshipped his oars, and began to row up-river.

Theodore took off his hat, and enjoyed the cool breeze which played about his hair. It was a lovely afternoon, the sky was clear and blue, and the sun was pleasantly warm.

When they came in sight of the houseboat which was moored in a backwater about fifty yards from the river bank, Theodore saw Naomi in a dainty yellow dress, leaning over the stern, watching their approach. He realised suddenly and uneasily that they would be entirely alone in the houseboat all afternoon: a disturbing circumstance which, oddly enough, he had not considered before.

He gave the waterman five shillings, and climbed up a precarious wooden ladder at the side of the ship to the deck. Naomi greeted him, with hands outstretched and eyes sparkling.

A table was laid upon the deck with a primrose-coloured cloth, and an amazing variety of edibles.

"I knew that you'd have no time for luncheon, if you caught that train," she said cheerfully. "Of course, you'd work till the last possible minute. "Confess now, aren't you starving?"

Her gaiety was infectious.

"Ravenous," he admitted, with a laugh. "I've digested nothing but a railway ham sandwich since breakfast."

She took his hat from him and put it in the cabin, then led him to the luncheon table. Two cane chairs were placed for them, opposite each other.

The luncheon consisted of cold salmon and salad, cold roast duck, olives, celery, lettuce, and a trifle, followed by coffee, made in a percolator heated by a spirit stove, and biscuits and cheese. There was even a bottle of cider, flanked by a bottle of champagne.

Naomi eyed him frankly as she filled her own glass with sparkling wine. "Won't you try a little, to please me?"

"I honestly prefer cider," he pleaded.

She laughed: "You're much too good to live, Theo. Have your cider, then."

After the meal she produced a Havana cigar for Theodore and some Turkish cigarettes for herself. She cleared away the luncheon things, and they sat side by side in the shade of the deck house and smoked in silence until there was only a bare inch and a half of the cigar left.

Naomi produced a portable gramophone and a pile of records, and squatted on the deck to play them.

Theodore, watching the mobile beauty of her pale, oval face, wondered why it was that he refrained from loving her. She was attractive and alluring, and yet she appealed to nothing in him except his compassion.

The afternoon went quickly, talking and playing the gramophone. Naomi had a seemingly inexhaustible fund of small-talk which was really amusing.

At last Theodore looked at his watch; it was eight o'clock. He rose. "I'll have to go," he said. "My train is in half-an-hour."

Naomi put a hand on his arm.

"Not yet," she replied. "The man is bringing his boat back for you at a quarter to ten. There's a train at half past ten."

She went into the cabin, and Theodore heard the clattering of plates, then she returned with a tray loaded with sandwiches, cakes, and coffee.

Theodore placed his watch upon the table, where it would serve to remind him of the time. With a laugh, Naomi picked it up and examined it.

"How solid it is!" she exclaimed. "Like you, Theo., solid and—and—dependable."

While his head was turned, she hastily put the hands back half an hour, then laid the watch on the table, face downwards. It was an hour before Theodore looked at his watch again, and he was surprised to see how slowly the time had gone.

It had grown dark, and Naomi had lit an acetylene deck-lamp, and was playing a dreamy sentimental record, when Theodore looked at his watch again and started up.

"Good lord!" he exclaimed. "It's ten o'clock and that fellow hasn't turned up yet."

She shrugged her shoulders.

"What does it matter? He'll be along directly."

"If he doesn't come soon, I'll miss my train."

He noticed a curious gleam in her eyes, and became uneasy.

"You're certain you told the man to come back for me?" he demanded.

She was silent. "Did you?" he insisted.

She shook her head.

He pursed his lips tightly. "I'll have to take the punt, then," he said quietly. "If I can push myself across to the bank, I may be able to find my way back to the village in time."

"You can't," she said, "your train is gone." She showed him her wristlet watch; the time was thirty-two minutes past ten. "I put your watch back half an hour. There isn't another train until morning."

"Why did you do that?" he demanded.

She faced him calmly. "Because I wanted you to stay."

He turned away abruptly. "I'll take the punt, and get across the bank. I'll probably be able to get a bed for the night at the village."

Naomi was at the stern before him, and cast off the punt. Helplessly, he watched it drifting away from the houseboat.

"You once told me that you couldn't swim." she said clearly. "And the river is eight feet deep just here. That's why I chose this spot. The water is quite calm, but there's twenty yards of it to the bank. You'll have to stay."

There was a tone of triumph in her voice.

"Do you realise what you've done?" he cried.

"I love you," she answered simply. "I love you."

Theodore walked all-round the boat, but could find no way of leaving it, except by swimming, which was impossible. Naomi followed him.

He ignored her, bitter at the trick which had been played upon him. She went into the cabin.

"You're behaving like a fool!" he said, harshly, and striding to the door, locked her in. Then, deaf to her cries, he walked up and down the deck.

The night darkened, and suddenly it began to rain. It poured as though it would never cease. The rain lasted for an hour, and when it was over, Theodore was soaked to the skin.

He spent the night walking up and down in his sopping garments trying to keep himself warm.

An hour or two after dawn he heard a hail from the river, and looking over the rail, saw the waterman in his boat below, with the punt in tow.

"I found the punt drifting a few miles downriver," the man shouted, "and I thought I'd best bring it back to you."

He eyed Theodore's wet clothes and dishevelled appearance curiously.

"I forgot to ask you to return for me last night," Theodore told him hoarsely. "And I've been punished for my carelessness. I've had to spend all night on deck."

There was a humorous gleam in the waterman's eyes, but he made no comment.

Theodore unlocked the door of the cabin Naomi opened the door, and looked out. She had been crying, but she was in a quiet, subdued mood.

"I'm a rotten little cheat!" she whispered. "I'm sorry. I—I—I didn't know your sort existed."

She held out a packet tied with blue ribbon. "Here are the letters."

*

On Monday Theodore posted the letters Naomi Dean had given him, to his cousin, enclosing a formal note asking Sir Anthony to be so good as to let him know that the packet had arrived safely.

CHAPTER 8

Theodore had written on the previous Friday to Esther White, the third and last woman on his list, under her married name of Hargreaves, stating that he would call upon her on the Monday if it was convenient to her.

At eleven o'clock he arrived in the quiet working-class suburb where Mrs. Hargreaves lived, and found the eminently respectable street where her home was situated. The house was a modest, two-story structure of red brick, and had a cared-for, tidy air. The tiny garden In front made a proud show, the result of many long evenings of loving toil. The path to the front door was free from weeds, the doorstep was spotlessly white, and the brass door knob and the bell were polished to a mirror-like brightness.

He rang the bell, and the door was opened in a few minutes by a tidy, cheerful-looking woman, who was wiping her hands on her apron.

Theodore raised his hat and presented his card, which she took gingerly, and examined with care.

"Oh, Mr. Wrenn," she said, with a smile, and opened the door wider.

"Won't you please come in?"

He followed her into a sparsely-furnished but homely-looking room.

Mrs. Hargreaves drew forward the most comfortable chair in the room for him, waited until he sat down, and then seated herself on the edge of a straight-backed armless chair.

"You wrote that you had something to discuss with me, Mr. Wrenn," she said questioningly. "I've been hoping that—well—that it was good news. We could do with a bit of luck, sir, Bill and me."

Theodore hesitated.

"As a matter of fact, Mrs. Hargreaves, I have called on behalf of Sir Anthony Ravenal," he said gently.

Mrs. Hargreaves became white, and rose to her feet unsteadily.

Theodore wished, not for the first time in the last week or two, that he had not accepted this mission from his cousin.

"I'm afraid you don't understand—" he stammered.

"Mebbe I don't. I know that the worst thing that ever happened to me was when I met the man you've just mentioned. I'm married now, sir, and trying to forget what's past it can't be mended, but it needn't be dragged up."

"I have no wish to drag it up, Mrs. Hargreaves," murmured Theodore apologetically. "I agree with you that the past is a closed book."

The woman looked at him doubtfully.

"Then why need he send you to remind me of it?" she demanded. "Why can't he leave me alone? That's all we ask, Bill and me, just to be left alone."

Theodore wished himself miles away.

"There were some letters—"

She laughed, a bitter note creeping into her tone.

"So that's it! He's worried about the things he wrote me! I noticed in the papers that he was getting married. I suppose he thought Bill and me would take the chance to blackmail him! Well, you can put his mind at rest, sir. We don't want anything from him, and never will. I don't wish him any harm, though goodness knows he did me harm enough. Mebbe he'll settle down decently after he's married, but most likely not. His sort doesn't. I'm sorry for the woman he's marrying if she's a decent body. Even if she is Lady Ravenal, perhaps she'll be the worse-off of the two of us."

Theodore coughed slightly. He hardly knew how to proceed.

"I don't want to hurt your feelings," he said hesitantly, "but, well, frankly speaking, wouldn't a little extra money be a help?"

The woman turned searching eyes upon him. "You mean Sir Anthony Ravenal's money?"

"He owes you something, I think," he replied gently.

Mrs. Hargreaves shook her head. "I know you're not trying to hurt my feelings, sir. You're not that sort. You've got kind eyes. But don't think for a moment that I'd take a penny from him, for I wouldn't—not a penny."

The declaration was made with such vehement sincerity that Theodore realised that there was nothing to be gained by pursuing the matter further.

"Your little boy?" he asked, looking through the window. "He's a fine little chap."

"Yes, isn't he, sir? That's our Billy. He's the image of his daddy, only he's got my eyes. He's a dear little chap, sir. Hasn't caused me a moment's worry since the day of his birth. My husband treasures that child, sir. Calls him his "hostage to fortune". Quite fanciful sometimes, is my Bill."

She was silent for a moment and then went on: "I'll tell you, sir, how I met Sir Anthony Ravenal. I was born and brought up on a farm in his estate. I'm not telling you that my father was a farmer, sir; he wasn't, but a decent hard-working farm labourer. I kept house for him as a girl, my mother having died when I was a baby. When my father died, he left me thirty pounds, the savings of a lifetime of hard work. After paying for his funeral, I had a few pounds left to me. I could have had plenty of jobs on the farms round about, and there were one or two lads who offered me marriage, but nothing would do me but to try my luck in London and I got a job in domestic service. One day the mistress lost a gold broach. She suspected me, for I hadn't been in the house long, and nothing had ever gone missing before.

They searched my box, and found nothing; but that didn't clear me, and out I was packed, bag and baggage, without a reference.

"I don't blame that mistress; she was a good woman, if hard, and she acted in the way she thought right, but without a reference I found it impossible to get another situation. I went everywhere looking for work, but no one would listen to me when they found out why I'd left my last place. It's natural for people not to want a suspected thief about the place.

"Things went from bad to worse, and I found myself on the streets one night, without a thing that I could sell, and with a hunger that hadn't been satisfied for nearly three days. There was no one I could turn to. They say there are places where girls in that plight can go, but I didn't find them, and I was scared to go to the police; poor people are, you know, sir. I was desperate with cold and hunger, when Sir Anthony Ravenal passed me. Almost midnight, it was.

"Goaded by my hunger, I hurried after him, told him who I was, and begged him for God's sake, to help me. He looked at me oddly, put his hand in his pocket, then laughed, and told me to come with him.

"I followed him to his flat, and there was food spread out upon the table when we got inside. He sat down and watched me eat. I ate until the table was bare. That food was good! I didn't care what happened to me, as long as I was allowed to eat and eat. I knew the stories that were told of Sir Anthony.

"He gave me some money, and I found cheap, decent lodgings. Later, I got work, making shirts at seven-pence an hour. Sir Anthony found out where I had gone to live, and called on me once, and wrote several letters asking me to go and see him, but I never went. Those are the letters he thinks I'll use against him now.

"When I met Bill—he was living in the same lodgings—I

did my best to keep him from liking me. I wasn't fit to be his wife, but Bill wanted me, and he's rare persistent, is Bill. I told him the whole truth about myself, and he still wanted me, so in the end I married him. That was two and a half years ago, just three months after the night I met Sir Anthony Ravenal, when I was desperate with hunger.

"After we'd been married a little over a year, our little boy was born, and he's made as forget what it doesn't do anything but harm to remember. We're happy, sir, very happy."

She looked up, and her eyes were filled with tears.

"I'm glad of that," said Theodore simply. His own eyes were smarting a little.

"I shouldn't have bored you so much about myself," she continued. "Only, I wanted you to understand about me—that I wasn't ever really bad."

"I do understand," he said sincerely.

With a little sigh, she rose.

"I think you do, sir," she said. "You can tell Sir Anthony Ravenal that I burnt his letters on the night that Bill proposed to me."

On the journey from the suburb in which Mrs. Hargreaves lived, to his office in the city, Theodore Wrenn was buried in thought too deeply to take an interest in his surroundings. Since the day a week or two before, when Sir Anthony Ravenal had come into his dusty little sanctum, Theodore had learnt more about life than in all his thirty-six years of living. His contact with the three women to whom his cousin had sent him had broadened his outlook, and taught him many things. He had learned humanity. Above all, he had been forced to the realization that life was not the narrow, shallow existence which he had made of it.

Since his mother died, he had retreated more and more into his shell. His work; a game of chess or a chat with a casual acquaintance; a game of patience, or a book when he was alone; three weeks of fishing in the summer, and a long walk on Sunday mornings had formed the sum of his existence. A futile, lifeless existence. A bachelor, he had never contemplated marrying; now it came to him that without marriage a man was incomplete, like a ship without a rudder, or a crusade without an ideal. He conceived a complete and utter contempt for Sir Anthony Ravenal.

Diana Marquis, the actress, was, as he had seen, entirely capable of taking care of herself. It was impossible to think of her as an innocent victim. She would go into her affairs with men with both eyes open. It was her nature to be selfish and avaricious, and to give only when she was able to receive what she wanted in return.

Naomi Dean was neither selfish nor avaricious, but her passionate, impulsive character made it inevitable that she should, love disastrously if the wrong man came her way—and he had come, in the person of Sir Anthony Ravenal.

For his cousin's treatment of the third woman, Theodore could conceive no excuse. Sir Anthony had simply taken brutal advantage of her distress. Hitherto, Theodore had surrounded his cousin with a certain glamour. He was a rich man; he had experience of the far cities of the world; he was expert at most sports; he lived life to the full. Now, Theodore could no longer blind himself to his cousin's essential baseness. Sir Anthony Ravenal was a cad, and a beast. On his return to the office, Theodore telephoned his cousin at Gay Ladies. Sir Anthony, when he realized the identity of the person who had rung him up, was inclined to be jovial. It was more than Theodore could do to infuse a friendly note into his voice. It remained cold and distant.

"You persuaded the Dean woman to part with the letters?" was Sir Anthony's first question.

"They are on the way to you; posted them this morning," Theodore replied.

"Good man! I knew you'd manage it. What did you think of Naomi? A charming girl, if a trifle exotic. I expect she tried to work her wiles on you. Probably didn't realize what a dry old misogynist you are. Did she hold out for much?"

Theodore repressed the inclination to be profane. "Miss Dean refused to accept a penny of your money," he replied coldly. "She regarded the suggestion as an insult."

"How unkind!" commented his cousin, mockingly. "Have you seen the other woman yet?"

"I have."

"Get the letters."

"The letters need not trouble you. You will require to part with some money, though, I am afraid.""

"Put on the screw, did she. I shouldn't have thought that of Esther. I expect her husband put her up to it. Taking advantage of my marriage, of course. How much did they hold out for?"

"If I had you here," thought Theodore bitterly, "I'd kick you—hard."

Aloud, he said: "Better send me a cheque for five hundred pounds."

Sir Anthony whistled. "As much as that, eh? Pretty steep."

"You are paying for something more precious than the Ravenal pearls," said Theodore dryly.

"Eh? I don't understand—"

"No," replied Theodore bluntly. I didn't think you would."

His cousin laughed: "You're a queer bird, Theodore. I could never quite get the hang of you. I'll post you a cheque at once."

"Thanks," said Theodore, and rang off abruptly.

The conversation had left a nasty taste in his mouth. When the cheque arrived, he cashed it at once, and went with the notes in his pocket to see a fellow lawyer, one Millar, of Messrs Harrow, Weald, Upton, Lewis and Millar.

This very junior partner in a struggling firm was a friend of Theodore, and under many obligations to him. In addition, he had a heart of gold, which was the reason why Theodore had decided to ask him to help in the matter of Mrs. Hargreaves.

He explained the position to Millar as far as was necessary. When the recital was concluded, his fellow lawyer leaned back in his chair and placed his fingertips together.

"What you suggest is irregular; extremely irregular," he said thoughtfully.

"I realise that," agreed Theodore.

"You say this cousin of yours has treated these people badly?" Theodore nodded; "Very badly."

"And this money is by way of making amends?"

"Exactly."

"But they won't touch it if they know who it's from?"

"Not a penny."

Millar looked thoughtful. "Um. In that case, the irregularity is almost justified. You realize that your plan wouldn't hold water for a moment with educated people?"

"Of course, but these people aren't educated."

His friend eyed him closely. "Not likely to be suspicious, or to ask awkward questions?"

Theodore shook his head. "Mrs. Hargreaves will be surprised, certainly; but not suspicious. I think you'll be able to concoct suitable answers to any question she may ask.

"You're queer fellow, Wrenn. I've always thought you the soul of orthodoxy and the slave of professional ethics, and now you ask me to lie like a trooper for you."

"Not for me," said Theodore quickly. "For a woman who deserves help."

"But who mustn't know where it comes from? Oh well."

"You'll do it?"

"Of course, I will. But heaven help me if Harrow or Lewis hear of it. They're strong on red-tape."

*

It was a week later that Gifford announced a caller about four o'clock in the afternoon. When ushered into Theodore's dusty sanctum, the visitor proved to be Mrs. Hargreaves, dressed in her best, and looking very happy.

"I had to come and see you, Mr. Wrenn, to tell you our good news," she began tremulously. "I thought you'd be interested, because you were so kind and sympathetic, It's too marvellous for words, sir. I can't believe yet that it's true. I feel like pinching myself to make sure that I'm awake."

Theodore laughed, and motioned the excited woman to a chair.

"And what is this wonderful news?" he asked.

"Just think! An uncle in Australia, whom I'd never even heard of, sir, far less seen, has died and left me five hundred pounds! Five hundred pounds!" she exclaimed impressively; "it seems too good to be true."

"But it is true evidently," said Theodore. "I'm very pleased to hear it."

"Thank you, sir. I thought you'd be pleased. We've had a hard time lately—how hard I didn't like to tell you when you called—but it's all over now."

"What are you going to do with the money?"

Mrs. Hargreaves frowned a little.

"We've thought of a little shop, sir. A newsagent and tobacconist's perhaps; there's money in that. With a sweetie counter. But we're going to be very careful. Luck like that only comes to you once in a blue moon.

"I can tell you now, sir. Just for a little, I was terribly tempted to take some of Sir Anthony's money. We were so very hard up. But now, I'm glad I didn't. It's like the Hand of God, sir, helping us in our hour of need."

CHAPTER 10

It was now early August, and the weather in London was sweleteringly hot. The sky was cloudless, and seemed to hang heavily upon the city, making it difficult to breathe. The sun beat down pitilessly on the narrow canyon of Chancery Lane.

It was time for Theodore's annual holiday, but he was at a loss where to go. He had become a victim to a vague discontent. He was bored with his old life, and did not know how to go about constructing his world afresh. Certainly, he had no desire to spend his holiday in the sleepy village where he had gone for three weeks every summer for ten years. He wanted something new and different.

The problem was settled for him by a letter from his cousin.

"Come down and stay with me for a week before I go north for the twelfth," Sir Anthony wrote. "There's a small party of us at Gay Ladies, including my fiancée and some fishing to be had, and the party is lively."

Theodore put down the letter, and looked round his gloomy little office. The atmosphere of it was like an oven.

"The party is lively," he said to himself reflectively. How attractive that sounded! The phrase decided him. He wrote his acceptance of the invitation at once.

One of his cousin's motor cars was waiting for him at Dorcombe station when he arrived two days later. He was driven speedily along the tree-lined country road to Gay Ladies. A lump came in his throat as the car swung in at the gates, and went smoothly up the drive to the terrace in front of the house. Everything was as he had remembered it so many times in the years since he had last been here.

It was like coming home after a long journey when the door

swung open, and he saw Dodds, the butler, waiting to receive him. Thirty years ago, when Theodore had visited Gay Ladies as a child of six, he had adored the butler, who had always a handful of biscuits in his pantry for a hungry little boy. One night Theodore had been troubled with an ugly nightmare, and it was Dodds who had heard his cries, and come to comfort him, and who sat with the little boy's tiny hand in his warm, encouraging palm long after the child dropped off into an untroubled sleep. The butler had scarcely changed in thirty years. He stooped a little, and his hair was now quite snowy, but his face was smooth and unwrinkled, and his expression was benevolent as ever.

"Welcome to Gay Ladies," Master Theodore," he said heartily. "I am delighted to see you back again, sir."

Theodore could not speak, but he pressed the old man's hand warmly.

The others were at tea upon the lawn, and after Theodore had removed the grime of the journey, he went to join them. As he approached, he heard voices, high and shrill, the first discordant notes. There were about a dozen young men and women seated in cane chairs about the tea table, which was laid in the shade of a huge old oak.

As Theodore approached, his cousin came to meet him with outstretched hand.

"Delighted to see you, old chap. Come and be introduced to the others."

Ravenal was looking well, remarkably well. His eyes were no longer bloodshot. Country air and abstention from alcohol had worked wonders on him.

"Anne, this is Theodore Wrenn, my cousin. I've talked of him often. Theodore, Miss Wilding, my fiancée."

Theodore shook hands with a tall woman in diaphanous

green tulle, who smiled dazzlingly. She was beautiful. Probably the most beautiful woman he had ever seen, and he felt dazed in her presence. The nearness of such radiant loveliness was a little bewildering. He shook hands with a number of other people, without being consciously aware of them. From the moment his eyes had met the clear, frank eyes of Anne Wilding, he was lost to everyone but her.

Anne Wilding was a woman of thirty, no more, no less. She had the poise and charm of maturity. She had a long, straight nose, with a thin bridge and fine, sensitive nostrils. Her mouth and oval jaw were small and delicately formed. Her lips were carmine velvet; her dark eyes, like deep pools, had a questing look which was intensified by the quaint angle of her arched eyebrows. She wore her glorious hair in two graceful, sweeping wings, and gathered it in a lobe at the nape of her neck. Like pink shells, her ears were tiny and hugged her head.

Theodore at first felt utterly bewildered in her presence, but she quickly put him at his ease. Soon he found out that he could talk to her, a rare discovery because he could talk to few women. But he spoke very little, for he liked to hear her voice which was low and musical.

Soon, with a muttered excuse, Ravenal left the group on the lawn, and went up to the house.

Theodore scarcely noticed that his cousin had gone, so engrossed was he with Anne Wilding.

"Do you know, Mr. Wrenn, we're not really strangers," she was saying. "I've known you by sight for years."

"Really?" He was surprised, for he was certain that he would not have forgotten this radiant creature if he had ever seen her before "

"Yes. In my early days in London, when I was lonely."

"You lonely!" He was frankly incredulous.

"Unbearably lonely. I scarcely knew a soul. I did magazine illustrations for a living, and a bare living it was. I used to come to Fleet-street, looking for work, and I had a little game, which consisted of spying on the people who passed, trying to form an impression of their characters, and following them in imagination to their homes. I used to see you in Fleet Street, hurrying towards the Embankment. You were a lawyer, of course, that much was obvious—"

"A lawyer's clerk, to be correct," said Theodore truthfully.

"—and I conceived you to be a married man, with two children, a girl and a boy, who were ruinously careless with their clothes."

"I'm not married."

"You looked too friendly for a bachelor," said Anne. "You were very dignified, of course, but it was a friendly dignity."

Some of the others were beginning to rise, and stroll down the lawn to where a stretch of water sparkled in the sunlight. A pretty girl, who had been introduced to Theodore as Alys Mercer, stretched herself and yawned.

"I want to go for a swim," she said plaintively. "Tommy, dash up to the house and see what's keeping Sir Anthony. He promised to come."

She was addressing Tommy Renfrew, a tall, loose-limbed youth, who sprawled on the grass at her feet. He shook his head lazily. "It's far too hot to tog all the way up to the house," he replied. "Let's go in without him. He'll be down later."

Alys pouted.

"He promised to teach me that swallow dive. Do go and fetch him."

"I'm certainly not going to exert myself on a hot day like this," retorted Tommy, "simply to find a man who'll monopolise you for the rest of the afternoon."

Alys snatched a handful of leaves from the tree above her head, and stuffed them down the back of his neck.

"Lazy oaf!" she exclaimed. "I'll go myself."

Theodore rose. "I'll go," he volunteered.

Without waiting for a reply, he strode briskly towards the house.

He found his cousin in the library. Ravenal had made himself comfortable with two arm chairs. He was sitting on his spine on one of them, with his legs propped up on the other. In one hand was a whisky-and-soda of impressive proportion, and by his elbow stood a half empty decanter, which had been full when he arrived at the house. His speech was thick, and there was a vacant smile upon his face.

He hailed Theodore cheerfully. "Have a drink, ol' chap?"

"No thanks."

Ravenal waved his hand cordially. "Very thoughtful of you to entertain my fiancée, Theodore. You've become quite a ladies' man."

"Miss Wilding had been making me feel at home," replied Theodore. He was unable to prevent a tinge of contempt creeping into his tone.

"You're been entertaining each other," said Ravenal. "An excellent arrangement. Leaves me free to have a drink when I want one. Do you realise Theodore that I've hardly had a drink for weeks? That's what love does to a fellow. I've been dancing attendance on Anne. No time for anything else. Now you're here, you can look after her for me. A fellow must have some freedom. And I trust you with her, Theodore. I trust you. You're the only fellow I would trust."

He wagged a solemn finger, and added: "Only don't forget, old feller, she's going to be Lady Ravenal—not Mrs. Theodore Wrenn."

Theodore felt a disgust too strong for utterance. He left the room without a reply, but after dinner asked for a few words with his cousin in private. They went into the library, and Ravenal helped himself to another whisky-and-soda.

"There's something I must tell you," said Theodore. "It's about Mrs. Hargreaves."

His cousin looted up sharply. "She's not going to make herself awkward, is she? You got the letters from her, didn't you?"

"You needn't worry on that score," retorted Theodore. "The letters were destroyed."

"Good! Did you destroy them?"

Theodore shook his head. "Mrs. Hargreaves burnt them long ago, just before her marriage."

Sir Anthony omitted a low whistle. "Good Lord! And she got you to pay five hundred pounds for letters that didn't exist. Dashed cunning of her!"

"Nothing of the sort," said Theodore sharply. "She refused to accept a penny of your money."

"Then why," asked Ravenal, not unreasonably, "why did you get five-hundred pounds from me?"

"She needed money, and I was able to give it to her in such a way that she did not suspect that it came from you."

"Dashed cool of you," remarked Sir Anthony, draining his whisky and soda. "So, you ran me in for five hundred pounds that wasn't necessary?"

"Yes."

Sir Anthony looked reflective. "I can understand why you did it," he said at last. "You always were a soft-hearted fellow. But why on earth are you telling me about it now? If you'd only shut up I'd never have known."

"I've told you," said Theodore, "because you regarded Mrs. Hargreaves as a blackmailer. She wasn't; she's a decent, respectable woman."

Sir Anthony laughed suddenly.

"You're a queer chap, Theodore," he declared. I've never understood you, and I don't suppose I ever will. Dashed cool of you to be so generous with my money. And the funny thing about it is that the recording angel will probably credit you with the good deed, instead of me."

"The thing is," said Theodore, "what are you going to do about it?"

"Nothing," said Sir Anthony. "Nothing at all. Except—except—drink another whisky-and-soda to your cool cheek!"

The day was young and fresh when Theodore Wrenn rose and dressed methodically. He put on a pair of old flannel trousers, a flannel shirt, canvas shoes, and a white woollen sweater which dated back to his university days. (How long ago they seemed now!)

These were scarcely garments which could be exhibited to the fashionable young people who were his fellow visitors at Gay Ladies, but the hour was Just 6 a.m., and none of them was likely to be out of bed for a good two hours at least. Carrying his most precious possession, a light, perfectly balanced cane rod, the product of skilled craftsmanship, a landing-net, basket, and his wallet of flies, he crept noiselessly downstairs. The front door was locked and barred, but he tiptoed into the drawing-room and let himself out by the French windows.

As Theodore crossed the three hundred yards of dewy lawn from the house to the meadows that flanked the river—a chalk stream—he felt as carefree and happy as a piece of thistledown that dances on the wind. The dignity of Chancery Lane and the Law was stripped from him like a cramping garment one tosses aside in warm weather, and he ran through the lush grass of the meadow as though he were sixteen instead of a sober thirty-six.

Fishing! The thought made him feel like a boy again. Warm blood tingled in his veins, his nostrils were keen for the morning scents; he carried his burdens more lightly than he had ever carried the rolled umbrella that was the insignia of his slavery in the city.

He had been passionately devoted to the gentle art from the day when, at the age of nine, he had landed his first diminutive troutling. Going in the opposite direction from the bathing pool, which was filled through an artificial channel from the stream, Theodore walked along the bank for perhaps half a mile. He was looking for the tiny dimple made out of the stream by the rising of a trout.

Soon he spotted a large fish rising steadily some thirty yards upstream, close under the near bank. He halted and watched it sucking down flies at the rate of about twelve a minute. To any but the eye of the enthusiastic fisher, the trout would have been invisible, for only a faint swirl on the surface of the water, and the disappearance of the floating flies betrayed its presence.

He withdrew discreetly, took sections of his rod from their canvas coverings, and fitted them together. Then, leaving his rod upon the grass, he slipped cautiously along the bank, looking for a fly. He found one, crept back, and matched it as closely as possible with an artificial fly from the collection in his wallet.

When the fly was attached to his line, he went along the bank above the place where his quarry was feeding, almost holding his breath lest he should disturb the trout. Cautiously he cast, and let the fly, floating on the surface of the water, drift down stream, over the spot where the fish was feeding. Nothing happened, and he let his line drift some 20 yards below the fish before taking it from the water and repeating the manoeuvre.

With infinite patience, he offered the fly to the trout four times in exactly the same way, going upstream for several yards, casting lightly, letting the fly float over the rising fish, and removing it from the water at a discreet distance from his quarry. The trout fed on undisturbed.

At his fifth cast the trout took Theodore's fly, and was hooked. It gave one mad rush upstream, and the line zoomed off the reel. Theodore's heart was in his mouth, but the trout suddenly turned and went downstream, coming to rest in the depths of a pool, where he played at his wild will for a time, straining and tugging. Again, he rushed off upstream, and jumped clean out of the water, showing his goodly proportions and excellent condition. As well as he could judge, as the trout flashed in the air, Theodore estimated that he was a five pounder and a beauty.

For the strain he put on line, he might have been a whale. With his rushes upstream and down he kept Theodore busy, alternately, reeling in and letting the line spin out.

In one of his mad rushes, the trout had nearly all the line off the reel, and Theodore was about to give him up when he turned again and dived deep into the pool. There he remained for some minutes, at the bottom. Only the weight of the fish on the line told that he was still on the hook. He remained perfectly still, and Theodore waited breathlessly for his next manoeuvre.

He had not long to wait. From being perfectly passive, the trout became a silver flash of speed. Up and down, back and forward he went, and for several minutes it took Theodore all his time to hold him. It seemed that the line would go; but it held, and the speed of the trout began to slacken. After his herculean efforts he was tired, and Theodore had decided that it was about time to get the landing net ready, when the trout went across to the other side of the stream, buried himself in a great clump of weeds, and remained immovable. For all that Theodore could do with him he might have been several hundred pounds in weight.

In reeling in a little, the line became caught on some rushes at the water's edge. Theodore slipped down among the rushes and disentangled it; no easy task, for the line seemed to be in league with devils. It seemed to take a fiendish delight in tangling itself afresh.

When he finally got the line free it went slack. A callous jerk met with no resistance. A wave of disappointment swept over him; his fish was off.

With a sigh he began to reel in.

Just then a feminine voice shouted: "He's still on! He's still on!"

Theodore looked round in amazement, and saw Anne Wilding standing up five yards downstream from him. She was dressed in a tweed skirt, woollen stockings, stout shoes, and a green pullover.

For a moment he could do nothing but stare, so unexpected was her appearance on the river bank so early in the morning.

Anne almost danced with excitement. "Didn't you hear me?" she cried. "He's still on! Don't let him get away!"

Theodore pulled at his line carefully, and was rewarded by feeling a distinct tug. Anne was right. His trout was still at the end of the line!

It is no easy matter to lure a reluctant trout from its refuge, especially when it feels too fatigued to put up a fight in midstream. The fish had found a temporary sanctuary with which it was quite satisfied, and it had no intention of moving it.

Anne and Theodore looked at each other. To attempt to haul the fish from the weeds would have resulted in breaking the line.

"I'm afraid we'll have to play a waiting game," said Theodore.

A little smile played at the corners of Anne's mouth. "I can show you a trick worth two of that," she replied gaily. "It's a poacher's trick I learned as a child."

She sat down on the bank and removed her shoes and stockings. Prudery demanded that Theodore should avert his eyes, but Mother Grundy was far from his mind. He stood watching the lithe movements of her slim body in frank admiration.

Anne met his gaze with candid eyes.

"I awoke early," she explained, "and couldn't sleep again. It was far too lovely a morning for sleep. There was a sound on the landing outside my room, then I heard footsteps go cautiously down the stairs. I looked out of the window and saw you crossing the lawn with your rod. Fishing was afoot, of course, and I've never been able to resist an early-morning fishing expedition. So, I dressed and followed. You don't mind?"

Theodore smiled and shook his head. "Why should I mind? I only wish I'd known you were there."

"The knowledge would probably have disturbed you," replied Anne. "I turned up just as you had hooked him, and I've been holding my breath ever since. What a fight he put up!"

She stood up, barefooted, and put one toe gingerly into the water. "Ooh!" she exclaimed. It was cold!

"You're not going in?" protested Theodore. "You'll catch a chill if you do."

Anne laughed. "Chill or no chill," she retorted, "I must show you my poacher's trick."

With the landing net in her hand, she waded into the stream. A yard from the bank, the water was over her ankles. A little further, and it was lapping at her calves. Midstream, it almost touched the hem of her skirt.

"Come back!" shouted Theodore. "You'll be soaked."

She waved her hand gaily, took a deep breath, and waded on. When she reached the opposite bank, her skirt was soaked almost to the waist.

Cautiously, she took the line in her hand, and felt her way along it, through the weeds, until she touched the fish. He lay perfectly still, and seemed to think that this was a legitimate part of the entertainment. By degrees, she worked the landing net through the weeds, which were very thick, until it was under the unsuspecting trout. With her fingers, she jockeyed him in to it, and hauled out the landing-net and fish, both buried under a pile of dripping weeds. With an air of triumph, she turned and waded back with her burden. With a laugh, Anne knelt on the grass beside the net, found the fish, and dexterously removed Theodore's hook and line. There was another hook embedded in the fish's mouth.

"This fellow's a warrior!" she exclaimed. "Someone's had him on before, and he's gone off, hook and all."

She shot an inquiring glance at Theodore, then with a swift movement turned the net and tipped the trout into the stream. They watched him flash downstream, then Anne gave a shaky laugh.

"Fancy eating so brave a fighter!" she exclaimed.

She gathered up her shoes and stockings. "Come on," she said, "I'll race you to the house!"

"Tell me about yourself," said Anne Wilding.

"I'm afraid there's nothing to tell," replied Theodore.

They were sitting on comfortable cane chairs under a shady tree on the cool green lawn of Gay Ladies. A hundred yards behind them was the house, grey and gabled and ivy-clad, with an air of dignity and grace and leisurely age, rather than the youth and joyousness which its name suggested.

In front of them stretched the velvet lawn, which undulated down to the river, where the other guests and their host were disporting themselves in the bathing pool.

Anne Wilding looked at Theodore with friendly interest. "How old are you?"

"Thirty-six."

"Then you must have lots to tell about yourself." She eyed him critically. "I should have said that you were a little older. You have a quiet dignity which is unusual in young men."

Theodore laughed: "I was born with it."

She nodded sagely. "I expect you were. But you're growing younger, I verily believe. When I used to see you striding down Fleet Street, you were 60 at least. But something's changed you. Today you're not more than 40."

"Tomorrow I may be 25!" Their laughter blended.

"You should be," she said quite seriously. "No man under 60 should be a day older than 30."

"And what about a woman?"

Her eyes mocked him. "Oh, women are knowing creatures. They realise that, after girlhood is over, a woman is most attractive at 30, so they hurry over the twenties quickly, and remain 30 for the rest of their lives."

Anne settled herself more comfortably. "Tell me about your-self," she repeated.

"There's very little to tell. I've done nothing of importance."

"Oh, it isn't the important things about one's friends which enables one to know them. I'd rather know what you think about in your bath than what you do in your office."

Theodore laughed: "In my bath," he said, "I chiefly think that someday I'd like to be the proud possessor of a real porcelain bathtub, nine feet long and four feet wide. The bath I use in London is a wretched thing, so small that it is necessary to sit bolt upright in it, and the paint has flaked off gradually, leaving a rough surface most ungracious to one's anatomy."

Anne Wilding laughed: "I begin to know you. You live in furnished rooms, then."

"I do," replied Theodore sadly. "In Haggard Street, West Kensington. How did you know?"

"Because I, too, once lived in rooms, and in that very street." she told him. "And my bath was the very twin of yours. Tell me, does Haggard Street still smell of cabbage, and fried sausage, and tar, and dust and old boots?"

"It does, mingled with the odour of cleaning. When did you live there?"

"Six years ago."

Theodore sat up. "Why," he said, "it is just six years since I went to live in Haggard Street. To think that I never knew you!"

"The tragedy of people who live in dismal rooms in dingy streets," said Anne, "is that they never do know each other."

They were silent for a little, looking at the brightly-clad bathers, a hundred and fifty yards away.

"Tell me," said Anne, "what are your ambitions? One lives on ambitions, you know, if one lives in Haggard Street."

"I am afraid they are very dull. I want a little house of my own someday, and a room full of books that I've read, and a dog."

Anne shook her head. "That isn't all," she said. "You want more than that. I can see it in your eyes. Tell me."

Theodore hesitated: "I want life," he replied lamely.

She nodded; "We all want life. Some of us are slower to realise it than others. Some realise it too late; some never realise it at all."

She drew a pattern on the lawn with her toe. "What sort of life do you want?" With a wave of her hand, she indicated the gay bathers, the vast lawn, the gleaming cars standing in the drive, the table where Dodds was shaking cocktails. "This?"

"Not quite. And yet I'd like to taste all this, too. It's entirely different from the rut I've been in for years, and its "different-ness" appeals."

"Then why don't you plunge into it whilst you're here?"

Theodore's expression was wistful. "Because I don't know how," he said regretfully. "I can't swim, or drive a car, or play tennis, or talk."

"I should have thought that you'd have learnt to swim when you stayed here during the holidays."

He laughed. "I was going to, once," he replied, "but Tony pushed me in, and I haven't been near the pool since."

Anne eyed him critically. "Did you and Tony ever have a fight?"

He shook his head. "Never. I was afraid of him," he admitted. "He could have licked me easily."

"I thought so. He had his own way; bossed you about, and ruled the roost, didn't he?"

"I suppose so."

She looked him straight in the eye. "Theodore Wrenn," she said forcefully, "you would be a better man if you had taken your courage in both hands as a boy, and hit Tony on the jaw, regardless of the licking he would have given you. You've got an inferiority complex that must be worked out of your system."

Theodore was silent; inwardly he admitted the truth of her words.

Ann rose suddenly. "The bathers are all coming out of the pool for tea," she said. "Go and borrow a bathing suit, and I'll teach you to swim."

He stood up, hesitating a little. "I'm afraid I may prove to be a stupid pupil."

"You won't. Meet me at the pool in ten minutes."

He was at the pool, garbed in a borrowed bathing suit, in less than eight minutes, but even so, Anne was there ahead of him. She came out, dripping wet, as he approached. A bright red cap covered her hair, and her trim suit clung to her body like a scarlet sheath. Not for the first time, he decided that she was the most beautiful woman he had ever seen.

She met his gaze with the frank friendliness of a young boy.

"I learned to swim by jumping in at the deep end," she said. "But you are more methodical than I am; you'd better begin by going through the motions on land."

Without a word, Theodore ran past her, and sprang headlong into the water at the deep end. He rose, spluttering and coughing, waving his arms and legs uselessly, and promptly sank again.

Again, he rose, and again the water closed over him. Desperation over took him—he was going to drown, and all because of a foolish gesture. As he rose for the third time, a hand grasped his arm, and Anne Wilding, swimming steadily, towed him to the shallow end.

He stood up spluttering, flushed with embarrassment.

"I'm sorry," he said, when he could speak. "I've made in utter fool of myself."

Anne smiled sympathetically.

"You're an idiot," she replied cheerfully. "But a courageous idiot. It was my fault. I'm afraid I egged you on. I knew you had it in you to be reckless of consequences, and I wanted to bring it out. We aren't all alike, you know, Theodore. You are the slow, thorough type which must take infinite pains. Let's continue the lesson on land until you've mastered the strokes."

Theodore agreed. "If you're still willing to teach me," he added.

"Of course, I am."

When they went up to the house half an hour later, Anne predicted that Theodore would be able to swim with one more lesson. In the grasp of a rush of new sensations, Theodore dressed slowly. Afterwards he met Anne in the hall.

"Tony's in the library," she said. "I'm not going in. Let's go into the garden again."

It was not difficult to guess that Sir Anthony had a rapidly emptying decanter with him for company.

He followed Anne out into the garden. She led the way to her blue two-seater, which was parked in front of the house.

"Shall I teach you to drive?" she suggested. "Or have you had enough of lessons for one day?"

He opened the door, and followed her into the car. "It's kind of you to trouble about me," he replied. "As long as you're willing to teach me, I'm anxious to learn."

Anne drove the car down the driveway and out into the road. Half a mile along the road, she stopped at a secluded spot.

For ten minutes, she explained the gears and clutch and the principal of steering to him, going over the same ground time after time. Theodore followed her closely, asking questions whenever he was not quite sure of a point.

"The great thing is to steer as little as possible," she explained. "Don't keep turning the wheel from left to right. The car will hold the road itself, pretty well."

She moved out of the driving seat, and Theodore took her

place. He put the car into first gear and let the clutch in—too sharply, however—for the engine stopped.

Anne explained what he had done.

"Let the clutch pedal up gently," she reminded him, "and depress the accelerator slightly at the same time. That's one mistake you won't make again."

She was right. The second time, the co-ordination between clutch and accelerator was perfect, and the car rolled off smoothly. Theodore engaged the second and third gears successfully without trouble, and drove along the road at 20 miles an hour.

At first, he was suspicious of the steering wheel. Holding it and letting the car steer itself seemed altogether too easy. The inclination was to jiggle the wheel; the beginner's greatest fault.

He picked up the art of driving so quickly and thoroughly that Anne let him drive back to the house. He was gaining confidence, and coming out of his shell.

"What a delightful husband he'll make for some lucky girl," she thought, a little jealously; "after I've taken him in hand for a while!"

And Theodore"s thoughts ran like this: "What a delightful wife she'll make; for a worthless husband like Anthony!"

Both of them sighed.

CHAPTER 13

A tall woman, with copper-coloured hair and curious green eyes, stepped out of a huge Rolls Royce limousine which had driven up to the terrace in front of Gay Ladies. Languidly she opened a green silk parasol, fringed with fine old lace. A dapper little man who wore horn-rimmed spectacles and an anxious look, followed her out of the car and stood behind her diffidently.

With no lack of confidence, the tall woman strolled casually across the lawn towards a large striped umbrella, beneath which Anne Wilding was dispensing tea to her fiancé's guests.

All eyes were turned upon the approaching figure. Theodore Wrenn, who had recognised the newcomer as Diana Marquis, stole a glance at his cousin, who, he observed, had turned red with fury.

Completely conscious of the stir she was creating, and taking a perverse delight in it, the actress advanced slowly until she was within a yard or two of the tea-table. There she halted, and putting up an elaborate lorgnette, glanced casually at each of the guests in turn. A look of malignity appeared in her eyes for a brief moment as they rested on Theodore, then her glance travelled on to Sir Anthony, who rose to his feet, glaring at her.

"My dear Tony," said Diana, quite unmoved. "What a charming picture you all make. Strawberries and cream, too! My favourite weakness. You must help me to some after I've met your guests. I'm afraid it's too positively rude for words, Izzy and I breaking in on you like this, but we were driving this way, and I felt that we really must stop and call. It's so long since I've been to Gay Ladies. I felt I simply must have another look at the dear old place."

Concealing his chagrin as well as he was able, Sir Anthony presented the actress to his fiancée and the other guests.

Anne was submitted to a searching scrutiny through the preposterous lorgnette, then the actress held out her hand limply.

"Dear Miss Wilding, I'm positively charmed to meet you. So strange that we never met before. I'm an admirer of your pictures—they're positively too sweet for words."

Without waiting for a reply, she turned to Theodore with a disarming smile.

"And, Mr. Wrenn! I haven't seen you lately. Your last call was so brief and so early." She laughed, and added with a glance at the others: "It was really too bad of Mr. Wrenn. He called on me early in the morning—hours before I usually rise. He hasn't called on me since. I think my black silk pyjamas frightened him away."

She took the chair which Sir Anthony had vacated, and waved her hand at the dapper little man who had accompanied her to Gay Ladies.

"This is Izzy Guilderstein," she said. "A delightful little man. He's writing my next play. Really a charming drama. I wear different pyjamas in each act."

Guilderstein bubbled nervously in response to this introduction.

"I am writing the play especially for Miss Marquis," he explained jerkily. "She is my inspiration."

"What is the name of the play?" asked Anne pleasantly.

"'The Naked Truth'," replied the dramatist simply.

There was a little titter of amusement. The actress flushed angrily.

"The title is not definitely decided," she said, controlling her voice admirably. In an intimate tone, she added, "You are not wearing the Ravenal pearls, Miss Wilding."

Anne looked at her frankly. "The Ravenal pearls?" she repeated blankly. "I am afraid I have never even heard of them."

Sir Anthony, his face red, and his fingers twitching, bent over the back of her chair.

"They are a family heirloom," he said. "They will be yours someday, my dear."

"My dear Tony," drawled the actress, "you don't mean to admit that you haven't even shown them to Miss Wilding? I should insist on wearing them at once, dear Miss Wilding. They are positively marvellous. When I used to wear them, they were greatly admired."

She sighed pensively. "I hated to part with them, but of course since Tony was getting married—and he hasn't even shown them to you? How perfectly beastly of him."

Anne pursed her lips. "I don't agree with you," she replied stiffly. "In any case, I shouldn't dream of wearing them at present."

"But how positively old-fashioned you are," she exclaimed mockingly." Of course, you should wear them. Any woman would go crazy over them. Why, I believe I should even have been willing to marry Tony, for the privilege of wearing them, only of course, that wasn't necessary."

Diana"s green eyes were fixed upon Anne's face.

"If Sir Anthony doesn't let you wear them—and I should insist, my dear—I shall be delighted to give you mine, as a wedding gift. Only I'm afraid they aren't real. They are perfect imitations though, of the Ravenal pearls." She turned to Theodore. "Aren't they, Mr. Wrenn? I had them made because I hated to part with the originals. Mr. Wrenn knows how unhappy I was at the very thought."

"It is very kind of you." said Anne in a strained voice, "but really, I don't care for jewellery."

"Oh, but you should, my dear," Diana protested. "Jewels are the birth right of every woman—of every beautiful woman, I mean."

There was a short silence. No one felt equal to the task of coping with Diana Marquis.

"So, you are really engaged to Tony," said the actress at length. "Becoming engaged is a step I shall never take. It makes a man so sure of one, and that is always fatal. Of course, I realise that there are some women who become engaged so as to be sure of their men."

With a muffled exclamation, Alys Mercer rose to her feet, and drew herself up to her full height.

"What a spiteful cat you are," she exclaimed indignantly. "I think you must have a soul the colour of your pyjamas."

There was an embarrassing silence, then the actress raised her lorgnette languidly.

"How charmingly frank you are, my dear," she commented. "It is really quite refreshing to encounter such engaging rudeness."

Alys turned to Tommy Renfrew. "Do come for a swim, Tommy," she said. "I can't bear the smell of cheap perfume any longer."

The actress's eyes glittered, but her expression was composed as she leant toward Sir Anthony.

"I seem to have broken up your charming little party," she murmured, "I am so sorry."

The others were drifting off in twos and threes.

Theodore rose, and offered the actress his arm.

"May I show you the rose garden?" he suggested. "It is quite delightful just now…"

Diana took his arm and languidly rose to her feet.

"How charming of you, Mr. Wrenn," she drawled.

She leant toward Anne.

"I can scarcely tear myself away from you for a moment, Miss Wilding. There is so much we have to say to each other. But I simply can't refuse Mr. Wrenn's charming invitation. Do excuse me for just a few minutes."

Anne bowed stiffly without a word.

With Izzy Guilderstein trailing behind them like a well-trained poodle, Diana Marquis and Theodore strolled round the corner of the house, and out of sight of the others.

Instead of leading the actress towards the rose garden, Theodore guided her round the other side of the house to the terrace where her car was waiting. She looked at him with a mocking light in her eyes.

"Oh, Mr. Wrenn, how obvious of you."

Theodore met her gaze quietly. "I really think you had better go."

She shrugged her shoulders. "Such a short visit. Oh, well—come along, Izzy."

With a patient sigh, Mr. Guilderstein followed her into the car. The actress leaned out of the, window as the car moved slowly away.

"Do come and see me in town, Mr. Wrenn. I think you are a very interesting type."

"Thank you. You are very kind."

"Not at all." She laughed. "And I really think I have put a spoke in Tony's wheel. I don't think the course of true love will run straight for a little while."

"Perhaps you're right." said Theodore. "Good day."

As he turned away, he met his cousin going into the house.

"So, you got her to leave!" said Sir Anthony. "Good man. Lord, that was the most awkward 10 minutes of my life. I could have strangled her for two pins." He mopped his forehead. "I need a drink badly after that. Join me?"

"No. And I don't think you should either."

Sir Anthony laughed. "Don't be a fool, man. A drink never harmed anyone."

"Perhaps not. But with you, "a drink" is always plural. Don't take too much."

Theodore went back to the tea table on the lawn. Alys Mercer and Tommy Renfrew had returned, and were chatting airily to Anne. Theodore's heart warmed towards these ultra-modern young people. They were doing their level best to take Anne's mind off the unpleasant incident which had happened. He noticed that Anne was looking white and a little strained. There was a tired look about her eyes. Theodore sincerely hoped that Sir Anthony would benefit by his advice. To drink too much at the moment would only make matters worse.

His worst fears were realised when he saw his cousin coming from the house. Sir Anthony was swaying as he walked, and his face was unnaturally flushed.

Ignoring the presence of the others, he wobbled up to Anne, supporting himself by clutching her chair.

"Most awkward incident, my dear," he murmured clumsily. "Wouldn't have had it happen for the world. Mustn't upset yourself, though. Don't be jealous, you know. That affair's all over—and I never really cared for her anyway. Closed book, my dear, closed book."

Anne rose and looked at him steadily. "I would rather you refrained from mentioning the subject," she replied scornfully.

Sir Anthony blinked. "Oh, I say. Don't be like that. Mustn't be so haughty. That wouldn't do at all."

"Do you realise what I've had to bear this afternoon?" she demanded icily.

He swayed a little.

"Sorry. Awfully sorry," he muttered. "But don't blame me,

my dear. "Twasn't my fault. Couldn't be helped. Must bear it." His bloodshot blue eyes assumed a cunning expression. "Don't forget Ronnie, my dear."

"Oh!" With a sudden exclamation, Anne slapped his face. The marks of her fingers showed livid upon his flushed face.

For a moment they stood facing each other, Sir Anthony swaying a little, with an incredulous expression in his eyes, Anne, very straight, her eyes alive with fury; then she turned, snatched her diamond engagement ring from her finger, and threw it from her as far as she could.

It flew through the air in a glittering arc, and fell into the bathing pool.

Then, with her head held high, Anne walked steadily up the lawn to the house.

The hour was 11 a.m. Sir Anthony Ravenal had not yet breakfasted or dressed. His head buzzed like a hive of bees, and his tongue felt like thick brown paper. Moreover, he was in a vile temper.

He sent for one of the gardeners, a strapping young fellow who could dive and swim like a fish.

"There's a ring in the bottom of the swimming pool," he said abruptly. "Get it for me."

The gardener hesitated, but quickly left the room when his master picked up a slipper and aimed it in his direction.

Ravenal sent for the butler. "Where's Miss Wilding?" he demanded.

"Out in her car, sir."

"With Mr. Wrenn, I suppose?"

"No, sir; Mr. Wrenn is reading in the rose garden."

"Get me a brandy and soda."

The butler hesitated: "If I may make the suggestion, sir, a light breakfast first—"

Ravenal swore. With a shrug of his shoulders, the butler left the room.

Until Dodds returned with the brandy-and-soda, his master paced the room feverishly. In his mind he was going over and over the events of the previous day, which had ended with his fiancé taking off her ring and throwing it from her as far as she could. He was cursing himself for the inability to refrain from alcohol which had brought the affair to a climax. For weeks he had abstained from his two favourite vices—drink and women—and his fall had come at last, with a sickening thud.

Something would have to be done at once, if he wanted to

hold Anne—and to marry Anne was the dominating impulse of his life.

The telephone in his bedroom was out of order—he had knocked it over the previous night in his struggles to prevent two of his servants and one of his guests from putting him to bed—so he went downstairs in his dressing gown, to the telephone in the library. On the stairs he met the butler, and drained off the brandy-and-soda at a gulp.

Now the rose garden was quite near to the library, the library window was open, and Ravenal"s voice was loud and harsh. Reading a book in the rose garden, Theodore could not help overhearing a fragment of his cousin's telephone conversation.

"Put on the screw—Yes, at once—" and "Goodbye, Salzman," were the exact words which Theodore overheard. At the time he paid little attention to them and shifted his chair to avoid hearing any more.

A little later, Dodds brought him a telegram.

It said simply: "Daniel Gentry died last night. Please come to office at once."

He sat very still for a little while after he had read it. Although his employer was very old, it had seemed impossible that he should ever die. The news came as a great shock. He had been very fond of the fussy, eccentric old lawyer.

His mind went back to the day when Daniel Gentry had first shown symptoms of the illness which had carried him off, and he remembered Miss Maudsley's words: "Oh, if anything should happen to him, Mr. Wrenn! It would be the end of the firm and of all of us!"

Miss Maudsley and poor old Gifford would feel this blow even more than he, he knew. Their lives had been so bound up with that of the old lawyer. They had even fancied that when he died, they, too would cease to exist.

He rose with a sigh and went into the house to pack. As he went through the hall Ravenal hailed him from the library. Theodore joined his cousin without enthusiasm. He would have been well pleased never to have seen Ravenal again.

"I'm afraid I must go today," he said. "I've received a telegram calling me back to the office. Please convey my farewells to the others."

"Sorry you're going," replied Ravenal. "But if you must, you must."

He hesitated. "Bit of a row yesterday, eh?" he added.

Theodore nodded silently.

"You mustn't think that Anne was serious when she broke off our engagement," continued his cousin. "I'm sure I can persuade her to change her mind."

"I hope not," replied Theodore bluntly. "It would be the worst thing she could possibly do."

He went upstairs, leaving his cousin staring, after him with an expression of amazement upon his face. Outside Anne's bedroom he saw a trunk which her maid had just packed and placed in the hall. The door was open, and he saw the girl wrestling with the strap of a suitcase. He went in and helped her.

"Miss Wilding leaving?" he asked casually.

The maid nodded and studied his face curiously.

"She has remembered an appointment in London which she must keep, sir."

Theodore felt happier as he went into his room to pack. If Anne was leaving at once it seemed unlikely that a reconciliation could be affected between her and Ravenal. That took a considerable load off his mind.

Since knowing Anne, be had mentally writhed at the thought that she was to marry Ravenal. He had tried to think of ways to prevent the union. It was impossible for him to reveal his cousin's true character to her; he could not be guilty of such a breach of confidence. Now that Ravenal himself had revealed his own essential brutality, a weight had been taken from Theodore's mind.

He packed his things, and had them carried down to the hall. Anne had come in; her little blue two-seater stood on the terrace in front of the house.

He went to look for her, and found her in the drawing room. She was standing by the fireplace, clutching a buff-coloured envelope in one hand. Her face was deathly white, and wore an expression of stark despair. She did not notice that he had come into the room, and before she looked up, he had withdrawn. It was not for him to intrude upon her at such a moment.

In a few moments she came out of the room, with her head held high.

Acting upon irresistible impulse, he went into the drawing room. In the fireplace he found the crumpled buff coloured envelope. He opened it and his mind went back to the words he had overheard. "Put on the screw. Yes, at once—"

Salzman had put on the screw. And at Ravenal's dictation.

But what hold over Anne had Salzman that could make her the picture of stark misery?

He felt an impulse to go to Ravenal and force the truth out of him, but decided that such an action would be fruitless and might rebound on Anne.

Later, he found Anne in the hall, dressed for the journey to London. She was still very pale, and the, smile she gave him was fleeting and listless. "I hear you're going up to London, too," she said. "I can give you a lift if you like."

He hesitated: "If it's quite convenient."

She nodded: "Quite. My maid will be quite comfortable in the dickey seat. "

Outside, Ravenal's big Rolls-Royce, loaded high with luggage, was parked behind the two-seater. The chauffeur was to deliver the luggage at the station to be sent to London by rail.

As Theodore and Anne climbed into the little car, Ravenal, clothed but unshaven, came running round the side of the house. He put his foot on the running board and held out his hand to Anne.

"Here's your ring," he said.

Anne was silent, and her clear, scornful eyes looked squarely into Ravenal's bloodshot, blue eyes.

"Your ring," Ravenal reiterated.

With a sudden flash of anger, she struck it from his hand. It fell tinkling to the ground.

Without a word, Ravenal retrieved the ring and handed it to her.

She looked straight ahead, and into her face crept the expression of despair which bad torn at Theodore's heart a little while before.

"Put it on," directed Ravenal.

Theodore made a move to interfere, but as he did so he was amazed to see Anne slipping the ring on the third linger of her left hand.

Ravenal stooped toward her. She averted her face, but he kissed the nape of her neck.

"Not goodbye, my dear, but au revoir," he said, with a note of triumph in his voice.

"I'll expect you next weekend. Quite a lively bunch is coming. See you later, Theodore."

The little car moved off down the drive.

Anne and Theodore were silent and miserable during the long drive toward London. They were preoccupied with thoughts—unpleasant thoughts.

Ten miles from London, there was a sharp report, and the car swerved. Anne drew it into the side of the road, and put on her brakes.

"One of my back tyres gone," she said ruefully. "That means messing with the spare."

Theodore slipped out of his seat quickly. "I'll do it," he replied.

"Are you sure you can?"

"I can manage. It isn't a job for you, anyway."

He looked at her, with ineffable longing in his eyes.

"I wish I could always be at hand to do these things for you."

Their eyes met for a moment, and seemed to kiss. Then, like a magnet, their gaze was drawn to the diamond which winked maliciously at them from the third finger on her left hand.

The end of the world had come to the dingy, old-fashioned office of Gentry, Green, and Gentry. For the first time in fifty-five years the worn brass plate was unpolished. The caretaker whose task it was to make the brass gleam like burnished copper sat still in his little attic-kitchen. To Gifford and Miss Maudsley, standing together by a window silently huddled like sheep, it was surprising that traffic roared in nearby Fleet Street as it had roared with ever increasing volume for 50 years and more.

Daniel Gentry was dead, and the end of the world had come. Yet the postman clattered noisily up the creaking wooden staircase, and left a thick bundle of letters; the office boy had come whistling into the office; the telephone rang incessantly. The bus conductor had asked Miss Maudsley for her fare three times that morning. She had been thinking of other things than having her correct change ready. As though a threepenny bus fare mattered when the end of the world had come! Gifford had walked to the office, arriving in a state of collapse, and had been amazed at the fact that tobacco and boots and cabbage and chemistry were still for sale. The shops were open, huge policemen still directed traffic; people chatted with one another about cricket scores and crochet patterns. It was amazing!

The two oldest employees of the late Daniel Gentry had the pale faces of those who are already dead. Their mental faculties were suspended. They seemed to be waiting for the summons to follow their employer.

Strangely enough, it was Miss Maudsley whose ears detected a strangeness in Theodore's footsteps as he came up the stairs. She went out to the landing to meet him.

"Why!" she exclaimed: "You're sunburnt!"

Here was cause for wonder. Sunburn at such a time! Could it be that after all the end of everything had not come?

A little colour came back to her withered cheeks as she looked at Theodore. Never had she seen him looking so purposeful, so hearteningly manly. His shoulders were squared, and his eyes had a determined expression.

"Oh, Mr. Wrenn! I'm so glad you've come," she stammered.

She opened the door of his little private room and followed him in. Somehow, she felt that she must be near him for a few minutes, and draw strength from his manliness.

"I've had glorious weather for my little holiday," said Theodore. "I hope this spell lasts. You'll be going away on holiday in a few days, won't you?"

Miss Maudsley gulped "Holidays!" she said. "Holidays! Well!"

It was amazing how much better she felt already. Really, young Mr. Wrenn had a marvellous effect upon one!

Her eyes brimmed with tears.

"Don't cry," said Theodore gently. "Don't cry. You'll make your nose all shiny."

With a sob and a tremulous laugh, she left the room.

A little later Gifford came in. "I suppose they wired you about the Guv'nor?" he mumbled.

Theodore nodded. "I was sorry," he said. "It was very sad."

"Sad!" exclaimed Gifford. "Sad! I should just say it is sad. About the worst thing that ever happened."

"I shouldn't say that," replied Theodore, shaking his head. "Death isn't the worst thing that can happen, by a long way."

"But Mr. Gentry?" protested Gifford.

"He was a very old man."

"Yes," agreed Gifford hastily. "But have you thought what it means to us?"

"I can't say that I have. What does it mean?"

"It means—" Gifford waved his arms helplessly. "It means the end of everything."

Theodore sat back in his chair, and looked at the bent, withered old clerk.

"In your time, Gifford, you must have seen death come to many people," he said gently. "Even in this office, there was Mr. Green, and Norman Gentry, and two clerks. Have you ever known it to make any real difference? Didn't everything go on just the same?"

"Yes, I suppose it did." This with another helpless gesture. "But Mr. Gentry—?"

"Daniel Gentry gave 55 years of his life to this firm," said Theodore. "Do you think he built up so weak a thing that it cannot stand now that he is gone?"

"He was the blood and bones of the business," stammered Gifford.

"New blood, new bones. That's the inexorable law of nature. Nothing stands still Gifford. Everything progresses. You'll see, Gentry, Green, and Gentry will continue stronger than ever. Death is a single step in the endless progression of human affairs. As natural and inevitable as birth, and no more terrible."

When Gifford had gone, Theodore automatically took up the work which had waited on his desk for his return.

He sighed as he applied himself to the old routine.

For a brief spell, he had been lifted out the rut, only to be dropped back into it with a sickening thud.

Like Gifford and Miss Maudsley, and the lately-released Daniel Gentry, he would be a slave to his work, soulless and monotonous, until death struck him off the chains, with a few weeks freedom every summer to tantalise him with the hopelessness of escape.

What was the use of realising the meaning of life, when life itself was out of his reach?

Everything changed, but nothing was new. The young assumed the shackles of the old, that was all. As Theodore had half expected, Daniel Gentry's executors approached him with an offer of the business. After all, he was a fully qualified lawyer, knew the firm's business thoroughly and (most important of all) had been saving a large part of his salary for over ten years.

Theodore was willing to purchase the business on the terms that were offered, but he required a partner.

Not unnaturally, he thought of his friend, Adrian Millar, very junior partner of Messrs. Harrow, Weald, Upton, Lewis, and Millar. So, on the afternoon on which the offer was made to him, he called at his friend's office.

Millar, bending over his desk with a pipe in his mouth, was frankly pleased to see Theodore.

"Sit down and put your feet up," was his cheerful greeting. "Don't tell me you've come on business. My conscience hasn't recovered yet from the shock of the last illegal affair you roped me in on."

"It's business, but quite regular."

"Good," Millar looked his friend over, frankly sizing him up. "You've changed remarkably, Theodore, and, I think, for the better. There's a look in your eye that wasn't there before. A woman, or a nerve tonic, old chap? Oh, I heard about Gentry's death. Dashed sorry. He wasn't a bad old stick."

"That"s what I've come about."

"Oh." Millar looked thoughtful, then with a sudden gesture, swept a litter of papers from his desk into a drawer. "I'm the willing donkey of this firm," he commented. "All the hard work tills to my lot, and the kudos and cash to Harrow and Lewis. But this afternoon I'll call a halt for an hour or two. Let's go and have a pint or two, and you can pour your troubles into my willing ear."

As they went through the outer office, Millar spoke to one of the clerks.

"If anyone calls, say I'm out for a couple of hours on urgent business." To Theodore he added under his breath: "What could be more urgent than slaking one's thirst in this weather."

When they were snugly ensconced in the cosiest bar in London, Theodore stated his case. Millar listened intently, with an interested expression on his chubby, pleasant face.

Afterwards.

"Average income for the last five years?" he asked.

Theodore mentioned a sum which considerably surprised his friend.

"As much as that, eh? I knew the old firm was still fairly prosperous, but I thought that it had fallen off a little. All from fat, juicy trusts, I suppose."

His expression became sober. "The executors will want a hefty sum."

Theodore mentioned the exact figure.

Millar nodded more happily. "Reasonable," he commented.

"Say four thousand apiece down, and half of the income for five years," Theodore added.

"Reasonable indeed," reiterated Millar. "What do you think yourself, quite frankly?"

Theodore took a deep breath. "There's nothing I'd rather do than buy an interest in the old firm," he said, and added in spite of himself; "except—?"

"Except!" repeated Millar. "Ahah! I knew there was a woman in it."

It must be admitted that Theodore blushed in spite of himself.

Millar tapped the stem of his pipe against his teeth. "I can sell out my share in the firm without much trouble," he commented. "Upton's rather keen on getting his son into the business.

Four thousand down, eh? —Yes. I think I can raise that. It's an attractive proposition, Theodore. And by George, won't we make the old firm sit up!"

"Then you'll come in with me?"

Millar slapped him on the back vigorously. "Like a shot! There's no one I'd rather have for a partner than you, old boy. Absolutely no one."

"Thanks," murmured Theodore.

He was happy, for the dream of his life was about to come true. He was going to be the new blood and bones of the old firm of Gentry, Green, and Gentry.

Ambition could carry him no higher!

CHAPTER 16

Mrs. Apps snorted indignantly. It was her proudest boast that hers was a quiet house. And so it was, except for the pounding of brooms, the rattling of milk trays, the roar of passing traffic, the crashing of china, when the undernourished overworked little "skivvy" thought of Ramon Navarro during working hours, and the consequent bellow of Mrs. Apps righteously rebuking her servant in no uncertain terms. The boarders were usually as quiet as mice—and as little appreciated by their landlady.

But this morning a new noise sounded through the house. Not an unpleasant noise if one had an air, for music—but an unusual noise, and to Mrs. Apps any noise which was, not hallowed by tradition (or made by herself) was an unbearable nuisance.

One of her lodgers was singing in his bath.

It couldn't be Mr. Haddock, who bathed only at night. Or the Second-Floor-Front, whose Friday night bath did duty for a week. Or the Attic-Bed-and-Breakfast, who didn't bath at all.

Could it possibly be Mr. Wrenn? Quiet, respectable, easy-done-by Mr. Wrenn?

It was Mr. Wrenn—noisy, rowdy, inconsiderate Mr. Wrenn!

As she hurried upstairs with Mr. Wrenn's meagre breakfast on a tray, Mrs. Apps asked herself if ever a landlady had been so "put upon" as she. It seemed hardly possible. Her ideal lodger was one who paid-up promptly, ate what was set before him without complaint, was not fussy about the regular turning of mattresses, and never, never raised his voice above a whisper.

Mr. Wrenn had almost seemed to be her ideal lodger. And now! Singing in his bath!

What, next? She wondered.

She plonked the breakfast tray upon the table in Theodore's sitting room, took a crumpled letter from her pocket and leaned it against the teapot.

Then she went and knocked loudly and aggressively upon the bathroom door. "Your breakfast, Mr. Wrenn."

All the sorrows of her oppressed condition were expressed in her tone.

Theodore rinsed the soap from his chest, and commenced to dry himself vigorously, and Mrs. Apps retired, describing his conduct to herself in a perfectly audible tone.

As usual, the breakfast was cold before Theodore was ready to eat it. Since it was a moot point whether Mrs. Apps's breakfasts were more indigestible hot or cold, this circumstance did not disturb his serenity.

It was a week since the executors of the late Daniel Gentry had approached him with their proposal that he should purchase the firm, negotiations were proceeding smoothly, and he was naturally jubilant as the ambition of his life came nearer to realisation. There was a further reason, for his cheerfulness. At the end of the week, he had "phoned to Anne Wilding's studio, and had learned that she was to be in town for the weekend. She was not going to Gay Ladies. There was still a chance, and by no means a bad one, that she would never marry Ravenal.

His heart leaped when he saw the handwriting, frank and flowing, in green ink, upon the square white envelope which Mrs. Apps had propped against his teapot. It was from Anne; and he hastened to open it.

Will you come to tea at 4 o'clock?

Would he? From that moment on, 4 o'clock was the only hour

which had any significance for him. He carried the note in his breast pocket to the office, and referred to it frequently during the day. Although he knew the wording by heart, he was thrilled afresh every time he read it.

At five minutes to four, he was standing on Anne's doorstep, having arrived in the street half an hour before, and walked round and round the block impatiently waiting for the prescribed hour to arrive.

Anne came to the door herself. She put out a slim, white hand. "I'm glad you could come."

There was something shy; and yet spontaneous and infectious about their smiles, it was like the meeting of two children who want to be friends, and welcome each other eloquently without words.

"Of course, I came," said Theodore, "Of course."

Which sounded rather silly, once he had said it.

Theodore was in an exquisite agony of embarrassment at first, but Anne quickly put him at his ease. Over tea they chatted gaily and spontaneously.

The first break in the easy flow of conversation came when Theodore's eyes fell upon the diamond ring on Anne's finger.

He flushed and looked up—and met Anne's gaze. Each knew what the other was thinking.

"Do you know," Theodore blurted out suddenly, "the bitterest moment of my life was when I watched you putting that ring back upon your finger?"

Anne was silent.

"And the happiest moment of my life," he went on, gaining confidence, "will be when I see you taking it off."

She shook her head. "Dear Theodore," she murmured, "but when I take it off it will be to replace it with another, which must stay on for keeps."

"Don't!" said Theodore. "You'll never marry Ravenal. Never. You couldn't. He's the last man in the world for you. Surely you see that."

"Whatever I see changes nothing. I've promised to marry him, and I must keep my promise."

"But the life he leads—" Theodore's voice trailed away as he remembered that it would be a breach of confidence to finish what he had been about to say.

Anne slipped off her ring and crossing the room, put it upon the mantelpiece behind a blue vase.

"Wretched ring," she said, "creating such an uncomfortable, atmosphere. There—it's gone! Now let's forget everything except our two selves—and your wonderful opportunity."

Theodore shook his head.

"I can't forget. It's still there, winking maliciously at me from behind that vase, and when I'm gone, you'll put it back on your finger."

She was silent.

"Back on your finger," he repeated bitterly. "Where it has no right to be."

He rose, went to her side, and took her hand.

"Anne," he whispered. "I'm not a clerk any more, or at least I won't be, in a little while. When these partnership negotiations are completed, I'll be in a position to offer you the things in life to which you have a right. Luxury, security, ease. I'm not much of a chap beside Ravenal, I know. I've no social graces, no looks to speak of, and when it comes to making love, I'm a fool. But I'd live for you, or die for you, if you'd let me. I love you, Anne."

She moved away. "Don't—please. "

"You don't love Ravenal. You couldn't."

"Love him?" her voice was bitter. "No, I don't suppose I do. Perhaps I hate him."

"Then you can't marry him!"

But her expression damned his hopes. "I must."

He begged her cajoled, entreated, but the only, reply she would give him was simply, "I must."

At last, she turned a white, haggard face toward him.

"Please, Theodore," she whispered. "Don't say anything more."

He was shocked and grieved by the pain he had caused her.

"I'm sorry," he said humbly, "I'm a cad. A selfish, thoughtless cad. I've hurt you like the blundering fool I am. Forgive me."

She winced at the sorrow in his eyes.

"You're so wonderful, Anne, so very, very wonderful. So straight, so fine, so true. I can't help loving you, and I hate myself for hurting you."

She drew back, her eyes wide with pain, and her lips trembling.

"No, no, Theodore, you don't know me! If you did, you would despise me, hate me. I'm not straight or true. I'm mean and despicable. Oh, you make me ashamed."

Sobbing bitterly, she threw herself upon the couch.

Theodore bent over her, stammering incoherently.

"Go, please go!" she whispered. "Please, Theodore, please."

With a white, set face, he stumbled from the room.

Three hours ago, Theodore had stumbled from Anne's presence, acutely miserable, and for three hours he had been in despair. Now he was facing the position courageously, and more hopefully.

He sat very still, staring straight ahead of him with a faraway look in his eyes. "In love," he soliloquized. "In love."

It was wonderful to be in love, even when it was a hopeless love, poignantly bittersweet. He sighed and pushing back his chair, rose from the table. He was still hungry, for he had eaten only a thin slice of bread, washed down with a single cup of tea, but not hungry enough to attempt the unpleasant-looking kipper, lying in a bath of congealed grease on a plate before him, or the seedy-looking seed cake.

He murmured vaguely: "If you can be something, something, something, something...and rumpty, tumpty, rumpty, tumpty, tum.

"You"re in the world, and everything that's in it,

"And what is more, you'll be a man, my son."

Leaning against the fireplace, he delved his hands deeply into his pockets.

"Oh, hell!" he summarised briefly.

"Pardon?" said a querulous voice from the door, and looking up he saw his landlady, Mrs. Apps, standing on the threshold with a large tin tray under her arm.

"I'm afraid I was thinking aloud," he stammered.

She gave him a cold, appraising glance.

"Bad habit, is talkin' to yourself. Y'never know where it'll end. I had a cousin what took to arguin' with hisself. Keep it up all night, he would, callin' hisself a liar and contradicking hisself something scandalous. He'd say something quite serious, and the next minute he'd turn round and call hisself names for sayin' it. Y'never know how to take him. Pore feller, it done for him in the end. They had to take him away. A case of dual personality, the doctors said. Two-faced I called it. Terrible fond of dogs, he was."

She plonked the tea tray upon the table, and began to place Theodore's tea things on it.

"You haven't eaten your kipper," she observed with an injured air, as though he had left it out of personal spite against her.

"I wasn't hungry."

She tossed her head. "There's no pleasing some folks! A nice kipper it is, too. Fi'pence a pair on Hammersmith Broadway. I thought it would be tasty for your tea. I always understood you liked kippers. I try to study my boarders. If they aren't pleased, I'm sure it's not my fault. Mr. Mellish, now, that had these rooms before you, would eat a kipper, seven nights a week, skin and all. Easily pleased he was, nothing faddy about him. "A nice kipper, Mrs. Apps," he would say, "that's the ticket for me. Can't get enough of 'em". A real gentleman he was, if a bit awkward when he had one of his bilious attacks. Poor gent, he had a kipper the night before he left. Real sudden it was. One in the morning, he woke up the whole house, hollering his head off with pain. Soon as I saw he really was ill an' not jus' tryin' to be awkward, I called in the doctor, and by 3 o'clock he was took to the West London Hospital. He died three days after. It was a shock. Keen on wireless, he was."

Picking up the loaded tray, she staggered to the door.

"You didn't ought to talk to yourself so much," she threw back over her shoulder. "Bad habit that is."

Theodore sighed and propped his feet against the mantelpiece when she had gone.

Mrs. Apps was another of the crosses he had to bear. He had never before noticed quite what a bore she was.

His eyes fell upon the bilious yellow wallpaper, and he shuddered. It was no relief to turn his eyes to the coloured enlargement of a photograph of Mrs. Apps's deceased husband, who had too much collar and too little neck. Fond of aspidistras he had been, and by no means averse to beer.

Theodore drew the curtains, but did not turn on the lights. The dusk was merciful to the shortcomings of the room. He dozed in his chair with an unlit pipe in his mouth.

The room was full of shadows and half tones. The lines of it melted into vagueness; the walls seemed to fade. He pictured himself in a country lane at twilight, not in a stuffy, drab room at all.

Out of the shadows came the shadow of Anne.

So clear-cut was his mental impression of her that he could almost see her slim, straight figure, and smell the fragrance of her hair. Her clear, candid eyes seemed to be looking at him from the shadows.

"My dear," he whispered, "My dear."

He closed his eyes, and the shadow of Anne came closer to him.

"There are so many, many things I long to tell you," he murmured.

"How precious you are, how beautiful. How much I love you. Sweet things I could tell you over and over again, and never grow tired of the telling. I have so much of love and devotion to tell you—if only you'd let me tell it."

The shadows gathered, and the dusk deepened. Twilight darkened into night.

Theodore lay in his chair and dreamed.

Pleasant dreams, in which his despised umbrella was changed to a shining sword, and his conservative garb to a coat of armour. And Anne was his Lady Fair.

He did not hear footsteps on the stairs, nor the rattle as the door handle was turned.

Rudely, he was brought back to reality by the voice of Mrs. Apps. "All in darkness, I declare! He can't have gone out, "cos I'd have seen him. Feeling queer, I shouldn't wonder; refusin' good food, and talkin' to hisself."

Theodore came to his feet, blinking as the light was turned on. On the threshold stood Mrs. Apps.

Behind her was Anne.

"A lady to see you, Mr. Wrenn," Mrs. Apps expressed the wrongs of long-suffering landladies who are born to be "put upon" in her tone.

Theodore cried: "Anne!" then, more soberly, said; "Thank you, Mrs. Apps."

The landlady withdrew, decorously leaving the door a little ajar. Theodore closed it, and led Anne to a chair.

"It isn't comfortable, but it's bearable," he stammered. "The other has a bit of the spring sticking through the seat."

Mrs. Apps opened the door a little, and popped her head in at the aperture.

"If you don't mind," she said querulously. "One has to be so particular."

She withdrew again, leaving the door ajar.

"Oh dear!" exclaimed Anne laughing a little. "If I'm to be compromised, I'd rather be compromised behind a closed door."

With an air of determination, Theodore crossed the room and closed the door with a convincingly loud bang. The retreating footsteps of Mrs. Apps on the stairs told them that she had given them up.

Theodore perched on the edge of a chair and feasted his eyes upon Anne.

"Poor man!" she said. "You look terribly uncomfortable."

"I'm not, really. Only those trousers are quite new, and that bit of spring—"

They both laughed.

"Thank you for making me laugh," said Anne. "I didn't expect to when I came."

Her expression changed, and the worried, anxious look came into her eyes. "I came to ask you a question. It's something I'm rather anxious over."

He leaned forward, with a world of sympathy in his eyes. "If I can answer it, I will."

She smiled: "I knew that. You're a dear, Theodore. Only you must promise not to ask me anything at all, simply to answer my question."

"I promise."

She frowned, and the anxious look in her eyes deepened.

"I want to know—it's rather hard to put into words—if someone had stolen a large sum of money, and run away when he was about to be found out, and someone else borrowed enough to pay back the stolen money, and worked hard to repay the loan, but couldn't, could the person who had lent the money do anything to the, to the—"

"The thief," suggested Theodore, as gently as the word permitted.

Anne nodded, her eyes brimming with tears. "Yes, I'm afraid that's the word. The—the thief."

Theodore furrowed his brow. "Has a warrant been issued against the—well, the person who took the money?"

She shook her head. "No. The company he stole from agreed not to prosecute, when they were repaid."

"Then I don't see what the lender can do," decided Theodore. "Except make it hot for the person who borrowed the money."

Some of the worry cleared from Anne's eyes.

"Then that's all right!" she said more cheerfully.

"No," said Theodore decisively. "It isn't all right. Anne, there's a lot behind that question of yours. My dear, won't you tell me, and let me help you?"

Anne stood up, shaking her head.

"I can't do that," she replied.

"But you are worried—a fool could see that."

She looked at him squarely. "I've got to face this worry alone. Goodnight, Theodore."

"But I want to help you."

"You promised to ask nothing," she reminded him.

With a little smile, she took his hand. "But I love you for wanting to help," she said softly.

As they went downstairs, they heard the kitchen door slam, a token of Mrs. Apps's displeasure.

"Don't come with me," said Anne. "I much prefer to go home alone—dear."

Their eyes met and lingered. Theodore leant forward, and for a wonderful, delirious moment their lips touched…

Then the front door opened and shut gently, and she was gone.

Sir Anthony's aim was becoming more than a little erratic. He was beginning to see two birds for every one that flew above him, and nine out of ten times he aimed at the wrong one.

"Sad, very said," confided Harker, the gamekeeper, to the gardener, who had been pressed into service for the afternoon. "He used to be far and away the best shot in the country, and look at him now. Couldn't hit a barn door at fifty paces."

The gamekeeper spoke louder than he had intended, and his master heard him.

"Harker, you're a liar!" he roared. "Couldn't hit a barn door, eh! By heaven, I'll show you!"

He looked round wildly for a target. To the left of the coppice which he was shooting was a meadow in which three prize rams were browsing. Raising his gun to his shoulder, he took aim at the nearest ram.

Barker gasped, and tried to strike up his master's weapon.

"For God's sake don't, sir!" he shouted. "You don't know what you're doing."

"Stand back, you fool! Do you want me to hit you?"

As he spoke, Sir Anthony pulled the trigger. There was a sharp report, and one of the prize rams threw up its heels, kicked, and slumped over, dead. With a witless chuckle, Sir Anthony fired the other barrel, which fortunately went wide. He handed the gun to Harker. "Reload," he ordered briefly.

The gamekeeper shook his head.

"Reload!" Ravenal shouted.

"I won't, sir," said Harker firmly. "Not if you was to sack me on the spot."

Ravenal clenched his fists and took a step forward.

At that moment there was a timely interruption. The butler came hurrying down from the house. "Mr. Wrenn to see you, Sir Anthony," he said, when he came up.

Sir Anthony pulled himself together with an effort. Taking out a silk handkerchief, he wiped his forehead.

"Tell him to come down here," he said.

He turned to the gamekeeper. "It's all right, man, the fun's over. Here, put that ram out of sight behind the hedge. It wouldn't do for Mr. Wrenn to see it."

When Theodore came striding down to the coppice, Ravenal waved his hand.

"Glad to see you, old man! I've got a spare gun down here. You might as well have a shot at a bird when you're here Harker, a gun for Mr. Wrenn."

"I don't shoot," replied Theodore.

Sir Anthony laughed. "That's all right. If you can't hit a barn door, we're on level terms today."

"Please don't insist," said Theodore coldly. "Because I really don't wish to shoot."

"But I do insist. So that's that. You'll take a pot at a bird to please me.""

"No," reported Theodore. "I'm hanged if I will."

"And I'll be hanged if you don't!" Ravenal exclaimed.

Theodore's expression became grim. "If I shot anything, Sir Anthony," he said in a level tone, "it would certainly be you!"

The loud, raucous laughter burst out again.

"What a bloodthirsty little man you've become! All right, let's go up to the house. We can talk over dinner.

"No," said Theodore. "We can't."

"Why on earth not?"

"Because I don't intend to dine with you. I think that a bite of your food would choke me. Now do you understand?"

Sir Anthony glared. "If you're trying to be insulting—"

Theodore shook his head. "Not at all. I'm just telling you how I feel, that's all."

They walked towards the house. In silence they went through the French windows into the library. Sir Anthony poured out a glass of brandy from a decanter which stood on the library table, and filled it up with soda. "No use offering you a drink!"

"No use at all."

They sat down, and for a moment they faced each other in silence. They were summing each other up mentally. As a basis for comparison, each had his mental picture of the other on the day when Sir Anthony had come to seek his cousin's help in the matter of the three women, Diana Marquis, Naomi Dean, and Mrs. Hargreaves.

Since then, Ravenal noted, Theodore's jaw seemed to have become squarer. His shoulders seemed to have filled out. His eyes had a more self-confident expression. He had changed, and the change was immeasurably for the better.

Ravenal, too, had changed. His eyes were blearier and more bloodshot than ever. His complexion was frankly unhealthy. His erect carriage had given place to an ungainly slump. Not a pleasant sight, this wreck of a man.

"I've come to see you," said Theodore in a cold, acid tone, "because I want to know who Salzman is, and in what way he "put on the screw" at your direction. And who "Ronnie" is."

Sir Anthony's eyes wore a sneering expression, and his lips twisted.

"You want to know a lot. Why don't you ask Anne?"

"I'm asking you."

Ravenal laughed contemptuously, and gulped a mouthful of brandy-and-soda.

"What if I refuse to tell you?"

"In that case," retorted Theodore grimly, "I'll wring the truth out of you, if I kill you in doing it."

"If I didn't want you to know," snarled Ravenal, "it would take more than a shrimp like you to make me tell you. But you might as well know. Anne's brother is a thief. How do you like that, eh? A low, dirty thief. Couldn't keep his hands from sticking to other people's money—"

Theodore clenched his fists. "That's quite enough of that."

Ravenal sneered, "Cuts you on the raw, eh? I knew you were soft on Anne."

"We'll leave Anne out of it, too!"

"How can we? She's the whole story. She borrowed from Salzman to pay back what her dear Ronnie stole, and I gave Salzman the money to make sure that she'd marry me."

"You utter skunk!" blazed Theodore. "So, you blackmailed her into agreeing to marry you!"

"Why not? Handy to be able to put on the screw at the right time, eh? Besides, she's lucky that I'm willing to marry her at all. The sister of a thief."

Theodore stood up, with a fierce expression in his face. "You're several stone heavier than I am," he said with awful distinctness. "That gives you some advantage, I suppose. But you're not in condition, and I am. Nothing in this world would please me better than to pound you into a pulp. I'd like to smash at your face, until it resembled nothing human. I'd like to feel my hands at your throat, squeezing the life out of you. If you make one more sneering reference to Anne, I'll do it. If you think I can't, just try me."

Ravenal shivered. There was no doubting the sincerity of Theodore's tone.

"You'd like to marry Anne," he whispered, "but she's going to marry me."

"No," said Theodore. "She isn't."

"There's always, Salzman—"

"I'll deal with Salzman," snapped Theodore. "How much was the loan?"

"With interest it amounts to five thousand pounds—a staggering amount for a clerk, my dear Theodore."

Theodore stood up.

"I'd kill you, if it was worthwhile," he said. "But it isn't. I'll leave you alone to kill yourself. It won't be long, at the rate you're going. Women and drink have finished off better men than you, and they'll get you—there's nothing surer."

Sir Anthony shivered again. "What do you mean?" he asked in a hoarse whisper.

"Remember Hugo, Mark, and your own namesake, Anthony," Theodore said. "And the Grey House in which they ended their days."

Sir Anthony did not hear the door shutting upon his cousin. He was shivering like a man in the grip of the ague.

He rose trembling to his feet, and crossed the room to the mirror that hung above the fireplace. He looked at the face, haggard and colourless, which stared at him from the mirror, and a hoarse scream rose in his throat.

Hugo, Mark and Anthony Ravenal were his ancestors, and their weakness, like his, had been for women and drink. And the Grey House in which they ended their days was in the dark place where the mad are confined.

With a sob, he swallowed the remainder of the contents of his glass. As he looked up, that white, terrified face met his gaze, and seemed to leer at him horribly. He seized a brass, candlestick from the mantelpiece, and smashed the mirror.

Samuel Marbury, manager of the Westminster branch of a famous bank, prided himself on knowing all that there was to know about the characters and private lives of most of his clients, and Theodore Wrenn was a favourite. For twelve years he had been a customer of the bank, and Mr. Marbury had taken an interest in watching the slow but sure progress of Theodore's fortunes. Thrifty, cautious, and eminently respectable, Theodore was a man after the bank manager's own heart. Of all his clients, he felt that he knew Theodore's character most intimately.

He was therefore pleased when Theodore was ushered into his private office at ten minutes past 10 on the morning after his visit to Ravenal. There was an unpleasant surprise in store for him, however.

Ignoring the customary preliminaries, Theodore laid a paper upon Marbury's desk and commenced to explain the business which had brought him to the bank.

"That is a list of the securities you are holding on my behalf," he said, "I want you to tell me, if possible, the exact sum they will realise at the moment,"

Marbury waved Theodore to a chair, carefully adjusted his pince-nez, and ran his eyes down the list of gratifying sound securities.

"With three or four weeks to dispose of them," he said at last in his dry, precise voice, "it will be possible to sell them all at par, or possibly a little above par."

"We haven't got three weeks to dispose of them," replied Theodore quietly. "I must sell them at once—today."

Mr. Marbury started, and looked up sharply. "My dear Wrenn, this is unusual, and, if we may say so, very unwise.

With so little notice, they would probably have to be sold at quite an appreciable loss."

Theodore nodded. "I realise that. Unfortunately, I need the money at once!"

The manager drummed on his desk-top with his fingers.

"One of our clients has requested us to assist him in the choice of certain sound securities. These are all excellent investments. We, think it exceedingly likely that he will be interested in them."

"And the price?"

Mr. Marbury made a quick pencilled calculation. "Roughly four thousand, four-hundred pounds. Less than you might receive if there were more time at your disposal, but a reasonable figure nevertheless."

Theodore rose. "Very well. If your client will take them at that figure, I'll accept. It's less than I require, but I can borrow on my endowment policy."

The bank manager looked pained. "If we might offer our advice—"

"I'm afraid," said Theodore, picking up his hat and gloves. "I'm afraid that my mind is quite made up."

A little piqued, Mr. Marbury bowed his client out.

"Now what," thought Mr. Marbury irritably, "has changed Wrenn? I had always considered him sound, reliable, and cautious. Cautious above all. Is there a woman? On second thoughts, no. Wrenn's not the type at all. Gambling—hardly. Speculation—he said not."

Then the bank manager remembered the recent death of Theodore's employer, and an unpleasant thought occurred to him. Now that the old lawyer was dead, there would necessarily be a strict examination of his accounts—and Theodore had virtually been in control of the office for several years. Could it be that he had been systematically embezzling funds, and that this large sum was required to cover a shortage? It seemed unlikely, and yet Mr. Marbury shook his head doubtfully.

From there Theodore went straight to the offices of his insurance company, and arranged a loan of six hundred pounds on the security of his endowment policy, and by 2 o'clock he was in possession of a certified cheque for five thousand pounds. At 10 minutes past 2 he was ushered into the private office of Bernard Salzman, a short, thin individual with a sallow complexion and a repulsive oiliness of manner, whose occupation was announced briefly upon the glass door of his outer office as that of 'Business Agent'.

As he scanned Theodore's card, his expression, genial and bland, masked his true feelings. Theodore was a lawyer, and he did not like to do business with lawyers—they knew too much.

"I have called on behalf of Miss Wilding," said Theodore quietly.

Salzman's eyes were glassy and expressionless. "Yeth?"

"She owes you £5000?""

"Yeth?"

"If you have her promissory note at hand, I will pay you the money and close the transaction."

Salzman blinked. "You have the money?" he demanded.

Theodore produced the certified cheque and laid it upon the money lender's desk.

Salzman looked at it and nodded. "Yeth?"

He went behind a screen, to his safe. The screen was a protection against a certain unscrupulous type of person who might not be averse to attempting to read the combination of the safe over his shoulder.

In a moment or two he returned, handed Theodore Anne's note, and took the cheque in exchange.

Theodore satisfied himself that the note was in order, put on his hat, and pocketed his gloves.

"If I can be of servith at any other time," remarked, Salzman suavely, "I shall be only too pleathed."

"You will greatly oblige me," replied Theodore calmly, "if you will be good enough to stand up for a moment."

Blinking in a surprised manner, the moneylender complied. Theodore's fist lashed out and gave the man a terrific smack on the point of the jaw. With an expression of injured amazement, Salzman collapsed like a pricked balloon. In falling, his head struck the screen in front of the safe, which toppled forward; and buried him.

"That, Mr. Bernard Salzman," said Theodore calmly, "that is for putting on the screw."

He went quietly out of the man's private room, through the outer office, smiling in a quiet, friendly way to the clerks, and typist who sat there and made his way sedately downstairs. He derived a certain satisfaction from the reflection that for at least a week the oily-mannered Mr. Salzman would look less prepossessing than ever.

At his own office, he put Anne's note in a plain envelope, addressed it to her, sealed it, and sent the office boy out to register and post it. There was nothing inside the envelope or out to indicate who had sent it. Anne, he hoped, would receive it next morning as a special dispensation of providence.

He hoped that the way would now be clear for her to do what she should long ago have done; break off her engagement to his cousin. He had now no doubts that drink and dissipation had driven Ravenal mad, and in any case, sane or insane, Ravenal was no husband for her. At best he was a scoundrel, and a beast.

With a sigh, he wrote a letter to the trustees of Daniel Gentry, stating briefly that he would not be able to buy the business, and a second letter somewhat longer, to his friend Millar, who would be deeply disappointed. He left the office that night in a contented frame of mind. Certainly, he had by his action, ruined his own career; but in doing so, he had made a supreme sacrifice to the woman he loved. His career meant nothing, compared with her happiness.

Chelsea did not lie in the direction of his usual homeward route, but that evening, he found himself in Cheyne Walk a little after 6 o'clock. He had been drawn there, as though by a magnet.

Outside Anne's studio, he stood looking up at the blue-curtained windows.

In a house nearby, someone was playing a piano. Someone who could play. He recognised the tune. Lebensraum. The music was in harmony with his mood. It found its way soothingly to his soul.

"Goodbye," he whispered to the blue-curtained window, "Goodbye."

What else could he say? He was a clerk, without a future, without even the certainty, of keeping his situation, since the firm would soon be sold. Six months from now he might be out of work, tramping the streets with worn, broken shoes; or seated on a high stool adding up figures, and copying deeds for three or four pounds a week.

He had sacrificed his future—for love.

So, he whispered, "Goodbye." What else could he say?

As he turned away with a little lump in his throat," he stumbled against a woman who had come swiftly, down the street. Raising his hat, he muttered an apology. Then he recognised her as Anne's maid. She had been shopping, and her arms were loaded with parcels.

She said: "Good evening, sir. Did you wish to see Miss Wilding?"

Theodore shook his head. "No," he replied, "that is— "

"She isn't in, sir. She went away half an hour ago in her car. Going to see Sir Anthony Ravenal, she said, at Gay Ladies. She didn't expect to be back tonight. Sleeping with friends at Southampton, she said, sir."

Theodore heard his own voice, hollow and dry, speaking, it seemed, at a great distance.

"Going to Gay Ladies." he repeated dully.

"Yes, sir."

His brain repeated the message again. Anne was going to Gay Ladies, and Sir Anthony Ravenal in his present mood was little better than a lunatic!

CHAPTER 20

As Anne Wilding's little blue two-seater drew up on the terrace in front of Gay Ladies, the door opened and Dodds, the butler, stood on the threshold looking out. His aged, benevolent face assumed an expression of consternation when be recognised Anne.

He hurried down the steps and opened the door of the little car. "I shouldn't come in, if I were you, Miss Wilding, ma'am," he quavered. "I really shouldn't, Sir Anthony—" his voice faltered.

A glance over his shoulder reassured him that the lighted hall was empty. "He's been rather—rather awkward since he returned, ma'am," he continued tremulously. "Not himself at all. He's—he's been upset. I really—really shouldn't advise you to come in."

Anne felt that the time had arrived to call a spade a spade. "I suppose you mean that he hasn't drawn a sober breath for days?" she said steadily,

A worried frown furrowed the old man's brow. Loyal to the core, he had done his best to conceal his master's weakness, although, heart and soul, he was contemptuous of it.

"I'm afraid—very much afraid, that you are right, ma'am," he replied in a low tone.

She walked up the steps. Dodds followed, his hands clasped, and his fingers twining nervously. "I assure you, ma'am, you had much better not come in. He's—he's in one of his moods."

Anne shrugged her shoulders, "I simply must see him, so I must put up with his moods."

The heads of half a dozen large pink roses were lying upon the hall Carpet. Anne stooped, picked one up, and gave the butler a questioning look.

"Sir Anthony?"

He nodded hopelessly. "Sir Anthony took a queer turn earlier in the evening, ma'am. He took a peculiar dislike to flowers. Went about with a cutlass, slashing their heads off ma'am. He did irreparable damage in the greenhouse before his mood changed."

Anne laughed nervously. "He must be mad," she exclaimed.

Dodds nodded his head. "I'm afraid so miss. Quite—quite mad. There is an—er—and unfortunate trait in the family, and prolonged drinking always brings it out in him."

"Where is Sir Anthony?"

"In the library ma'am. But I assure you—"

The library door opened, and Ravenal appeared on the threshold, with a cutlass in his hand, swaying from side to side. He failed to notice Anne.

"Dodds," he cried harshly. "I sent you half an hour ago to refill that decanter. Where is it?"

Anne walked forward calmly. "You've had quite enough to drink," she said.

Sir Anthony blinked, and focussed his bloodshot blue eyes upon her. For a moment he looked at her like a stuffed owl. Then he grinned, and walked forward with a swaying gait.

"Anne! Of all pe-pe-people! Splendid!"

He would have touched her but the contempt in her eyes struck home and he blundered back a pace or two.

"I've come down to see you," said Anne. "There quite a lot to be said."

He gestured clumsily towards the open door of the library.

"We can have a q-quiet chat in here," he replied. "Dodds, bring that decanter!"

Anne shook her head. "Dodds will do nothing of the sort," she said scornfully. "When a man has already drunk more than he can carry like a gentleman, to continue merely makes him more like a pig. It won't take long to say what must be said—after that, you can drink yourself unconscious."

Ravenal's complexion became purple, but he followed her into the library, and closed the door. For a moment, he stood before the fireplace, swinging his cutlass, then he plunged it into the upholstery of an armchair. The hair stuffing bulged out. Ravenal laughed uproariously.

Anne's quiet voice struck him, with the sting of a whiplash. "I've disturbed your game," she said scornfully. "You were playing at Pirates, weren't you? I'm so sorry."

Leaving the cutlass stuck in the chair, Ravenal lurched heavily to another. "Don't be so sarcastic," he growled. "I hate women who are sar-sarcastic. After we're married—"

Anne looked down at his sprawling figure contemptuously. "We never will be married," she said slowly and distinctly. "Please understand that. Nothing would persuade me to marry you." She laid a package upon the arm of his chair. "Your ring is in this, and your letters, and everything you have given me."

Ravenal looked at her owlishly, scarcely comprehending. "Cool! Dashed Cool!" he exclaimed.

Her eyes expressed a great loathing for him. "When you proposed to me," she continued, in an even tone, "I was perfectly honest with you. I told you that I didn't love you. You said that it didn't matter, that love would come. I was less sure of that, and told you so, but you were insistent. I went even further, and admitted that I was almost desperate over money, and said frankly that otherwise I should not have considered your proposal. Still, you were insistent. We made a bargain. A despicable bargain. I have never ceased to be ashamed of it. But I had to accept. There was a reason."

"You didn't tell me the reason."

"Why should I? That was no part of our bargain. But you

found out, somehow. You taunted me with it once."

He laughed, a laugh in which there was no genuine mirth. "Of course, I knew. It was to my advantage to know. Your darling brother, Ronnie. He was the reason. The worthless, good-for-nothing thief."

Her eyes lit up with fury, but her self-control was perfect, and she restrained herself. "We will leave Ronnie out of this."

He nodded slyly: "Certainly, my dear. He wasn't expressly mentioned in the bargain. A damned good bargain for you, my dear. You were to marry me, and in return, I was to give you five thousand pounds. You set a high price upon yourself. A damned good bargain."

"A shameful bargain," she blazed, "a despicable bargain."

He eyed her craftily. "But having made it, my dear, you will keep it."

"No," she retorted. "I won't. I owe you nothing. I have a perfect right to withdraw."

"But what about the man who lent you the money to square Ronnie's little theft? How will you repay him?"

"I'll manage somehow. I'll work day and night until I've paid him. He'll have to wait for his money, but he'll get it—every penny of it."

"He won't wait," said Ravenal.

"How do you know?"

"Because I will give him his orders. That money came from me, my dear."

"From you?" she gasped.

"Of course. You don't suppose that moneylender's part with large sums of money without security, do you? They must have their pound of flesh my dear. I gave them the money—and you were my pound of flesh.

"If you go back on our bargain, I'll put on the screw. You'll realise the hell it can be to owe what you can't pay. You'll have a taste of Courts. I'll strip you of everything you own, and every penny you earn. You'll realise what poverty is, and hopelessness. Better think it over."

She squared her shoulders, and looked at him with flashing eyes. "Do anything you please," she retorted. "Nothing will ever persuade me to marry you."

"You were willing enough to marry me at one time—"

"Don't remind me of it," she cried. "The shame is mine."

"Why have you changed your mind?"

She looked at him squarely. "I've swallowed my pride," she said. "I've expressed my feelings; I've accepted my shame, but it is beyond me to swallow your essential beastliness."

His expression was fury incarnate. "Are you sure," he retorted, speaking with an effort, "are you quite sure that my dear cousin Theodore has had no hand in this?"

"That is the sort of suggestion I should expect from you!"

"You love him!"

She did not reply, but a momentary change in the expression of her eyes spoke volumes.

"You do love him!" he cried.

"He has made me see my soul, and it's shame," she replied shakily. "He is all man—just as you are all beast!" She turned towards the door.

"Don't go!" he snapped.

"I've said what I came to say," she replied. "Now I'm going."

With amazing quickness, he heaved himself out of his chair, and moved to the door, blocking her way.

"Let me pass!" she exclaimed.

He shook his head. "No; you'll stay here."

She backed away, her hands involuntarily clutching at her bosom.

He advanced steadily, with his blood-shot eyes fixed on her white face. His arms reached out toward her.

She could retreat no further. A chair was behind her. Instinctively, her hand clutched the arm of the chair. Her fingers touched something smooth and hard—the handle of the cutlass.

Scarcely knowing what she was doing, she grabbed the cutlass, and held it before her.

The point of the gleaming blade pressed against the resistant surface of Ravenal's starched white shirt.

"Back!" she cried. "Back! Or I'll kill you."

He hesitated, and retreated a step.

Still holding the cutlass, she attempted to pass him, and gain to the door.

Ravenal clutched at her, and to save herself she swung the glittering blade. It hit into his forehead. A stream of blood trickled down his brow and into his eyes.

Blinded he stepped back, blundered against a chair, and fell heavily to the floor.

With a cry, Anne dropped the cutlass, and darted to the door.

With unseeing eyes, Anne stumbled out of the library into the hall. She would have fallen had not Dodds caught her as she swayed.

"What has he done to you, miss!" he cried. "What has he done to you?" His expression was worried and anxious, and his tone was strained.

Anne passed a limp hand across her pale forehead. "I've wounded him," she gasped. "We quarrelled and he—I had to defend myself. I wounded him—with the cutlass—perhaps—perhaps I've killed him."

She stood up straight, to the relief of the old butler, who had feared that she was badly hurt.

"A good job, too, miss, if you have killed him," he declared fiercely. "But his sort doesn't die easily. Most likely he's only scratched."

Anne turned back reluctantly towards the library door. "I—I'd better go and see."

Dodds put a gnarled, withered hand upon her arm. "Not you, miss. This is my job. I'll go."

Gently, he guided her to a chair. Squaring his shoulders with a pathetic air of determination, he went into the library.

While he was gone Anne waited with bated breath, hoping against hope that Ravenal was not seriously hurt. She detested, loathed, despised him; but to kill or seriously wound him was not her wish. The moments went slowly. Scarcely a minute had elapsed before the aged servitor returned, but the brief lapse of time seemed interminable. At last, he came out of the library with the key in his hand and locked the door behind him.

An involuntary gasp escaped Anne when she saw that there was blood on one of his hands.

Dodds looked at the stain and smiled wryly. "He hasn't lost much of that, miss," he told her, in a soothing tone. "He could have lost a lot more, and come to no harm. The wound is only a scratch, miss, just a little scratch. He's stunned—hit his head on something, I suppose—but there's nothing much wrong with him. The drink more than anything else. He'll be all right directly."

Anne sighed with relief; she had gone through a brief but tense period of anxiety.

"You'd better go now miss," the butler urged. "I've locked the library door, but Sir Anthony will be a fair demon when he comes round."

She nodded: "All right."

As they went down the front steps to her car, they heard a shuffling, scraping sound from the direction of the library. They listened. It was repeated, then followed by a vicious, urgent rattling on the handle of the library door.

The butler's hand quivered. "He's come round already," he gasped. "Get away, miss, while the door holds."

Anne climbed into the car and pressed on the self-starter. As the engine came to life with a roar, they heard a furious pounding—Sir Anthony, was using a chair upon the panels of the library door.

Crash! Crash! Crash!

It seemed as though each blow would make it unnecessary for another to be struck. They were savage blows, dealt by an infuriated man who was more like an angry beast than a human being.

"Go! Please go!" the butler pleaded.

Anne leant out of the car. "He'll take his rage out of you!" she exclaimed.

Dodds shook his head. "It's you he's after! For heaven's sake, get away!"

Reluctantly, she put the car into gear, released the clutch, accelerated, and drove off towards the gates.

As the car moved away, there was a deafening crash. Sir Anthony, reckless of consequences, had taken a blundering run at one of the long widows of the library, and bad dived through in a shower of splintered glass.

With a roar of fury, he came round the corner of the house in time to see the tail light of Anne's car disappearing down the drive.

He turned on the butler. "Why didn't you let me out of that room?" he raged.

Before Dodds could reply, Ravenal struck him a brutal, vicious blow on the jaw. The old man dropped to his knees, and crumpled forward, unconscious, on the gravelled terrace.

Without a glance, Ravenal ran heavily past the limp body, towards the garage. The doors were locked, but he battered in a window with a large stone, clambered through, and opened them from the inside.

He chose the faster of his two cars and the beautiful engine sprang quivering to life at his first jab at the starter. Without ceremony, he crashed in the gears, and literally jumped the big car off the mark. It went roaring down the drive at 80 miles an hour in first gear.

Anne had reached the gates at too fast a speed, and had found it impossible to swing on to the road heading towards London. Barely missing a gate post, she had swerved to the left, and faced in the opposite direction. Her principal concern, however, was to get as far as possible from Gay Ladies, and she continued to drive, oblivious to all else.

At the foot of the driveway, Ravenal, who had noticed the direction in which she had gone, applied his brakes harshly, and skidded round in to the road in the same direction. He snicked the gear lever across to engage second gear, pressed the accelerator down as far as it would go, and the big car roared down the road in pursuit of the bobbing rear-light some three hundred yards in front.

The pursuit would have been over almost as quickly as it began had not the narrow, winding road made it impossible for Ravenal to push the car to the 90 miles an hour of which it was capable.

As it was, the speedometer needle on the big car jumped from 50 to 70 miles an hour, dropped back to 65, dropped back again, and settled at 60 miles an hour along a road full of potholes, awkward turns, and treacherous bends.

With the powerful headlights of the pursuing car sending out twin beacons to warn her on, Anne drove her little two-seater with grim determination. Naturally fearless, she threw caution to the winds, rocked, swayed, and skidded round corners at a suicidal speed. Grimly, remorselessly, the white beams of light crept nearer. She almost stood on the accelerator and used her brakes to help her steering at corners.

The road became narrower. It wound and twisted along the side of the hill. On one side it was bounded by a stout blackthorn hedge, and on the other side, protected only by a flimsy wooden fence, by a sheer drop of a hundred and fifty feet.

The speed of the racing cars slackened.

Even a drunken maniac like the fiend who drove the limousine did not dare to do more than reckless 45 miles an hour along this narrow death trap of a road. Anne, terror-stricken as her car slid and slithered and skidded, saw the lights of the pursuing car coming nearer and nearer, and desperately accelerated too fast at a corner, with the result that the near side mudguard struck the trail wooden fence, and was crumpled like card board. It took all of her strength to straighten the car after the impact and hold it to the road, and an additional hazard had resulted—her lamps fused, and she was forced to drive on at suicidal speed without lights.

Behind, Ravenal skidded round the corner, looked for the bobbing tail light which should have been less than a hundred yards in front, failed to see it, and with a muffled oath, stepped on the accelerator.

With a lurch and a roar, the car shot forward. Forty-five, fifty-five, sixty frantic miles an hour. Swaying, bucking and bumping like a mad thing, the big car hummed to destruction with a drink-crazed lunatic at the wheel.

The pace was too hot to last. On such a road, at such a speed, disaster was inevitable.

Looking back, Anne saw what must happen. Icy fingers plucked at her heart. To delay what must come, she urged yet more speed out of her engine.

Her eyes travelled desperately from side to side. She was looking instinctively for a place in the hedge into which she might swerve with a chance of escaping the worst of the consequences.

At a few yards' distance, everything was a curtain of black. Had she not known the road well, she must long ago have been over the precipice. As it was, she could not expect the little car to hold the road much longer.

The inevitable came.

Speeding crazily, his eyes searching for nothing but the tail light in front, which had so suddenly and mysteriously disappeared, Ravenal perceived a moving shape in the gloom—Anne's car—scarcely 15 yards away. Why he had not made it out before he could not have explained. At the moment he could have explained nothing. His brain was fogged and bemused. His head felt like a jungle of red-hot wires. There was a crazy hum in it urging him on, without rhyme or reason.

Instead of jamming on his brakes, he held his car to its mad speed. It came nearer and nearer to the one in front.

Looking back, Anne saw the headlight glare just behind. She heard the growl of the engine, like a furious beast, threatening her with annihilation.

A moment of terrified horror, then the crash came.

Her little car started and shuddered as the limousine struck it in the rear with all the force of frantic speed. It swerved, and the steering wheel was wrenched from her hands, as though by giant fingers.

She closed her eyes, and her lips moved silently in prayer. There was a roar in her ears as her car plunged off the road.

CHAPTER 22

Anne's maid shook Theodore's arm.

"What's the matter, sir?" she asked in a frightened tone; "you look queer."

Theodore looked down at her, and forced a wan smile. "I'm quite all right. It's—It's nothing."

He raised his hat, and walked away a little unsteadily. The girl watched him go with a puzzled expression in her eyes.

"He isn't drunk, I hope," she thought vaguely. "A nice, quiet spoken gentleman like that, and so early in the evening, too. He seemed to come all over queer when I told him Miss Wilding had gone to Gay Ladies."

The news had come to Theodore as an unpleasant shock. Anne had gone to Gay Ladies!

She had gone in her car at half past five, and could not possibly arrive at her destination before nine o'clock. And for weeks, Sir Anthony had not been sober at that hour. Worse, the steady drinking which had been his daily habit lately was bringing out in him the Ravenal curse—the curse of insanity!

It was not pleasant to think of Anne alone at the mercy of Ravenal when he was in such a condition. There was no limit to the brutalities which his drink-crazed mind might suggest.

Making up his mind quickly, Theodore hailed a taxi, and was driven to Euston Station. There he inquired about trains for Dorcombe. There was none for several hours, and it was fully two hours before one would leave for Southampton, which was thirty miles from Dorcombe.

He went out of the station in a considerable state of anxiety, and found his taxi driver looking for him in a distinctly unpleasant mood.

"'Ee, wot abaht my money?" that worthy demanded. "Cough up, or I'll call a cop."

Theodore looked at him vaguely. "Your money!" he repeated. "Of course, I forgot to pay you. I'm sorry. Will five shillings cover it?"

Five shillings more than covered it. The taxi-driver expressed his satisfaction. Theodore started to walk away; then returned suddenly and clutched the man's arm.

"Can you drive me down to Hampshire?" he demanded.

The taxi-driver blinked and nodded. "If the fare's big enough."

"How much do you want?" Theodore asked.

The other pushed back his cap and frankly sized up his prospective fare. "A shilling a mile," he ventured at last.

"All right. I want to go to Dorcombe—it's about 20 miles from Southampton."

The taxi-driver was a man of few words. He opened the door of his taxi and jerked his thumb towards the interior.

"Get in, sir," he said. "I'd drive you to Hades for a shilling a mile."

He was almost as good as his word. With a long journey before him, and darkness fast approaching, he put on speed; and the taxi was not built for speed. It swayed perilously, and threatened to capsize at the corners. One or two narrow shaves as they passed other cars made Theodore's scalp tingle, but he made no protest. Nothing mattered except that they get to Gay Ladies as soon as possible.

At Dorcombe, Theodore took the seat beside the driver, and directed him for the rest of the journey. His anxiety had grown with every mile of the long drive from London. One hope was in his mind—to reach Gay Ladies, and to find Anne safe.

It was dark when they turned in at the gates of his cousin's house at last. He strained his eyes trying to see Anne's car on the terrace, but it was not there. Perhaps she had changed her mind and come on further than Southampton, he thought—without much hope, however. Perhaps she had seen his cousin and already left the house safely. Perhaps—oh, anything might have happened.

He jumped out of the taxi as it lumbered to a halt, ran up the steps to the door, and rang the bell furiously. The house was silent, although he could see through the glass panels of the door that the hall was brilliantly lit.

He rang again—and again. Still silence—a silence that filled him with a sense of foreboding. A heavy, ominous silence. He had the feeling that someone was in the hall; someone who listened to his frantic ringing but did not stir. At last, he abandoned the front door and walked round the house looking for another means of entry. At the rear of the house, he found the lawn littered with shattered glass—and the paneless library window.

He climbed in at the window, and noted with an anxious quiver the blood-stained cutlass which lay upon the carpet. It was enough to confirm his worst forebodings. Anne had been here, and something terrible had happened. Something terrible—

The library door was locked, and he pounded upon it savagely.

There was a faint rustling in the hall.

"Open the door."

"Open the door!" he cried loudly.

Silence. He pounded upon the door again. "Who's there!" he shouted. "Open the door."

He heard a footstep. The key turned in the lock, and the door swung open. Dodds, the old butler, looker in nervously.

"It's you, Master Theodore," he quavered. "Thank God! I was afraid—"

His legs seemed to go from under him. Theodore caught the old man as he collapsed and guided him to a chair.

Some moments passed before Dodds could speak, then his story came jerkily and incoherently.

"I asked her not to see him, sir. I begged her to go away. He was in a mad, devilish mood. He's been terrible lately, sir. You know what he's like."

"What happened?" Theodore demanded hoarsely.

The old man shivered. "She would see him sir, and they had words. He attacked her, I think, and she wounded him in the forehead with the cutlass. At first she thought she had killed him—"

"I wish she had!" exclaimed Theodore vehemently.

"But he was only stunned. I locked him in the library, but before she had got away in her car, he had escaped through the window. He followed her in his. That's all I know. I shudder to think what may have happened, sir."

Theodore could visualise the possibilities, and he shuddered, too.

"How long ago did this happen?" he demanded.

Dodds tried desperately to think. "Not long, sir. About five or ten minutes, I think. It seems longer, but then, I've been on tenterhooks all the time."

Without further ado, Theodore hastened into the ball, opened the front door, and hurried down the steps. He brushed past the taxi-driver who was beginning to be anxious about his money without noticing him, climbed into the driving seat of the taxi, and drove off. At the gates, he stopped, got out, and examined the marks on the road which showed him which way the cars had taken.

As he returned to the driving seat, the cabman came hurrying up.

"Hi!" he cried. "Wot the dickens are you up to? Wot's the game, hey!"

"I can't explain now," said Theodore hoarsely, "but if you'll get in beside me, you'll know all about it soon."

The taxi driver was inclined to argue, but gripping his shoulder firmly, Theodore yanked him into the taxi, manipulated the gear-lever, and drove off quickly.

"You didn't ought to do this!" grumbled the taxi-driver. "It's against the law, that's what it is. Stealing a man's cab, an doin' him out of his fare. You can get gaol for this!"

Theodore was driving the vehicle as fast as it would go."

"If you'll only, shut up," he shouted impatiently, "You'll get your money and your cab." Fear was clutching at his heart. It drove him on madly, at an insane speed.

The taxi driver complained incessantly: "You didn't ought to do this. It's against the law, that's what!"

Theodore paid no attention to the man's grumbling. With his foot jamming the accelerator down as far as it would go, all his attention was devoted to keeping the swaying, lumbering vehicle on the road.

Corners were taken on two wheels, and more than once he narrowly missed the ditch which bounded one side of the road.

The engine was wheezing and grunting as though every revolution would be its last.

"You didn't ought to do this!"

The car swerved suddenly, as Theodore, cornering rapidly, just scraped a tree trunk.

"For heaven's sake shut up!" he cried.

Now they were on the part of the road which wound round the side of the hill. Looking out, the taxi driver saw the sheer drop which awaited them if a wheel went close to the side of the road. He clutched desperately at the steering-wheel.

"Slow down!" he cried. "You'll kill us both if you don't."

With one hand, Theodore pushed him back roughly.

He pushed rather harder than he intended, and with a wild yell, the taxi driver fell out, and sprawled helplessly at the side of the road. Theodore slowed down and looked back. He saw the man rising slowly to his feet. With a sigh of relief, he accelerated again.

A few hundred yards farther on the beam of the headlights showed him that a motor-wheel was lying in the middle of the road. He jammed on the brakes and skidded to a halt.

Jumping out, he examined the wheel. With a sinking feeling he recognised it as belonging to Anne's little two-seater.

There was a skid mark across the surface of the road, and about twenty feet of the flimsy fencing at the edge of the cliff was smashed away.

Gulping back a desperate sob, Theodore ran to a gap in the fence and peered down. A hundred and fifty feet below he saw the blazing wreck of a car, which was sending up long tongues of flame.

Not fifteen feet from the roaring inferno Anne lay upon her face with her arms sprawled out lifelessly.

CHAPTER 23

Twenty yards along the road, Theodore found a path which led down the precipitous hillside. Near this path, and on the other side of the road, he saw a car which had crashed into the hedge. It was Anne's car—buried for half its length in ditch and hedge.

With something between a sob and a sigh, he realised that, whatever had happened, it was not Anne's car which had gone over the cliff.

Fear plucked at his heart, however, as he scrambled down the steep path to the clearing where Anne lay, beside a twisted heap of blazing machinery. From above Anne had looked very frail and lifeless.

The heat and fumes from the flaming car—now unrecognisable as a car—were almost suffocating as Theodore approached. A gaping hole at the back testified to the explosion which had wrecked the petrol tank.

At the end of its wild dash over the cliff the car had landed on its nose, collapsed forward, somersaulted, and come to rest on its four wheels, with tongues of flame already beginning to lick at its coachwork. Now it was a mangled heap of twisted metal and wood and rubber.

Theodore ran to Anne, and knelt by her side. Her face was blackened with smoke, her hands were scorched and her hair was singed.

She was in a dead faint.

Putting his arms under and around her, Theodore managed to lift and carry her twenty yards from the blazing wreck. He laid her gently on the grass, and arranged his jacket under her. Then, pulling off his hat, he ran to search for water. He found a stream, filled his hat, and hurried back. Anne still lay as he had left her, and there was a tortured frown on her brow. Gently he bathed her forehead and moistened her lips with water. She moaned, and moved a little, but did not open her eyes. He took her hands and rubbed them gently.

How little she looked, how pathetically frail!

Her expression was that of a tired, frightened child. Something tugged at his heartstrings as he bent over and kissed her lips tenderly.

"My dear," he murmured. "My dear."

Anne moved a little, and her eyelids quivered but did not open. A little of the colour seemed to return to her wan cheeks.

Theodore slipped his arm round her shoulders and raised her head tenderly.

He touched her cheek with his lips, and as he did so, her eyes opened. She started up at him with a puzzled expression, then her eyes brightened, and her lips framed the word "Theodore."

Almost simultaneously, her expression darkened, and she clutched at Theodore's shoulders convulsively.

"Don't let him find me!" she cried. "Don't—"

The roar of the flames attracted her attention. She turned her head and stared frantically at the fury which had been a car.

"Anthony's in there!" she cried suddenly. "He's in the middle of all that! I tried to get him out and failed. My hands hurt so, and he was unconscious. I couldn't move him."

She stared into Theodore's eye, and shook him vigorously.

"Do you hear? Do you hear? Anthony's in there: In that furnace!"

Theodore stroked her forehead gently.

"He doesn't feel it," he murmured soothingly. "He never felt it. God was merciful. He died at once, Anne, and this is his Viking's funeral."

The tortured expression faded from Anne's eyes. "Dead!" she murmured. "Poor, poor, Anthony!"

Remembering what had happened so recently, she shivered.

Now it was all over; and Anthony poor, mad Anthony—was dead!

"It was for the best," said Theodore gently. "A nightmare was pursuing him. The nightmare of a hereditary failing, and a Grey House. He has escaped that doom."

A voice hailed them from the road. Looking up, Theodore saw a hand waving a motor lamp about.

"Come down here!" he shouted, cupping his hands.

The motor lamp disappeared, and a few moments later he saw the taxi driver, whom he had completely forgotten, coming stumbling down the path.

The taxi driver firmly believed that Theodore was to blame for the blazing wreck, for the smashed car in the ditch on the road above, and for Anne's weak condition.

"I knoo something terrible would 'appen in the end," he said accusingly, when his startled gaze had transmitted the amazing features of the scene to his mind. "I knoo it. Askin' for it, that's what you were. Stealin' a man"s cab, and drivin' it reckless like that. You didn't ought to have done it."

"Don't be a fool," retorted Theodore irritably. "Your cab's all right."

"Yes," said the driver, "yes, me cab"s all right" His eye wandered from the white face of Anne to the twisted ruins of Ravenal's car, and he said, "But what price this little lot?"

"This," replied Theodore, "is what I was trying to prevent."

A world of suspicion dwelt in the eye which the taxi driver cocked at Theodore.

"Ho!" he snorted, disbelievingly. "Ho! Well, it's my opinion that this wouldn't 'ave 'appened if you 'adn"t tried to prevent it.

I knoo you'd commit suicide or murder, the way you was goin'. Mad, that's what you was."

"Instead of talking like a fool," snapped Theodore icily, "don't you think you could help me to carry this lady up to the road?"

The driver stared at Anne. Her eyes, filled with pain, touched him. He put a grubby finger to his cap.

"Don't you worry, ma'am!" he declared. "We'll 'ave you out of this in a jiffy. Now then, sir, tell me what to do and I'll do it."

Supporting Anne on each side, they managed to carry her up the rough path to the road and placed her in the taxi.

Theodore gave certain directions to the driver, then climbed in beside Anne and put his arm round her. She smiled tremulously at him and murmured something which was inaudible.

She closed her eyes, the lines of her tired face relaxed, and her head dropped back on his shoulder.

She had fainted again.

Theodore tapped on the dividing with his free hand.

"As fast as you can go!" he cried. "The lady has fainted!"

The driver started up his cab, climbed in, and responded to Theodore's appeal with a respectable turn of speed. They jogged and jolted along the winding cliff road for a few miles to where the road rejoined the highway. Two miles further along, the main road brought them to a village.

In a mercifully short time Anne was lying on a couch in a doctor's consulting room, while the medical man bent over her gravely. Then she was put to bed in the spare room of the doctor's house with four hot water bottles grouped round her. She was suffering from nerve strain, shock, and severe burns.

"I'm afraid she's in for a bad illness," said the doctor gloomily.

Theodore suddenly felt a desire for air. He went outside, and found the taxi driver standing beside his cab.

"Wot next?" asked that worthy patiently.

"We'll have to report the accident to the police," replied Theodore mechanically.

He swayed as he spoke and stumbled against the taxi. The driver gripped his arm.

"'Ere, guv'nor," he cried, "'old up, there. 'Ere, sit down for a bit...all-in, that's what you are."

Theodore sat down upon the running board, and wearily supported his head with a grubby hand. He was feeling sick and faint.

The taxi driver left him, and returned in a few minutes with a small glass of brandy.

"'Ere you are, guv'nor, drink this," he commanded. "It'll set you up properly. Fit for anything after, you'll be. Only—" this an effort to cheer Theodore up—"only don't go raisin' Cain anymore."

Theodore winced and bit his lip. The driver touched his hand.

"Sorry, sir," he muttered. "Only trying to amuse you, sir."

Theodore gripped the other man's arm. "You're a good soul," he said.

He rose swaying to his feet "Let's go in and interview the village policeman," he added.

CHAPTER 24

For days Anne Wilding tossed in delirium. She was kept at the house of the kindly doctor, and three or four times every day Theodore was allowed to tiptoe into the room to see her for a few minutes. These visits by no means cheered him, for he found a white haggard invalid whose mind had temporarily ceased to function coherently, and who seemed to be hovering upon the hairbreadth borderline between life and death, but it consoled him to be near her, although she was not conscious of his presence.

Theodore put up at the village inn, and spent his waking hours haunting the doctor's house and wandering about the nearby hills and fields. Until Anne recovered, he was in a state of suspended mental animation.

At times Anne lay still and white, perfectly motionless, with the placid calm of death. At, others, she moaned and struggled in the grip of a nightmare, and her agony was pitiful to watch.

These nightmares began with the obsession that her brother Ronnie, whom she loved passionately, was standing his trial for embezzlement. She could feel the atmosphere of the court, see the stern grim face of the judge, and hear the prosecuting counsel saying "Thief!— Thief!— Thief!" in tones of terrible monotony, which increased in volume until they were deafening.

"Thief! Thief! Thief!"

Then she would start up wildly and cry out: "No, no! He didn't mean to do it! He was weak—not bad. Just weak. He isn't a thief! He isn't! He isn't!"

The face of Bernard Salzman, the moneylender, with eyes heavy-lidded like those of a bird of prey, would follow, and sometimes she confused his cruel face with that of the judge, and fancied that he was passing judgment on Ronnie, and knew that he would find her poor brother guilty.

"No!—no! Don't send him to prison!" she would shriek. "I'll pay! I'll pay! Anything you ask. Only—not that. Not prison for Ronnie."

Her delusion about Ravenal caused her the greatest anguish. She lived over and over that frantic, terrible chase along the side of the hill. The car in which Ravenal pursued her was a flaming furnace, as she had seen it after the crash, and Ravenal, wreathed round with tongues of fire, drove like a devil in a fiery chariot.

Then the awful feeling as the front wheels of his car had crashed into the back of hers, and the grinding noise as it crashed over the precipice; and the unconscious form of Ravenal, as the hungry flames consumed him—

With a wild cry she would lapse into unconsciousness, and lie, white and still, hovering between life and death.

Sometimes Theodore would come into her troubled, tortured mind, and her lips would part in a tremulous, pathetic smile.

"Theodore!" she would whisper.

"Theodore, my dear!"

And then, if Theodore tiptoed into the room and took her thin, limp hand, she would fall into a deep, untroubled sleep, which helped her to weather her days of delirium.

On the fifth day, when Anne was losing strength quickly in the terrible battle, the lawyers of the dead baronet called on Theodore. They found him white and shaken, drifting on a sea of despair, like a ship without an anchor.

They found it difficult to make him understand that he was the new baronet, Sir Theodore Wrenn. He shook his head and begged them to leave him alone.

"But don't you understand?" they insisted, "you inherited the baronetcy on your cousin's death.

Theodore laughed mirthlessly. "That's funny!" he exclaimed.

"What a good story for the papers! Sir Theodore Wrenn, the pauper baronet! The titled clerk!"

Mortimer Fosdyke, the senior partner in the firm of Fosdyke and Loam, glanced at his junior partner with raised eyebrows.

"I'm afraid you don't understand, Sir Theodore," he said smoothly. "Sir Anthony died intestate, and his entire fortune reverts to you, as the next of kin. I congratulate you. After death duties are paid, your inheritance will amount to over a quarter of a million pounds."

Trembling a little, Theodore dropped into a chair.

"A quarter of a million pounds!" he repeated dully.

"Exactly."

It was almost unbelievable.

"A quarter of a million pounds!"

He looked from the silver-haired Fosdyke to the younger, cherubic Loam.

"You really mean it?" he whispered. "It's—it's really true?"

"Absolutely true," Mortimer Fosdyke assured him.

Theodore took a deep breath, and rose slowly to his feet. He went to the door, and as though on second thoughts, turned for a moment before leaving the room:

"Pardon me, please."

As the new baronet went out, Mr. Loam looked at his partner, and tapped his forehead significantly. The older man shook his head.

"He's dazed, that's all," he said. "So would you be, if you inherited a quarter of a million as suddenly as that."

The other nodded.

"I suppose so. But there's no such luck for a poor devil like me."

"I've found out that there is an enormous sum of money at

my disposal," he said. "Is there any way I can use it for Miss Wilding's sake?"

The doctor stroked his chin.

"We can call in a London specialist. The chances are that he could do no more than we are doing, but he might help."

"Very well, will you call in the best man you can get?"

The doctor nodded. "I'll phone at once. But, I say, Wrenn…"

"Yes?"

"Well, doctors can only go so far. We're not miracle-workers, you know. I think well be able to save Miss Wilding, to an extent. Beyond that, the case rests with you. You've seen what you mean to her, how she is soothed when thoughts of you enter those terrible deliriums of hers. She's been through a lot—enough to have killed the average woman. When she's on her feet again, there'll still be a lot to do. That's your job. Look after her, man."

Theodore gripped the doctor's hand convulsively. "I'd give my life for her!" he exclaimed.

A famous specialist was called, and spent two days in the village. On the second day, the delirium that tortured Anne had past. She was ill, and very weak, but conscious. On the third morning the specialist left, and Theodore was allowed to see Anne and talk to her for five minutes.

She was pitifully pleased to see him. Her eyes lit up as he came into the room.

"Theodore! How splendid!" she exclaimed, and a glow suffused her cheeks.

"It's splendid to see you looking so well," murmured Theodore huskily.

A tear fell upon her hand and she saw that his eyes were wet.

"My dear, you're crying! Don't! I'm all right now. I'm going to get well. You mustn't cry."

Theodore wiped his eyes roughly.

"I'm crying for happiness, my dear. Sheer joy! I don't know when I've been so happy. Of course, you're going to be well and strong again, soon. And we're going away. Far away to the sun. To the shores of the Mediterranean, where the sun will warm your blood, and melt your heart"

She looked at him with misty eyes. "Dear Theodore! It sounds like a wonderful dream."

"It isn't a dream. It's all right. We're going to travel and travel for years."

There was a tiny sob in her laugh. "Oh, my dear, have you found the pot of gold at the end of the rainbow? Or a magic carpet, to carry us wherever we wish?"

Theodore blundered. He should have matched her airy fantasy with romancing equally as fantastic. Instead, he blurted out the truth, and could have kicked himself for it afterwards.

"A quarter of a million pounds," he said. "All yours and mine, my dear, to buy us happiness for ever and ever."

Her eyes questioned him. "A quarter of a million pounds!" Then intuition told her the truth. "Ravenal's money?"

His face expressed acute misery. "I didn't mean to remind you, my dear. Forgive me."

She shook her head. "There's nothing to forgive. It doesn't hurt me to think of Ravenal now."

But she remembered, and during the next few days, she thought often of the wealth which Theodore had inherited from Ravenal. And she knew what would be said of her if she married Theodore. That she had been willing to marry Ravenal for his money, and had "hooked" Theodore when the money went to him—

Soon she was able to go home to her studio in Cheyne Walk, and Theodore called there daily, full of his plans for their happiness. But they never quite regained the old intimate footing.

Something was lacking in their comradeship. The dead man's money had come between them.

Anne learned that someone had paid the money which she owed to Bernard Salzman, and she knew that that "someone" was Theodore. Also, she knew what sacrifice it had meant to him at the time. They never spoke of it, but she loved him the more for it. But loving him, and knowing the things which would be said of them, she decided that he and she must never marry.

Theodore was worried about the inquest on Sir Anthony Ravenal. He was afraid that Anne's part in the accident must necessarily be revealed and that a scandal would result. To prevent that, he discussed the matter with Dodds, Sir Anthony's butler, and they agreed upon a story which shielded Anne's name and was more or less merciful to the memory of the dead man.

When called as a witness at the inquest, Dodds explained that Miss Wilding had been calling on her fiancée, his master, and that after she had departed it was discovered that she had left her handbag, containing the latchkey of her London house, behind her. Sir Anthony had followed her to return it. A little later, Mr. Wrenn had called to see Sir Anthony on business, and on being informed of the circumstances had decided to go to meet Sir Anthony, since he wished to see him as soon as possible.

In reply to a question from the coroner, Dodds stated that his master had taken 'a little brandy' that evening.

"He was not intoxicated?" suggested the coroner.

The butler rolled his eyes in a shocked manner. "He had no more than his usual, sir," he replied, from which the coroner concluded that the late baronet had been quite sober when he met his death.

Theodore then gave evidence to the effect that he had discovered Anne's wrecked car at the side of the road, and the blazing limousine at the foot of the cliffs. The headlights of

Miss Wilding's car were on when he found it, he added, but the tail-light had failed. He had examined the bulb and discovered that it was not broken, but burnt out. He had concluded that it had gone out before the accident and that Sir Anthony, failing to see the red tail-light ahead, had driven too fast, with disastrous results.

"Miss Wilding is seriously ill?" asked the coroner.

"Yes, she was badly hurt," agreed Theodore.

"She will not be able to give evidence for some time?"

"Not for months, according to the doctor," replied Theodore, and added: "But if my theory is correct, it is unlikely that she will be able to throw any light on the affair. The accident presumably took place before she realised that Sir Anthony's car was following. Had she known that her fiancé was attempting to overtake her she would naturally have stopped to ascertain his mission, and the tragedy would have been averted."

"Quite," agreed the Coroner.

The taxi driver, who had returned to London, was not called.

After some slight consultation with the police the coroner announced that he considered it neither necessary, or desirable to postpone the inquest until Miss Wilding's return to health. The cause of the tragedy seemed obvious enough—the burnt-out tail-light had prevented Sir Anthony from realising the nearness of the car in front until it was too late.

The jury brought in a verdict of 'Accidental death' without leaving the court.

Theodore was complimented by the coroner for the lucid manner in which he had given evidence. The case was reported briefly in the morning papers, and in a day or so was forgotten…

CHAPTER 25

If you stand, up here, sir, on this bit of a rise, and look over there, to the left a bit, you'll see the steeple of the parish church of Little Monktop. Just there's the south boundary of the estate, Sir Theodore."

Beale, the bailiff, a little man in riding breeches, with mouse-coloured hair, and wrinkled, weather-beaten features, was speaking. He pointed a thick ash stick towards a tall spire, half a mile away.

Sir Theodore Wrenn, very countrified in a suit of shaggy brown tweeds, looked in the direction of the pointing stick, and felt a thrill of pride as his eye travelled over the broad acres which were his, to the church steeple which identified the boundary of his domains. These fields, laid out like neat pocket handkerchiefs in various shades of green and gold and putty, were his—his! It was wonderful, this first taste of good, honest soil.

Anne had gone the day before to spend a few weeks with some friends in Cornwall, leaving Theodore at a loose end in London. She had suggested that the time was ripe for him to go down to Gay Ladies and inspect the estate which he had inherited. He had been none too eager to return to the place which held so many unpleasant memories for him, but it was remarkable how enthusiastic he was now that he actually, stood upon his own solid earth.

"That's a neat little steading over yonder." Theodore pointed to a farm house in the valley, surrounded by well-fenced fields in which sleek cows were browsing.

Beale nodded. "You're right, Sir Theodore, a neat little property it is," he replied. "Been in one family for eighty years, too. Pity we'll have to be seeking a new tenant soon. Old farmer wants to retire."

"By the way, Beale," said Theodore reflectively. "Do you remember an Esther White, whose father was a labourer on one of the farms about here?"

The bailiff looked at his new master oddly. "Now it's funny that you should ask that, Sir Theodore," he commented. "For that very farm was the one old White worked on for the best part of his life. A stone's throw from the farmhouse you can see the cottage he lived in with Esther, his daughter. A decent, nice girl she was, if a little inclined to keep herself to herself, which didn't please everybody around her, if you understand me, Sir Theodore. She hasn't been in these parts since her father died a few years ago. Went to London, so some said."

Theodore nodded, and looked again at the well-kept farmstead where Mrs. Hargreaves had spent her girlhood. An idea was beginning to take shape in his mind. He spent a happy weekend at Gay Ladies, and went up to London filled with pride about his new possessions.

The first morning he was back he met a client of Gentry, Green, and Gentry while walking down the Strand. That worthy submitted him to a searching scrutiny.

"You're looking well, Mr. Wrenn—Sir Theodore, I should say. Heard about your stroke of luck. Congratulations. You deserved it." With a quizzical glance, he added: "The old firm's going a bit to the dogs. Still for sale, I hear. I'm withdrawing my business, of course. 'Fraid Gentry, Green, and Gentry are just about at their last gasp. Pity."

With a pang of remorse, Theodore realised how he had deserted the firm for which he had worked for a dozen years, and which had meant so much in his life. When he left his friend, he went straight to Chancery Lane. He stopped outside the dingy, two storied building, sandwiched between its taller, more imposing neighbours, and surveyed the worn brass plate, which had evidently not been polished for weeks. The building had a more dilapidated air than ever before. It was almost as though it realised that it had been deserted.

Clenching his fists, Theodore ran lightly up the stairs, past the first landing and on to the second storey, where the caretaker had his room. The caretaker was in, and sitting in an old armchair with his feet on the mantelpiece and a pipe in his mouth. He looked up with a ridiculous expression of amazement on his features.

"The plate downstairs hasn't been polished for weeks," said Theodora tersely. "Do it at once—and see that you make a job of it." He walked to the window, and drew a circle on the grime which almost rendered the glass opaque. "'Phone the window cleaners, and tell them to come over at once, and give the stairs and landings a good scrubbing tonight. No more slacking in future, if you want to keep your job."

He went downstairs and into the main office. There was a dead hush as he came in. Then Miss Maudsley sprang up with a startled cry:

"Mr. Wrenn!"

Theodore looked round the room, noting the depressed, beaten look on all of the faces. He was touched to see how pathetically broken both Gifford and Miss Maudsley looked.

"Yes, I'm back," he said in a kindly tone. "Back for good. I just wanted to tell you all that we're going to give Gentry, Green and Gentry a new lease of life. The old firm is good for another hundred years. Someone said to me a little while ago that it is going to the dogs. Well, we're going to put our backs into the job of showing the world that it isn't,"

With a little lump in his throat, he went into his old room and sat down at the dusty desk. He telephoned to Millar.

"It's Wrenn," he said when he heard his friend's voice.

"Wrenn—Theodore! It's good to hear your voice again. I heard about your good fortune. Congratulations, old boy. I wish it was a million."

"Millar, old man," said Theodore huskily. "I want you to come round here at once. To Chancery-lane. Yes, I'm back, and you and I are going to be partners after all. Will you come?"

There was an excited gasp from the other end of the wire.

"Will I come?" repeated Millar. "Will I? In ten minutes, I'll be with you."

The executors of the late Daniel Gentry got the surprise of their lives when Sir Theodore Wrenn telephoned them and announced that he and his partner, Mr. Millar, would buy the business of Gentry, Green and Gentry after all, at the price agreed upon at their last meeting. A conference was quickly arranged for the following morning.

Then Theodore 'phoned a firm of builders and decorators, and made arrangements for the building to be decorated inside and out. The old firm was to have a new lease of life with a vengeance!

He had a scheme for turning some of the cottages on his property into weekend houses for his employees, and eventually retiring the oldest (if they could be persuaded to retire) to spend their last years in comfort and peace in the country.

Late that afternoon, Theodore took a taxi to the quiet, working-class suburb in which Mrs. Hargreaves lived. Mrs. Hargreaves, cheerful and tidy as before, was weeding her front garden path when Theodore arrived. Her plump, rosy little baby boy was basking in the sun upon the tiny lawn.

Mrs. Hargreaves flushed with pleasure as she recognised Theodore.

"I'm delighted to see, you, Mr. Wrenn, sir," she exclaimed, offering her hand diffidently (Theodore wrung it with warmth). "Billy," she called to the child, "come and shake hands with Mr.

Wrenn. Oh, I'm sorry, sir, it's Sir Theodore now, isn't it? I read about Sir Anthony's death in the paper. I won't say I'm sorry, for I'm not, but I'm real pleased that you've inherited his estate. You'll be a good squire, I'm sure. Better than him, in a hundred ways. Excuse me for running on like this, sir, only I do know you'll love Gay Ladies, and the land about it."

"I love, it already," said Theodore, "and I know that you love it, too. That is why what I have to say will probably interest you. By the way, have you found an investment for your five hundred pounds yet? That legacy from your uncle in Australia, I mean?"

Mrs. Hargreaves shook her head. "Not yet, sir. It isn't very easy to decide. We want something safe, you see, and yet, we want to get on in life, does Bill and me—mostly for the sake of little Billy, here. First, we thought of a newsagent's business, but neither of us knows anything about the trade. And we've thought of poultry-farming and going in for pigs, and, and—but it isn't easy to decide."

Theodore looked down at the gravel path.

"The farm on which you spent your girlhood will shortly be tenantless," he said. "I wonder if you'd care to consider it?"

He heard a gasp of delighted amazement, then his hand was seized in a warm clasp.

"Oh, sir, do you really mean it? Why, that would be paradise for Bill and me, and the youngster. Oh, it sounds too good to be true. We'd never dared to set our hopes as high as that!"

"Then in that case," said Theodore, with a little cough, "the place is yours. It won't be empty for three months, but if you like, I'll lend you a cottage in the neighbourhood meantime, so that you can get accustomed again to the district."

He left, very much embarrassed, with the praises of the good woman ringing in his ears.

He wrote a long letter to Anne that night, telling her all about his hopes and plans, and hinting (though he didn't dare voice the hope too plainly) that he wanted her to share them with him.

For the next few days, he was very busy with the work of rehabilitating the firm of Gentry, Green and Gentry.

One morning, on arriving at the office, he found a letter awaiting him from Anne.

A letter which brought his castles crashing about him.

CHAPTER 26

Dear Theodore, —

I am delighted to hear how you are rebuilding the lives of other people, and incidentally your own. You seem to have found your feet, and your place in the world. I had hoped that money would not make you forget your old ambitions, and I am pleased to see that it has not.

There isn't enough money in the world, my dear, to make it worthwhile for a real man to be idle. With idleness comes indigestion and gout and mental degeneration. Work is one of the most vital factors for health that exists.

I, too, am working again. By the time you read this letter, I shall be on my way to Scotland to fulfil a commission. After that, I am going abroad, so you see, we may not meet for quite a long time. But I will remember you—and I hope that you will remember me.

In our daydreams when I was recovering from my illness, we talked as though we should never be parted again, as though we were going to be companions through life. It was a lovely dream, but it was only a dream, and dreams don't come true in real life. Let's be frank; although we never mentioned it, our dream included marriage, and I can never marry you, my dear. Never.

I want you to understand why, for I am not simply trying to hurt you. Until poor Ravenal's tragic death, I was engaged to him, and for one reason only; his money. I should be ashamed to admit anything so sordid to anyone but you, but it is true. If I married you now, it would be as though I were not marrying you at all, but the Ravenal money. Everybody would credit me with a purely mercenary spirit and perhaps (only perhaps) even you in time might come to doubt me. It would be quite natural if you did.

If you were still a lawyer's managing clerk, or even a partner, without the appendage of Anthony Ravenal's money; I should be proud and happy to be your wife. But in the present circumstances, I should never respect myself again if I married you.

This is the first mention of marriage there has been between us; let's make it the last. Let's be good companions; we can never be anything more.

And now I have to thank you for the finest action I have known in all my life. Of course, I knew, when I received the promissory note I gave to that moneylender Salzman, who had redeemed it for me. You, of course, and you sacrificed what was at that time your whole future for me. Ambition, security, everything. It was wonderful of you, Theodore. Oh, if only Ravenal had not died, so that I might share poverty and happiness with you!

It may be months or even years before we meet again, but I shall be thinking of you, and cherishing your memory.

Anne

For minutes, Theodore, sat like one who has been stunned, reading Anne's letter over and over. It was the worst blow which fate had ever dealt him. He had so many plans for the future—and they all included Anne. Without her, they meant nothing to him.

So numb were his senses that he did not notice, that the telephone bell was ringing. Its clamour filled the tiny room, but it was not until an anxious head was popped in at the door, and an anxious voice said: "Telephone, Mr. Wrenn. Sorry, Sir Theodore, I mean. Telephone, Sir Theodore," that he roused himself and took the receiver off the hook.

A pleasant but determined feminine voice came to him from the other end of the wire. "Is that Theodore Wrenn?"

"It is," he replied listlessly.

"Good. Well, you don't know me, but I've something to tell you. I'm speaking from Cornwall. Anne Wilding has been visiting me for a week or two, and she hasn't been her old sunny, self, at all. I found her crying yesterday over a letter she was writing. And it's all your fault."

"Mine?" gasped Theodore incredulously.

"Yes, yours!" (This severely). "She has some idiotic idea that your money is an insurmountable barrier between you. Such nonsense! And it's your fault. Any intelligent man would give her a good shaking and drag her to the altar by sheer brute force!"

"I would," said Theodore grimly, "if I knew where to find her."

"Oh good! I hoped you'd say that. Well, Anne will never forgive me for betraying, her confidences, but if you really mean what you say—"

"I do!"

"Well, you'll find her at Euston Station at two o'clock this afternoon. Platform eight."

"I say," Theodore gulped. "I don't know how to thank you."

The feminine voice laughed happily. "Thank me by persuading my dearest woman friend not to be an idiot; I like your voice, Theodore Wrenn. I think it's just possible that you are worthy of Anne."

"Thanks!"

Theodore hung up the receiver, and was out of his chair like a shot. He looked at his watch. Eleven o'clock.

There was much to do before two o'clock." He grabbed his hat, and hurried out of the office.

At five minutes to two, he was at Euston station standing at the entrance to: platform eight. Two minutes later, Anne arrived.

She stopped short with a gasp when she saw him. "Theodore! You!"

Theodore nodded. "Me," he said briefly, then turned to the porter who was wheeling Anne's luggage in a hand cart.

"You'll find a newly-painted yellow taxi outside," he said curtly. "It's the third on the rank, number eight-one-three, and the driver's name is Bert. Take the lady's luggage there."

The porter glanced hesitantly at Anne.

"Theodore!" she exclaimed angrily. "How dare you!"

Theodore squared his jaw. "Please, Anne!" he said.

He turned to the porter and handed him a ten-shilling note.

"My wife will not travel by this train," he said. "Take her luggage to the taxi."

With an amazed incredulous expression Anne watched her luggage being wheeled briskly away, then she wheeled on Theodore.

"Will you please explain?" she demanded. "Why have you interfered with my luggage, and why did you tell that porter that I am your wife?"

"A little premature," said Theodore steadily. "But it will be the truth within the hour."

"Theodore, it's impossible. Didn't you get my letter?"

"Yes. And of all the sweet, idiotic letters I have seen, it was the sweetest and silliest."

"But, Theodore—"

He held up a warning hand. "We're wasting time," he declared. "We're taking an aeroplane to Paris at four, and we've lots to do before that."

"Your dear idiot, I'm catching this train to Scotland."

"My dear, you are mistaken."

She produced a cardboard slip, and held it up before his eyes.

"You see, I've got my ticket and everything."

He took the ticket from her and calmly tore it up. "That disposes of the ticket. Now do come on. We can talk in the taxi."

"But, Theodore, I can't. I wrote—"

"We won't discuss what you wrote," retorted Theodore. "I wouldn't dream of taking a letter like that seriously. As though money could make any difference. Money! I'll promise never to give you any, if you think it would hurt your feelings."

He produced a little pile of papers. "There's our ticket," he said, displaying a ticket made out in the names of "Sir Theodore and Lady Wrenn."

Anne laughed helplessly. "But, Theodore, dear, we aren't married."

Theodore produced a diamond ring, and slipped it on the third finger of her left hand. Then he put his arms round her, and kissed her on the lips.

"Now we're engaged, my dear," he said. "And by three o'clock we'll be man and wife. I've got a special licence."

He looked at her sternly. "No more nonsense, please. Don't make me carry you to the taxi!"

There was a world of love in her eyes. "Theodore, I believe you would."

For reply, he put his arms round her and lifted her up. He kissed her, then carried her through the station (much to the amusement of the officials and no few travellers) and placed her in the newly-painted yellow taxi.

"To the registrar's office in Hanover square," he instructed the grinning Bert.

Then he climbed into the taxi, beside his literally blushing bride.

THE END

THE BABY AND THE GORILLA

A long shaft of sunlight, shot with dancing specks of dust and wreathed with tendrils of steam, shone through a glass panel in the high ceiling of New Street Station, and chased the shadows that lurk in its cavernous gloom. In and out of the ray bobbed human beings, hurrying like ants; porters wheeling trucks piled high with luggage; stout, fussy businessmen, glancing at their watches; gaily dressed youths, laden with golf bags and tennis rackets; darting boys, with trays of magazines, chocolates, cigarettes, and fruit. In and out they weaved, jostling one another, stumbling over suitcases, stepping on each other's toes: mumbling, apologising, blaspheming. Hurrying to catch trains that weren't yet due and trains that had already steamed out of the station.

Through the ray Detectives Kelly and Brown marched ponderously, and between them slouched the Gorilla, attached to each of them by the stout links of regulation handcuffs. As an additional precaution his thick wrists were manacled together. And in the hip packet of each of the Scotland Yard men reposed a neat little leather blackjack, packed with steel shot. Detectives Kelly and Brown were taking no chances with the Gorilla.

The station was crowded, but a way cleared for them like magic. One glance at the shambling figure between his burly custodians, and the jostling crowd melted like snow on a stove, leaving a clear passage to the platform for the London train. No one felt the slightest inclination to jostle the Gorilla.

Although he was tall above the average, the Gorilla's huge

shoulders and barrel like torso made him look almost short. His bullet-shaped head seemed to rest directly on his shoulders, so short was his neck. His arms reached almost to his knees, and terminated in huge, hairy paws, tanned like leather, seamed and cracked and calloused, with twisted, broken nails.

The Gorilla's forehead was flat, and the thatch of matted hair which covered his head grew down to within an inch or so of his jutting eyebrows. His little black eyes, which could gleam with cunning, were now as dull as those of a caged animal. His wide, thick-lipped mouth hung loosely open, and revealed his irregular, blackened stumps of teeth, with many cans between them. A week's growth of stubble disfigured his jaws and chin.

There were rust-like stains on the ready-made suit, which stretched almost to splitting across the Gorilla's massive shoulders, and bagged grotesquely under his armpits. The stains were the blood of the young policeman who had recognised the Gorilla in a Birmingham Street, and had rashly attempted to detain him. That had happened three days ago and the young policeman was still lying unconscious in a hospital ward. The Gorilla's flight had been intercepted by a lumbering truck, which had struck him between the shoulder-blades as he lurched into the street. A strip of sticking-plaster over his right eye testified to the fact that even the Gorilla could not escape unscathed from an encounter with five tons of slow-moving force. He had been unconscious for three full minutes, and had come to in a police van, efficiently bound, and surrounded by five grim and burly policemen.

Now he was bound for London, where he was wanted for robbery with violence on a night a month previously. Detective Sergeant Kelly entered the reserved third-class carriage first, dragging the Gorilla after him; Detective Brown brought up the rear. The Gorilla was pushed down on a seat unceremoniously, and Kelly unlocked the handcuffs which attached the criminal to Brown. The handcuffs were clicked over the Gorilla's ankles before the pair that linked him to Kelly was removed.

Detective Sergeant Kelly produced his blackjack and reflectively thwacked the cushions with it, knocking out a cloud of dust. He sat down opposite the Gorilla and placed the blackjack on the seat beside him. Detective Brown closed the carriage door and sat down beside Kelly, placing his blackjack on the seat. They looked meaningly at the Gorilla.

His beady eyes flickered for a moment toward the wicked-looking leather-covered implements which lay so conveniently close to the capable hands of his captors, then they became dull and expressionless again.

"Gimme a chew of 'baccy," he growled.

Kelly cut a liberal chunk from the black, tarry plug, and inserted it between the Gorilla's thick lips. The massive jaws of the Gorilla champed steadily. Occasionally he leaned over and squirted mahogany tobacco juice on the floor.

The guard blew his whistle and waved his flag. Steam hissed and curled beneath the footplate of the giant locomotive. The whole length of the train shuddered and creaked as the engine strained at it. The platform receded slowly, then more quickly, as the train gathered speed.

Detective Sergeant Kelly pushed his bowler back from his forehead and lit his pipe.

"Think we'll have any trouble?" whispered Brown.

The older man shook his head. "He's a fool, but not a blasted fool," he murmured. "He's shrewd enough to know when the odds are too heavy. Besides, what could he do? —handcuffed hand and foot. Before he could rise, we'd put him out for the count with our blackjacks."

Brown was doubtful.

"I wouldn't trust any cosh ever made to put a dent in that thick skull!"

Kelly sucked on his pipe drowsily and watched the Gorilla through drooping eyelids. Twenty years older than his colleague, Kelly had a seamed, weather-beaten face, and short, iron-grey hair. Long service on the Metropolitan Police Force, and later with Scotland Yard, had taught him to take things as they come. The younger detective was in the jumpy mood of one who must talk, to be reassured by the sound of his own voice.

"There's no doubt of a conviction, I suppose?" he whispered.

"None whatever."

"What'll he get?"

The older man drew on his pipe reflectively. "About seven years hard," he prophesied. "And you and I and the rest of the rate payers will have to pay for food and lodging for that animal for seven years!" commented Brown disgustedly. "And within a month of his release he'll be in gaol again, for cracking another poor beggar's skull. They ought to put him away for good, with chloroform or gas, that's what they ought to do. Same as they would a mad dog.

"I've been looking over his record and it's as long as your arm. Assault, attempted murder, robbery with violence; he hasn't the brains to pinch a pin without beating up the owner. No one seems to know what his right name is— 'the Gorilla' is good enough for him. It fits, and it's stuck. He was pinched first at the age of 15, when he was running the streets with a gang of bruisers. Nobody claimed him; as far as it was known, he belonged to nobody. He was sent to Borstal for three years, but half killed a warder in his first six months, and escaped. Since then, he's been in and out of gaol at intervals of from one to six months. Always for using those murderous maulers. He's a public menace. There ought to be some way of disposing of him for good. His type—the really hardened criminal—never reforms."

Sleepily, Kelly watched the curling blue smoke from hit pipe writhing and twisting to the ceiling, vanishing suddenly, sucked through the ventilator into the rushing air.

"Ever hear of Basher' Griggs?" he drawled lazily.

"Can't say I have," admitted Brown.

"Before your time," said Kelly.

The grey-haired detective's shrewd eyes were dreamily retrospective. "He was a tough criminal. As tough as they're made. Bad, you'd have said, right to the core. And he reformed, utterly and completely. Became a model citizen. All on account of eight pounds of squalling flesh, red as a boiled lobster and wrinkled as a prune…"

The train rushed toward London, shrieking at intervals like a soul in torment; the wheels pounding and clattering, the springs creaking and wheezing, the windows rattling, and high above it all a sixty-mile-an-hour gale wailing, battling the iron giant, buffeting the sides of the long carriages.

"Basher Griggs was a holy terror. Of the first thirty years of his life, he spent twelve in prison. He's speciality was robbing shopkeepers. He'd walk into a shop with a length of gas-pipe wrapped in newspaper under his arm and make a small purchase, tendering half-a-crown. When the shopkeeper opened the till to make change the Basher would lean over and swipe him across the head with the gas-pipe. Then he'd reach across, clean oat the till, and make his getaway, leaving his victim to bleed on the floor until the crime was discovered. A messy worker was the Basher.

"In no time we got so that we could spot his work at a glance, and then it was only a matter of ferreting him out, laying him out (it used to take four or five of us to do it), and locking him up. If he'd had the brains of a performing flea, he'd have realised that his game didn't pay. But you couldn't have found his brains with a pneumatic drill and a microscope. The Basher was one criminal you'd have said would never reform. But he did…

"One morning we were called to the scene of a crime which had the Basher's trademark all over it. I wasn't as tough then as I am now. One look at the inside of the shop and I nearly lost my breakfast. A swinging job, it was. The shopkeeper, a little chap who lived alone above his premises, was lying in a crumpled heap; on the floor, dressed in his nightshirt, with his head crushed in like an eggshell. The floor and counter were spattered with blood and grey matter. According to the doctor, the poor little beggar had been done in about midnight.

"Well, it didn't take us long to figure out what had happened. He'd obviously surprised an intruder in the act of rifling his till. And, by all the earmarks, the intruder had been the Basher.

"I went round the slum street where the Basher lived and knocked at his door. To my surprise, it was opened by the Basher himself. I had a truncheon in my hand, and four constables at my back, but I don't mind telling you I was in a blue funk. I knew the gentleman of old.

"I want you, Griggs," I said, putting my foot in the door.

"To my surprise he didn't slam the door or swing his great fist at me or any of the things I had expected: He just stood there, looking stupid and grinning vacantly.

"'Me?' he responded, 'Whatever for, Mr. Kelly?'

"You'll find that out at the station," I snapped, talking boldly, though my knees were like jelly. "It's that little job you turned last night."

"'Last night?' he repeated. 'I didn't put foot over the door last night, Mr. Kelly, not after' 8 o'clock. I've got witnesses to prove it.'

"You can tell that to the Chief, I retorted.

"'It's true,' he declared. And 'ere's Doctor Grierson; 'ell tell you the same.'

"You'll remember Doctor Grierson, Brown? The best old chap that ever breathed. Gave his life to the slums. When he died, it took four motor-lorries to carry the flowers, and half the East End followed the coffin to the cemetery. Well, sure enough. Doctor Grierson showed up in the corridor behind the Basher, and bore out every word he said. Griggs hadn't been out of doors since the previous evening. And why hadn't he? Because his wife had given birth to a baby!

"The Basher made me come in and see it. And if you'd seen the great, hulking brute dancing round the cradle with a broad beam on his ugly face, like a blessed lunatic, you'd have laughed yourself sick. It was his first kid, and he was pretty near delirious about it.

"Mind you, I don't say it wasn't an attractive little, beggar. As kids go, it wasn't at all a bad specimen. There was something about the way it smiled and crinkled its little blue eyes that would have touched the heart of a blessed stone image. It clutched my finger in a little fist like—like a—a crumpled rosebud."

Meeting the reproving eyes of his subordinate, Detective Sergeant Kelly looked distinctly sheepish.

"In a manner of speaking," he added apologetically.

"As I was saying," he continued hurriedly, "the Basher was crazy about the kid. From that day onwards he went straight. He wouldn't have, stooped in the street to pick up a pin, unless he'd dropped it himself. He got a job as a warehouse porter, and worked like the devil for the first time in his life. He saved a bit of cash and bought a small lockup shop. Bought for cash and sold for cash, and made money. It was a treat to see him and his missus, prim as you please, mincing in at the door of the Bow Road Wesleyan Mission: they were regular attenders at all three services every Sunday.

"Later they moved to Barnet, I think it was—and bought a larger shop. The Basher settled down like a respectable, citizen and joined a local church. In due course he became a sidesman; frock-coat, striped trousers, silk hat, and all. And all because of a baby—eight pounds of squalling flesh, as red as a lobster and as wrinkled as a prune!"

The train roared on. While Detective Sergeant Kelly scraped his pipe with a penknife and knocked it out on the heel of his boot.

"I haven't seen Griggs for over twenty-five years now," he murmured. "Lord, how time flies! That kid will be a big follow by now. Helping his Daddy to run the business, I expect."

The Gorilla leaned forward and squirted tobacco juice through a gap in his broken stumps of teeth.

"Oh, no he ain't," he growled.

"What the devil do you know about it?" demanded Kelly.

"Hell!" exclaimed the Gorilla. "I'm the baby!"

THE END

www.ingramcontent.com/pod-product-compliance
Lightning Source LLC
Chambersburg PA
CBHW071117180726
48291CB00007B/2074